WHAT HAPPENS IN VEGAS…

ASHE BARKER

ASHE BARKER BOOKS

Copyright © 2021 by Ashe Barker

All rights reserved.

No part of this book may be reproduced in any form or by any electronic or mechanical means, including information storage and retrieval systems, without written permission from the author, except for the use of brief quotations in a book review.

Cover art by https://www.fiverr.com/designrans

WHAT HAPPENS IN VEGAS...

I'm not the first man and I don't suppose I'll be the last to be confronted by a beautiful woman demanding a divorce. The problem is, I've never seen Fern Daniels before in my life. I don't care if she does have the wedding certificate and photographs to prove her ridiculous claims.

This is a scam.

The scheming Ms Daniels is up to something.

I mean to find out what, and when I do, she'll realise she chose the wrong man to try her tricks on.

ABOUT THE AUTHOR

USA Today best-selling author Ashe Barker has been an avid reader of fiction for many years, erotic and other genres. She still loves reading, the hotter the better. But now she has a good excuse for her guilty pleasure – research.

Ashe lives in the North of England, on the edge of the Brontë moors and enjoys the occasional flirtation with pole dancing and drinking Earl Grey tea. When not writing – which is not very often these days - her time is divided between her role as taxi driver for her teenage daughter, and caring for a menagerie of dogs, a tortoise, gerbils. And a very grumpy cockatiel.

At the last count Ashe had around sixty titles on general release with publishers on both sides of the Atlantic, and several more in the pipeline. She writes M/f, M/M, and occasionally rings the changes with a little M/M/f. Ashe's books invariably feature BDSM. She writes explicit stories, always hot, but offering far more than just sizzling sex. Ashe likes to read about complex characters, and to lose herself in compelling plots, so that's what she writes too.

Ashe has a pile of story ideas still to work through and keeps thinking of new ones at the most unlikely moments, so you can expect to see a lot more from her.

Ashe loves to hear from readers. Feel free to follow her on social media or drop in on her little bit of the internet.

www.ashebarker.com

Or you can email her direct on ashe.barker1@gmail.com

Better still, sign up for Ashe's newsletter to be the first to hear about new releases, competitions, giveaways and other fun stuff. You'll find the link on her website

PROLOGUE

Halstead Grange Clinic, near Edinburgh
1990

THE REVERENT SILENCE of the sanitised, white-tiled corridor rang with screams. It was most unbecoming, not the usual sort of thing at all.

Aldrich Digby Saunders slowed his stride to study his Rolex for a moment, assessing how much longer this din was likely to go on. He much preferred to leave the loud ones to his staff, but Alister McPherson would hardly expect his son and heir to enter the world assisted only by a humble midwife. No, Alister McPherson expected the best, and the best was Aldrich D. Saunders, consultant gynaecologist and obstetrician to the rich and famous.

And, occasionally, the infamous.

He quickened his step, though only slightly. The great Mr Saunders was never seen to hurry. Haste implied fuss and a lack of control. These were not the qualities upon which he had founded his reputation, nor his not inconsiderable fortune pandering to the feminine idiosyncrasies of the Scottish and English elite. He had delivered half the royal grandchildren of

Europe here at Halstead Grange, and there was hardly a celebrity infant who saw the first light of day in anyone else's hands.

Mr Saunders was the best. Everyone knew it. They all came here, to his clinic, if they could afford the exorbitant fees. Most left with a squalling infant upon which to dote and lavish yet more expensive gifts, and their bank accounts lighter by a cool hundred thousand pounds.

Meryl McPherson was different, though. She was not at all the usual brand of pampered trophy wife he was accustomed to dealing with, not least because she made her contempt for her husband abundantly clear. It was not, in Aldrich's experience, unusual for wives to be at odds with their husbands, especially during childbirth, but Meryl McPherson had never expressed anything but loathing for Alister during the seven months she had been under the care of Aldrich's exclusive practice. This, he considered odd. Most of the women he attended understood which side their bread was buttered and would at least pay lip service to their meal ticket.

Not Meryl McPherson.

Aldrich had the impression the feeling was mutual. Alister McPherson had never attended any of the appointments. He had not been at his wife's side during her scans, nor had he so much as acknowledged the phone calls from Halstead Grange to inform him that his wife was in labour. Aldrich was given to understand that the happy father-to-be was in the United Stated on business and not expected to return for a month or more.

Christ, he hoped that was true. There was no way he wanted to actually face Alister McPherson once this awkward business was done with.

The consultant entered the room where his patient had been in labour for close to forty-eight hours. Two midwives were with her, one of them busily engaged between the woman's legs which were suspended in stirrups. She straightened to regard her boss.

"Eight centimetres, Mr Saunders. No change now for almost two hours."

Meryl McPherson let out another blood-curdling screech and groped for his sleeve. "You... Have...To...Make it... Stop..." she ground out between contractions. "Help me..."

"Any indications of foetal distress?" Saunders asked, calmly picking up the clipboard at the end of the bed to examine the scrawled notes.

"No, sir," the midwife confirmed, "but it has been almost two days now."

There was a groan from the bed. "Fuck how many days it's been. I'm paying you, and I want this sorted. Now." Meryl grasped Aldrich's arm again. "If you want that fat fee you were so keen on, you'll get on with doing exactly what I told you to do."

"Mrs McPherson, this really is most irregular," Saunders began, employing the condescending tone he had honed to perfection over his years of telling women what was good for them, only to break off when she fixed him with her cobalt-blue stare.

"Fucking do it. Now. Aaagh!"

He made up his mind. After all, a deal was a deal, and her money was as good as anyone's. "Prep for theatre. We'll see this one out through the skylight."

"But don't you think we should wait a little longer?" observed one of the midwives. "It's been slow, but she is making progress."

"I thought there had been no further dilation for two hours."

"Yes, but—"

"Theatre," he repeated. "Let's get on with this."

Meryl writhed in the bed as Saunders and two orderlies wheeled her along the corridor. The gynaecologist took the opportunity to bend over the trolley and speak to her in a low tone.

"You are quite certain no one else is aware of...the circumstances?"

"There's been no leak at my end. If you or your staff ever breathe a word, I shall...aaaagh!"

"I can assure you of absolute confidentiality, here at Halstead Grange."

"You had fucking better. If *he* ever finds out..."

There was no need to remind him. Aldrich knew his lucrative business would tank in a matter of days if Alister McPherson were to ever discover what had gone on here today.

"Quite so." He patted her shoulder.

"No records. Nothing to attract attention," she insisted, perspiration beading on her forehead.

For a woman in the advanced stages of a difficult labour, Aldrich had to afford a grudging respect to Meryl McPherson. She knew what she wanted, and her focus was undimmed, her attention to detail as sharp as ever.

"Of course. We understand perfectly."

The orderlies swung the trolley around at a right angle, and Meryl was wheeled into the operating theatre to be bathed in the harsh white light of the overhead lamps. The anaesthetist was already there, waiting for them, his instruments laid out in readiness to perform the epidural.

Aldrich dealt with his own preparations speedily, the procedure perfected over years of practice. He followed Meryl into the sterile theatre, already scrubbed up, masked and gowned. He took his place at the foot of the trolley whilst the anaesthetist and midwife positioned Meryl, first on one side, then the other. At the anaesthetist's brief nod, Aldrich called for the screens to be set up to prevent Meryl actually witnessing him slicing her abdomen open.

She would be conscious throughout the procedure, and would feel something, though not pain. She would be aware of

What Happens in Vegas…

the pushing and tugging, and, provided there were no complications, she would be able to hold her baby immediately.

Aldrich took his place alongside his patient, flanked by the two midwives. He picked up his scalpel. "Okay, let's get this done."

There was silence as he drew the blade across Meryl's abdomen, just below her navel. He set the scalpel aside and stretched out his hand to have a clamp slapped into it by the well-trained midwife. It was the work of just a few moments to create the necessary opening, revealing the tangle of thin limbs within. The medical professionals exchanged a glance, then Aldrich reached in to grasp the squirming, blood-stained scrap of humanity.

"A boy," he announced, straightening. "Would you like to hold him, Mrs McPherson?"

She reached for the infant, a sad smile on her lips. The consultant dumped her tiny son in her arms.

"Is he…? Is he all right?" she whispered. Her voice was close to breaking.

"As far as I can see. We'll need to check him properly, of course." The newborn chose that moment to let out a high-pitched, disgruntled squeal.

One of the midwives stepped forward. "I expect he's hungry. Would you like me to help you—?"

"No. I can't." Meryl took one last look at the crying baby, then turned her head to stare at the wall. "Take him. Please."

"But surely you—"

"Take him," the mother insisted. "Now."

The midwife scooped up the tiny form and wrapped him in a clean blanket. She looked to her boss for instructions.

"Do it. Do what we agreed," Meryl ground out.

Aldrich's lips flattened, but he gave a brief nod. "See that Mr McPherson is informed of the birth and ask him to make arrangements to collect his son at his earliest convenience. Also, you will inform him that, despite all best efforts on our part, his wife unfortunately did not survive the labour. You will offer our deepest condolences on his loss."

The midwife was not unduly surprised at her instructions. After all, the deal had been agreed. They were all party to it. But right up to this point, Aldrich had expected Meryl to change her mind. It is one thing to make plans, however bizarre, quite another to give up a baby, moments after it is born.

His patient's stony features betrayed not a hint of wavering. She met the surgeon's gaze, unblinking.

"Now, finish it off."

CHAPTER 1

January 2018
Bond Court, Manchester

I SCRAMBLE FROM THE TAXI, then pause to hand the driver a ten-pound note. He tips his hat in a cheery salute, advises me to have a nice day, and whirrs off to be swallowed up in the bustling city centre traffic. I am left standing on the broad expanse of pavement, gazing up at the North West offices of Messrs Ingram, Albright, and Smartt, Investment Analysts. The name of the company is engraved in sleek black lettering on a brushed silver plate beside the wide glass doors.

I suppose they must have a better class of thief around here. Where I live in downtown Stockport, a plaque like that would be prised off and melted down for scrap quicker than you could say corporate takeover.

I hug my oversized bag to my chest as I climb the short flight of stairs to the doors. They glide apart to allow me entry, and I step forward onto the plush carpeting. Three men in sharp suits stride in behind me and make for the bank of glass-fronted lifts at the far side of the foyer. I'm less certain of where

I need to be, so I make my way to the reception desk to be greeted by a man dressed in a starched white shirt, black tailcoat and pinstriped trousers.

A fucking butler! Could this place get any more pretentious?

I thrust my letter of invitation under his nose. "I'm here for the shareholder's meeting."

He leans forward to examine my letter. I can't blame him, not really. I doubt if I look the part of a shareholder in an investment analysis company, not in my skinny black jeans, red-and-black-striped top, and faux leather jacket. In fairness, the jacket is my best one and usually passes for reasonably smart. And I have taken the trouble to fasten my hair in a sort of messy bun for the occasion. If I had had a bit more time to prepare I might have invested in a matching skirt and jacket, but I've only been a shareholder for a week, and I doubt if I'll find it necessary to show up for many more of these functions.

I'm only here now to see *him*.

"You are Miss Daniels?" The butler raises one supercilious eyebrow. "Do you have any other form of identification on you?"

"Yes. Miss Fern Daniels," I reply, dragging my phone from my bag. "Here, will this do?" I slide my driving licence from its pocket in my phone case and hand it over.

He takes the photocard, peers from it to me then, double-checks the photo. He hands it back. "First floor, room one. Refreshments are being served in the ante-room. The meeting begins at two-thirty."

I start for the lift, but he calls me back. "Miss Daniels, your lanyard."

He hands me a visitor ID encased in a rigid plastic holder and dangling from a lanyard sporting the company's logo. "Wear this at all times whilst in the building, and hand it back when you leave."

"Yes, Right." I hang it around my neck and make for the lifts.

I emerge on the first floor and follow a little arrow on the wall pointing me in the direction of the meeting rooms. To my left are open-plan offices populated by smartly dressed executives. They lean back in their leather swivel chairs, most with phones to their ears, all with fancy laptops or tablets on their desks. It strikes me that they all seem happy enough, though I know it would be my worst nightmare to work in an environment like this. It's all too pristine, too efficient and businesslike.

I suppose it has to be. This is the world of high finance. Wealth and power ooze everywhere. Not my cup of tea, but I'm a curious soul, so this glimpse into another world holds a degree of fascination for me. I slow my pace and take a good look around. To my right a balcony overlooks the foyer I just left. The butler is greeting the next set of new arrivals, and as far as I can tell he is no more pleased to see them than he was me.

I turn a corner at the end of the suite of offices to find myself in what I assume must be the ante-room to room one. A table is set up with rows of dainty corporate teacups and saucers. Two smiling young men in dark suits offer tea or coffee to everyone who enters the space. I'm early, but already a few people are milling around, including the suits who came in from the street with me. I accept the offer of a coffee and hope not to spill it as I juggle the cup, the saucer, a spoon I don't need, and the Shareholder's pack which I am directed to pick up from the tower of files at the end of the long table.

The pack consists of a folder, again emblazoned with the Ingram, Albright, and Smartt corporate livery, containing an agenda for the shareholders' meeting, and several sheets covered in figures. I find a spot close to a window and dump my cup and saucer on the windowsill, leaving my hands free to flick through the printed sheets. I'm only interested in the agenda.

The meeting will be opened at two-thirty sharp by the chair of the Board, Mr William Smartt. Following the chairman's opening remarks, the Director of Finance will present the year end accounts. Then comes the main item of business, and the reason I am here.

I have read a bit about the issue online, enough to grasp the key points. A bid has been made to take over Ingram, Albright, and Smartt, and the shareholders are to be invited to vote on whether or not to accept this proposal. The current board oppose the move, but the offer is for an eye-watering amount of money and it is expected that a fair proportion of the shareholders will be tempted by the quick profit they can expect if the deal goes through. The share price will rocket, and anyone who sells at the right time stands to make a decent killing. I suppose that includes me, though I only hold thirty shares, the minimum required to afford me the right to attend this meeting and cast my vote.

It all came about by accident really. I was in the hairdressing salon thumbing through glossy society magazines as I waited for my stylist to be free, when I spotted his picture under the caption *The UK's Youngest Tycoon Goes After Old Money*.

I recognised him at once, even though I haven't seen him for over five years. Caleb McPherson, a man I knew intimately, though briefly, but expected never to see again. Mr McPherson and I have unfinished business. He disappeared out of my life without leaving so much as his phone number, and all attempts to track him down on social media have drawn a blank. To say that he is, allegedly, one of the richest men under thirty in the UK, it would seem he lives an exceptionally quiet, invisible life. According to the article I discovered at the hairdressers, Caleb McPherson is head of McPherson Holdings who are the company seeking to take over this long-established firm of investment analysts. And what's more, given the knife-edge upon which the negotiations were teetering, he announced his intention to be here in person to seek to convince the Ingram, Albright, and Smartt shareholders to vote in favour of his deal.

What Happens in Vegas...

It was a chance not to be missed. If I couldn't reach him by phone or online, how much better to confront him in the flesh, so to speak. The headquarters of Ingram et al are in Manchester, just a few miles from where I live. I'll never have a better opportunity. I wasted no time in contacting a broker and instructing them to acquire for me enough shares to get me a place at this meeting. Twenty-four hours and one bank transfer later, it was done.

I finish my coffee and take the cup back to the serving table. Then, I wander into the meeting room to find a good place to sit before it gets too full.

The seats are laid out in ten or a dozen rows. I choose to sit at the end of a row about halfway back. From here I have an uninterrupted view of the speakers' table and the lectern which I assume will be used for the presentations. The meeting will not start for twenty minutes, so I settle myself down to wait.

By half past two the room is full. I'm glad I opted for an end seat. If all else fails I can get out quickly and waylay Caleb McPherson when he leaves the meeting.

At two-thirty precisely, a door behind the speakers' table opens, and five men troop out to take their seats. They are all well dressed, perfectly groomed, exuding a collective air of power and authority, but my attention is riveted on just one of them.

Caleb has not changed at all. I expected him to look...older. I'm sure I do. His hair is still so dark as to be almost black, and his eyes are still a rich shade of brown that reminds me of chocolate. Or whisky. His mouth is firm, his jaw angular, his nose straight, the nostrils flaring slightly as he regards his audience. It is an expression I remember well. He used to look at me just the same way, somewhere between hunger and a desire to dominate, to control. Now, he sweeps his deep-brown gaze across the assembled shareholders, and I fully expect him to react when he sees me.

He must see me. I'm not hiding.

What will he do? What will he say?

His composure doesn't waver one iota. He returns his gaze to the papers before him, then shifts his posture slightly to watch the chairman make his way to the podium.

Mr Smartt's words of welcome are mercifully brief, and he passes the mantle on almost immediately to a tall, gaunt-looking man who attempts to dazzle us all with a PowerPoint slideshow. The director of finance draws our attention to the formidable financial projections we shareholders can look forward to whilst enjoying the benefit of a risk-free trading environment. Money for old rope, or so it sounds.

Stick with us. Don't be fooled by this Johnny-come-lately.

He doesn't actually say it, but it's there in his closing arguments, plain enough.

The director of finance sits back down after about a quarter of an hour, and the chairman gets to his feet again to call for a vote. We all stick our hands in the air to accept the annual accounts and reappoint some old and established firm of accountants to keep up the good work and do next year's audit.

The routine business now concluded, we are on to the main event. Mr Smartt introduces Caleb McPherson to the shareholders and briefly outlines the main terms of the takeover. McPherson Holdings are prepared to pay just over two million pounds to acquire a controlling interest in the company. If the deal goes through, these proud and respected Manchester headquarters would be sold, and the bulk of the business relocated to Edinburgh. Many jobs would be lost, not to mention the goodwill, reputation, and invaluable web of trading networks built up over generations.

The chairman subsides back into his seat amid much shuffling of agendas among the audience, who I sense are not warming to the idea of foregoing the windfall apparently coming their way. He invites Caleb to take over the podium.

Caleb McPherson gets to his feet, flashes a film-star-worthy

What Happens in Vegas...

smile at the rows of eager shareholders, and ambles confidently to the lectern. I note he does not seem to have a speech to read out. I hope we are not to be treated to Death by PowerPoint, yet more slides showing columns of numbers.

Caleb does have slides, but they are pictures of Edinburgh, the graceful city he hopes will be the new home of Ingram, Albright, and Smartt. He reminds the shareholders what a firm of investment analysts is there to do. Their mission is to help others to prosper, to understand global market trends, and make sure their clients have access to the best possible advice to enable them to invest wisely, whether those clients be the corporate multinational giants or a widow wondering how best to invest the pension left by her deceased husband. It all matters. Competent investment analysis means things get done, but great analysis, inspirational analysis, that would move mountains, quite literally (cue the slide depicting a tunnel through a mountain in Africa allowing a much-needed single track road to reach isolated communities). Ingram, Albright, and Smartt had the potential to make a difference on a global scale, but that potential needed to be unlocked. It was no longer good enough to rest on the laurels of safety and security. What was investment analysis about if not risk?

Caleb paused, surveyed his audience.

"I have no quarrel with profit," he continued. "I know that is why each and every one of us is in this room this afternoon. I invite you to share in the prosperity and potential of this fine established firm, whilst at the same time unlocking the opportunities we can offer to others. Prosperity does not need to come at the expense of ethics or solid social values. I say, we can have it all. And we will, if you back my proposal to acquire this company."

He returns to his seat, applause ringing around the meeting room. The chairman's expression is thunderous, but he manages to collect himself sufficiently to invite questions.

I ready myself to stick my hand in the air.

Whilst I am composing my lines, a couple of others get their questions in. Caleb listens, fields their objections or corrects their misunderstandings. He is remarkably patient and extremely well-informed.

And utterly formidable. I begin to wonder if I may be making a mistake, confronting him here, on his own turf, among his colleagues and employees.

The meeting is ending. The chairman starts to wind up the proceedings, thanking everyone for their contributions. There will be a vote on whether or not to accept Caleb's generous offer, then we will all go our separate ways.

It's now or never. I get to my feet.

"Excuse me. I have a question for Mr McPherson."

The chairman peers at me over his rimless spectacles. "I'm afraid the questions are now concluded."

I stand my ground. "Just one question, please." I address my words to Caleb, not Mr Smartt.

Dark eyebrows lower. He meets my gaze, and still...nothing, No reaction, no flash of recognition, no sharing of a memory, however fleeting. But he does nod.

"Go on," he says. "What would you like to know?"

I take a breath. "Do you remember me, Cal?"

He frowns, clearly taken aback by my use of his shortened name.

"Should I?"

Arrogant bastard.

I straighten my spine, ready to do battle with him if I must. And it seems it has come to that.

"You should, but it changes nothing either way. I am here to tell you that our marriage is over. I want a divorce."

THERE IS SILENCE, just for a moment. Caleb's dark eyes lock on mine, and I swear if I was within his reach he might just throttle me. Then the room erupts.

The chairman's attempts to call for calm and proceed with the vote are futile. Everyone is talking at once, and the dizzying flash of press cameras is everywhere. I had entirely overlooked the possibility that this meeting might attract media interest. Well, it certainly will now, and they got a lot more than they bargained for.

Caleb and the man seated closest to him, an aide of some sort, get to their feet and leave by the door at the rear, the way they came in. I swear softly to myself. The elusive bastard is slipping away. Again.

I get up, my bag clutched to my chest, and try to follow, but I am prevented from approaching the table by a burly security guard who appears from somewhere in the shadows.

"Sorry, miss. No unauthorised personnel past this point."

"But I—"

"Sorry. Speakers only."

I spin on my heel and make a dash for the exit at the front of the room, leading back to the ante-chamber. I rush along the corridor, searching for any sign of Caleb McPherson making his escape by some other exit. My way is blocked by a dead end. I turn and sprint back the other way, only to find myself passing other meeting rooms, all locked.

Panting, I come to a halt. I have to face it. He bloody ran out on me. Again.

I start to make my way towards the lifts. There's no point in hanging about here. They'll probably want to throw me out anyway for disrupting the meeting. The rest of the shareholders are pouring from room one as I pass that door, and I attract more than a few curious stares. A reporter catches me by the elbow and shoves a microphone under my nose.

"What do you have to say to Caleb McPherson now, miss?"

I back away, shaking my head. I'm not here for fame and glory. I simply want my freedom.

I am almost at the lift when I am again grasped by the

elbow. I attempt to shake off this latest intrusion, but the grip tightens.

"Let go of me. I'm leaving."

"Not yet, miss. We need a word with you first?"

"A word? Who wants to talk to me?" I take a proper look at the mountain of a man decked out in a sharp silk suit and dazzling white shirt. He may be dressed like a stockbroker, but he has the rugged features of a bare-knuckle fighter and the strength to match.

"Caleb McPherson. This way, please."

A prickle of genuine fear arcs down my spine. *Shit, what have I got myself into?*

"I'm going nowhere with you, I don't even know you," I protest.

"I suggest you do as you're told. You are coming with me." It is an instruction, not an invitation. "Mr McPherson wants to talk to you."

I give an inelegant snort. "Well, you could have fooled me. He couldn't get out of there fast enough."

He ignores my jibe. "This way, please," he repeats, the semblance of courtesy somewhat undermined by the sharp shove between my shoulder blades.

He keeps hold of my arm as we march back in the direction of the meeting rooms, past number one and number two, but entering the third door along. This is a much smaller space, more seminar than conference size. There is just one table in the centre, surrounded by six chairs.

An entire wall is taken up with a floor-to-ceiling panoramic window. Caleb leans with one hip resting on the glass pane, his arms folded. His suit jacket now removed, he watches me enter but offers no word of greeting.

I glare at him. His little sham is over. There is no point in continuing to deny he even knows me.

"Hello, Cal." I meet his cold gaze. "Long time no see. You're looking well."

His eyes narrow. He steps away from the window to be silhouetted briefly against the late summer sunshine streaming in at his back. He frowns at me, his expression hard.

"You can stop the play-acting now. Just who the fuck are you? And what do you want?"

CHAPTER 2

Her eyes darken. They are green, the perfect counterpoint to her wild mass of rich, red hair. She's a sassy little thing, I'll grant her that. I might even be attracted to her if I didn't know for a fact that she's a grubby, grasping thief, out to make a quick buck out of me.

I've come across her type before. I suspect most wealthy men have. It goes with the territory. Women who claim some sort of relationship in the dim and distant past and crawl back out of the woodwork years later to claim compensation. Or worse, maintenance for some kid I'm supposed to be responsible for.

I've never been involved with this female before, and I certainly haven't fucked her. I would have remembered.

She dumps her large bag on the table and rummages inside. Her attention is on the contents, and I have to restrain the urge to march over to her, cup her chin, and force her gaze up.

Eyes on me, girl!

If we were alone, I would test this, explore her responses a bit more. My instincts are rarely wrong, all the more reason for my conviction that she and I have never met before today. My relationships tend to be somewhat intense. I like to dominate, to control, in my personal life as well as business. This cute redhead would have been no exception.

"I told you what I want," she snaps, "back there in the meeting. A divorce."

I let out a mirthless laugh. "Yeah. Right."

She glowers at me. "What's the matter with you, anyway? Why keep on behaving as though we never met? You must remember."

"There is nothing *to* remember. I never set eyes on you before this afternoon. I don't even know your name."

Except I do. It's there on her visitor's pass swinging from the lanyard. Fern Daniels.

Her emerald glare hardens. "You're a liar, Caleb. And I can prove it." She drags a thick bundle of papers from her bag and dumps them on the table. "There. All the evidence you need. Or rather, all the evidence a divorce court will need to establish that we were married on the twenty-first of August, twenty thirteen, in Las Vegas." She unpeels the top-most sheet of paper and unfolds it, then lays it flat on the table. "Our marriage certificate. Caleb McPherson and Fern Daniels. That's me," she announces, "though you already knew that."

"I do. It's on your badge."

I don't move to examine her so-called proof. Instead, I gesture to my companion, Simon Waters, the McPherson Holdings corporate lawyer who sat beside me in the shareholders meeting just now, to do those honours. He'll expose the forgeries in moments.

"May I?" Simon picks up the marriage certificate and scrutinises it. Then, he sets it down and extends his hand to request the rest of the bundle.

The girl—Fern—looks to me.

"Simon's my lawyer. Show him your papers."

Satisfied seemingly, she hands the bundle over, then sits down to wait.

No one speaks for the several minutes it takes Simon to

work through the papers. The respite gives me ample opportunity to study this audacious would-be thief who is clearly convinced she can somehow extort money from me, presumably in exchange for promising not to sell her fictitious story to a tabloid newspaper.

Is that even still a thing? Isn't it all social media and YouTube now?

She appears confident enough, though I note her hands are shaking slightly. She sees me watching and moves them into her lap. Her hair is escaping from the loose knot she has made of it, no doubt caused when Harry, my driver and general odd-job man, bundled her unceremoniously along the corridor. Her clothing is more casual shopping trip than corporate boardroom, though I have to admit her style suits her. She has the look of someone comfortable in her skin, which I suppose makes her current escapade all the more baffling.

Especially as she hasn't a snowball's chance in hell of pulling it off. She really should have settled for the make-believe lovechild, although even that would have been unlikely to stick, given the wonders of DNA. A whole bloody marriage, though…

"These seem genuine." Simon lifts his gaze from the papers. "It would appear, based on these documents, that a ceremony of marriage did take place, in the Sunset Garden Chapel in Las Vegas, in August, two thousand and thirteen. The licence was duly purchased from the Clark County Marriage Bureau on that same date, valid for the state of Nevada. It was paid for in cash. The wedding certificate shows the marriage taking place, witnessed by a Mr James Chiltern and Miss Juliette Feldmann."

Fern nods. "Yes. Witnesses provided by the chapel. It's all above board and legal."

"Like fuck it is." I reach for the certificate. "I wasn't even there." I examine the sheet of thick embossed paper, alarmed to see a perfectly good approximation of my signature on it.

Holy fuck, she's good.

"I've never heard of you, or of this Sunset Garden Chapel."

"No?" Her eyes flash in temper. "Then you did well to get on all the photographs."

She produces another bundle from what is beginning to seem like a bottomless bag of tricks, this time a reinforced card wallet containing perhaps a dozen professional photos. I cannot start to imagine how she's managed to produce this lot. Photoshop, I suppose. But they do all include me, suited and booted for the occasion, looking every inch the part of the devoted bridegroom. And beside me, the lovely Fern in an elegant off-white cocktail dress, smiling for the camera and sipping champagne.

Simon and Harry exchange a glance. It's clear they are warming to this tale of hers in the face of her expertly produced and presented 'evidence'.

I try another tack. "I wasn't even in Nevada in August, twenty thirteen. That was the year we acquired Routledges Brewery in Seattle. I was there for nearly two months, sorting out the deal."

"Yes, I remember. But, if you were in the US, then," Simon murmurs, "Nevada is just a flight away..."

I glare at him. His job here is to find the lie in all of this, not back up this fantasy.

"I was not fucking there," I grind out. "I have no idea how the resourceful Miss Daniels managed to come by all of...this, but it never happened."

"Caleb, I—"

The girl starts to get to her feet, but I stride away, back to the window. I gaze out over the swarming street below.

"What are you wanting out of this?" I demand. "Some generous payoff? An allowance, even? Forget it. Or are you about to claim I'm the father of your child and you want Christ knows what in back-dated child support?"

"I don't want anything," she replies quietly. "Just the

divorce. Then we can go our separate ways. You will never see or hear from me again."

Does she think I was born yesterday?

"Oh no, that isn't how these things work. You have an angle, and I want to know what it is. What's in this for you?"

"My freedom. I want to rule a line under what happened five years ago and get on with my life."

"Nothing happened five years ago. What you do with your life has nothing to do with me."

"This says different." She sweeps her hand over the papers and photographs scattered across the table. "And you can deny it all you like, but I remember every detail. I remember how we met, where we met…"

"Yeah? Go on, then," I challenge her.

"I was eighteen and doing a gap year before college. I got a job in an art gallery in Las Vegas. Nothing grand, just helping to set up exhibitions. You came in, looking for a present for your mother. You bought a figurine. A ballet dancer…"

"My mother's been dead for nearly thirty years."

"Well, that was what you said. You bought the figurine and asked me out for a drink with you. You seemed nice…then. So, I agreed, but we settled for a coffee instead because I wasn't twenty-one. Not old enough to drink in the US. We spent three weeks together, you even gave up your hotel room and moved into my studio flat. We were…very happy. You proposed, and I was young enough and silly enough to agree. So, we went downtown, to the Clark County Marriage Bureau, and you bought the licence. We got it on the spot, and it was valid immediately. We went into a boutique in one of the hotels and bought the clothes you see here, in the photos. Then we crossed the road and marched into the nearest wedding chapel which just happened to be the Sunset Gardens. They had a free slot, so we were married there and then, with the chapel staff as witnesses. They even laid on the champagne and photographer."

"Bloody hell. You've certainly given this story of yours some thought." I have to hand it to her. She has an eye for the detail.

"It's true. All of it. That's exactly how it all happened."

"A whirlwind romance? Love at first sight? You're saying I swept you off your feet, a barely legal bit of a kid."

"Well, you did."

"Hell, no I did not. I would have remembered."

"After the wedding, we went back to the flat, and...and..."

"Fucked like bunnies?"

"Do you have to be quite so crude?"

I shrug, unrepentant."

"In the morning, I woke up and you were gone. All your stuff, too. I tried your phone, but it was unobtainable. I went to the hotel where you'd been staying before you moved in with me, but they hadn't seen you and they refused to give me any details about where I might contact you. I was stuck, no ideas where you went, or why. But you'd gone. You made your position clear, your views on our marriage perfectly obvious. I cried for a week, then started to pull myself together. I saw you for the heartless lowlife you actually are and decided to get on with my own life."

She pauses to draw breath, then launches back into her tirade.

"But you're baggage, Caleb McPherson. I want rid of you. I brought you this. You can have it back." She produces a gold wedding ring from her pocket and flings it at me.

It lands at my feet, but I don't bother to pick it up. Instead, I take the mobile phone which Harry offers me. It really is time to put a stop to this nonsense.

I spend a few moments scrolling through the information on the screen, deciding how best to make use of it.

Miss Fern Daniels, meanwhile, is not giving up. "I have ample proof here to convince a court. I could apply for a decree nisi tomorrow. I don't even need you to agree, but I thought it polite to at least talk to you first."

"Do not even think about it," I growl, my patience at an end. "No way are you dragging my family name through the courts with this fairy story. Neither are you getting a penny out of me."

"I told you, I don't want—"

"Save it. I don't believe you. You're a liar. Everything you've said, all of this…it's a lie. You haven't gone to all this trouble for nothing." I stalk back to tower over her. She can't be more than five feet four, I have almost a whole twelve inches on her. "It ends here, Miss Daniels. If it doesn't, you have my word you will live to regret having tried to pull a stunt like this with me. I will ruin you, be assured of that."

She tips up her chin, never once breaking eye contact with me. The green darkens from warm moss to brittle, cold emerald. "Ruin me? And how do you plan to do that, Mr High and Mighty McPherson?"

"While you've been entertaining us with your fairy tale of Las Vegas, Harry here has been checking you out on Google, stalking you on social media. You're a freelance artist, I gather."

Her eyes narrow, wary suddenly. Too little, too late.

"Yes. Why?"

"A potter, to be exact." I consider the images of her work displayed on the small screen. "You make tableware. Very nice, too, if you like that sort of thing."

"What has any of this to do with—?"

"Does it sell well?"

"Mind your own business."

"Hmm, thought not. Oh well, it's a good thing you have your other sideline, then."

"I make a decent living," she protests, her chin up and her eyes blazing. "People will pay good money for quality products, unique designs…"

"Will they?" Actually, I do think her work is rather attractive, in a rustic sort of way. I might even buy a set of mugs myself. "You run a studio in Stockport," I continue. "You rent out space to other artists. Potters, painters, sculptors. A nice little business, by the sound of it."

"My business has nothing to do with this. Or with you."

"If you pursue this sham divorce, the clapped-out old warehouse where you rent space will be bought out. The new owners will have other plans, and they will not include a tinpot artists' workshop. And if that isn't enough to make you think twice, try this. You live in a house in Stockport. A rented house. You can expect a change of landlord soon, and some unwelcome amendments to your tenancy agreement. Homeless, your business gone. Will it all have been worth it, do you think?"

"You can't bully me."

"No? Try me."

"You bastard."

"Hardly. You're the one who came after me with your trumped-up story and forged papers, demanding a divorce from some fictitious marriage. I've a better idea. I suggest you walk away now, drop all of this, and you need never hear from me again. I don't want your business or your house, but I will take whatever steps are necessary to make sure you are out of my hair. For good. Do you understand me, Fern?"

"You can be rid of me by agreeing to the divorce. Or not agreeing, even. Either way, I'm gone."

I shake my head. "There was no marriage, so there can be no divorce. End of. So, we'll do this my way."

"But I—"

"That's the deal, Miss Daniels. The only deal on the table."

She glares at me, her green eyes filling with angry, defeated tears. And I know we're done here.

"Harry, would you see Miss Daniels back to the main entrance, please."

She starts to scoop her papers together.

"You can leave those. After all, you won't be needing them, will you?"

"I can get more copies," she mutters,

"I wouldn't bother. Drop it, Miss Daniels. All of it. And make sure it stays dropped."

"Thank you for that helpful remark, about Seattle being just a flight away from Nevada." I round on Simon as soon as the door closes behind Harry and Fern Daniels. "What the fuck? You don't actually believe that crap, do you?"

He shrugs, which does nothing at all to appease my irritation. He's my lawyer, for Christ's sake. I pay him good money to believe me in matters such as this and keep me on the right side of the law. Now, he regards me with a serious expression which I do not much care for.

"There's nothing at all wrong with those documents. She was right about convincing a court."

"It's me she needs to convince. I'm not in the habit of dossing around in Las Vegas for weeks on end, screwing jailbait adolescents, marrying them, then walking out the next day. You know that, Simon. How long have we worked together now?"

"Ten years."

"Ten years. So, think about it for a moment, will you? Have you ever known me take a holiday, let alone even consider marriage? Why the fuck would I do any of that?"

"I'm lawyer, Cal, not a psychiatrist. All I'm telling you is this, those documents would stand up in court if she ever does decide to pursue that course."

"So, let's make sure she doesn't. I need you to pay her a little visit, in a few days, when she's had time to consider her options. Remind her of what's at stake and make sure she knows I mean business."

"Do you want me to take Harry along, too? He could rough her up a bit, make sure we have her full attention."

I sigh. Sometimes I swear I'm surrounded by idiots.

"No, do I fuck. You've been overdoing it on Netflix with the

US gangster movies. I'm a businessman, not a hoodlum. Just explain things to her and make sure she gets it. And then, once the penny has dropped, it wouldn't hurt to keep an eye on her for a while. Hire someone discreet, but thorough. Have her watched and let me know if she does anything I might not approve of."

"What sort of thing?"

"Jesus, Simon, Work it out. Or, better still, let whoever you hire work it out. And I want you to go over that stuff again. And again. Those papers are forged. They must be. I want to know exactly how she acquired them just in case she does call my bluff and go for that decree nisi."

"But you said—"

"You've worked with me long enough to know my style by now. I prefer to do business by boxing off every possibility apart from the outcome I want. See to it, Simon, or I shall have to find someone who can."

CHAPTER 3

The thug in a silk suit marches me back to the foyer of Ingram, Albright, and Smartt. He lets me stop at the front desk for long enough to hand back my lanyard, then he escorts me out of the door.

As soon as we get outside, I shake his hand off my elbow and try to stride away along the pavement with some semblance of dignity intact, but he grabs my arm again.

"Where are you going?" he asks me.

"Mind your own business," I snap back.

He flags down a passing cab and opens the rear door. "Get in."

"I don't want—"

"Take her to Piccadilly Station," he instructs the driver.

I cease my protests, since I do, actually, need to get to the station. Once there, I can hop on the intercity headed for Euston, and get off at the first stop, Stockport. So I allow him to bundle me into the taxi, my now depleted bag dumped on my lap. My escort hands the driver a ten-pound note then closes the door and watches calmly from the pavement as the cab glides away into the traffic. I peer back through the rear window to see him hike back into the building, his duty apparently done.

"Animals," I mutter. "All of them."

How did it all go so wrong? I know the papers were all right, everything perfectly in order. Even Caleb McPherson's own lawyer agreed with me on that. He can't deny that any of it happened, but somehow, he managed to do just that. Worse, he now has my evidence, which is probably already in the shredder. And he's called me a liar, a thief, Christ knows what else, as well as threatening to ruin my business and put me out on the streets.

How could I have ever thought I loved him?
I don't even like him.

A sharp bolt of something painful stabs at me. Not anger, not even resentment. With a start, I realise it's disappointment. Bitter, gnawing disappointment. I had, God help me, actually looked forward to seeing Caleb again. In what I can only now describe as an abject fit of naivety, I can acknowledge, if only to myself, that I anticipated some sort of reunion. Not necessarily the happy ever after sort, not after the way he dumped me followed by five years of total silence, but I had been hoping for closure. I wanted to tie off the loose ends, leave it all tidy.

I wanted us to be...okay. Friends, perhaps.

Despite this afternoon's unpleasantness, I have no trouble at all in remembering how he managed to charm me out of my knickers and into that marriage chapel. Even now, five years older and a lot more experienced, I would struggle to resist him. He was always attractive, but today he was simply devastating on every level. Sexy, self-assured, built like an athlete, but it was always his eyes that got to me. He had only to look at me, and I would be drowning.

And the truly awful thing, the most shameful admission, he still could.

It was different today, though. More...unsettling, I was in the right. I was telling the truth, not him. But somehow, I still found myself wanting to apologise to him, ask him to forgive me. Or fuck me. Or both. I don't remember feeling like that about him before, though maybe I did. I was under his spell, for sure, but I remember it as a purely physical attraction rather than this emotional, compulsive tug I sensed from him today.

I shake my head as though that might help me regain some perspective, but it doesn't. I have to face it, arrogant bastard or not, I'm still as much enthralled by Caleb McPherson as I was back there in Vegas.

I get out if the cab and make my way to the platform for my train, still in something of a daze. Nothing about this adds up.

Why did he deny it? And carry on denying it, despite the clear evidence. Even his own staff believed me, I'm sure of it. Why is he so certain I want to extort money from him? I never said that, would never even consider such a thing. I don't need his money.

I wanted him, once. Maybe I still do, but I'm a realist and I know that ship has sailed. I told him the absolute truth, I just want that divorce and to move on. I would never have contacted him again.

He sneered at me, at my account of our time together, but even so, he possesses more than enough self-confidence in his little finger to overcome any temporary embarrassment I might have caused him. Maybe a whirlwind romance in Las Vegas was totally out of character for him. Me too, come to think of it. Neither of us has much to be proud of, but even so I would have thought he would be big enough to face what he did. What *we* did.

I stare out of the train at the outer suburbs of south Manchester as they whizz past. Within minutes we slow down and stop in Stockport where I exit the train. I should go straight home, I suppose, but I need a bit more time to think about what has happened and to process this afternoon's events. So instead of heading for the bus stop I walk across the town centre in the direction of the converted mill where my studio workshops are located.

What Happens in Vegas…

Acorn Arts is my pride and joy. A potter myself, I nevertheless love the visual arts in all forms, and it made perfect sense to me to split the space, which is much larger than I need just for my own studio, into individual workshops and invite others to join me. I signed up for a ten-year lease and found myself flooded with requests for the space. It's a good, steady income, with the added bonus that every day I am surrounded by painters, sculptors, illustrators, all gifted creatives starting out on their careers. Just like me.

Yes, he threatened to wreck all of this, to keep me quiet. To stop me from telling the world the truth about him.

And he succeeded. There's no way I'll jeopardise what I've started to build here, let alone the roof over my head. I have responsibilities, people who depend on me.

I wander down to my own private workshop space and start up my potter's wheel. I pull a stained smock on over my clothes, an old shirt that once belonged to my father, and scoop a handful of wet clay from a large barrel I keep beside the wheel.

My foot operates a pump, to keep the clay wet enough to work with, but the wheel itself runs on electricity. It whirrs quietly as I knead the clay, tugging at the edges and digging my thumbs into the centre to create the shape I want. This will be a cup, part of a set of six. Decorated in a bright, geometric pattern, this is one of my best sellers at the various craft fairs I frequent up and down the country. I can almost create the shape blindfold.

I slow the wheel and make the final adjustments to be quite certain the cup matches the rest, then I separate it from the face of the wheel using a length of thin wire, rather like slicing cheese. I turn it upside down and etch my initials into the base, then set it on a rack to air dry. Tomorrow, I'll stick a handle on with liquid clay, then glaze it before applying the final colours to create the familiar design.

My brief burst of art therapy is over. I slump onto a low,

sagging sofa and bury my face in my hands. For the first time since I saw him on that stage, I allow my guard to drop.

Alone, in the gathering dusk, I weep for what I still like to think might once have been love.

Three months later…

THE WAITING AREA IS SOLEMN. The half dozen or so of us huddled in the small space speak little, then only in hushed tones. In pairs, we keep to ourselves. Non-intrusive, respecting of each other's privacy and fearfulness in the face of formidable odds.

Beside me, my mother sits, her shoulders hunched and her delicate features pale. This is her third visit to the clinic in as many weeks.

I didn't come the first time. It was routine, after all, her regular three-yearly mammogram. There had never been any issues before. But when she got a letter a few days later calling her back for further tests and examinations, I came with her. Of course I did, though I had to wait outside the examination suite with the other anxious relatives. Husbands, mainly, men in their fifties and sixties confronting the prospect of losing those they love.

I face the same potential tragedy, the same crushing loss, and I have not the first notion how I will cope. How will *we* cope, if this turns out to be…?

The tests that day took over an hour, and my mum was ashen when she finally emerged from the examination suite. Much prodding, poking, ultrasound scanning, and a biopsy later, she now faced a week's wait for the results. It felt like months, but at last, here we are, waiting our turn to see the consultant.

The door opens, and a female voice calls my mother's name.

"Poppy Daniels?"

What Happens in Vegas...

"Yes, that's me." My mum gets up and follows the nurse. I trail behind.

Is it a good sign that we are seeing a nurse rather than the consultant himself? I decide it must be and take a seat beside my mum. I reach for her hand as the nurse settles herself on the other side of the desk and scans the file in front of her.

My misplaced optimism is dispelled in mere moments. We both sit, silent, letting words like 'carcinoma', 'malignant', 'invasive', wash over us. It seems my mother has never been one for self-examination. Had she been, she might have discovered the lump herself and sought treatment earlier. As it is, she has already reached stage two or possibly three. The cancer has spread to her lymph nodes and surrounding muscle tissues. The treatment options are laid out for our consideration—chemotherapy, radiation and surgery, probably a combination of the three. The cancer is becoming aggressive, the nurse warns, but the prognosis could still be good.

"This is beatable," she assures us. "We'll start treatment at once. I can make you an appointment with a specialist oncologist for..." she peers at her computer screen, "this coming Tuesday. She'll talk through all the options and help determine the best course of treatment for you."

I find my voice, at last. "She...she'll be all right, though? You're saying it's still treatable."

"Outcomes are much improved, even in the last five years or so. You're in good hands, Mrs Daniels, and we're going to do all we can to beat this."

"But...what are the likely odds?" I begin, only to shake my head and think better of it. I'm not even going there. My mum can't be dying. I won't have it.

She is made of sterner stuff. Or maybe she is just numbed with the shock. It's clear she wants out of here. "Next Tuesday? Right, then." She takes the sheet of paper which is already humming out of the printer. It has the appointment details on it. She folds it, shoves it in her handbag, and gets to her feet. "Is that it? For now?"

"Yes, but here's a card for our helpline. Feel free to phone us if you have questions or need to talk. About anything."

The card follows the appointment sheet into her handbag, and moments later we are making our way back to the car park.

Despite having had a week to get used to the idea, I'm still in shock. I can't believe my mum has taken this news so calmly.

I hold out my and for her car keys when she attempts to open the door to her Ford Fiesta. "I'll drive."

I suspect she's more shaken than she's letting on because she allows me to slip into the driver's seat unchallenged. Neither of us speaks during the half-hour drive back to the terraced house we share in the outskirts of Stockport.

It's not until we're facing each other across the kitchen table, mugs of steaming tea at the ready, before I manage to say anything.

"Stage two. That's not too bad. We'll beat this, we really will."

She nods. "I mean to."

"They can do wonders these days," I continue. "You hear about it all the time. New advances, better treatments. Maybe we should think about going private."

She shakes her head. "The National Health is good enough for me. Best in the world. I'll see this oncologist on Tuesday and sort out what's what." She pauses, takes a tentative sip of her tea, then, "But all of this sort of brings matters to a head. It's not just me who has things to sort out. What about your life?"

I pause, my mug suspended between the table and my lips. "Me? What do you mean?"

"I mean, that leftover business from Las Vegas. It's time you ruled a line under it, once and for all."

I meet her eyes. "I tried that. You know I did. And you know why I can't press it any further."

"I know you've found yourself hitched up to a high-handed

bully who thinks he can threaten and scare you into doing as he wants." She shakes her head, irritated. "I should never have let you go on your own that day."

"It would have made no difference. And I doubt you'd have been allowed into the shareholders' meeting anyway."

"Moral support, love. I should have been there."

"Mum, you know what he'll do if I try to take matters to court. We can't deal with all of that, especially not now. We have other priorities."

"You were always my priority, Fern, and that won't ever stop. I do mean to beat this cancer, but just in case I can't, what then? You'll need your life back. You'll need to move on. What if you meet someone else and you're still shackled to this Caleb McPherson?"

"Don't even think about not beating the cancer," I protest. "And there's no one else. There won't ever be."

"You don't know that, love. How could you?"

But I do know. Those weeks with Caleb were the best sex of my life. The only sex of my life, in fact. There was no one before, and apart from a couple of lacklustre encounters with other budding artists, none since. I can't imagine ever wanting to get married again after my experiences so far. I've learned my lesson.

My mum is not letting up. "It's a mess, Fern. You know it, I know it. You can't go on like this, stuck in some sort of half-life. Married to a heartless, spineless bastard who pretends he doesn't even know you."

"But he said—"

She grabs my hand. "Think about it. The tenancy of this house is in my name, not yours. I've never been so much as a day late with my rent, never had a wrong word. And I rent from a housing association, not some grubby little private landlord. There's no way he can get us out of here. And you have a ten-year lease at the workshop, bought and paid for. They can't just chuck you out. He might be wealthy and ready to throw his weight about, but we have rights, too. I say we take him on."

"Okay, we will." *Anything for a quiet life right now.* "But, Mum, one battle at a time. Let's get you well again, then I can—"

"No, I brought you up to have backbone, to stand up for yourself. And if there's one thing I've learned today, it's that time might be shorter than we think. Your dad found that out, dropping dead with a heart attack at forty-seven. He'd say the same, if he was still here. Don't put this off, love."

"Caleb has all my documents, the papers from the chapel…"

"So, it was all a matter of public record. We can get duplicates."

She's right. I know, I already checked that. The US authorities will issue replacement papers, for an admin fee. It'll take a couple of weeks but shouldn't be a problem. I can even get replacement wedding photos from the Sunset Garden chapel.

My mum reaches for my hand, her grip surprisingly strong. "Please, Fern. Do this. Do it for me. Stand your ground, go after what you want. I'll get free of cancer. You get free of him. Please, do it for me."

She makes it all sound so simple, so straightforward. Perhaps it is.

I sigh and make up my mind. "I'll send a fax to the Clark County Marriage Bureau tomorrow."

CHAPTER 4

"Come in."

I glance at the door to my office, expecting to see my housekeeper peering around it. Sally Parsons has worked for me for the last five years, overseeing the domestic arrangements here at the large house a few miles from Edinburgh which serves both as my home and my main place of business. I also have offices in Edinburgh itself where most of my corporate staff are based and a smaller suite in The Shard in London. The right address can work wonders, I've found.

But I prefer to work mainly at home, controlling my business interests from my office and conference rooms which cover the ground floor of one wing in my extensive home. The privacy suits me. I get more done without the hassle of traffic, commuting, and office politics. I like to think of myself as a workaholic with a work/life balance.

But it isn't Sally disturbing my morning.

"Simon? What brings you out here? Did we have an appointment?" I bring up my electronic calendar and do a quick check but find my day supposedly clear.

He shakes his head and enters the room. "Something came up. I thought I'd better tell you about it in person."

I set aside the iPad I had been working on and lean back in my leather chair. "What sort of a something?"

"That girl. Fern Daniels."

I frown. "What about her?"

"She instructed solicitors. Graham and Mahony, based in Stockport. She's petitioning for a divorce."

"Bloody hell." I flatten my lips, lean back, close my eyes. "How is she doing that? I have her so-called documents locked up in my safe."

Simon shrugs. "I assume she got duplicates. From the US."

"And how did she do that, exactly, without us knowing? I thought you had someone watching her, tracking her."

"I did. I do."

"So?"

"We hacked into her phone and emails, but she dealt with it all over fax."

I shake my head, wondering why I still employ Simon Waters.

He continues, undaunted. "The first we knew of it was when she phoned her solicitor to confirm that she wanted to go ahead. The papers were filed at the Family Court in Stockport the same day. Yesterday, in fact."

"So, it's done. The wheels are in motion?"

Simon nods. He does at least have the grace to look uncomfortable.

"What can we do to stop it?"

"Nothing, not now..."

I get to my feet and pace to the window to gaze out over my wild meadow. Normally, I prefer this view to the more manicured formal gardens at the front of the house, but not today. Today, I long for the predictable neatness of the clipped lawns and cultivated flowerbeds. And for a woman who will do as she is damned well told.

"Do you want me to get in touch with her landlord, Cal?"

Simon appears almost eager. "And the development company who own that mill she squats in?"

I pinch the bridge of my nose between my finger and thumb and draw in several deep breaths before shaking my head.

"Those measures were intended as a deterrent. They didn't work. She's called our bluff. Any retribution now would be just that, revenge and punishment, hardly very constructive. I don't want vengeance. I just want this fixed."

"Maybe Harry could—"

I glare at him, and Simon falls silent at last. "I do have a job for Harry, but I'll deal with that. What I want you to do is draw up a legal agreement, something watertight that our Miss Daniels can be convinced to sign, swearing that all her previous claims are false. That no wedding took place, and she and I never met prior to the Ingram, Albright, and Smartt shareholders' meeting."

"But she'd never sign that."

"Let me worry about getting her to cooperate. I'm reasonably certain that I can convince her."

"Cal, you can't mean to…"

I raise one eyebrow. Simon is aware of my personal preferences in matters of intimacy. He has shared them, on occasion, though he's something of a submissive himself.

"Just draw up the contract, Simon."

"You might be needing a non-disclosure agreement, too. In case she accuses you of assault."

"We both know those aren't worth the paper they're written on. And it won't come to that. I can be persuasive whilst still respecting boundaries. It's just a matter of pressing the right buttons."

"But you don't know her. You don't know her buttons."

"I will." I don't know her well, this is true, but even on such scant acquaintance I'm fairly sure of my intuition about her. She will respond to my brand of dominance. But it may take a little time to establish quite the right level of rapport, and this is where Harry comes in.

"Thank you, Simon. I'll expect to be looking over the first draft of that agreement by this evening." I wait until he closes the door behind him, then I pull out my mobile phone. Harry is on speed dial.

"Hey, boss. What's up?"

"Miss Daniels is causing us problems again."

"Ah." He waits for my instructions.

"I need you to find a nice craft fair. Something fairly high-end, prestigious. And it needs to be happening in the next week or so."

He never questions my order. "Okay. I'll let you know what I come up with."

YOUR TAXI IS HERE." My mum separates the slats of the Venetian blind with her fingers and peers down into the street. "Best not keep him waiting. He'll have his meter running."

I reach for my overnight bag, then pause. I really should not be doing this.

"I'm not happy about leaving you."

"Don't be ridiculous. I'll be fine."

"You're having major surgery next week. How can you be fine?"

"I'll need you fussing over me when I come out of hospital, and when they start pumping me full of chemicals and radiation. Right now, I feel just as I always did." She leaves her spot by the window to come and take my hand. "This is a big chance for you, and you were lucky to be offered the stall."

"I still don't understand…"

"You were recommended. Just be glad of it. Camden Art Fair is one of the biggest indie events in the country, you said it yourself. Lots of exposure, lots of potential new outlets. Now you just need to get yourself down there and knock 'em dead with your stuff."

"But, Mum..."

"Go. Now. Or you'll miss your train. Text me when you arrive."

I grasp the handle of my bag, lean down, and kiss her on her still-smooth cheek. "Where would I be without you?" I murmur. I desperately hope I'm not going to find out anytime soon.

She kisses me back. "Get on with you."

"I'll be back in two days, but if you need me before that you have only to—"

"Just go."

She more or less bundles me out onto the front steps. I make my way down to the waiting taxi and climb into the back. Her determined smile never wavering, Mum waves to me from the doorstep as the car pulls away.

"Piccadilly Station," I call to the driver, who nods. I already told the firm my destination when I booked the cab. I have just over an hour before my train leaves for Euston, plenty of time to grab a latte and plan how best to lay out my three-square metres of display space in Camden Lock's bustling arts and crafts gallery.

The car turns out of my quiet side road and joins the main route heading towards Manchester. I settle back in the soft leather rear seat and for the first time I register what a particularly nice car this is. I detect none of the usual questionable odours associated with minicabs. No hint of stale beer, three-day-old curry, or the lingering aroma of vomit and disinfectant.

Oh no, don't say I booked a limo by mistake...

I lean forward to peer between the front seats, looking for the meter. I don't see one.

"Excuse me," I begin...

The car slows, then takes a left turn.

"Is this the quickest way to Piccadilly Station?" I peer left and right, unable to fathom this route. "I think you may have taken a wrong turning…"

The car glides to a halt, and the door to my right opens. A large man slides in beside me. Horrified, stunned, and outraged in equal measure, I stifle a scream and make a dash for the other door, just as the central locking system gives a decisive clunk, sealing me inside. I grab the handle, rattle it in mounting desperation.

"Let me out. Let me out," I demand. "What are you doing? Get out of my cab…"

"Miss Daniels. How nice to see you again."

I recoil into the farthest corner of the large car, gaping at the man beside me. "Who…? "What…?"

"I am saddened that you don't remember me, Miss Daniels, though I appreciate you will have had other matters to concern you on the occasion of our first meeting. That was a few weeks ago, at Ingram, Albright, and Smartt. I recall that you were most anxious to speak with my employer."

I recognise him now. This is the huge baboon of a man who escorted me from the offices that day and put me in a taxi. He was terrifying enough then, but my insides turn to liquid now.

"Why are you doing this? You have to let me out. I don't want—"

"Mr McPherson wishes to speak with you." He offers the terse explanation as though that accounts for everything, justifies this…this outrageous behaviour."

"You can't just…just abduct people off the street. Even Caleb can't expect—"

"But he does. Mr McPherson is expecting you at his headquarters in Scotland, so I am afraid you won't be going anywhere else, at least not for a while."

"This is ridiculous. I have a train to catch. I'm on my way to—"

"Camden Lock. Yes, I know. For the UK Indie Arts and Crafts Pageant or whatever it's called. I arranged it for you. You should do very well, though sadly you will not be present yourself."

My head is whirling. "You? How did you arrange it? I was—"

"You were offered a short notice cancellation slot."

"Yes, but..."

"The organisers were happy enough to squeeze you in, for a fee."

"A fee?" I squeak. "What fee? I can't afford—"

My heart sinks. The fee is the least of my worries. I packed up all my very best work, placed it in crates and shipped it off to London on the strength of this 'opportunity'. I've lost thousands of pounds worth of stock, items I should have been selling all over the north-west of England and which could now be anywhere. It will take me months to replace it all.

"The fee has been paid. Your wares have been transported to the venue, and agency staff will look after your stall. In the meantime, you will be enjoying a short break. In Scotland."

I claw at the handle again and hurl myself against the door. "I can't go to Scotland. I can't go anywhere. I need to be here. My mother is ill, and—"

The baboon grabs me and pulls me back into the seat. His arms are around me, like clamps. I can barely breathe.

"Miss Daniels, I cannot permit you to carry on like this. You might injure yourself, which Mr McPherson would not like. Or you might damage our vehicle, which I would not like. Worst of all, you might succeed in attracting unwelcome attention from other road users which would seriously piss off all of us."

"Then let me go. You have no right—"

"I appreciate that this is somewhat unexpected, but you *are* coming with us to Scotland to meet with Mr McPherson. There are, I gather, a number of unresolved issued to be discussed."

"I have nothing more to say to that bastard..."

The baboon does not even answer me. His next words are directed to our driver, who has been silent up until now.

"We'll make a stop in the warehouse to get her properly secured, then continue on."

Warehouse? Secured? I wriggle with renewed energy, but to no avail. The man with his arms locked around me is as strong as an ox.

Too soon, we leave the busy traffic. The buildings on either side of the wide roads are huge industrial units with gaping goods entrances, each one surrounded by acres of tarmac. The car purrs through a set of heavy electric gates and glides into one such unit, coming to a stop beside a towering stack of pallets.

The baboon lets me go, and the driver unlocks the doors. He gets out, then walks around the car to open the door closest to the other man. My captor slides out, dragging me effortlessly behind him.

I scream and kick, try to bite him.

"For fuck's sake, are you serious?"

Three times my size, he bundles me facedown over the bonnet and pulls both my hands into the small of my back. Moments later, he has secured them with something. I lay panting, my cheek against the cool metal, shocked to my core, utterly terrified.

The driver opens the boot, then hands the baboon an item. It's a roll of tape. He tears off a strip a few inches long and lays it across my mouth.

Helpless, I can only gaze up at my abductors, silently pleading with them not to harm me.

"Miss Daniels," the baboon begins. He takes my elbow and assists me in standing up straight, then he marches me around to the still-open boot. "One way or another, you are coming with us to Scotland. The journey will take perhaps four hours, and you may spend that time in the car, with us. Or, you can travel in the boot, bound and gagged, like this. There's plenty of room, as you can see, though I don't suppose it will be very comfortable. So, which is it to be?"

What Happens in Vegas...

I close my eyes, and my legs start to buckle.

"Do I have your promise that there will be no more kicking and screaming? No more attempts to escape? No more unseemly displays likely to cause a traffic hazard? You may nod if you agree."

I nod desperately, too scared to even contemplate defiance.

"In that case I shall remove the gag and allow you to sit in the car. Any more trouble from you, and the gag goes back on and you will be in the boot. Is this absolutely clear?"

Again, I nod. Will he keep his word?

He rips the tape away with one swift, painful tug. I gasp in huge lungfuls of air and stagger as my knees threaten to give way. The baboon steadies me again and assists me back into the rear seat.

The driver has already taken my overnight bag and dumped it in the boot. The baboon removes my shoes, and those, too, are stowed with the rest of my things. "Just to discourage you from making a run for it when we have to stop for petrol," he explains. "Not foolproof, but every little helps." He slides back in beside me.

The driver slips into the front seat and starts the engine. Moments later, we are back outside, in the daylight, and presumably headed for Scotland.

The baboon smiles at me, a not unpleasant expression, all things considered. "I apologise for the necessity of all of this, Miss Daniels. It is not my wish to frighten you unduly, or that you should be uncomfortable on the journey. If you require a comfort break, or something to eat or drink, you have only to say so."

I gaze at him, unable to find words to answer. He doesn't seem especially cruel or violent, but all of this...

"My name is Harry. As you will have gathered, I work for Mr McPherson. And this is Jared, our driver. If you require anything on the journey, please feel free to say so." He leans forward to open a storage unit fitted into the rear of the front passenger seat. It's a small fridge, and from it he extracts a bottle of still water. "I expect you will appreciate a drink, Miss Daniels."

He snaps open the top and holds it out to me. My hands are still bound so I can't take it, but he places it by my lips and tips it gently. I swallow a few drops.

"Enough?" he asks.

I nod.

He replaces the cap and slots the bottle into the door pocket. "You might try getting some sleep. I'll wake you when we get near."

I can't even start to imagine going to sleep, but the opportunity to close my eyes and shut all of this out, at least for a while, isn't unwelcome. I turn away from him and rest my cheek against the door panel as the car glides down the slip road to join the motorway heading north.

"Would you like a cushion?"

I shake my head and blink back tears.

In the next moment, gentle fingers cup my chin, and he has produced a spotless cotton handkerchief. He wipes my eyes.

"There's no need for all of this, Miss Daniels. We won't hurt you."

"Y-you abducted me," I protest. "In what universe would I not be scared?"

"I take your point, but you have my word that as long as you cause me no trouble, everything will be fine."

My tears continue to flow. "I need to be at home. My mother needs me…"

"Does she? You already arranged to be away for three days."

"I know, but…she's not well, and I ought to be there. I never should have agreed to the London trip."

"Well, I'm glad you did. It saved me the bother of coming up with another cover story for you." He smiles at me, and it's rather like dealing with a kindly uncle. He's not young, mid-forties, probably, but he has strong features and an eminently capable look about him. It doesn't surprise me that Caleb sends this Harry to do his dirty work. I suspect he is very efficient.

"Pass me a cushion and a blanket, Jared."

The driver reaches into the passenger seat and tosses both items over the back.

"I said I didn't want—"

"Humour me." Harry tucks the cushion between my cheek and the car door, then spreads the blanket over me. "Just take things easy, Miss Daniels."

CHAPTER 5

I open my eyes, startled.
"Miss Daniels, do you want to come inside?"

Inside? I peer at Harry the baboon, bewildered and confused. "Inside where?"

"Time for a toilet stop. And they do excellent coffee here. And cakes. Do you fancy that?"

The prospect of the loo appeals. I nod.

"Okay. Here are your shoes." He places my battered Nike trainers beside me on the car seat. "I'll need you on your best behaviour, mind. It would be a pity to arrive at Linn Mill in the boot after all, don't you agree?" As he issues his warning, Harry reaches behind me, and with a swift tug he releases my bound hands. He emerges with a tie dangling from his fingers.

I flex my aching wrists, then bend forward to pull on my shoes. "Linn Mill? "What's that?"

"Mr McPherson's estate. It's where we're headed."

"An estate? Like, landed gentry?" I'd already worked out that the man I married five years ago is apparently as rich as Croesus, but I hadn't expected this lord of the manor stuff.

Harry grins. "Maybe, though he bought the property rather than inheriting it. Linn Mill is both Caleb's home and his business headquarters." He smiles at me. "Shall we go and treat ourselves to a latte, then?"

The small tearoom is very comfortable, a little olde worlde, and not exactly the sort of place I would have associated with a paid thug such as Harry. The small, round tables are covered with a red-and-green tartan cloth and a jar of wild flowers decorates each one. The teacups on the counter are delicate, the pretty floral pattern lending its own aura of elegant permanence. They are made of porcelain with saucers to match. The cutlery is decorated with ornate thistles, all very Scottish.

Harry lays his hand on my elbow as he escorts me inside, then selects the table closest to the toilets.

"Wait here," he instructs me.

I sit, and Jared takes the seat opposite. The driver picks up the menu while Harry ducks through the low door leading to the toilets. He emerges a moment or two later.

"All clear. In you go."

I enter the toilet to find one door with a female image on it, and next to it the men's cubicle. Harry leans against the outside of the men's door and gestures me into the ladies' cubicle with a tilt of his chin. It's clear he intends to wait here for me.

For want of a better option, I use the facilities as quickly, and quietly, as I can. I emerge to find Harry at the wash basin.

I rinse my hands, lather in a bit of soap, then rinse again. He hands me a paper towel, then we return to the main tearoom where Jared is deep in conversation with a short woman wearing a grey apron. She beams at Harry.

"Ah, Mr Fowlds, it's so nice tae see ye again. Ye'll be havin' yer usual, I daresay...?"

"Indeed I will, Agnes. A double-shot latte and a generous slice of your lemon drizzle cake."

She nods enthusiastically. "And for the young lady?"

"Miss Daniels?" Harry guides me back into my seat. "I can recommend the coffee here, and any of the cakes. Agnes's shortbread is especially wonderful, mind."

"I'm fine. Really."

Agnes is having none of that. "Ee, the lass is fair worn out. Ye've come a long way, I expect. Maybe a nice cup o' herbal tea'll pick 'er up. I have peppermint, jasmine, oh, an' a nice lemon just in."

I rally sufficiently to ask for a pot of normal tea and agree to try a scone. Jared orders an Americano and a slice of something particularly exotic and gooey from the chilled cabinet. Agnes convinces us that a round of toasted buttered teacakes would be in order as well, and I find myself actually looking forward to that by the time the plates are set before us.

There is little in the way of conversation. After all, what small talk might we make? Agnes more than compensates with her friendly chatter from behind her cluttered counter, and the food does its part, too. The teacakes melt in my mouth, and the scone comes with a generous tub of clotted cream. Despite not feeling especially hungry, I manage to clear all of mine, and all to soon we stroll back out into the late afternoon sunshine and get back in the car.

"You did well," Harry concedes. "For that, I'll let you keep your shoes and I'll leave your hands unbound."

I almost thank him but bite back the words in time.

"How much farther is it to this Linn Mill?"

"About an hour," Harry answers. "You'll be there in time for dinner."

"I don't want dinner. I want to go home."

He shrugs.

Jared starts the engine, and we purr out onto the main road again.

I HADN'T REALLY FORMED any mental picture of what Linn Mill might be like, but even so, I gasp as the car rounds the final bend on the wide, gravelled driveway which must be at least two miles long, and the house comes into view. Linn Mill is a sprawling, gracious residence constructed of pale-grey granite. The stately home rises to four storeys overlooking an elegant terrace and manicured gardens. There is a central main facade, and two additional wings which may have been added later. The overall appearance is Georgian, though architecture is not my speciality.

What Linn Mill is, without a doubt, is impressive. And huge.

"Does Cal live here?" I breathe. "Alone?"

"There's a housekeeper and a few other staff to take care of the grounds, but yes. Pretty much." Harry waits for Jared to bring the vehicle to a halt and get out to open our doors, then he offers me his hand. "Come on. Let's go and find Caleb and get you settled in."

I extricate my hand, but Harry takes my elbow instead. Jared retrieves my bag from the boot whilst we climb the half dozen or so stone steps onto the front terrace. The main entrance, a pair of immense double doors painted immaculate white, loom before us. I half expect the door to open as we approach, but it doesn't. Instead, Harry grabs the handle, turns it, and gestures me to precede him inside.

"Shouldn't we—?"

"Caleb's expecting us," he replies. "This way."

I'M in my office checking over the due diligence for a takeover I'm contemplating when the car cruises along my drive and glides to a halt in front of my terrace. I check my watch. Harry made good time. I close the accounts I just downloaded from Companies House, leave my desk, and stroll to the tinted window to observe. The glass allows light to get in but appears black from the outside. I can see them, but they can't see me.

Harry emerges first, from the back seat. He leans back into

the rear to help Fern Daniels out, while Jared collects her luggage from the boot.

She appears ridiculously tiny next to my men, barely reaching Harry's shoulder. And even from this distance I can see that she is scared.

Utterly terrified would be a better description. And well she might be, though not for the reasons she probably suspects. I don't intend to harm her. I don't even mean to hurt her. Well, not much. And not without her consent. I mean to fuck with her mind, expose her to a whole new perspective on truth and falsehood. By the time we are finished, I have no doubt she will see matters with sufficient clarity and be ready to sign Simon's agreement.

I take in her appearance. The description that comes most readily to mind is unprepossessing. The waist-length leather jacket is familiar. I think it's probably the same one she wore at our previous meeting, and it suits her. This time, though, she's teamed it with a short denim skirt and thick, black tights. Her choice of footwear lacks much in the way of elegance, but again, the well-worn trainers speak of comfort and familiarity and a 'fuck you' attitude to what anyone else might think. I suspect I will be able to adjust that mindset, too, before we are done.

Her bright-auburn hair is loose and lifts in the slight breeze. She sweeps it from her face as she mounts my front steps and tries to take in the scale of my house. I can imagine what she might be thinking. I still vividly recall my own awe when I first came here to view the property. And I've added a whole new wing since then.

Her gaze scans from left to right as Harry nudges her forward and through the front door.

Time to greet my reluctant guest.

I return briefly to my desk to close down my laptop, then I exit the office, passing through my conference room to reach the external corridor which leads to the main entrance foyer. I emerge through a discreet door behind the central staircase.

Harry sees me at once, but Fern Daniels is too busy gazing up at my elaborately carved ceiling, cut-glass chandelier, and gold-leaf cornices. I know they are bit on the ostentatious side, but the original period features do suit the architecture of the house so I prefer to leave them.

I step forward. "How nice to see you again, Miss Daniels. Welcome to Linn Mill. I trust your journey wasn't too...arduous."

She spins around, wide-eyed. "I can't believe you did this."

I make no pretence of not understanding. "Ah, yes. I didn't think you would agree to come here of your own free will. I apologise for the need to take more direct action."

"Direct action?" She approaches me, emerald-coloured eyes blazing now. "You had me kidnapped. Snatched off the street. I could have you arrested. The whole lot of you."

"I'm sure it won't come to that," I murmur, suppressing a smile. She was not exactly seized on the street, though I will grant that she has reason to be aggrieved. I attempt to appease her. "Can I offer you some refreshment?"

"No, you can't. I won't be staying. I insist that you—"

"Jared, would you put Miss Daniels' bag in the Rose Room, please?"

The driver nods and sets off up the stairs.

"Now, hold it right there. I don't want—"

"Please, come and sit down. You must be tired after the journey." I gesture towards the drawing room where I asked Sally to lay out tea and coffee. "We have a lot to talk about."

"No, we don't." She starts to back up in the opposite direction. "I said all I had to say to you back there in Manchester. If there's more, take it up with my lawyer. I'm leaving. Now."

She manages two paces towards the door before Harry grasps her by the arm and steers her in the direction of my drawing room. She struggles, forcing him to firm up his hold.

She is beginning to fight in earnest, not exactly how I had hoped to commence our encounter.

"Okay, Harry. I'll take it from here."

He releases her at once but takes the precaution of blocking her way to the door.

"Miss Daniels. I know you're upset. You have every reason to be. I—"

"That man tied me up." She jabs a finger at Harry. "He gagged me and threatened to make me travel all the way here in the boot. The bloody boot of a car..." Her voice is rising, and she is close to tears. "I hate being closed in, and I hate the dark. I was so scared. I thought... I thought..."

I wrap my arm around her shoulder. "I know, and I'm sorry it had to be like that."

"He even took my shoes," she sobs.

"But he gave them back," I point out. "And you didn't ride in the boot, did you?"

"No, but—"

I give Harry a nod as I manage to bundle Fern through the drawing room door. Despite Miss Daniels' complaints, he did a good job. He may look the part of a hired thug, and he can play it well enough when occasion demands. But he is also intelligent, sensitive, and not inclined towards mindless violence. He clearly scared her but still managed to get her here unharmed and not as traumatized as she might have been.

Well, I hope not.

Harry follows us into the drawing room and adopts his position by the door.

"May I take your coat?" I offer her a warm smile by way of reassurance.

She shakes her head and hugs the leather jacket closer.

I let the matter of her jacket go for now and settle for easing my unwilling guest onto a sofa, then I sit beside her. "Do you prefer tea or coffee?"

"Tea," she sniffles.

Ah, now we're getting somewhere. "Milk? Sugar?"

"Just milk."

I pour for her and get a black coffee for myself.

"I... I can't stay here. You have to let me go home."

"Of course I'll let you go home." *Eventually.*

"Now. I need to go now. My mother is ill, you see. She needs me."

I raise an eyebrow. "Oh? I understood that you made arrangements for a three-day trip to London. She won't be expecting you back until late on Sunday."

She puts her teacup down with a clatter and starts to get up. "I should never have agreed to it. I have to go back. Now."

Time to assert a little authority. "That won't be happening, Fern." I ease her back onto the sofa and cup her chin in my palm. "You're going to be spending a couple of days with me. We need to talk, to resolve some matters. Then you can go home. Understood?"

"You can't make me stay if I don't want to." The hint of defiance in her eyes is not even remotely convincing.

"I think we both know that I can. You'll be spending the weekend here so get used to it. You might even enjoy yourself."

"Enjoy being called a liar and a gold-digger," she grumbles. "I doubt it."

"There will be no name-calling, on either side. Agreed?"

"Then what are we going to find to talk about?"

"I thought we might start with a tour of Linn Mill, but first, do you want to let your mother know you're all right?"

"I said I'd text her..."

"Do that, then." I glance over at Harry. "I assume you have Miss Daniels' phone."

He produces it from his jacket pocket and hands it to me. I pass it onto Fern. "Keep it simple. No need to worry her. Just tell her you arrived safe and you'll see her on Sunday."

I watch as she types in the message, but I take the phone from her before she has a chance to press 'send'.

Mum. Call the police. Kidnapped. In Scotland.

I'm not surprised. Not even disappointed, I really can't blame her, but in the world she's going to inhabit for the next couple of days, actions have consequences.

I delete the message and type in another.

Arrived safe. Nice hotel. See you Sunday. I press 'send' then slip the phone into my jeans pocket.

"Hey, that's mine."

I shoot a wry smile her way. You can have it back on Sunday. Have you finished your tea?"

She nods.

"Good. In that case, first we need to deal with the matter of your disobedience, then I'll give you the tour I promised."

"Disobedience? What are you talking about?"

"The text. Not especially helpful. And definitely not what I told you to write."

"You can't expect me to—"

"I expect you to do as you're told. You didn't, so you're going to be punished. It really is that simple."

"You've no right to punish me."

"My house, my rules."

"But I didn't want to come here. I didn't ask to come. I don't accept your rules."

Her protests are all fair enough, but beside the point. I harden my tone. "For the next two days, I strongly suggest that you reconsider that position, Fern, and accept what you can't change. Submit to your punishment, learn from it, and we can all move on."

"What...what do you mean to do?"

"A spanking will be sufficient, this time. Nothing too heavy."

"Spanking?" she squeaks. "You mean to spank me?"

"I do, yes. Shall we get on with it?"

She shakes her head, backing away from me along the sofa. "Are you mad? You can't just... I mean..."

"Harry, would you leave us, please." It's clear we have plenty of barriers to get past without adding an audience to the mix.

He bows his head and exits.

"So, it's just the two of us. If you would lay across my lap we can soon be done with this unpleasantness."

"I won't. It's ridiculous. What do you think—?

"I think you need to do as I say. I believe I already made that clear." I harden my tone yet further. The sooner she gets her head around who is actually in charge here, the better. "My lap. Now."

She stares at me. Seconds tick past. I give her time. This is a big deal for her. I get that and I don't want to rush it. But I *will* have my way.

She begins to edge towards me, her gaze locked on my lap.

"You might like to remove your jacket now," I suggest.

Wordlessly, she slips it off and hands it to me. I drape it over the arm of the sofa.

"How should I...?"

I shift forward on the sofa. "Hands and feet on the floor. I'll raise your skirt and lower your tights and underwear. Once we start, you will remain still until I tell you we're done."

"You mean to spank my bare bottom?" Her shocked expression is almost comical.

"Oh yes," I confirm. "I'd be short-changing you otherwise. Be assured, Fern, I intend to make this a truly memorable experience for you."

CHAPTER 6

Have I slipped into some sort of parallel universe? Some world where people can be abducted, held against their will, spanked for the slightest disobedience?

In the entire three weeks of my torrid affair with Caleb before our wedding, and our relationship was pretty full-on and intense, he never so much as hinted at any of this. He never came across as the sort of man who would…who would…

"Be quick, Fern. I'm sure you're just as keen to get this done with as I am. Maybe even more so since I confess I expect to rather enjoy myself."

He sounds very…firm, suddenly. Not in a threatening, bullying sort of a way, but in a way that says he expects to be obeyed. And fast.

I could argue. I *should* argue, I'm sure of it. But I am equally sure that I won't. There's something in that measured tone, that raised eyebrow, that expectant glint in his dark-chocolate eyes that is both compelling and reassuring.

This will be all right, as long as I do as I am told.

So, I don't do the sensible thing and scream blue murder. I don't scramble for the door, screeching at the top of my lungs or threaten to call the police the first chance I get. Instead, I sidle forward, slowly but surely, and I slither across his lap.

"Good girl," he murmurs, gently positioning me to his satisfaction. "Can you put your hands and feet on the floor?"

I can, just about. "Yes, I think so."

"Good. Keep them there. Don't kick out, and don't reach back to protect your bottom. Do you understand?"

"Yes," I whisper.

His fingers brush the backs of my thighs when he lifts my short shirt up and arranges the fabric in the small of my back.

"I'm going to pull your tights and underwear down to your knees. Then, when you're nice and bared for me, I want you to lift up your bottom to receive your spanking."

Oh. My. God.

I lie still, my eyes tight shut, while he does exactly what he just described. The cool waft of air across my buttocks proclaims my state of utter humiliation and absolute vulnerability.

"Lift up for me. Offer me your bottom to spank." His voice is low, deceptively soft.

I obey, because to not do so is unthinkable.

How on earth did I ever get myself into this?

"Fern, are you ready?"

As much as I'll ever be. I manage a nod.

"Say it, if you would, please."

"I... I'm ready."

The first slap is soft, more a caress than a spank. He brings his palm down on my right buttock, then spends the next few moments rubbing the faint sting away.

I let out a breath, not even aware until that moment I had been holding it. Maybe a spanking isn't so awful, after all.

The next slap is just as gentle as the first, the third one, too. Each is followed by a few moments spent massaging away the hurt, though I could not exactly describe the sensation as painful. The impact, if that is the right way to describe this experience, is not on my rear end, at least, not yet. Rather, it is between my ears. Somewhere in my head, for reasons I cannot even start to unravel, I am reacting in a wholly inappropriate manner to the indignity and intimacy of being treated this way, made to display myself, to surrender to his will.

It's...almost as though I actually enjoy what he is doing to me.

Dear Lord, Vegas was never like this!

He continues to spank me, and gradually the pressure builds. He slaps me a little harder, sharpening the crack when his hand meets my flesh, and the slither of pain which dances across my tender skin becomes hotter with each stroke.

He still smooths the sting away, but residual heat remains. The sensation starts to build, and I let out a grunt.

"Did that one hurt?" he enquires.

"Yes," I mutter, though my throat feels clogged somehow.

"Is it too much?" he asks me. "Do you want me to stop?"

I shake my head without thinking. "No, It's fine."

Fine? In what world is this fine?

"Okay, then."

He continues to drop spank after spank onto my upturned bottom while I writhe and whimper across his lap. It never occurs to me to ask him to stop, especially when he takes more and more time between spanks just rubbing my buttocks in slow, lazy circles. The contrast between the sharp prickles of discomfort with each new spank, and the languid sensuality of the rubbing is almost hypnotic, a heady, erotic clash of baffling, conflicting sensations which turn my brain to cotton wool.

Eventually, the intensity of each slap is enough to make me gasp, then squeal, then cry out.

He slows, resting his palm on my heated flesh.

"Enough, yet?"

"I'm not sure. I think..." I try to clear my head, but it might as well be stuffed with feathers. It's all I can do to remember my own name.

"Enough," he repeats, though it's not a question this time.

He eases his arm under my body and lifts me to a standing

What Happens in Vegas…

position. My skirt is still tucked into its own waistband, and my tights are around my knees. My backside feels to be on fire, though I don't think he spanked me that hard. My perspective must be all wrong.

He turns me to face away from him, and my bum is now at his eye level.

"Your bottom looks beautiful, all freshly spanked. Such a pretty shade of pink. Now, I want you to stand there until I tell you to move. I have a couple of calls to make and I'll enjoy admiring my handiwork while I'm on the phone."

If draping myself across his lap has been a challenge, to be made to stand here, my underwear lowered and my skirt raised, my punished bottom on proud display, is excruciating. What if Harry should come back? Or someone else…?

Caleb, the arrogant pig, ignores my discomfort and dials a number on his phone.

I soon start to fidget.

"Simon? Yes, she's here. Do you have the paperwork we discussed?" Caleb's tone is neutral as he speaks to his colleague. "Email it to me, please. I also need the articles of incorporation for MNQ and dates of forthcoming board meetings." There's a short pause, then, "Increase our offer by seven percent, and…excuse me. Fern, put your hands on your head and your feet apart. Don't squirm about."

I'm mortified. Whoever he's speaking to knows about me, knows I'm here, recently spanked and being made to stand like a naughty schoolgirl. I send him a baleful look over my shoulder before adopting the position required.

"Eye-rolling and scowls won't help you to get your underwear pulled back up any sooner. Don't be a brat, Fern."

I clench my jaw but succeed in not making matters any worse. Caleb returns to his conversation.

"I can sign the deeds on Tuesday. And, yes, pencil him in for Thursday. Okay. Bye."

He ends his call and immediately makes another, this time

to a bank as far as I can work out, though I suspect not in this country as he lapses into speaking German several times.

"*Auf veidersehn.*" He closes that call, too, and at last, mercifully, sets his phone down on the low table beside the sofa. "You can restore your clothing now and sit down again. That is, if you feel you want to, obviously."

I bend to pull up my tights and knickers and release my skirt from around my waist. Then, I turn to face him.

"Can I ...? I mean, did you say I was to have a room here? My bag...?"

"You want some time on your own?"

I nod.

He meets my gaze, shaking his head. "Not a good idea, in my experience. You'd only brood and become upset if left to yourself. It's my responsibility to take care of you, since it was me who punished you, and I can't do that it I leave you to cower in your room."

I stiffen my spine. "I wasn't thinking of cowering. I'm tired. I just want..."

He gets to his feet, pockets his phone again, and extends his hand to me. "There's something I need to show you, then you can have a short rest before dinner."

I scowl at him, deliberately ignoring his outstretched hand.

He shrugs and strolls to the door. "After you, Fern."

I should feel better after my mini victory over refusing to take his hand, but I don't. I feel like a sulky child when I stalk past him to go back into the airport hangar of a hallway.

The entire house is built on a huge scale, the ceilings, the curving main staircase, the expanse of marble tiled floor. The house I share with my mum would easily fit into one corner of this vast foyer. I try not to stare as Caleb leads the way across the imposing space, though I know my eyes must have been out on stalks the first time I stepped in here.

"I... I never realised your house was so big," I blurt out, hurrying to keep up with him.

What Happens in Vegas…

He pauses, sends a wry glance my way. "Maybe you're regretting filing for that divorce, after all."

I stop dead, and in that moment any residual vestiges of composure crumble. "You bastard," I hurl at him before I spin around and make a run for it, seeking the relative if somewhat dubious safety of the drawing room.

He catches up with me in two strides and wraps his arms around me. I kick out, try to elbow him in the gut, but he turns me in his arms and holds me against his solid chest. I give up the fight and settle for what seems to be my next-best option. Sobbing. Loud, ugly sobbing, the sort to leave distasteful stains on the front of his light-grey T-shirt.

"Y-you promised," I manage between huge, gulping sobs. "No name-calling."

"I know, I'm sorry," he murmurs, from somewhere above my head.

"I d-don't care how rich you are," I howl into his chest. "I never said I want anything. Nothing…!"

"You're right. It was uncalled for. No name-calling, I promise."

"I'm not after your money," I wail. "I wouldn't have your bloody money if you begged me. Or your house. But I was interested, that's all. In the…the history…"

"It's okay," he murmurs. "Just let it out."

I don't quite get what he means about letting it out, but I do feel better for having had a good weep. Odd, this is so not like me, but that tsunami of emotion erupted out of nowhere and I just couldn't stop myself. I was…overwhelmed. Eventually, though, my sobs diminish. I manage a few gasping hiccoughs, then start to wish I had a box of paper handkerchiefs close by. I must look such a wreck.

"I… I don't suppose you have a tissue," I ask, not especially hopeful.

He steers me back into the drawing room and lets go of me, just long enough for him to open a couple of drawers and find a full box of tissues. He pulls back the cardboard top and hands them to me. "There you are. Would you like some more tea? Or maybe a glass of water?"

"Some water would be nice. Thank you."

He somehow manoeuvres me back onto the same sofa where he spanked me just a few minutes ago. I wince as I settle on it. He goes over to a side table by the window where a cut-glass jug and several glasses have been placed. He pours water into one of the glasses, then brings it over to where I am dabbing at my cheeks with handfuls of tissues, wiping my eyes, trying to blow my nose without being too loud about it. He drops onto his haunches before me.

"Drink that, then I'll give you the history lesson on the way to my office."

The water is delicious, lightly flavoured with fresh lemon and very refreshing. Much nicer than the bottled stuff he gave me earlier. I finish the whole glass in two gulps.

"Do you want some more?"

"Yes, please. And... I'm sorry about your shirt."

He straightens, then glances at the crumpled, damp front of his clothing. I wince when I catch sight of the Gucci label on the sleeve and know it has to be genuine.

His lip quirks. He takes my glass and refills it, then waits for me to drink the water. "Feeling better?"

I nod, embarrassed now. "You speak different," I blurt.

"Excuse me?"

"In Las Vegas, you sounded different. There's something... maybe your accent...?"

His expression hardens. "I was never in Las Vegas."

He offers me his hand, and this time I do take it. I'm learning to pick my battles. But I'm not wrong. The man I married spoke with a definite drawl, I assumed it to be American, whereas Caleb's accent is distinctly English, with the occasional hint of a Scots brogue. Just another of his little games, I suppose, intended to confuse me. It won't work. Anyone can

What Happens in Vegas...

mimic an accent. I can manage a passable American twang myself if I put my mind to it.

I set that puzzle aside for now and we continue our tour of his house. Caleb briefly outlines the history of the place.

"Linn Mill, or at least, the original house, was built between seventeen twenty and seventeen twenty-three," he tells me when we arrive back in the entrance foyer. "The early Georgian period in England, though the architecture of the time was influential in Scotland, too, at least in the borders. The original house was just this central section, which was constructed on the site of a much earlier manor house. The place was built by the Carson family who had acquired considerable wealth through mining interests topped up by the slave trade. That particular Mr Carson found himself in need of a big house because he and his wife were blessed with thirteen daughters, all demanding dowries and fine husbands. He had no option but to adopt a lavish lifestyle if he was to succeed in marrying them all off and could afford it. Linn Mill was home to the Carsons and their descendants for over two hundred years, until it was sold to settle unpaid taxes and gambling debts incurred by the last Carson incumbent."

He crosses the marble tiles and throws open a pair of double doors.

I gasp. "Is that an actual ballroom?"

He grins. "It is. Remember those thirteen Miss Carsons? They were all determined to catch suitable husbands so there were balls and other parties here virtually every weekend. Nowadays I like to use it for playing tennis."

"What about the old masters on the walls? Don't they object to being pelted with tennis balls?" Traditional landscapes aren't really my thing, but I know enough to be able to pick out a Gainsborough or two, and a Lowry.

"I try not to do too much damage, and it's only in wet weather. There's more to see." He tugs me back out into the hall and along to the next pair of double doors. These open onto a gracious dining room which would easily seat eighty without anyone feeling squashed.

"All those prospective husbands and their families needed wining and dining, as did the monarch and other pillars of society. Queen Victoria was a regular visitor here, and I gather Edward the Eighth, too, before he decided that being a king wasn't for him. He and Wallace Simpson threw some legendary parties." He trails his fingers along the polished edge of the gleaming table. "The original silverware was sold off long ago, but some pieces of the Carsons' dinner services are still here."

"Do you use them?"

He shakes his head. "We tend to prefer to eat in a much smaller dining room, part of the orangery at the back of the house."

"You have an orangery?"

"I do. You'll see that when we eat."

"What even is an orangery?" I mutter, following him back out into the foyer.

He smiles at me and simply shakes his head. His gaze sweeps the foyer, taking in the airy space. "The final chapter of your potted history tour... The house was extended at some stage to include the east wing which mainly consists of leisure and spa facilities... I'll show you that later, and after the Carsons sold up, Linn Mill was converted into a hotel. The house changed hands several times, went through refurbishment after refurbishment, not always especially sympathetic, and was actually destined to be converted again into retirement apartments when I acquired it four years ago. I constructed the west wing, my business headquarters, and I'm working to restore the rest to something not unlike its original form, but it will probably take years to complete."

"It...it looks good, so far."

"Thank you."

"Harry said that you work from here as well as live here."

"That's right. I have offices in Edinburgh and London and

What Happens in Vegas...

employ over two hundred people who work in those locations, but I prefer relative seclusion for myself. That said, Edinburgh airport is only half an hour away. I can be in London in a couple of hours or so, and pretty much anywhere else in the world within a day. Linn Mill is private but not remote."

As we talked, he has led me over to the main stairs, but instead of mounting the steps he keys a code into a discreet little door behind them.

"This is the business wing. My offices are through here. Come with me, please."

I follow him along the carpeted corridor, past several closed doors, until we reach a window through which I can see a decent-sized conference room with all the facilities imaginable. Drop-down screen, projector, visual display, catering station. It all looks very efficient, and no less than I would expect.

And a world away from my cluttered, converted mill, complete with painted bare brick walls and wrought-iron beams, the faint aroma of lanolin still lingering from the bales of wool stored there over almost two centuries. The smaller workspaces are separated by a hotch-potch of DIY partition walls, and my only nod at modern convenience so far has been the installation of a disabled loo and a kitchenette.

But I worked hard to get as far as I have, and once again I cringe at the thought of my precious stock ending up God knows where. Harry gave me to understand that my crates will be delivered to the craft fair in Camden, but even so...

"Do you know if my work arrived safely?" I ask.

He pauses. "Your work?"

"The stuff I sent to the craft fair. Those pieces took me months to make. They're worth a lot of money..." *Well, they are to me. These things are all relative.*

"Ah, right. That work. I expect so, but I could check if that would make you feel better."

"It would. Please."

He halts at the next door along, keys in another code, then gestures me inside.

I find myself in what must be the very nerve centre of McPherson Holdings. the CEO's private office. The furniture is modern, all sleek greys and blacks. The desk is wide, lots of space but ruthlessly uncluttered. I can't imagine a greater contrast with my own cramped workspace in my studio in Stockport. Only a tablet litters Caleb's otherwise pristine desk. He seats himself in the huge black leather swivel chair and picks up the tablet. He fires it up with a couple of swift taps. Moments later, the laser printer behind him whirrs into life and two sheets of paper emerge.

Caleb picks them up, scans them over, the hands them to me.

"Read this, please."

I sink onto a low sofa and peer at the top sheet. It's clearly a legal contract. I see my name, and Caleb's there. I glance at him, puzzled.

"What is this?"

"Just read, Fern."

So, I do. I sit in silence for several minutes perusing documents which declare me a liar and a fantasist. *So much for no more name-calling!* If I sign this 'agreement' I will be accepting that my claims regarding what happened in Las Vegas are untrue. I will be confirming that no marriage ever took place between myself and Caleb McPherson and I will, with a stroke, relinquish any present or future claim on any part of his estate or businesses.

I set the papers down on the couch and look him in the eye. "You baffle me. Really, you do."

He lifts that sardonic eyebrow again, and I barely resist the urge to march over there and slap him across his arrogant face.

"I get it," I say, attempting to blunt the icy edge to my voice, though I suspect with little success. I really don't want to antagonise him, I've seen where that leads, but this is just too much. "I get that you don't want to be married to me. You made that perfectly clear when you voted with your feet the morning after our wedding. I wish you'd arrived at that conclusion a few hours earlier, but we are where we are. But here's the thing, Caleb, you don't need to be married to me. I'm offering you a way out, no strings. I'll even meet all the costs, despite..." I wave my arm in the general direction of his Gainsboroughs, Lowries, and goodness knows what other precious objects bear witness to his wealth. "There's no need for any of this. I'm ready to go quietly. I always was. I want nothing of yours."

He regards me for several long moments, his dark eyes boring into mine.

"I... I won't sign," I blurt out. "I won't deny what happened. I'm offering you a divorce, what more could you want? You need never see me again."

"You're mistaken, Fern," he says, his tone quiet.

"I don't think so," I protest. "I was there."

"And I was not. But that isn't what I meant. You said just now that I don't want to be married to you. I don't recall ever saying that."

"But you..."

"I have said on many occasions that I am not married to you, and that remains my position. But that is not the same as not wanting to be. If I was looking for a wife, Fern, I suspect she would be very much like you...feisty, submissive, and drop-dead gorgeous. And on one thing I want you to be absolutely certain, had *I* been with you in Las Vegas, I would not have disappeared the morning after. I would have held you in my arms and never let you go."

"You...? Would you?" I gape at him, beyond astonished.

"Oh, yes."

"But why?"

"Because I want you. I wanted you from the moment you stood up in that meeting and dropped your bombshell."

"But you were horrible to me. You don't even like me. You… you spanked me, just now."

"None of that alters the simple fact that I want you so much my balls ache. You may be a thorn in my side, but I still like you. Why would I not?" He pauses, then levels a sexy grin at me. "Once I start fucking you, I doubt I could ever stop."

"We are not going to—"

"Dream on, Fern. We don't have a happy ever after waiting for us, I grant you that. There's too much baggage piled up everywhere for that to be a possibility. But we both have an itch that the other can scratch, and the fucking will be part of it. And so will signing that agreement. Eventually."

"I will never sign your bloody contract." To show him I mean business, I snatch it up from the sofa and tear it into pieces before his eyes. I scatter the shreds of paper on the floor. "We're done here. I… I want to go to my room."

"Clear up the mess you made first."

He nails me with his dark velvet eyes. There is nothing rough or even remotely menacing in his tone, but I am compelled to obey. I crouch, gather up the bits of paper, and dump them on the corner of his desk. He collects them in his fist and drops them into a drawer.

"I shall print off another agreement. And, Fern, the next time you see this particular version," he taps the front of the drawer, "it will be rolled up inside a butt plug, ready to go in your arse."

CHAPTER 7

I text Harry and ask him to come to my office. He shows up a couple of minutes later, still brushing the crumbs from Sally Parson's gingerbread from his fingers, if my guess is right.

"Mrs Parsons said to tell you she's done a vegetarian lasagne for dinner."

"Okay," I say.

"She wasn't sure what Miss Daniels likes, so she decided to stay safe."

"I see." I turn to my guest. "Do you eat meat, Miss Daniels?"

"What?" She looks up at me, still obviously startled.

"My cook is wondering if you have any special dietary requirements she should know about. Do you eat meat? Are you allergic to anything?"

"No. Anything is fine," she replies.

"Please pass that on to Sally, and would you show Miss Daniels to the Rose Room, please?"

Fern is still perching on the edge of the sofa, her features a mask of astonishment, whether at my declaration of lust for her, or my promise to reintroduce the legal agreement in a most intimate manner, I cannot be sure. Either way, I'm well satisfied with my progress thus far.

Harry nods and invites Fern to follow him. She does so, sparing a fulminating glare for me as she exits the room.

Once we are deeper into the relationship, I mean to develop with her, a look like that will earn her a few stokes with a cane. We are not at that stage yet, though.

Even so, I am content with my progress so far. I begin to tick off my triumphs one by one.

First and foremost, I have established beyond any doubt that she is a submissive by nature. I suspect her to be totally without experience and certainly untrained, but the innate response is there.

Second, she can be obedient, with the right encouragement.

Third, she is not so painfully modest as to make getting inside her knickers a mission akin to a lunar landing. She let me bare her bottom with relatively little protest. Getting her naked will be more of a challenge, but I see no obvious reason for any lack of optimism.

Four, she now knows how I feel about her, and something of my plans for her whilst she is here. She will be shocked, and not especially cooperative, I daresay, but she will soon become accustomed to the idea. I expect my evening to be filled with much in the way of outrage, denial, and demands that I let her go at once, but by tomorrow morning I suspect she will be less determined to cut short her visit.

And five, her natural and completely involuntary response to the spanking was glorious to watch. Despite that nonsense with the text, I administered an erotic spanking, not a punishment. Her body knew the difference, even if she didn't. She wanted it, wanted more. Asked for more. And the tears later? Whilst they were triggered by my careless remark—and I really will need to watch that, I have no wish to upset her unnecessarily—the root cause was her emotional reaction to the wicked, forbidden pleasure of being spanked.

I was right not to allow her to scuttle off to her room. If I had done so, she might be up there now, still weeping, still confused and unhappy and not knowing why she felt like that. I doubt if she understands her mini-meltdown even now, but I do, and it is all part of understanding *her*. I can be ready for a similar reaction again.

I leave my desk and go to stand by the floor-to-ceiling tinted windows. Outside, the dusk is just beginning to gather, and I watch several rabbits enjoying their first foray into the early evening. During the day I mainly get to watch squirrels from my window, but at night my grounds are overrun by rabbits, badgers, bats, and the occasional fox.

The rabbits come right up to the window, unable to detect me on the other side. They scurry about just inches from my feet, ears flat against their heads as they nibble on the grass and an occasional daisy or dandelion. Their misplaced cocky confidence reminds me of Fern Daniels.

Like the rabbits, she has much to learn. Unlike them, she doesn't have all the time in the world.

DESPITE MY DETERMINATION to despise everything about Caleb McPherson, I have to admit, the room allocated to me is beautiful.

The Rose Room, so named, I suspect, because the paintwork and linens are all a delicate shade of pastel pink, with occasional darker highlights in the lampshades and rugs. The carpet, which feels to be ankle-deep shag pile, is a subtle blend of baby pink and pearly grey, the curtains which hang at two sets of French windows an exact match in colour and pattern.

I can't quite believe that, as well as running his multinational empire, Caleb has sufficient attention to detail left to have selected every item himself. He must employ interior designers to model his home, but it is clear he has spared no expense.

My scruffy-looking bag appears totally out of place dumped on the exquisite silk counterpane, framed by the curtains adorning the posts at each corner of the bed. It is still zipped up, but I am under no illusions. Someone will have rifled through to check what I have with me. Harry probably. No sharp implements. No spare phone. No handy rope ladder for escaping from second-floor windows.

I have an hour and a half before we eat, apparently. Harry told me that much on the way up here, and advised me to take a shower, better still, a bath, then get some rest.

I do none of those things. Instead, I pace across the costly carpet considering how I can possibly get away from here.

I try the door and find it locked. That comes as no real surprise, but all the same, my stomach churns. I'm a prisoner. They locked me in.

I go to one of the French windows and find that is easily opened from the inside. I unlock it and step out onto a small balcony, but my heart sinks when I peer over the railings. The ground is at least thirty feet below me, and beneath are what seem to be granite flags. I'd break my neck if I attempted to jump.

I look to my left and right. Similar balconies extend from what I assume are more guest rooms. And about three rooms, or six balconies along, on my left, an ancient apple tree stretches up far enough to brush against the painted metal railings.

It's a pity I wasn't allocated that room. I might even be able to shin down that tree and make a run for it.

I go back inside and perch on the end of my bed to assess my options. They are sparse indeed.

I could just sign that bloody agreement, and hopefully he would let me walk away. I would, in effect, have admitted to lying earlier and he would be entirely vindicated.

I could defy him, whatever that might entail. Despite his willingness to spank me, I somehow doubt he means me real harm, because if he did, he would have done something about it by now, surely.

I could do whatever he says, short of signing that agreement. I suspect that would expose me to the prospect of spending the next three days naked, my legs spread for him. He said as much, more or less.

"*When* we fuck." Not if.

I get to my feet. *When we fuck, indeed*. I need to get out of here.

Back on the balcony, I again estimate the distance to the ground and contemplate making a rope from the expensive bed linen. I abandon that plan and concentrate instead on the apple tree. I need to somehow find a way of hopping from one balcony to the next, until I can reach it. Some sort of bridge…

That's when I spot it. On the other balcony, also extending from my room, is a sun lounger. It's perhaps six feet long, enough to just reach the next balcony. If I'm very careful, maybe I could use it to make my way along the outside of the house…

The notion crystalises in my head. I am convinced it is doable. I have to try. And I have to try now. It's already getting dark.

I open the other French windows and step out to inspect my equipment. The sun lounger looks sturdy enough. The frame is made of polished wood and it is upholstered in a thick hessian style of fabric. It is fairly solid, but not so heavy that I can't manoeuvre it. The main question is, will it be long enough to reach the next balcony?

One way to find out. I have to just hope the other rooms are unoccupied.

I fold the sun lounger flat and lift it onto the railings. One factor in my favour, the top of the balustrade is not flat. Rather, it is decorated with spiky metal tulips at the top of each vertical rail, and these provide a secure anchor for my improvised bridge. I might fall off, but my sun lounger probably won't.

I rush back inside to grab my bag and curse softly when I remember I left my jacket in the drawing room. I check the side pocket in my bag and find my wallet is still there, complete with the fifty pounds in cash I thought I might need on my journey. Unfortunately, my credit and debit cards are tucked in pockets in my phone case, and Caleb has that. Still, fifty quid will get me on a train headed south. All I need to do is reach Edinburgh and find the station.

But first...

I lean out over the side of the balcony and hurl my bag across the six-foot gap to land on the next one. The clatter seems ear-splitting to me. I wait, motionless, for any reaction from the next room.

Nothing.

I allow myself to breathe again, and manhandle the sun lounger into position. It takes more strength than I anticipated to hold it out, horizontal, and far enough to hook the top of the wooden frame over the tulips. But I'm desperate, and that counts for a lot. I manage to get my bridge in place, then rattle it nervously to satisfy myself it's secure enough.

"Do not give way," I instruct the object sternly, then I set my foot on the horizontal balcony rail and carefully ease myself onto the edge of the hessian.

On all fours, I make my way across. I keep my knees and hands on the outer wooden framework and shuffle slowly forward. I will myself not to look down but can't resist a quick, masochistic glance when I reach the halfway point.

I am actually doing this!

My heart in my mouth and my limbs shaking, I somehow, miraculously, complete the first crossing and scramble down onto the next-door balcony.

Panting hard from the effort, I assess my progress. So far, so good. I've proved it can be done. Now all I need to do is somehow unhook my bridge and drag it across after me to use again.

This turns out to be the most strenuous part of the entire escapade. I have to push the sun lounger away from myself so that it is clear of the tulips and then somehow lever it upwards from my end before gently hauling it back towards me, but this requires me to abuse muscles I never even knew I had. Still, I can't give up now, I simply can't.

You can do it. You can do it.

I grit my teeth, flex my core muscles, then find the strength to lift the sun lounger straight up, high enough to clear the railings, then I drag it after me onto the next balcony. My biceps feel to be on fire, but I manage to achieve my objective. As soon as the sun lounger is clear I stumble back, still gripping the wooden frame. It clatters against the outer rail of the balcony, dangling dangerously from my aching hands. I hang on as though my life depends on it and lean over to hoist it onto the small platform.

Then, I do it all again.

By the time I reach the next balcony I am already exhausted. I don't wear a watch, and without my phone I can't be sure of the time, but I suspect I've used up a decent portion of that hour and a half. I want to take a breather, but I don't dare. I need to be on the ground and running for the main road. Hopefully, I can put some distance between myself and Linn Mill before anyone misses me.

I grab my bag and fling it onto the final balcony, then position my bridge. I may be tired, but I've become quite adept at getting it in place, and at least now I'm confident it's going to hold. I climb up and shuffle across much more quickly now, my thoughts already turning to an assessment of the actual distance I'll need to leap through mid-air to reach the tree, the final obstacle between myself and freedom.

"Miss Daniels has expressed some concern regarding the whereabouts of her artwork, the items she dispatched to the fair in Camden. Could you check with the organisers that the pieces have arrived safely, please?"

"Will do, boss." Harry, seated across my desk from me, pulls out his phone. "I know the crates were delivered but I can ask for pictures of her stall if that will make her feel better."

"I expect it would. And an update on any sales. I think—"

I stop short when my own phone buzzes, a distinct signal I rarely hear but never ignore.

"The intruder alarm has been triggered." I reach for my tablet and open the CCTV app. "Holy fuck..."

I turn the tablet around and hand it to Harry. He lets out a low whistle.

"The idiot," I mutter, already striding for the door. "One slip and she'll break her neck."

"What the fuck does she think she's doing?" Harry follows me. We both break into a sprint as we head for the main foyer.

We charge up the two flights to reach the second floor. The door leading to the Rose Room is almost at the far end of the upper hallway, but that isn't where we head. No point, she's no longer there. I check my tablet again, to see she's already reached the balcony next door and is scrambling over the railings onto her rickety homemade bridge. I allow myself a brief sigh of relief. I half expected to see her crumpled and broken on the unforgiving granite flags.

"She's making for the tree," Harry suggests. "I bet she means to climb down there."

He's right. It's a mad idea, but the only one that make sense. "Third room along, then. We'll intercept her there."

For fuck's sake, don't let her fall...

I signal Harry to silence and I slowly open the door to the guest room which we assume to be her destination. The last thing we want is to startle her while she's still teetering on the flimsy affair she's rigged up to climb over. We enter the room

What Happens in Vegas...

and edge close to the window. The curtains are partially open, perfect for hiding us from sight but affording enough of a view to be able to see when she slips safely onto the balcony outside.

The French window is locked, but the mechanism operates from inside. The moment I spot her feet safely connect with the balcony beyond, I turn the lock and open the door.

Fern stifles a scream. She staggers back, but I grab her before she can topple over the railings. I haul her inside the guest room, and Harry shuts the French window behind her.

"H-how did you...?" She glares at the pair of us, then eyes the door to the balcony as though she still thinks she might escape that way.

"Did you imagine a house of this size wouldn't have a decent intruder alarm system? The moment you started clambering from one balcony to another it was triggered. CCTV did the rest."

She sinks onto the bed, head lowered. Clearly, she had never considered such a possibility. If I wasn't so fucking angry, my absolute terror at what might have happened to her barely starting to abate despite the fact that she is now safe, I might even feel sorry for her.

"What were you thinking? Have you any idea how dangerous that was? One slip, and you could have been killed."

"But I wasn't. I was careful, and—"

"Careful?" I heave in a breath. "I can't believe you would do something so stupid. That little stunt was so fucking dangerous. Why would you even do that?"

"I... I wanted to go home. I told you that. And...you locked me in."

"Locked you in?"

"Yes. In that bedroom."

I turn to Harry, one eyebrow raised.

He shrugs. "I assumed..."

It was a fair enough assumption, I suppose. In the circumstances. I turn my attention back to the belligerent female who now perches miserably on the guest bed. "If you wanted to be let out, you had only to ask."

"How could I ask? You weren't there."

"The phone," I suggest through gritted teeth.

"You took my phone," she retorts.

"The phone in the bloody room." I point to the one beside the bed where she now sits. The system links up, and had she lifted the receiver, Sally would have answered and I don't doubt let her out at once. My cook-cum-housekeeper is not accustomed to guests being locked in their rooms. Or she would have passed the call to me and I would have unlocked the door. It had not been my intention to treat her as a prisoner.

Until now. Now, she has shown that she can't be trusted, left to her own devices.

"Thank you, Harry. I can deal with this from here."

He lifts his hand in a salute and leaves us.

"You. Come with me," I instruct, still fighting to control my temper. Christ, she scared me. I had horrific visions of scraping her up off my granite terrace. The image is still locked in my imagination.

"I don't want to be locked in again. You have no right—"

"You'll be lucky if I don't tie you to the bed, let alone lock you in."

"You wouldn't..."

Well, actually, I would. Though I would have no intention of leaving her alone.

My patience, such as it was, is exhausted. "Come. Now." I take her elbow and pull her to her feet. She will come with me, willingly or not.

"Let go. There's no need to manhandle me."

She tries to escape from my grip, but I have no intention whatsoever of letting her go. As for manhandling...she really has no idea.

I steer her out into the hallway and along the corridor to the end opposite where her room was. We turn a corner, into a wider hallway, the main upper landing. Halfway along is the entrance to my private domain. I open the door and bundle her inside.

"What...? Whose room is this?" she asks, eying the huge bed in the centre of the master suite.

"Mine. And now yours, for the duration of your stay."

"I won't sleep with you," she declares "You can't expect me to..."

"I expect you to do as you are fucking told. Have I not made that clear already? And when you don't there will be consequences."

"C-consequences?"

She's beginning to catch on to the reality of her current predicament.

"Consequences. Starting now. Take off your clothes."

She gapes at me. "I will not!"

"No? I'm sure Harry and Jared will be delighted to assist if you don't feel able to cooperate."

"You wouldn't."

I raise my eyebrow. She knows better than that by now, surely.

"You have a count of ten in which to get naked," I tell her, a deliberate note of Dom steel injected into my tone. "Then, you'll kneel. Here." I point to a spot right in front of me. "With your knees apart and your hands on your head."

"What do you mean to do?"

"I mean to provide you with another much-needed lesson in obedience. And self-preservation."

CHAPTER 8

I stare at him, open-mouthed. He means it. He actually means to have his men come in here and... Christ, what does he intend to do?

"Two." His tone is implacable.

I meet his gaze. His eyes are even darker than I remember, deep mahogany, and just as hard.

In this moment, I truly know what fear is. The sort of fear that paralyses, gags, the sort you can taste.

"Three. Four."

I lose it, Totally. In a blind panic, I whirl and dive for the door. He reaches it at the same time as I do, his hand over my shoulder, holding it firmly closed. I rattle uselessly at the handle.

"No, please...let me go. Please..."

I'm sobbing, hammering on the door, then on his chest as he turns me to face him.

"Don't, please... I'm sorry. I..."

The fight goes out of me. I can't win. He's stronger, this is his home, his room. His domain. No one here will lift a finger to help me, to defend me. He can do as he likes, no one will care.

"I j-just want to go home," I wail. "You can't blame me for that. I'm sorry, I won't try to escape again. Just, please don't hurt me..."

He lifts me in his arms, and I go limp. This is it...

"Fern? Fern, sweetheart...look at me."

I squeeze my eyes tighter shut. The softness in his tone is a ruse, another of his cruel tricks, his sudden mercurial mood shifts.

He lays me on the bed and smooths tangles of damp hair from my face. "Open your eyes, love."

I shake my head. "Please, leave me alone."

"That's not happening, but we do need to talk."

Talk? I whimper, as much in confusion as terror.

"I scared you, I know that. I hit some sort of trigger without meaning to, but you need to know you are safe."

I shake my head. I may be many things, but safe is not one of them.

"You...you were going to rape me." There. I've said it. "Even though we're married, you can't just... I don't want you to..."

"Rape you? No. No, Fern, I was not going to do any such thing. I swear it."

"But you said..."

"What? What did I say to make you think that?" His voice has softened even more.

"You ordered me to strip. Threatened to have your men undress me by force if I didn't do it."

"Yes, I did, but—"

"Why else would you do that?"

"Maybe just because I want you naked."

"By force. Tearing my clothes from me. Hurting me. I could fight you. I would have fought you. Fought them. But it would do no good. You're stronger, there are three of you. It would happen anyway. I can't... I can't..."

"Okay, I get it. And I think I know what the trigger was."

"Trigger?"

"Hmmm. I'm thinking that perhaps something happened to you before, and just now, you were reminded of it. Something frightened you in the past. You were powerless, weak, vulnerable. Maybe you were hurt by someone and it was like it was all happening again. Our minds can play tricks on us. I suspect it was the fear of being forced that set you off, or of being outnumbered, perhaps."

Now, at last, I do open my eyes. I gaze up at him, horrified. It's as though he can see right through me, see into my dark places, poke at the monsters haunting me, wake them all over again.

"No. You're wrong."

"I'm guessing at the details, but I'm not wrong. I can see it, in your face, your eyes. You don't have to tell me if you don't want to, but now I know what scares you, I can avoid it."

"Avoid it?" I am more baffled by the second. "Why would you do that? Surely, now that you know how to really send me batshit crazy, you would use that."

He shakes his head. "I mean to punish you, and I need you to understand why, to accept that you deserve what is happening to you. To learn from it. You won't learn anything in a blind panic. No one ever learned from being abused, terrorised. My purpose is not to scare you half to death, or even to harm you. I do, though, mean to teach you to take better care of yourself. Not to put yourself in danger." He pauses, shakes his head. "God, Fern, I almost died myself when I saw you out there, teetering on that bloody contraption you rigged up. If you'd fallen before we got to you..."

"Caleb? I..."

He cups my chin, turns my face towards his, and holds my gaze. "Never, ever, scare me like that again."

"I didn't mean to scare you. I never even thought you'd see me..."

His lip quirks. "Now that I can believe. But the image of you lying unconscious, or worse, on my terrace is one I'll never get out of my head."

"You were so worried about me? Truly?"

"You took ten years off my life, girl. Truly."

"I... I'm sorry about that. I didn't think... But I'm not sorry I tried to escape. You had no right to lock me in, or even to bring me here at all. I'm an inconvenient wife, not your prisoner."

"That's true, well, the prisoner bit. And I'm not angry that you tried to escape. Hell, I would probably do the same in your position. But I can't, I *won't* allow you to put yourself in danger. Whilst you're here, I'm responsible for you. I mean to keep you safe. And that stunt on the balcony...there's no way you're getting away with that."

I frown up at him. "Are you going to spank me again?"

He grins. "You know, I think you'd like that. Wouldn't you?"

"No. It hurts."

He narrows his eyes, obviously not buying my denial. "I do intend to spank you, but a little differently this time. So, are you ready to accept your punishment?"

"Just a spanking?" I eye him warily, my mindless panic of moments before almost entirely gone. "You promise?"

"I do. But I can also promise you that despite what you may be thinking, and believe me, I know what that is, it won't be pleasant this time. It will hurt, and it's natural that you should be scared. But you need to know that you can trust me never to do you any lasting harm. Pain is temporary. It goes away, and I would never hurt you more than you can bear."

"How would you know?"

"Because I'm going to give you a safe word."

"How would that work?"

"Your safe word is 'red'. If you say that, I stop. Whatever's happening, whatever the reason, it stops if you say 'red'. No questions, no argument. From now on, the power is in your hands, to accept, to surrender, or not."

I remain still, silent, processing this piece of information. This...opportunity.

I've not led an entirely sheltered existence. I've heard of safe words, read kinky books. I even went to see the *Fifty Shades* films with a couple of other artist friends, not that those are hours any of us will ever get back. But I know what he means. I understand the theory of it, at least.

With a safe word, I can...be curious. I can taste what Caleb might be offering, allow him to do things to me, knowing it will never go further than I want, never be more than I can cope with. As long as I trust him.

But why should I trust him? Caleb McPherson lied to me before, in Las Vegas. He said he loved me, romanced me into a marriage chapel, then dumped me the first chance he got. He denies even knowing me, yet he brings me here, to his house. He says he wants to fuck me but also demands that I sign an agreement swearing that we never met before.

None of it makes sense. And the most bizarre, senseless thing of all? I still want him.

I never stopped loving the man who swept the naive, eighteen-year-old me off my feet. Even if there's to be no happy ever after for me, for us, there is, at least, our here and now.

I have an itch. Caleb will scratch it for me. I'm curious, he can teach me, show me, share with me. Even if this weekend is all we'll ever have, why should I not take it?

He's offering me an experience, maybe of the once-in-a-lifetime variety, and I want to accept. He wants honesty from me. He said as much. This is authentic, genuine. There will be a sort of sincerity in this bargain. Will it be enough?

I make up my mind.

"If I accept your punishment, I want more from you. I want something in exchange."

"More?" He tilts his head, waiting.

"I... I want the pleasure, too. I know you can do that. You can give me that."

His brow furrows. "Are you sure? Do you understand what it is that you're asking me for? What might happen? What *will* happen, between us, if you consent to this?"

I nod. "Yes. And I want it. Three days to...to experiment. To explore, to experience. And on Sunday, I'll sign your agreement, and leave. That will be the end."

His eyebrow rises. His sensual mouth curls in a smile. "Not exactly the way I intended to convince you to sign, but it will do."

"So, you agree?"

"Hell, yes, I agree. We're going to have an interesting weekend together. And it starts now, where we left off a little while ago. With you getting naked for me. Can you do that now, do you think?"

I manage a smile, though I suspect it's somewhat shaky. "Yes, I can do that."

He nods, slowly. Then kisses my forehead. Then, he steps away to lean on the windowsill, the closed curtains at his back. He folds his arms and waits.

I slide off the bed and stand in the centre of the huge room. "You still want me to...to kneel. There?"

"Yes," he replies.

I start at the waistband of my short denim skirt, unfasten it, and drop the garment to pool at my feet. Next, I toe off my trainers, then unpeel my thick woollen tights. I roll them to my knees, then, without hurrying, I tug them off each foot. They join my skirt in a heap on the floor.

Clad now in just my underwear and a plain black T-shirt, I glance over at him. He hasn't moved, though his eyes rake my body, and he is watching every move I make.

I grasp the hem of my T-shirt and pull it over my head. I feel very exposed, even though he has had ample opportunity already to study my bare bottom. This is different. Now, I have to look him in the eye while I lower all my barriers and surrender everything. My choice. My decision.

I drop the T-shirt and reach behind me to unfasten my bra. It's a pretty, lacy affair, ruby red in colour, a treat to myself from Victoria's Secret with panties to match. I offer up thanks to whatever divine intervention persuaded me to wear this combination today.

The slight quirk of his sensual mouth suggests my efforts were not wasted. I take my time removing the bra, then, once that has joined the rest of my clothing on the floor, I hook my thumbs into the elastic of my knickers and push them to my knees. I let them fall the rest of the way, then step out.

I bend to pick up my clothes.

"No, you can leave them there. Kneel, please. Just there." He points to a spot a couple of feet in front of him. "That was nicely done, though you took your time over it. For the rest of the weekend, if I instruct you to strip and kneel, you will do it quicker. Is that understood?"

"Yes. I'm sorry…"

"No problem, and no need to apologise. You're learning, I'll make allowances for what you don't yet know. But as soon as you do know my requirements, my expectations, you will do your best to satisfy them. In return for what I can share with you, I demand obedience, Fern. And submission."

"Yes," I whisper. "I understand."

"And, in circumstances such as these, it's customary for a sub to call her Dom 'Sir'. Will you be comfortable with that?"

I consider for a moment, roll the word around on my tongue. "Yes, I can do that. Sir."

He pushes away from the window and crosses the room, to a blanket box at the foot of his bed. He lifts the lid, peers inside, and retrieves a short riding crop. Fashioned from stiff brown leather plaited into a solid handle and a supple blade, the short flick of leather hangs from the end.

"You…you mean to beat me with a riding crop?" Inexplicably, desire coils deep within me.

What Happens in Vegas...

"I do." He returns to stand before me, flexing the crop between his hands. "Place your hands on your head, Fern. Shoulders back, look up at me. Eyes on me throughout. Do *not* look away."

I gnaw on my lower lip. I'm not scared, not exactly. Apprehensive, perhaps. He's right, this isn't like last time. This is more...intrusive. And more intense. More personal, even.

He circles me, slowly. I have to strain my neck to keep him in sight. The crop dangles from his right hand, the wicked-looking tail swaying ominously. Without warning, he flicks his wrist, and the tip of the crop strikes my shoulder.

I flinch, but more from surprise, the sudden if not unexpected surge of sensation. It wasn't especially painful.

He moves around to stand in front of me and flicks his wrist again. This time, the crop stripes the edge of my hip. It stings, but not much. He really is being very gentle with me.

"Okay so far?"

"Yes, Sir." I tilt my head back to meet his gaze. "I'm fine."

"I'm glad to hear it. Don't move."

I have barely a moment to process that final command, before his wrist jerks again, but this time the tip of the crop catches my swollen nipple.

It hurts. It really fucking hurts. I yelp, and rear backwards, my hands instinctively coming down to cover my breasts.

"I said, don't move. Back in position, Fern."

"But... But you..."

"I told you, this is a punishment. You're not supposed to like it."

"It's horrible. It hurts. You can't hit me there."

"Are you using your safe word?"

"No, but—"

"Then get back in position, Now."

"Please, Caleb. Sir..."

"You agreed to accept my punishment, in exchange for

what you want from me. This is it. This is the reality, Fern. Punishment means pain. Pleasure can also mean pain. It's up to you to decide where one ends and the other begins. And I get to decide how much you can take, unless you use your safe word. So, last chance, Fern. Do we continue, or are we done here? Do we have a bargain or not?"

I blink. Tears are already forming. Was I always such a cry-baby or is this just one of the qualities he brings out in me?

"W-we have a bargain," I whisper, lifting my hands to my head again.

"Three more, on each nipple." He waits, eyebrow raised.

"Yes, Sir. I... I'm ready."

I grit my teeth, clench my jaw, and stiffen. I won't wriggle, I won't cower. If it's too much, I can always say 'red', though I know I won't do that. I refuse to be defeated at the first hurdle.

The next stroke is every bit as cruel as the first. My nipples, despite the abuse, seem to lengthen and firm, as though inviting more punishment. I chew on my lower lip, try to distract myself with more pain, but I'm no match for that vicious little riding crop.

The leather tip catches my left nipple again, this time wrapping itself around. The slight tug as Caleb pulls it away adds to the pain. I cry out but manage to remain in place.

The next stroke is a backhand, catching my right nipple hard and fast. Fiery agony snakes through me, driving a direct course to my clit which throbs in helpless arousal.

"Oh God," I moan.

He takes a few moments to circle me again, affording me the opportunity to get my breath back and steel myself for what is still to come. Three more. Just three more. I can do this.

His aim is uncannily accurate. He delivers the next stroke to my left nipple from above, a perfect swipe that sends waves of conflicting sensations pulsing to my core. It hurts, but it's intensely erotic even so. My arousal is spiking off the scale even as I kneel here, trembling, dreading the final two strokes.

He doesn't waste time. With a deft but deadly flick of his wrist, the crop catches the underside of my right breast, the lower curve, and the firm nipple. It's brutal, agonising. I let out a keening moan.

"Last one," he murmurs, and I know he means to make this one count.

I'm not wrong. The final swipe of the crop paints a vivid crimson line across my breast and sends an arc of devastating heat from my nipple to my clit. I scream, sway backwards, but succeed in remaining upright. Every instinct demands that I cover my breasts, seek to protect, to comfort, to somehow soothe away the pain, but instead I meet his dark gaze.

His image blurs. I cannot see him clearly through my tears. He tosses the crop onto the bed, then bends to swipe away my tears with his thumbs. "Welcome to my world, Fern. Is submission all that you expected?"

"That was awful," I reply.

"Good. It might just serve as an effective punishment, then."

"I... I don't ever want that to happen to me again. Can I...? Am I allowed to say that?"

"A hard limit? Yes, you can have hard limits. Duly noted." He takes a handful of my hair, tips my head back, and kisses my mouth. "You can get up now. But no touching your breasts. Or your clit. I shall deal with that later. Now, I think we should eat."

"Eat?" I take the hand he offers and stagger to my feet. "I don't think I..."

He picks up a shirt which had been draped over a chair. It's one of his. He drops it around my shoulders. "I'll ask Sally to send up our meal. We'll eat in here."

"Oh." Relief floods me when I realise I am not to be taken downstairs, paraded in front of Harry, Jared, and whoever else might be about, humiliated and hurting.

He pulls his phone from his jeans pocket and hits one key. At once a female voice comes on the line.

"Hello, Mr McPherson."

"Hi, Sally. Can you send up two trays, please?"

"Of course, Five minutes."

"Thank you." He ends the call, shoves the phone away, and wraps me in his arms. "You did well, Fern. I'm proud of you."

CHAPTER 9

D*elightful.* I regard Fern across the small dinner table set up for us by my housekeeper.

Sexy, sassy, just the right degree of apprehension. But courageous, too. Determined, and curious as fuck.

Fern had a sudden rush of modesty when Sally knocked at the door, and I permitted her, on this one occasion, to dive into the bathroom until the housekeeper had gone. As well as the vegetable lasagne, Sally had prepared a spicy tomato soup and a sort of peach ice cream thing for dessert. She added a bottle of crisp, chilled Chardonnay and a pot of coffee. The tempting aromas brought Fern out of hiding, and she more than did justice to the meal.

"You seem to have worked up an appetite after all," I observe as I watch her eat.

"This is wonderful," she replies around a mouthful of pasta. The soup is, by now, just a memory. "So creamy. Do you think your cook would give me the recipe?"

"I daresay. You can ask her tomorrow."

"Do you have a lot of staff? I mean, with a place this size…"

I shake my head. "Only Sally living here, at the house full time. There are any number of cleaners and maintenance crew, but they just come as needed. Sally hires them and supervises all of that. When it's just me here, she does the cooking, too, but when I entertain more guests, business dinners and the like, she hires in cooking and waiting staff. Harry has his own house in Edinburgh, but he spends a lot of time here, so he has an apartment as well. But that's all. Otherwise, I prefer to have the place to myself. And exclusive, invited guests, too, of course."

"Don't you get lonely?"

The question surprises me slightly. It has never occurred to me to view my self-imposed solitude as anything other than positive, a lifestyle choice. "No. I'm busy with work usually, and I spend a fair bit of my time in Edinburgh or London. Linn Mill is my retreat."

"I see." She scoops up the final mouthful of pasta. "Will I get to look around properly soon?"

"Tomorrow. The grand tour. Do you want some of this ice cream?"

"Too right, I do."

I serve her a generous portion but settle for just coffee myself, and the final half glass of wine.

At last, Fern sets her spoon aside and grins across at me. "I'm beat. But that was wonderful." She stifles a yawn. "Sorry…"

"You'll need to be well fed this weekend and get plenty of rest. I mean to see to both. You need a shower, then bed."

A flicker of apprehension clouds her expression briefly. She swallows, then, "I know I said I wouldn't sleep with you…"

"By which I think you meant you didn't want me to fuck you. But we will share a bed. My bed."

"Yes. I know that. And, as for the rest. The other thing…"

"The matter of fucking you?"

She reddens. "Yes. That. I don't think… I mean, I…"

I'm all for letting a submissive's imagination run riot on occasions, but I need to put a stop to this. "Fern, you don't have to do that. Fucking is off the agenda, not part of the bargain. I promised that you'll be safe. Nothing will happen that you

What Happens in Vegas…

don't want to have happen. Consent is everything here. Is that clear?"

She nods. "Yes. Perfectly. Thank you. But… I'm not so sure now. About the no fucking bit. That's what I was trying to say."

I grin. "Okay. We'll see how it goes, then. Now, since I don't believe in allowing punishments to fester or be delayed unduly, we have one remaining item of business still to deal with this evening."

"Another punishment? Oh…" Her mossy eyes widen.

"Remember the agreement you tore up?"

"Ah." She drops her gaze.

"Ah. Exactly. So now, I have a little job for you."

She looks up at me, waiting,

"You'll find the scraps of paper, a stainless-steel butt plug, and some lubricant in a tray on my bedside table. I want you to unscrew the finger grip from the butt plug and stuff the paper inside, and then you can go to the drinks fridge and take some ice from the icebox. Fill up the rest of the plug with crushed ice, as much as you can get in there, and screw the end back on. Then, you can put the plug in the freezer to cool down a bit more and bring me the lubricant so I can start preparing you to receive it."

"Ice? You mean to put a freezing cold plug in my arse?" Her eyes are like saucers.

"Yes. I think the combination of that, and a hot shower, will prove interesting. And memorable."

"You're such a pervert. How did I never notice that before?"

"And you're glad of it. Go on, Fern. You have work to do." I choose not to respond to the second part of her comment as that discussion has become somewhat stale. And superfluous.

She gets up and pads barefoot over to the bed. The tray is there, just as I left it, in readiness for this part in our proceedings. Fern perches on the edge of my bed, the tray balancing on her lap. She picks up the butt plug and unscrews the end, then places the torn scraps of paper inside. They mean nothing, just symbolism really. It's the ice that will create the challenge and push her boundaries, that and the indignity of allowing me to penetrate her rear hole. I'm reasonably certain she's a virgin there.

"Have you done any anal before?" I ask. Best to find out.

She shakes her head. "Will it hurt?"

"Not hurt, exactly, because you'll be well lubed and the plug isn't too big. We'll take our time getting it inside you. I promise to be very gentle, as long as you cooperate."

"I don't know what to do."

"It's my job to teach you, to help you to do these things. And yours to do as I say. So, the ice?"

She swallows, sets the tray aside, and takes the plug over to the small drinks fridge beside my sofa. I keep my stock of cold beers and water in there for evenings spent watching sport on the television, and Sally can always be relied upon to keep the ice topped up.

There's a large jug of crushed ice in the icebox. Fern sets it on top of the fridge and uses the spoon provided to shovel several scoops of it into the plug.

"Will that be enough?" She shows me her progress so far.

"I think you can get more in. I want it packed solid."

She nods dutifully and works several more scoops in before finally pressing it down with her thumbs. "It's full."

"Good. Put it in the freezer then and get over here. Don't forget the lube."

She screws the end on and places the plug in the icebox. Then, she returns to the tray, picks up the tube of lubricant gel, and comes to where I am now seated on the long leather sofa which fills most of one wall.

"Kneel beside me, on the sofa, facing away."

She's still wearing nothing but my shirt, and it looks absolutely adorable on her but leaves noting to the imagination. Her nipples, still sore, I imagine, are clearly defined beneath the lightweight linen. There is no darker shadow where her

What Happens in Vegas...

slender thighs and groin meet because she is beautifully bared. I was surprised to see that, but pleased. I prefer the smooth look, the absolute nudity of a perfectly waxed body.

Fern scrambles onto the leather cushion to my right. I help her to bend forward, her knees as wide apart as the sofa will allow so her bottom is poised just where I need it. I lift the shirt to expose her pretty backside. There remains a slight flush from my earlier attentions.

"Reach back and part your buttocks for me." I could manage all of that perfectly well myself, but this is a trick I learned from a much more experienced Dom some years ago. It helps to establish the right mindset if the submissive is involved in delivering her own punishment, if she contributes to her humiliation.

Obedience, it seems, is coming more easily now. Fern stretches her small hands behind her, grasps her creamy buttocks, and eases them apart to expose her puckered rear hole.

"Beautiful. Now, hold still. This might be a bit cold."

I squirt a generous fingerful of the gel onto my hands, then smear it around her arsehole.

"Oooh!" Fern flinches but manages to keep still.

I squirt some more lube onto my fingertip and lay that against the tight ring of muscle. She lets out a quick hiss when I start to press.

"Am I hurting you?"

"N-no, but...it feels odd."

I twist my finger, press harder, and manage to ease the tip inside. I hold there, let her become accustomed to the new sensation before burrowing further. Once I am sure she's still with me, I work my finger a bit deeper, to the first knuckle, then the second. Then, I withdraw to reload.

It's easier to penetrate her the second time, aided by the copious amount of lubricant, as well as the slackening of her entrance. I manage to insert my middle finger fully with little resistance, so I add a second digit. This elicits a gasp or two as I stretch her inner channel, but Fern is still managing to relax and tolerate the intrusion.

"You're doing well, sweetheart. Still not hurting?"

"I... I'm fine. It's a bit tight, though."

She's not wrong there. We will only have a short space of time together, and I wonder if three days will be enough for me to get to fuck her arse and really take advantage of that tight little channel. Probably not. A pity…

I withdraw one last time to collect another squirt of lube, and work that into her rear hole for good measure, then I drop a playful pat on her buttock.

"Go and fetch the plug, love."

She gets to her feet, her movements awkward, and crouches before the fridge. She retrieves the plug, quickly tossing it from one hand to the other, then holds it out to me by the grip at the end.

"You can lie across my lap for this bit, if you prefer."

She nods and drapes her body over my legs. There is no protest, no last-minute pleading, no attempt to delay matters and allow the plug to warm up slightly. Given her commitment to our endeavour, the least I can do is ensure she gains the maximum impact from this.

I could have made her lube up the plug but prefer to deal with that myself. I start by thoroughly drying it with a wad of tissues. It's vital to ensure no moisture is on the outside which might freeze and cause injury to her delicate inner walls. Once I'm satisfied, I coat the plug in lubricant. Then I part her buttocks with my fingers and place the bulbous head at her loosened entrance.

"When I press, you'll need to push back against the plug. Try to relax, don't tense up or squeeze shut."

"I... I'll try."

I pat her bottom by way of encouragement, then start the serious work.

What Happens in Vegas...

As soon as the cold plug connects with her hole, she lets out a shriek.

"Shit, it's cold!"

I ignore the outburst and continue to turn the plug, left then right, all the time easing it forward.

"Push back, Fern. Accept it. Let it in."

She whimpers but manages to do as I ask. She's been well prepared, and the plug slides home easily, to settle deep inside her rear channel. Her entrance closes snugly around the narrower neck, holding it in place.

"Ooooh," she groans. "That feels horrible, I hate it."

"This is a punishment, remember. It's not supposed to be fun. Yet. You can cope."

I wiggle the plug, creating a stirring motion to drag the head around her inner space, applying pressure on the walls. "Try to ignore the cold," I advise her, knowing full well that this will be the main sensation, at least at first, and it will feel really weird in her delicate, virgin arse. The pleasant, erotic fullness will come later.

"It's so cold..."

"I know. Time for your shower."

I roll her over and scoop her up in my arms, then head for the en suite. I pull back the glass sliding door and turn on the jets. The hot water is instant. I set her under the steaming showerheads and grasp the bottom of her shirt. Fern allows me to draw it up and over her head, baring her body to me again, then lets her head drop back and her eyes close as the water streams over her auburn locks.

I step away, take a few moments to remove my own jeans, shirt, and underwear, then step in beside her.

She jerks when I wrap my arms around her waist, then she moves around to nestle within the circle of my arms.

"How does it feel now?" I murmur.

"Still cold."

I kiss her wet hair and reach for the shampoo.

Fern stands motionless as I soap her hair, then rinse it before working conditioner through it. I don't tend to use the stuff myself, but generally keep some handy. Then I direct one of the showerheads to her scalp and carefully rinse all the products away to leave her russet curls sleek and soft, spiralling gently around my fingers.

Next, I turn my attention to the rest of her. I tell her to face the tiles, then place her hands on the wall at shoulder height.

"Don't move." I instruct.

She rests her forehead on the smooth marble while I work soap into her shoulders, her back, her buttocks, then down each slender thigh and calf, finally lifting her feet to wash the soles and between her toes. I make a thorough job it, then I have her face me and lean back on the shower wall, and I start all over again from her neck down.

I rinse the soap from her shoulders, pause to admire the rivulets streaming over the curves of her small breasts. I pinch her tender nipples, then, when she winces, I bend to take each in my mouth, one after the other, and gently suck. Fern's fingers tangle in my wet hair, and she arches for me.

"Still sore?" I murmur.

"Yes. Christ, that feels good…"

I increase the suction and use my tongue to press each pebbled bud against the roof of my mouth as she groans and writhes under the hot spray. Then, I drop to my knees to complete my journey, tasting first her navel, then the tantalising slit just visible between her thighs.

"Open for me," I command.

She spreads her legs, and I part her folds with my thumbs, then lap at her exposed clit.

"Caleb… Sir…" Her voice is ragged, breathy. She's close. Very close.

I reach around to grasp the finger grip on the plug and twist it, then start to drag it in and out, leisurely fucking her arse with the toy.

"Oh, ooooh," she moans, the sound one of unadulterated pleasure now, her grip on my hair tightening.

I continue to flick her clit with my tongue, at the same time sliding one finger inside her channel, quickly followed by two more.

She comes with a high-pitched cry, her body bucking, convulsing, her inner muscles squeezing down hard on my fingers and the plug. Not letting up, I rub and flick, tease and play until her body stills and she slumps, limp and thoroughly sated, against the shower wall. Then, I slowly pull the plug out and drop it onto the shower floor.

I stand, kill the jets, then grab a large towel from the hook outside the cubicle. I wrap Fern in it, then choose another smaller one for around my waist. I pick her up and carry her back to my bed and set her down on the end of it.

She sways slightly, exhaustion taking its toll.

"Do you have a hairbrush in your bag?" If not, I'll need to ask Sally for one.

Fern nods and reaches for the holdall. She extracts a wooden-handled paddle brush, exactly the sort I like. I store that snippet for later and take the brush from her.

"Let me."

I towel some of the excess dampness form her hair, then spend the next few minutes gently teasing out the snarls and tangles. Fern is silent, her eyes closed, just the faintest hint of a contented, sated smile on her lips. I squeeze her hair in the towel again to dry it a little more then set the brush aside and go back into the bathroom to tidy up. By the time I return to the bedroom she has crawled between the sheets, the large towel discarded on the floor.

"Fern?" I crouch beside the bed and lay my hand on her cheek.

She opens her eyes and reaches for my shoulder. "When did you get this?" she murmurs sleepily, stroking the tattoo on my right biceps. "It wasn't there before..."

I glance down at the stylised balletic figure inked into my arm. I got the tattoo almost twelve years ago on my eighteenth birthday, an act of defiance deliberately calculated to annoy my father.

"I've had it a while," I answer. I know I'm being evasive, but I really don't want to get into another discussion right now of what may or may not have happened in Las Vegas, and what she thinks she remembers of it.

"Oh." She drops her hand and closes her eyes. Moments later, she's fast asleep.

CHAPTER 10

I open my eyes to bright daylight. I am alone in the bed, though I sense Caleb close by, maybe because of the delicious aroma of fresh coffee hovering in the air.

I wrinkle my nose and shove myself up on my elbows. Is he in the shower? Or out on the veranda? The French windows are open, and the full-length curtains flutter in the slight breeze.

I roll over and glance around for a clock but can't see one. There's nothing for it but to get out of my snug nest and face the morning properly.

"You're awake." Caleb strolls back through the French window, wearing nothing but a pair of jeans, unzipped. He has a mug in his hand and looks like pure sex on a stick. "Did you sleep well?"

"Like a top." I sit up and try not to stare, clutching the duvet against my chest when I realise, belatedly, that I am naked. "What time is it?"

"Almost ten. Coffee?"

I stare at him. "Ten o'clock? I never sleep that late!"

"Well, you did today." He saunters across the room to where a coffee-maker perches on a side counter, gurgling merrily. "I was just about to get myself a top up." He picks up an empty cup and waggles it at me.

"Please," I reply, my mouth watering. "I just need the loo…"

"You know where it is." He proceeds to pour the coffees as I scramble from the bed, dragging the duvet around me in a sudden and unaccountable fit of modesty.

When I emerge from the en suite, my teeth brushed, my hair finger-combed into a degree of compliance, he has disappeared again and taken my coffee with him. I quickly swap the duvet for the shirt he was wearing yesterday and apparently has no pressing need for this morning and follow him out onto the veranda.

He is seated at a small wrought-iron table, the two mugs in front of him. He shoves a spare chair out with his foot, and I settle myself next to him.

"You have a beautiful view," I observe, scanning the flat Scottish borders landscape extending for miles beyond the cultivated grounds.

"I do," he agrees, though he is looking at me, not the scenery.

"You should have woken me," I complain. I reach reach for my coffee and take a long, appreciative inhale before tasting it.

"I added milk and one sugar. That's right, isn't it?"

It sounds perfect. I nod and take my first hit of the caffeine. "Ah, that's good."

He says nothing, and for the next few minutes we sip our coffee in companionable silence. He empties his mug first and goes back inside to fetch the pot.

"What do you want to do today?" he asks me, once the mugs are refreshed.

I furrow my brow, a little surprised to be consulted. I'm hardly an authority when it comes to planning a weekend of kink. "Well, I assumed we would…carry on from where we left off."

"Insatiable wench," he mutters. "There's plenty of time for all of that. I wondered about a spot of fresh air this morning, since it's such a nice day."

What Happens in Vegas...

The late springtime sun is just beginning to make itself felt. The day promises to be pleasantly warm. An excursion would be rather nice.

"What do you have in mind? A walk?"

"Riding," he clarifies. "Do you ride, Fern?"

"What? Horses?"

He nods.

"You have a horse?" I don't know why I am so surprised, but I am.

"I have several. Including a sweet little mare that would suit you very well. So, do you ride at all?"

"I had about half a dozen lessons when I was a child. My dad paid for me to go to a stable near where we lived. It was a birthday present."

"But you didn't continue?"

"No. We weren't poor exactly, but we were never going to be part of the horsey set. I wouldn't be joining the Pony Club. I enjoyed the horse riding but joined an art club instead." I pause. "I'd love to come riding with you, though." And hopefully I might even manage not to fall off and make a total idiot of myself.

"Right. That's the plan, then. Did you pack jeans for your weekend in London?"

"Yes."

"Put them on. You'll need a warm jumper, too, but I can lend you one."

"Are we going now? Straight away?" I set down my cup.

"First, I thought we'd stop by the kitchen and see if we can't convince Sally to rustle up some breakfast. I'm fancying eggs Benedict myself."

"Oooh." My stomach growls in approval. "Give me two minutes to dig out my jeans."

. . .

AFTER THE GRANDEUR of the rest of the house, I find the cluttered informality of the kitchen refreshing. Naturally, the place is huge, dominated by a bank of professional-quality ovens and other equipment required to entertain on an industrial scale. But there is also a microwave, a toaster, and a sophisticated little grill upon which the cook and housekeeper is preparing bacon when we arrive in her domain.

"Sally, let me introduce you to our guest for the weekend. This is Fern Daniels."

The middle-aged woman turns with a warm smile. "Eeeh, it's grand tae meet ye, lass. Did ye sleep well?" Her lilting Scottish brogue suits her friendly demeanour.

"I did, thank you. And thank you for the meal last night. It was wonderful, Mrs...?"

"Parsons, but ye shall call me Sally. Now, what can I get for ye? I have some decent smoked bacon here, or I could manage an omelette."

"We were wondering about your famous eggs Benedict," Caleb suggests.

"Aye, ye shall ha' that, then. Sit ye down, the pair o' ye. I shall nae be a minute." She gestures to the long wooden table which runs the length of her kitchen. Harry is already seated at one end, enthusiastically tucking into bacon, eggs, and mushrooms washed down with a pint-sized mug of tea.

Caleb greets him, and we join him at the table.

"There's coffee fresh if ye want some," Sally calls from her station by the grill. "Or I could make ye a pot o' tea."

"Coffee's good. I'll get it." Caleb strolls across the flagged floor to extract two mugs from a cupboard and pours for both of us. Then he gets the milk from the fridge and splashes a drop in to mine. It's obvious he is accustomed to helping himself, despite the housekeeper's offers to serve him.

He sits down again, just as Harry shoves his phone across the table.

What Happens in Vegas…

"That information you wanted, Mr McPherson," he offers, by way of explanation.

Caleb picks up the phone, studies the screen for a moment, then passes it to me. "Your stall in Camden. Looks good."

"My…?" I peer at the little screen. It's a picture of my stall, laid out just as I would have arranged it. My pieces are displayed to best effect, well-lit and each aligned so the handles are all in a straight row. The colours are grouped attractively, and proper space afforded to the larger pieces with the higher price tags. There even appear to be a couple of potential customers hovering.

"When was this taken?" I ask.

"Just now. It's a live feed," Harry explains.

"Crikey! That woman is buying something." I watch, entranced, while a smartly dressed woman turns one of my Borealis vases over in her hands, examining the work for any flaws. She won't find anything wrong. The piece is part of a series I designed, inspired by a visit to Norway last year where I saw the Northern Lights and sought to capture their essence in the blues and greens of this glaze. It's a delightful effect, one of my finest creations.

It appears she thinks so, too. What's more, she's prepared to stump up two hundred pounds in order to acquire the piece. I watch the money change hands, to be placed in the pocket of some stranger.

"Who is that? He has my money," I protest.

"He's one of the agency staff," Caleb explains. "He'll keep a record of what's been sold and see that you get your money. What's the tally so far, Harry?"

Harry takes back the phone, scrolls through a few pages. "Fourteen hundred and seventy-seven pounds. So far Miss Daniels has sold a set of goblets, five sets of coasters, that vase just now, thirteen mugs, a set of wind chimes, eight salad bowls, three—"

"Did you say fourteen hundred, as in, one thousand, four

hundred?" I am gaping at him, astonished. The most I ever made at a weekend fair was two thousand pounds, and this is only the first morning in Camden.

"Yes," Harry confirms. "And seventy-seven pounds. Plus, whatever that vase cost."

"Crikey. At this rate I'll be sold out by close of play today." And I'll have enough cash in hand to replenish my materials and go on a creative spree. I'll need to, I'll have nothing left to sell at the other fairs and outlets I'm booked to attend over the summer. I might even bring forward my plans to start work on that small exhibition space I've promised myself.

"Here ye are, eggs Benedict. Would ye like anything else?"

Sally interrupts my planning to deposit two plates of food before us. The tangy Hollandaise sauce pools beside the fresh toasted muffins, all topped off by generous slices of succulent ham and soft poached eggs. The aroma is mouth-watering.

"Oh, wow..." is all I can manage.

"Eat up," the cook urges, "while it's hot."

Caleb punctures his egg with his fork to let the runny yolk ooze out. "Do we have plenty of apples?" he asks.

Apples?

Sally nods. "Aye, I should think so. Shall I go find ye a bag i' the larder?"

"Let Harry do that, when he's finished his breakfast. If you have a minute just now, Fern wanted to ask you about your recipe for vegetable lasagne."

HALF AN HOUR LATER, we leave by the rear door. Caleb has a plastic carrier bag full of small green apples dangling from his hand, which I gather are intended for the horses.

"How far is it to the stables?" I ask.

"About a ten-minute walk," he replies. "Or I could drive us there if you prefer."

"No. The walk will be good."

We set off across the springy grass, skirting a copse of trees. In the shadows cast by the new leaves, a carpet of bright bluebells shimmer in the slight breeze.

"Do you have my phone with you?" I ask.

Caleb shakes his head. "No, do you need it?"

"I wanted to take a picture. Of the bluebells. I could use it in a design..."

"Ah. Use mine."

He passes me his iPhone, and I spend the next few minutes crouching in the grass and happily snapping close-ups of the tiny azure flowers and their contrasting dark-green leaves. I can already envision them reproduced onto lampshades, or maybe printed on tea towels. I am starting to consider a new range of fabric-based artwork, items I can produce in bulk and with a decent profit margin.

I don't intend to remain a starving artist in a garret if I can help it.

Satisfied I have enough inspiration to be going on with, I hand the phone back and we continue on our walk.

"So, tell me about your dad," Caleb says, suddenly and without preamble.

"My dad." I halt. "What about him?"

"You said he paid for the riding lessons."

"Yes, he did. For my twelfth birthday, I think it was."

"And you said you weren't poor but would never join the horsey set."

"That's right."

"What does he do? For a living?"

"He...he *was* a policeman. A sergeant."

"Was?"

"He died when I was sixteen. A heart attack at work. It was just three weeks before he was to retire."

He pauses and takes my hand. "That's grim."

I nod. "It was...a shock. We had no idea. One moment he was fine, the next... gone."

"Were you close?"

"Very," I whisper. "I still miss him every day. My mum does, too, though she doesn't say much."

"And now, your mum is ill. I think that was what you said when you arrived yesterday."

I nod. "She was just recently diagnosed with breast cancer. Stage two." I meet his concerned gazed, my jaw tightening. "We mean to beat it. She has surgery coming up soon, and….other treatments. There's lots they can do for her."

"Yes, I know. The prognosis gets better all the time." He offers me an encouraging smile and squeezes my hand. "What about other family?"

I stare up at him. What is he asking me? What else does he know about me? He has his sources, his spies. Surely he can't…

I shake my head. "There's no one. Just me and my mum."

We crest a grassy slope, and I gasp. "Oh. Are they yours?"

Below us, in a meadow beside a wide stream, are four horses. Five, if the gangly foal also counts.

"They are," he says. "Brace yourself. As soon as they get wind of us they'll be over for their apples."

Sure enough, the largest of the group raises his head and sniffs the air, then starts towards us at a slow canter.

"That's Roman. My gelding. I've had him for seven years, since he was a two-year-old."

"He looks very big," I observe nervously. I recall the horses at the riding school were somewhat more stubby and squat than this huge beast approaching fast.

"Yes. Sixteen hands. He's a gentle giant, though."

I certainly hope so. The horse slows to a trot a few paces from us and ignores me completely, preferring to butt Caleb in the shoulder by way of a greeting.

He runs his hand down the animal's long neck and reaches into the bag. The first apple disappears in moments.

"Ah, here comes Bella."

The mare with the foal is next to arrive, her baby tiptoeing delicately behind her. She looks a lot less threatening, and the foal is adorable.

"What's his name?" I ask, extending my fingers for him to sniff at.

"Her," Caleb corrects me. "She hasn't got her official name yet, but we call her The Princess for now."

"How old is she?"

"Six weeks."

"Will you keep her?"

"Probably," Caleb replies. He tugs on the foal's ears. "She's from fine stock, good for breeding."

I suspect it's more than that. He clearly adores his horses. Soon, several more apples have gone. I even manage to work up enough courage to offer one to Roman, who is really very well-mannered, despite his size.

"Ah, here's Pumpkin." The next to join us on his short legs is a pony, his once-bright amber coat contrasting with his long, dark mane and black feet. Despite his diminutive stature, the Shetland muscles his way between the larger animals to reach his share of the apples. They allow him to shove them aside, and it's perfectly clear who is the leader of this little pack.

"He looks quite old." Close up, the grey is visible in the pony's rough coat, and his eyes are semi-opaque.

"Yes." Caleb tugs at the pony's ears and rubs his shoulder. "He's thirty-two years old. A geriatric in the horse world. He's living out his retirement now. Pumpkin was the pony I learned to ride on."

"Oh. And you've kept him, all this time."

Caleb shakes his head. "Sadly, no. My father sold him as soon as I outgrew him. I was about eleven, I think. He bought me another, bigger pony and said there was no point keeping a useless animal that no one could ride."

"Poor Pumpkin."

"Yes. And poor me. I liked the new pony well enough, but I missed Pumpkin. So, a few years later when I had the chance, I bought him back."

"What happened to the other pony?"

"He died two years ago at the ripe old age of twenty-five. He's buried down by the stream."

"You're really a big softie, aren't you?"

"Where horses are concerned, guilty as charged. Which explains this old buzzard. And those two, over by the trees."

The last of the four adult horses is just ambling over. A dark-grey colour, and about the same size as Bella, this one has an edge of wariness to him. He circles us, sniffing the air and coming to a halt a few feet away.

"Cole's a rescue," Caleb explains. "He's been very badly treated, half starved for years, tied up in a grotty builder's yard until the rope almost cut through his fetlock. The owner got six months for it and banned from keeping horses for life, though that hasn't helped Cole much. He's nervous around people, doesn't trust easily. He seems to enjoy the company of other horses but needs a lot of space. The equine rescue centre where he ended up couldn't find him a big enough field that he could share, so I agreed to give him a try here. He's settled well, gets on with Pumpkin especially, and he'll tolerate a bit of affection from me occasionally. Mostly, for Cole, it's just the freedom he wants, and a bit of horsey company. And plenty to eat."

I'm horrified. "Who could treat a horse like that?"

"The world has its share of heartless bastards, and they often find their way to animals. Animals can't defend themselves. Well, not usually. The same can't really be said of my other two guests."

He points to the corner of the meadow where, in the distance, close to a stand of trees, I can just make out two more equine shapes.

"Why don't they come for their apples?"

"Because they're idle slugs and consider themselves above all of that nonsense. They'll wait for me to go to them. Peggy and Walter are donkeys. Retired now, from a fairground where they used to do children's rides for hours on end. I reckon they think they've done their share and others can put in the hard graft now. They're fostered, from a donkey sanctuary a couple of miles away, but I expect they'll live out their days here as well."

"Oh, I see."

"We'll call and visit them on our ride. Come on, let's go and get Roman and Bella saddled up."

I feel a bit like the Pied Piper as we make our way across the meadow to the stone-built stables and yard at the far end. An elderly man is ambling around the cobbled courtyard with a wheelbarrow. He waves as we get near.

"That's old William," Caleb explains as we approach. "He was head lad in my father's stables and agreed to come to Linn Mill when I bought the place and help me set things up here. He's the only other employee who lives on the premises, in a loft over the stable block. He's also the only human Cole has any real time for, so I suppose that qualifies him as a true horse whisperer."

"Ye'll be wantin' Roman, I expect," William calls, setting down the barrow full of manure.

"And Bella," Caleb replies. "I'll help you get them saddled.

I never got as far as helping with saddling up in the course of my brief equine-related education, so I perch on a low wall and watch through the open door as the two horses are fitted with their saddles and other tack. The foal skitters around them, prancing nervously.

"What about The Princess?" I ask. "Will she be upset at being separated from her mum?"

"She'll come with us," Caleb replies. "She'll enjoy the outing."

He's right. The foal has a wonderful time trotting behind

the two larger horses. In deference to her gangling gait and my lack of experience, Caleb holds Roman to a slow canter which I can just about match. We visit the two donkeys who turn out to be every bit as aloof and attitude-filled as Caleb suggested. But they appreciate the offering of apples which they treat as no more than their due, munching their way through all that are left, then turning their haughty bottoms towards us.

"I think we're dismissed." Caleb offers me his clasped hands to make a step so I can get back on Bella, then he remounts Roman with one practised stride. "Time to get back, I think. I've yet to complete your tour of Linn Mill."

"Ah, yes. The rest of the grand staterooms. And maybe the billiards room."

He slants me a glance. "You may joke, but I do have a billiards table, though I can think of better things to do on it than roll coloured balls about. In fact, I think it's high time I showed you my favourite games room. The one in the basement."

"Your games room? You mean…"

"You might prefer to call it a dungeon. So, are you ready to explore a little more?"

CHAPTER 11

"There are four floors, but the top one is just bedrooms. Servants, mainly, in the past, though there is the old nursery and schoolroom up there as well. From the days when children were seen but not heard."

We returned to the house to find Sally gone—a meeting with some corporate catering supplier, apparently—and a pile of smoked salmon sandwiches in the fridge. Caleb brewed coffee to go with it, dug out a bottle of chilled Chianti, and we finished the whole lot off with the remains of last night's peach ice cream.

It's late afternoon by the time Caleb begins my tour. He starts on the third floor, where he does, indeed, have a beautiful billiards room complete with wraparound plush benches and a low-hanging overhead lighting system.

"Do you play?" I ask him.

"I know the rules, but I'm not great at it. I prefer snooker."

"I can play snooker," I reply. "Do you fancy a game?"

"Snooker? Do I detect evidence of a misspent youth?"

"Not really. I used to go to a snooker hall near our house, with my dad. I had my own cue and everything."

"I see. Are you any good?" he asks, looking cautious.

I take one of the cues down from a rack on the wall and

peer down its length, before leaning over the table for a couple of experimental air shots. "I once scored twenty-seven. That was my highest ever break."

"Hmm, Not too bad. Later, perhaps."

There's also a library, the walls lined with glass-fronted book cabinets. Behind the glazed panels are thousands upon thousands of leatherbound volumes, their gnarled spines sporting such august names as Chaucer, Dante, and Shakespeare.

"Have you read any of these?" I ask him.

"Well, a bit of Shakespeare, obviously. At school. And I did enjoy learning the Beowulf poem when I was about ten, I seem to recall. But mostly I tend to prefer the more modern classics. I keep my own books either in my room or in my office."

"So, what's this all for?" I ask. I turn in a circle to better view the finest pillars of English literature down the centuries, towering above me.

"Because they belong here," he replies. "Shall we continue?"

We move along into a hall-like space which Caleb calls the gallery. Here, portraits line the walls, interspersed with statues and figurines."

"Who are all of these?" I ask. "Your family?"

"No. Apart from me, there is no McPherson family connection to Linn Mill. I only bought the place five years ago. These are previous owners, the Carsons, mainly. And some of the artworks and souvenirs they collected on their travels."

"And you keep them because they belong here?" I'm fast getting the idea.

"Exactly." He takes my hand. "That's the classical part of the tour done. Shall we go downstairs now?"

We bypass the main entrance and staircase in favour of a discreet lift tucked away at the rear of the property, another of Caleb's modernising touches. It is his mission to make the place fit for the twenty-first century but without unduly

What Happens in Vegas...

disturbing the timeless serenity of his home. He will have his creature comforts. Even so, he conceals them discreetly behind a veneer of sophisticated elegance.

We exit the lift into a tiled corridor, and my nostrils are at once filled by the familiar scent of chlorine.

"You have a pool?"

"Of course." He tows me along to the end of the corridor where a glass door leads to a well-proportioned spa. The rectangular pool forms the centrepiece, but there is also a whirlpool bath, a sauna, and a steam room. The space is pleasantly warm, made to feel even cosier by the floor-to-ceiling tinted windows offering an unrestricted view of the landscape beyond,

"Mmm, this is nice," I murmur. *Peaceful, private. Utterly chilled.*

"We'll come back later," he promises. "You might appreciate a soak in the whirlpool."

He leads me back along the tiled corridor, pausing to show me a small home gym. I get the impression weights are not his thing. There's a treadmill, a bicycle, and a rowing machine, but not much else.

The final door at the end of the corridor is locked. Caleb operates a keypad to gain entry, then stands back to allow me to pass him.

Unlike the other suites in the basement, this one is windowless. And carpeted, in the main. Dim lighting kicks in as we enter, no doubt motion-activated. It is enough to illuminate the walls lined with shelving and storage racks, and the islands of apparatus situated in various locations around the large space. I have never encountered a BDSM dungeon before, but I have no doubt that is what I have just walked into.

"Oh...my..." I can only stand. And stare.

"Are you all right, Fern?"

"I.... Oh." I take in the padded bench a few paces to my right, and the large cross close to the far wall. Right in front of me is a wooden chair, any number of ominous-looking traps dangling from it. There's a double bed, too, set high off the floor with a pair of stocks built into the footboard. And, if I'm not mistaken, a cage built underneath it.

Bloody hell! A cage. I turn to him, scared suddenly. "You're not locking me in a cage."

"Of course not. Nothing's going to happen that you don't want."

"That I don't want? How could anyone want...this?" I swing my arm around to indicate the entire intimidating environment. it's all just...just...medieval."

He grins. "I think I can prove you wrong there. Unless...do you want to leave, Fern? You don't have to stay in here."

I breath in, give my head a shake. These are just things. Things I don't have to go near if I don't want to. I'm over-reacting, surely.

"I'm fine," I reply. "I just... I've never seen any of...this before. At least, not close up. In the flesh."

"Let's have a wander around then. You can ask me questions if you like, or just ignore anything you don't fancy the look of."

I manage a nod, my attention fixed on the wooden chair closest to us. "What's that for?"

"Just for restraint. And positioning. It allows the submissive to relax and forget about holding position themselves. Great for newbies."

"But what if I want to move?"

I? Did I just actually say 'I'?

"Then, you simply say so. A lot of submissives enjoy being restrained. Tied up. Strapped down. If that's not your thing, then that's fine as well."

"Oh. And what about the benches? For spanking? Right?"

"Right. Handy for anal play, too."

I ignore that remark. "And the cross?"

"That's a St Andrew's cross. Great for impact play."

"Impact play? That's like, hitting me with things?"

He takes my hand and leads me over to the far wall where a heady collection of 'things' are stored on racks and shelves. Paddles, crops, several whips, a set of half a dozen canes that could have come straight out of a Victorian schoolroom. There are leather straps, too, and less daunting items made of brightly coloured silicon, suede, or even feathers.

I reach out to finger the soft downy texture. "You mean to tickle me into submission?"

"Ah, Fern, you'd be amazed what I can achieve with a few feathers." His grin is lop-sided, utterly sexy. Something curls in the pit of my stomach.

"Amaze me, then," I whisper.

He inclines his head in a slow nod. "We'll keep this very simple. Play around with some interesting sensations, find out what you like, what cranks your chain, so to speak. Are you up for that, Fern?"

"Yes," I reply. "Okay."

"Some simple rules, then. First, you need to get naked. When you're in here, your clothes will be in a tidy pile by the door."

"Do I do that now?" *When did I become so eager?*

"Yes. Then return and kneel on the floor, Just there." He indicates a spot just in front of him. "I'll show you how to kneel properly in a moment. Once you've been shown the way, that's how you do it from then on. Understood?"

I nod.

"Okay. Clothes by the door, then."

It felt strange, uncomfortable, to be naked in his bedroom this morning. But any sense of modesty seems to evaporate here in this room, steeped in the apparatus of sinful sex and dirty desiring. Lust is a powerful force, I'm finding. That and rampant curiosity.

I tug off the sweater lent to me for our outdoor excursion, glad to be rid of it. The temperature in Caleb's dungeon is a balmy twenty-odd degrees, far more comfortable against naked skin. My jeans, socks, and training shoes soon follow. I crouch in my underwear to fold the discarded items and place them on a low stool beside the door.

I glance back over my shoulder at Caleb. "Just here?"

"Yes," he replies. "That's fine."

I straighten, remove my bra and add that to the pile, then my knickers. Nude, I saunter back to drop to my knees before him.

"Nicely done, Fern." He bends to cup my chin. "How do you feel?"

"Good," I reply quickly. "Really good…"

"Can you fasten your hair up in some sort of knot?"

"I… I'm not sure?" I grab it, twist it around the top of my head, and tuck the end in. "Like this?" It falls down as soon as I let go.

"Allow me." He moves behind me and pulls the mass of curls behind my ears then splits it into three strands. He forms those into a loose plait which he arranges over my shoulder. "There, that should do. The necklace will need to come off, though."

"Oh?" I clutch the delicate silver chain around my neck. "But I always wear it."

"It could get snagged and be damaged. Or cause you an injury. Best if I take care of it, for now." He holds out his hand.

"It was a present. From my father." The chain and charm which dangles from it, in the shape of an artist's palette and paintbrush, were a gift to celebrate the sale of my first commercial piece of artwork, a picture of a dormouse asleep in a cup. The design was snapped up by a card manufacturer, and they paid me the princely sum of fifty pounds for it. My father went out and bought me the chain and a frame to keep the cheque in. I never cashed it. And I never take the chain off.

"I'll take care of it for you," Caleb repeats. "It will be quite safe, I promise."

What Happens in Vegas...

I reach behind my neck to unfasten the clasp, then drop the necklace into his palm. He pockets it. "Thank you. Now, I said I'd explain how you should kneel. Your knees need to be about a foot apart, and you lay your hands on your thighs, palms upward. That's the resting pose. Your spine will be straight, your shoulders back, and you will look down at the floor unless I tell you, 'eyes on me'. Then, you will look me in the eye and not break your gaze unless I give permission. Is all of this clear?"

"I think so."

His eyes narrow slightly. "Is it clear, Fern? Do you need me to explain anything again?"

"No. It's clear."

"Right, then. Assume the resting position."

I shuffle about until I'm kneeling just as he described. "Is this all right?"

"Yes. That's good. Now for the rest of the rules. When we're in here, you don't speak without permission unless it's to answer a direct question. Or to use your safe word. Is that also clear?"

"Not speak? But...?"

"But what?"

"What if I need to ask you something?"

"Then you start by asking for permission to speak to me. I will always grant you permission if you ask politely and have a good reason."

"Oh. This feels really...odd. Does it have to be so formal?"

"No, it doesn't have to be. But this is how I like it, and since I'm the Dom here, I get to do things my way. Do you have any objections to this?"

I shake my head.

"Say it."

"No. No objections."

"One last thing. We touched on this yesterday. In here, you will always refer to me as Sir."

I take a pace back to regard her. She really is quite perfect, and a quick learner. Her resting pose is pretty much spot on, and her submissive demeanour positively glows. I had wondered about the no speaking rule and I'm not surprised she queried that. Fern loves to talk, I'm finding, and is full of questions. She won't be able to contain herself once we get started.

The discipline will do her good. I know I'll enjoy it.

Sensation play. I mean to make her tingle, but not to frighten her unduly. This needs to be challenging, edgy, sufficient to push her boundaries, but not too far. Tomorrow will be somewhat intense, so I need to ease her in gently today, build her confidence and indulge her thirst for knowledge.

I'm not entirely sure why and how this wannabe sub with the delusional tendencies and tendency to fantasise has captured my interest or imagination, but she has. I want to show her some of these things, help her to experience and enjoy her submissive nature, to appreciate the gifts she possesses. Ours will be a temporary liaison, but it already means something to me. I intend to leave a lasting impression on her.

I remove my thick sweater and my shirt. I always prefer to wear as little as possible in my dungeon, though jeans are a given unless I'm actually fucking my sub. I lose the shoes and socks, though. Silent footsteps are an asset, I find.

Fern's eyes are on the floor in front of her, though I suspect her gaze does secretly follow me as I move about collecting the items I mean to use. I could be firmer with her, require her to lean forward and lift her bottom for a few well-deserved swats, but I prefer not to. At least, not yet. Instead, I busy myself with the preparations, then return to stand in front of her.

"Eyes on me."

Her head bobs up. Her mossy gaze is bright. Eager.

"Stand up and go over to the cross."

Her eyes widen.

I wait.

Slowly, with rather less grace than when she descended into the kneel, she gets to her feet. She makes her way over to the cross, then pauses to look at me. "What should I do...?"

"You should be quiet, unless I ask you a question. And did I say that you could look away?"

"Oh." The flush rises from her chest. "I'm sorry. I didn't..."

"You said you understood my instructions. I don't like to repeat myself."

"No, Sir. I just... It's hard to get used to everything, that's all."

"I know that. You need to concentrate."

"I will. I promise. Sir."

I move towards her. "On this occasion, I think you'll find it easier if I fasten you to the cross. Is that okay with you?"

"Fasten me?"

"Yes. Using these straps." The cross is fitted with plenty of restraints, all made of soft leather, lined with faux fur. "You'll be perfectly comfortable."

"I see. Yes. Yes, okay."

I take each of her wrists and attach them to the upper arms of the diagonal cross, then her ankles to the lower points. I position her feet as far apart as she can comfortably manage. The cross is far enough away from the wall that I can easily walk all around her, and since it is open at the front, I have access to her entire body.

"I mean to touch you. Everywhere. Nowhere is off limits, unless you say so now."

I wait, but there is no response.

"Fern? Did you understand me? Is there anywhere you would prefer I not touch you?"

She shakes her head. "No, Sir. I just..."

"Go on."

"If it's going to hurt, please tell me. I... I don't like shocks."

"No shocks, I promise. And remember, pain can be pleasure, too."

Her expression suggests she remains unconvinced of this, but time will tell.

I reach into the back pocket of my jeans for my first item of equipment.

A blindfold.

"May I?"

"Oh? You mean to cover my eyes?"

"It heightens the sensations. And will help you to concentrate."

"I'm not sure…"

"Trust me, Fern. And remember, you have your safe word if you need it."

The mention of her get-out-of-jail-free card seems to do the trick. She calms and nods. "Okay, I'll try it."

"Brave girl." I kiss her lightly on the mouth, then quickly secure the soft suede blindfold around her head. "Is that okay? You can't see anything?"

"No," she whispers. "Please. Don't go too far away."

"I'll be right here. All the time."

"Will you speak to me? I don't want it to be quiet and dark."

"Yes, I'll speak to you." I kiss her shoulder, then the nape of her neck. "If you need to hear my voice you have permission to ask."

She allows her head to drop forward. "Thank you, Sir."

I step away to pick up the first of my chosen implements. Since she was particularly interested in feathers, we might as well start with those. I return to sweep the delicate fronds of the boa across her shoulders.

Fern twitches under the gossamer caress. I repeat it, drawing the nest of downy feathers first to the right, then the left. Her head sways from side to side, in tune with my strokes.

I trace a pattern down her ribcage next, keeping the contact so light as to be almost not there at all. Soon, she is wriggling, seeking more. I maintain the ethereal touch, teasing her, tempting her, forcing her to shift and seek, to go in search of the friction her skin craves. Only when she is almost panting with a need she can barely describe do I ramp up the pressure.

I move around to the front and draw the boa across her breasts, the upper curves first, then the lower. Then, I use the tips of the feathers to graze her pebbled nipples. Fern lets out a sigh; her lips remain parted. Her pink tongue slips out, and she licks her lower lip.

Time to dial it all up a notch. I raise the feather boa and with a flick of my wrist strike her across the breasts.

Her sigh is ragged, one of surprise but not pain. I do it again, then shift my attention to her bottom. I use the boa as a whip, striking her tender buttocks. It's so light that her skin barely ripples, but she feels it.

Revels in it.

Her back arches. She pushes her bottom towards me, silently begging for more, begging for harder, faster.

I set the boa aside and reach for a soft flogger. Made of suede, this is still light, still designed to pleasure and to tantalise but with the capacity, in the right hands, to bite.

We're not there yet, though.

I circle her, swirling the tails in a slow figure of eight, slapping them against her torso from all directions. I avoid her kidney area, even though the flogger is so light. There is plenty to go at in her shoulders, her ribs, her luscious buttocks and thighs.

Her skin starts to take on a delicate shade of pink. I lay the backs of my fingers on her shoulder blade, feel the first flickers of heat and know that she is becoming sensitised, receptive.

"How are you doing, Fern?" I lean in to murmur directly into her ear.

"It's... I'm fine, Sir."

"Okay. Tell me if that changes."

"Yes, Sir."

I swap the flogger for a crop. I remember her dislike of having her breasts spanked yesterday. That was a punishment, intended to hurt. Today is all about pleasure, sensuality. I'll restrict this to her bottom and thighs. I deliver a series of quick, light taps to her bum, and enjoy watching her dance and quiver under the onslaught. Her bottom is glowing crimson by now, but still, she doesn't complain.

I reach for another item I set aside, the vampire glove. A leather mitt, the palm is covered in small spikes. I slide it onto my left hand then draw my palm slowly across both cheeks of her bottom.

"Caleb! Sir..." She flinches, then relaxes into my touch.

I continue to caress her, alternating the sharp scratch of the mitt with not especially light strokes of the crop.

Slap. Sting. Stroke.

Slap. Sting. Stroke.

"Oh. Oh, wow..."

"Does that feel good?" I nuzzle her shoulder with my mouth.

"So good..." she sighs.

I allow myself a wry grin. This is intense, and without the build-up it would be fairly painful. She'll bear the marks from this for at least a couple of days, yet her senses are so scrambled now that all she experiences is pleasure.

I continue to tease and torment her delicate skin until we reach a point where I'm close to drawing blood. That will never do. I set the glove and crop aside and begin my next phase.

Without preamble, I swipe my palm through her pussy folds. My hand comes away soaking wet, as I knew it would.

"Tut, tut," I admonish her. "So sloppy. You're leaking all over my nice clean cross."

"Sir...?" she almost wails. "I need... I need..."

"You need to come. Don't you?"

"Yes."

"Do you deserve to come, though? Have you earned it yet?"

"I don't know. Please..."

I retrieve a bullet vibrator from my jeans pocket and flick the switch at the end. It bursts into life, and I slide it between her spread thighs, applying just enough pressure to tease her clit but afford no real satisfaction. When she tries to press down onto it, I lower my hand a fraction.

"Please..." she moans, "I need it..."

"Where do you need it?" I ask, lowering my hand yet more, breaking the contact.

"Against my clit," she grinds out. "Hard."

"Not this time," I answer. "This time, it goes inside. Like this." I crouch in front of her and part her pussy lips with my fingers. I insert the toy, making sure it rests nicely against her G-spot before standing again. Then, I take her face between my palms and kiss her mouth, plunging my tongue inside.

"Come for me, Fern," I command her, my voice, low, urgent. At the same time, I grasp her tender arse cheeks, scratch them with my fingernails, reignite the ripples of pleasure and pain that have become indistinguishable. She is pure sensation now, pure lustful energy. An orgasm desperate to happen.

Her features contort in a grimace. Her mouth sags open, her breathing is laboured. Her buttocks clench under my hands, and I know her inner channel is clamping down hard on the small toy. I'm making her work for it, but the rewards will be there for her.

"Sir. Sir. *Sir...*"

"Come for me. Now."

She shudders violently, then shatters. Her entire body convulses. She lets out a keening moan, her fists clenching and unclenching as the waves of sensation punch through her. A deep flush rises from her breasts to engulf her, totally involuntary, utterly impossible to fake.

Fern Daniels' absolute surrender is a glorious sight, one I swear I would never get tired of even if we had a lifetime and not just this one weekend.

CHAPTER 12

I drop to my haunches to release her ankles, then wrap my arms around her waist and undo the wrist cuffs. Fern drops from the cross like a stone, collapsing against me. I pick her up and carry her to the bed, then stretch out alongside her.

I tug the blindfold up and away from her face. She blinks in the dim light, peering up at me.

"You seemed to enjoy that," I observe.

"Mmm," is the best she seems able to manage in response.

"Shall I take this?" I part her thighs to reach the finger cord attached to the bullet, still whirring inside her.

She arches as I draw the toy from her body.

"Maybe I should buy one of those," she murmurs, the hint of a smile playing on her pretty lips.

"You can have this one," I reply. I'm feeling generous. "I mean to fuck you now."

"You should," is her succinct response. "You were always very good at that."

I bite back any sharp retort. I no longer think she is trying to trick me, though that is of little comfort really. She genuinely believes what she is saying regarding our previous relationship, however bizarre.

I half expect her to protest when I take her wrists and

fasten them to the headboard, but her smile widens. We both know she's going nowhere.

"Spread for me," I command her, my voice soft.

She parts her thighs, lying open beneath me. Ready. Waiting. Willing.

My cock throbs like a bitch, and my balls ache. I can barely unfasten my jeans fast enough. I shove them to my ankles, then kick them off. My underwear goes, too. I lean over to reach into the bedside drawer for a condom. This is not going to take long.

I get into position and spear her in one long thrust.

Fern cries out, her body arches, then clamps tight around me. She's snug, so small, and wet. All liquid heat and soft, quivering flesh.

"Christ, that feels so good..."

She writhes against me, her hips swivelling. "Harder, Cal. I need more..."

I draw back, make her wait for a few moments before I plunge deep again. And again. She moves with me, meeting my thrusts with her own. She lifts her legs and wraps them around my waist and grasps my shoulders with her hands as though she expects me to slip away at any moment.

Not. A. Chance.

I grope on the mattress and find the discarded bullet. I flick the switch again, then slide the toy between us, wedging it hard against her clit.

Fern lets out an appreciative moan and comes all over my cock.

I return her guttural shout. My cock lurches, my balls twist painfully. Long streams of cum spurt into the condom, and I sink into blessed oblivion.

The moment of peace is short-lived. I flop onto my back, peel off the condom for disposal later, and reach for another. It only takes one tug on the cuffs to release her wrists from the headboard.

"Roll over."

"Sir?" She nestles into my side.

"Over. We're not done yet."

"Oh." She shoves a hank of curls back from her face. "So soon?"

"So soon. On all fours, girl."

She smiles and gets into position. I kneel behind her, pause just long enough to appreciate the rosy glow of her buttocks, the delicate scratches traced into her porcelain skin by my vampire mitt, then I part her pussy lips and penetrate her slowly. Just the head of my cock at first, teasing her, opening her, holding her there. Ready and waiting…

I swipe my hand through her folds, gathering moisture, then I press the tip of my middle finger against her arsehole. She can take me in two holes this time. I press forward, and her rear hole parts to let me in. I finger-fuck her arse a few times, then sink my cock into her pussy.

Mine. All mine.

Our second round lasts marginally longer than the first, though it's close.

After, we lie tangled in the sheets. My breathing returns to something like normal, I even consider dozing off.

"Tell me about the tattoo."

Fern's voice is soft, barely a whisper. Her fingers are resting against my biceps, and she traces the outline of the figure etched there.

"It's just a tattoo," I reply, "Nothing special."

"It's unusual. A ballet dancer."

"Yes." Well, sort of. It's more stylised figure suggestive of a dancer. Not a tutu in sight. "It's for my mother."

"Oh? She was a dancer, then?"

I shrug. "I think so. I'm not sure."

Fern leans up on one elbow. I have her full attention now. "Not sure?"

"I never knew her. She died giving birth to me."

What Happens in Vegas...

"Oh. Oh, I'm so sorry. I never meant—"

"It's okay. It was over thirty years ago, and obviously, I've no memory of it. Or of her."

"But your father told you about her? That she was a ballet dancer?"

"No. He refused to ever speak of her. They...they did not get on. She'd already left him by the time I was born. He was in America, I gather, which is where he spent most of his time when I was growing up. He had to hire a nanny to come and pick me up from the hospital. That sort of set the pattern. I was cared for by servants, and eventually sent off to school, first in England, then in America."

"It sounds very..."

"Cold," I fill in for her. "Detached."

"Well, yes."

"It was. Those words describe my father perfectly. He did his best, I daresay, but it wasn't much. He was an emotional embryo. He saw to my physical wellbeing, my education, but he had no paternal instincts at all. No affection, no time for a son. Or a wife, I suppose. That was probably why my mother got out while she could."

"What was her name?"

"Meryl, according to my birth certificate. She was just twenty when she died."

"So, why the ballet, then?"

"I found a pair of ballet slippers in a drawer in the room she used to use, in my father's house near Aberdeen. I don't know how they got missed, because he had everything of hers cleared out. It was as though he tried to just erase her from his life. I'm not even sure the slippers were hers, and I couldn't ask him. He refused to ever tell me anything about her or even let her name be mentioned. So, I assumed, built up my own mental picture. It might be pure fantasy, but it's the one I have. And I had the tattoo done when I was eighteen. My dad was livid, which I suspect means I guessed right.

He resented her being commemorated in any way, shape or form."

"He hated her so much?"

"I always had the impression, from the servants we had at the time, that it was entirely mutual."

"So, that tattoo was a sort of act of rebellion, then? A way of making him remember her?"

"I could never make my father do anything. But yes, I suppose I was striking a blow for my own freedom."

"What happened to your father? Is he still alive?"

I shake my head. "He died six years ago when his light plane came down in the desert in Arizona. No survivors."

"And soon after that, you bought Linn Mill."

"Yes. I sold our old house near Aberdeen and my father's apartment in Manhattan, invited anyone who worked for us and wanted to stay on to come here with me, and started over, minus all the bitterness and recriminations. Sally Parsons relocated, so did Harry. And old William, obviously."

"And the horses."

"Naturally, the horses, though it was only Roman and Bella then, and Stardance. He's the one buried by the stream."

"I think I understand now why your horses mean so much to you."

I roll her onto her back and smooth the hair from her face. "I'm not sure you do. I love my horses, but they are no substitute for anything else. My father was not a man to be admired, even less loved. He wouldn't have known what to do with anything like that. But he was resilient, and he taught me to be the same. He was a successful businessman, and I inherited those skills, too. He made sure I knew how to earn money and keep what I earned through shrewd investment and surrounding myself with the best advisers. I enjoy being wealthy, it gives me the life I want."

"But don't you get lonely?"

"You asked me that before. The answer is still 'no'."

She doesn't reply. Her eyes are wide, the green glowing in the dim light of my dungeon. She doesn't believe me, not that it matters. I answer to no one, not anymore.

"Aaah..." My lips part on a soft sigh. Something warm yet compelling curls deep in my core. I should be awake. I should pay attention...

"Ah, you're coming round. At last."

"Mmm," I writhe on the mattress. "What...?"

"Wake up, Fern. You might miss the good bit."

I come fully alert when Caleb lifts me, his palms under my buttocks, and draws the flat of his tongue the entire length of my slit, from anus to clit.

"Cal..."

"Do you want me to stop?" He pauses to look up at me from his position between my thighs.

I shake my head. "Please don't."

His lip quirks in that sexy way he has. "Thought not. And now that I have your full attention..."

He makes a spear of his tongue and inserts that into my pussy, at the same time placing the pad of his thumb over my throbbing, swollen clit. He rubs in slow, lazy circles, tongue-fucking me as he does.

My bones turn to liquid. I'm melting, dissolving in a puddle of undiluted pleasure.

"I need to come..."

"Not yet," he replies before taking my clit between his lips and sucking gently.

"Yes. Now..."

"Wait," he commands. He scrapes his teeth across the tip of my sensitive bud. "I'll tell you when to come."

How is that supposed to work? I grit my teeth, try to contain my mounting desperation in the face of his relentless onslaught.

"Cal, please…"

"Sir, please," he corrects me.

"I can't help it. You need to stop. Or slow down…"

"And you need to learn to control yourself. Wait until I tell you, like a good girl."

"I can't, I can't," I wail, just in time to shatter as my orgasms finally breaks through any fragile resistance I might have put up.

Caleb continues to lick and suck, to tease and caress until the final shudders have died away. Only then does he lean up on one elbow to fix me with a cool, stern glare.

"Naughty subs who steal orgasms get punished."

"I didn't mean to. I just—"

"I told you to wait. You disobeyed me."

"I know, but—"

"Are you hungry?"

"What?"

"Hungry? Food?"

My stomach growls. "I'm famished."

"Okay. I have it on good authority that you and I have an appointment with a rather succulent duck drowning in orange sauce, but after that, I mean to see to your continuing education."

"Duck? In orange sauce? I guess Sally's back from the caterer's then?"

"She certainly is. And it'll be ready in an hour."

"Oh. What time is it now?"

"Almost eight in the evening."

"You mean, we slept for over two hours?"

"Well, you did. I thought I'd better wake you, in case you fancy a dip in that whirlpool bath you were oohing and aahing over, before getting dressed."

What Happens in Vegas…

"Oh, that would be so good." I stretch, exploring the myriad of sensations. "I ache in places I never knew I had."

"Lightweight," he replies, with a smirk. "Come on, then."

He rolls from the bed and turns to lift me bodily from the mattress.

"Hey, I can walk."

"But why bother?" He strides from the room, pausing only to make sure the door closes behind us with a decisive click, then he marches along the tiled corridor to the other end where the spa is situated. We are both gloriously naked, not that this seems to concern Caleb in the least.

"Someone might see," I whisper, clinging to his neck.

"There's only us here. I value my privacy, remember." He elbows open the door to the spa and only stops for long enough to settle me in one of the several loungers dotted around the place.

I watch, appreciative, as he operates the controls on the whirlpool. He has his back to me so I am afforded an unrestricted view of his tight arse and muscled shoulders. The absence of weights in the gym suggests other forms of exercise. I know he rides, and I suppose he might swim as well. However he achieves it, he's perfectly toned.

I recall this was one of the things that drew me to him back in Las Vegas. Not an ounce of spare fat, muscles sharply defined, athletic, brimming with energy and raw sex appeal. Cal always exuded a verve for life. He was exciting to be around, a powerhouse of enthusiasm and vitality. I became entangled, sort of caught up in his aura, and I was swept along, right through the doors of the Sunset Chapel in Las Vegas.

I dismiss that errant memory. It means nothing, not anymore.

Caleb shoots me a glance over his shoulder and beckons to me. By the time I reach him, he has already lowered his body into the foaming water. Steam rises from the bubbling surface as he offers me his hand to help me step over the edge and into the pool.

"Aah," I sigh. The water is warm and delicately scented. Beyond sensual, the feeling is one of utter decadence. Aromas of pine and something more floral tease my nostrils. I sink onto his lap.

"Turn around and straddle me," he whispers.

I do as he asks, looping my hands around his neck and linking my fingers in the damp strands of his hair. His cock, hard again, nudges my bottom.

Does he never get tired?

I wriggle my arse. Caleb groans.

I reach down, between us, and fist his engorged cock. Holding it at what seems to be the correct angle, I slowly sink down onto it, taking the crown inside me.

"Fern…" My name comes out as a low growl, and he tenses, ready to thrust.

"No, let me…"

"Condom?" he mutters. "In the locker…"

"I'm on the pill," I reply. "And I'm clean, I swear." *After all, it's not as though I make a habit if this sort of thing.*

"Me, too," he concedes.

The matter seemingly settled, I continue to lower myself onto his cock, taking him inch by inch. My body stretches to enfold him. I wrap him in my tightness, lower, deeper, until my tender buttocks come to rest on his thighs.

"Christ, girl, I can't…"

I squeeze, hard, and wriggle my hips again.

"Jesus," he exhales. "For fuck's sake, don't do that."

"But I like to." I treat him to another sensuous shimmy. "I'm so full, I could burst."

"You're so full of fucking attitude you might earn yourself a close encounter with a cane," he grinds out. "I know just the one."

I'm not sure if he means it. He might, and I've seen his

impressive collection of canes so I don't doubt he has a favourite among them, but I can't help rolling my hips again, savouring the sensation of being stretched, impaled, wrapped impossibly taut around his magnificent cock.

"Please, I want to fuck you. Just this once. Let me..."

He grasps a handful of my hair and drags my head back. He's not gentle, forcing me to meet his gaze. His dark-chocolate-hued eyes are narrowed, glinting dangerously and hinting at every sort of retribution. Have I pushed too far, too fast?

The corner of his mouth quirks, creating a dimple I never noticed before. "Be sure to make a decent job of it, then, little sub."

"You mean...?"

He nods, just once. "Go for it. Show me what you can do."

I need no further permission. Bending my legs at the knees, I find a toehold on the step below the one where he is seated. It's not much, but enough to give me a bit of leverage, and the water helps to take my weight. I lift my body, releasing him from my snug inner embrace, only to slam back down again as hard as I can.

"Holy fuck..." he breathes, his nose buried in my hair.

I take that as a sign of approval and do it again. And again. I find a rhythm and sink into it, adding a slight swirl of my hips to each downward stroke.

Caleb cups my breasts in both his hands and pushes them together, then takes my nipple between his lips. The crackle of sexual electricity arcs straight to my clit, nearly derailing my carefully orchestrated private dance. I gather my wits and continue, shorter, sharper thrusts now, and I lean forward in the hope that I might find that place he seems to always connect with.

Yes! There!

I clamp down hard, my inner muscles aching now with the frenzied activity. My arousal spikes. My desperation soars. I need to come, but not until...

I reach down again and this time cup his balls. I roll them in my palm, massage them, relish the sense that I have him, however briefly, right here in my hands.

His cock lurches inside me. The movement is sharp, violent, involuntary. He's close, very close. So am I.

I rest my forehead against his chest, drag in a steam-filled breath. "Caleb, I...."

"Fern," he groans, "Fuck, girl..."

I squeeze down hard, grind my hips against him, and deliver one final, driving thrust.

Caleb shouts something distinctly Scottish, and his cock lurches again. His balls contract in my hand, and the heat of his semen fills me.

My own climax erupts just moments later. Waves of pleasure pulse through me, right out to my fingers and toes, reaching every nerve ending and hovering there. I cling to Caleb, quivering, shaking, my body convulsing around his until slowly, eventually, my world rights itself.

"Nicely done," he murmurs.

I'm too wrung out to come up with anything in response, but Caleb seems not to mind. He lifts me from him, achingly gentle now in contrast to his earlier roughness, then turns me around and cradles me in his arms.

I wish...

"Mmm, what do you wish, sweetheart?"

"Nothing," I whisper.

I wish we had more than just this weekend. I wish... I wish we had Las Vegas again. Somehow, I'd do it differently this time, somehow I'd make it right...

CHAPTER 13

For a small woman, Fern Daniels is blessed with a seriously healthy appetite. Not that I'm complaining, I like a woman who appreciates the delights of the senses, whether that's a mind-blowing orgasm precisely crafted, the perfect culmination of pleasure and pain in exquisite harmony, or a gourmet meal where the flavours are artfully orchestrated to explode on the tongue.

I can provide the former, my cook and housekeeper, the latter.

Sally Parsons could probably walk into a job in any high-end restaurant. I'm lucky to have her, and she has outdone herself this evening. The duck is perfect, the sauce simply sublime. The zesty aroma of Seville oranges laced with ginger, garlic and, if I'm not mistaken, a dash of cinnamon, gives way to sultry notes of chocolate and coffee as we nibble our way through the dessert of fluffy mousse and brandy snap biscuits.

"Have you had enough?" I ask when Fern at last sets her spoon aside. "There's some of the mousse left, I think."

She leans back in her chair with a contented sigh. "I'm stuffed. That was wonderful, though. I wish I could cook like that..."

"Each to their own. I'm reasonably certain that Sally can't paint."

"I'm a potter these days."

"Pot, then. More coffee?"

She shakes her head. "I'll be buzzing all night if I do."

I meet her gaze, hold it. "You may find you'll be buzzing all night anyway."

She frowns at me. "Oh?"

"There remains the small matter of a stolen orgasm," I remind her. "We need to work on your self-control issues."

"It was your fault," she protests. "I told you to stop."

"Well, there's the thing, you see. Telling me to stop means fuck all. That's what a safe word is for, to avoid any misunderstandings. I didn't hear you say 'red'." I lean towards her, daring her to avert her gaze. "Did you say 'red', Fern?"

She shakes her head. "I didn't think..."

"Okay. So, we're clear on that. Which means we need to address the matter of your sloppiness, teach you to control yourself a little better."

Her expression falls, her joy of just moments ago disintegrating before my eyes. She looks close to tears. I reach over the table to cup her chin.

"Tell me what you're thinking right now, Fern."

"It...it doesn't matter."

"It does. Tell me."

"Okay. I... I was wishing, after the lovely day we've had, and the meal and everything, that it would have been nice to end it...in bed. Together."

"And so we will."

"But I'll be sore. Hurting..."

"Is that a problem?"

"I suppose not." Despite her reply, she does not appear in the least bit enthusiastic about what she believes the next few minutes hold for her.

She glances about the room. "Will we stay here? Or go down to your other room?"

"Here. I brought a few bits and pieces up that I thought might come in useful."

"Bits and pieces?" she repeats. "What sort of bits and pieces?"

"Not the sort you have in mind, sweetheart." I release her jaw and get to my feet, then offer her my hand. "Come with me. I'll show you my toy cupboard."

Not so much a cupboard, more a polished oak chest, dating from, I think, the early Victorian period, I like to keep my collection of erotic toys where I can find just what I need at a moment's notice. I drag the box out from beneath my bed and open the lid. Behind me, Fern gasps.

"See anything you fancy?" I ask her.

"Wow!"

Not especially incisive. I decide to make a few selections of my own. The toys are all new, many still in their packaging. Submissives tend to be choosy about such thigs and I don't blame them. I can afford to replace items as I use them, often going back for old favourites. I choose a small internal vibrator, curved to access the G-spot, and an external device which simulates a sucking sensation, very effective when applied to a particularly sensitive clit.

I happen to know that Fern's clit is likely to appreciate the attention.

I consider butt plugs, and do set one aside, just to get started with, but opt for anal beads as well. I also pick out a large wand-style vibrator, always a reliable choice, and a couple of tubes of lubricant.

"I thought you meant to punish me," Fern whispers. "These…these are for… Well, you know."

"I do know. I know very well. I also know that punishment comes in many forms, and that the most effective discipline is that which best fits the crime."

"I'm totally confused." Fern sits on the edge of my bed. "You say I'm in trouble, yet you start preparing for an orgy."

"Then, let me explain. You stole an orgasm from me. I mean to steal one from you."

Her expression would be comical if there was not a serious angle to this. She shakes her head, utterly perplexed. "You don't need to steal orgasms. Well, not from me. You can make me come just by…by looking at me. You always could."

Ouch. I let that one go.

"A stolen orgasm is the one you don't want to give."

"Why would I not want…?"

"When you're tired. Exhausted. When you've already come Christ knows how many times, and you can't face even one more climax. When every touch feels like fire, when every lick or kiss feels like sandpaper. When you beg me to stop, but I force one more from you. One. Last. Orgasm. That's the one that I mean to steal. So, the next time I tell you to wait, you'll remember how a forced orgasm feels, and you'll do as you're told."

"Oh."

She regards me with new interest and a fair degree of trepidation. As well she might.

"I'll need you to undress and lie on the bed. On your back, legs spread wide."

She doesn't move.

"Fern, I don't like to be kept waiting. And I definitely don't appreciate having to repeat myself."

She jumps up. "Sorry, I… I was just…"

She seems about ready to bolt. I need to settle her, bring her into the moment, with me.

I wrap my arms around her and ease her back to sit on the bed. "It's okay. Calm down. This will be intense, and intimate, but you *can* do this."

"Intense? Yes… I suppose…"

"Fern, do you remember your safe word?"

"Yes."

"And you know to use it if you need to."

"Why would I need to? This is…different from before."

"Yes. A different challenge, different boundaries. If you need me to stop, you can make that happen."

"I know." Her voice is barely a whisper now. "I trust you."

I kiss her hair. "Are you ready to undress, then?"

She nods, then, "Will you…will I be tied down?"

I consider that for a few moments. "Yes. You will be restrained in the position I choose. Open, and accessible."

This is a punishment I could take a long, long time over. With a more experienced submissive, and one I know much more intimately than I do Fern Daniels, I would certainly go that route. Hours of edging will bring even the brattiest sub to heel. My gut instinct tells me that Fern won't be able to tolerate that approach. She needs this to be over, quickly, and to know that she survived the ordeal. That she did well, that she met this emotional and personal test just as she managed to overcome the physical challenges earlier.

Tied to my bed, she will be helpless, vulnerable. She will experience being exposed and laid bare to anything, everything I might choose to do to her, her choices gone, her responses no longer hers to own or to give. She might hate it, never want to experience anything similar again, rather like the breast torture of earlier.

Or she may love it. The experience might feed her innermost and most secret fantasies. And maybe…that's what frightens her the most.

I leave the toys I selected on the duvet and settle myself in a chair to watch Fern undress. She's speedy about it, and even remembers to fold her clothes and leave them in a neat pile on a low footstool. Then, she climbs onto the bed and lies down, her gaze fixed on the ceiling.

Fastening her wrists to the headboard takes just a few

moments as I like to I keep plenty of cuffs and restraints to hand. Practicalities sorted, I grab a couple of pillows.

"I need to slip these under your bottom. Can you lift up for me?"

She plants her heels against the mattress and pushes her hips up, enough that I can shove the pillows under her. The effect is to raise her off the bed and make her pussy and anus easier to reach.

Fern extends her legs, feet wide apart.

"No. You need to bring your feet up closer to your hips and bend your knees. Then, just let your legs flop apart. Nice and wide, as far as you can."

She gnaws on her lower lip but manages to arrange herself just as I want her. The trick, naturally, is to keep her there. And for this, I have help.

Two long leather straps are attached to the base of my bed, on either side, about halfway down. I take the first one, on the left-hand side, loop the strap around her knee, and fasten the buckle, effectively immobilising that leg. Then, I walk around and repeat the action on the other side. I stand at the foot of the bed to admire the scene before me.

"Perfect. You look beautiful, Fern."

Her gaze remains fixed on some fascinating spot above us.

"Eyes on me," I command, my tone sharper.

She turns her head. Her emerald-green eyes have darkened. Arousal? Fear? I can't be sure.

"We'll start with something simple. And familiar." I pick up a tube of lubricating gel and squirt some onto my finger. "I think we'll put a plug in your arse, just to get your attention."

The plug I'm using this time is quite big, but I have no doubt she'll cope. I sit beside her, lean over to admire her puckered arsehole, then slip my lubed finger right inside. I drive it in and out a few times, noting the vaguely startled but definitely not overly bothered expression. She has become accustomed to this intimate handling already. I withdraw my fingers to replace them with the plug, suitably lubed, of course.

Even though this is wider than my finger, it's still relatively tame. It slips easily into place, then her tight sphincter closes around the neck to hold it firm.

"Feel okay?"

She manages a nod.

"We'll rub out the first one or two climaxes quickly. I'm going for five in total so not too daunting, really."

"Five?" Her eyes widen. "I've never come that many times, at least, not in one session."

"A novel experience then." I select the internal device to start with and squirt lubricant onto it.

Fern watches nervously.

"Have you ever used one of these before?" I ask her.

She shakes her head.

"Okay. I'll insert it. You just need to relax and let me do this. Ready?"

"I think so..."

I slide my finger into her pussy to test her wetness. Not as much as I might have liked. Nerves, no doubt. I load my fingers with lube and drive them into her again. Her response is almost instantaneous. Her pussy tightens around my fingers, and she lets out a low moan.

I place the head of the toy against her entrance and ease it very slowly inside. It's small, a novice piece, really. She can take it easily, but the hardness of the silicon will feel odd. Intrusive, perhaps.

I watch her face as I slide the toy deeper, alert for any sign of real discomfort. She seems to be managing fine, and the head of the vibrator is soon nestling against her G-spot. I tilt the thing to make sure the rubbery ears are in contact with her clit, check that it's on the lowest setting, then I press the button on the end of the handle.

"Aaah?!" Fern jerks within her restraints, "Caleb! Oh..."

I'm confident she can handle the sensation, though it is probably more intense than she expected. This particular toy has a very...direct approach. No lead-in, no preamble. Straight to business.

I use the handle to shift the toy to and fro, causing the head to rub against her inner sweet spot. At the same time, I peel back the hood shielding her clit, to ensure she receives maximum benefit from the rabbit effect.

"Oh God, that feels... "

"Nice?"

"Yes. No. It's too much..."

"I don't think so, but you know the rules. Do you need to use your safe word?"

She bites on her lower lip and shakes her head. "I just... Oh Christ, I'm going to come."

"Excellent. Whenever you're ready."

"You bastard... Aaaagh!" She rocks her hips back and forth, writhing in her cuffs as her first orgasm overwhelms her.

I wait until the final tremors die down, then I hit the switch again to stop the internal vibrations, but I don't remove the toy. Instead, I grasp the finger grip of the butt plug and gently pull that out.

I pick up the anal beads, seven inches of jelly-like round balls, fastened together on a silicon string. I dangle the item in front of Fern. "Three guesses where these are going."

She gulps. "No..."

"Yes." I dip my fingertip into her anus. "One at a time, in here."

I don't ask if she's ready this time. I apply a generous coating of lube, then simply start easing the beads into her. They go in easily, and I am able to work the entire length inside with no trouble.

"You're doing well, Fern. How does that feel?"

"Sort of...deep."

"Mmm. You'll love the sensation when you come. So, shall

What Happens in Vegas...

we switch this back on now, and get ready for the next instalment?"

I press the button on the vibrator handle twice, once to turn it on, the second time to increase the intensity.

"Oh. God..."

Fern closes her eyes, a slight frown across her forehead.

I'm holding the handle of the toy, swirling it inside her, and I feel the moment her arousal begin to spike. It really doesn't take long. She bites on her lower lip, then suddenly jerks her hips forward and clamps down hard as she comes for the second time.

Again, I wait until her shudders cease before turning the toy back to its lowest setting. I don't turn it off, though. Not this time. Instead, I settle down to watch while the gentler vibrations continue to tease and arouse, not quite enough to catapult her into the sort of explosive climaxes she has been having, but enough to keep her on the edge.

"Please, turn it off. I need to rest for a few minutes..."

I shake my head. "Come for me again."

"I can't."

"You can. And you will. I'm in no hurry." I stand and cross the room to pour myself a glass of water, then I settle down in the chair I used earlier.

"What are you doing?" she demands, irritable now.

"Watching. Waiting. I have all night."

"Caleb," she wails. "I can't. I need more..."

"Concentrate. Block out everything else."

"You make me nervous, self-conscious, knowing you're watching me."

"Tough. I enjoy watching you come," I sip my water, at the same time relishing the play of emotions across her features. Irritation, frustration, annoyance, then interest as her arousal builds again. Next comes concentration when the inexorable buzzing and vibrating eventually begins to have the desired effect, followed by a slackening of her jaw and relaxing of her muscles when her third orgasm looms.

Not as powerful or overwhelming as the previous two, I witness the moment she lets out a contented sigh and her body stiffens before going absolutely still. She lies motionless, eyes closed, her breathing slowly returning to normal.

I glance at the clock on the mantelpiece. The third climax has taken nearly twelve minutes to achieve.

I return to the bed, and now I do switch off the vibrator. "Time to try a different approach."

I draw the toy out of her pussy and set it aside, then pick up the clitoral suction device. One of my personal favourites, its quiet, understated approach disguises a seriously punchy performance. The small handheld device has a rubber cup which sits nicely on the clit, sucking gently. Or, not so gently. I lube it up, then position it on Fern's plump clit, and set it off on its lowest setting to see how she reacts.

Nothing, at first. Then, a few seconds later, her eyes open wide.

"Oh! That feels…"

"Intense enough? We can turn it up if you like."

She shakes her head. "No, it's quite all right. It's enough…"

She thrusts her hips as though seeking to increase the pressure, gain more stimulation. I press the 'plus' button on the handle then clamp the toy hard over her sensitive nubbin. This won't take twelve minutes. She'll be lucky to last twelve seconds.

Sure enough, Fern lets out a shriek from deep in her throat, and her body starts to convulse. I maintain the pressure until her arousal crests, then, as her orgasm erupts, I slide my finger into the ring on the end of the string of anal beads and tug sharply. The combined effect sends Fern into orbit. The shriek rises to a scream. She bucks and thrashes against the mattress, and the pillow beneath her hips is now damp with her juices.

"How was that?" I enquire when she has managed to regain some semblance of equilibrium.

"Weird," she breathes after a few moments' thought. "Just... weird. And fierce. Severe. It was too much."

"Pity you think that, since I need one more from you still."

"I can't, Caleb. I really can't." Tears form. She looks ready to use that safe word.

"You can, and you will. If you want to please me."

"Just give me a few minutes, then."

I shake my head and pick up the trusty wand vibrator. Potent and compelling, this piece of kit never fails to bring about the desired result, however reluctant the sub on the receiving end.

I lube up the bulbous head and apply it direct to Fern's clit.

She shakes her head. "I can't. I'm done."

"Not until I say so." I start the device, on a modest setting, then ramp it up fast.

"Cal, no. It hurts..."

I squirt extra lube on and angle the wand to apply more pressure to the tip of her clit. Fern's involuntary jerk suggests I may be getting somewhere.

"That's it, sweetheart. One more time." I roll the wand across her clit and pussy, varying the pressure.

"I can't, I can't..."

Even as she moans and pleads, her body responds. I change things up again, pressing hard, then lifting the wand away. Hard. Away. Hard. Away.

Fern pants. She runs her tongue over her lower lip and shakes her head from side to side. "Stop. Please, stop..."

"Are you wanting to say 'red'?" I don't think so, but I need to be sure.

"No, I just...oh! Aaaaah!" She lets out a sound, somewhere between a groan and howl, and her body shudders as she tumbles into one, final, clenching orgasm. I continue to draw the wand back and forth, teasing the final tremors from her body before finally calling a halt.

The pile of discarded toys litters the floor. I scoop them up and dump them in the bathroom for cleaning later, then I return to release Fern from the cuffs and leather straps. She lies silent in my arms.

"Speak to me, sweetheart." I stroke damp strands of hair from her face. "Tell me what you're thinking."

"I'm too exhausted to think." Her tone is dull, flat.

"Have a sip of water, then." I hold the uncapped bottle to her mouth, and she takes a few gulps. I draw the duvet over her, and she snuggles closer to me. "I need to know that you're okay."

"I'm fine. Just tired. And sore. That last one..."

"The one I stole?"

"I came, but I hated it." She pauses. "You must feel very smug."

"Smug?"

"As in, you told me so, and you were right." I detect a note of bitterness now.

"You resent that?"

"Of course. I just... I just..." She buries her face against me and starts to sob.

Weeping after an intense scene isn't unusual. I half expected it and just pull her in closer. She can cry herself out, then we'll talk again. I wait until the tears subside, then tip her face up so she has to look at me.

"I'm not smug. But, I am your Dom, so it's my job to be right."

Her eyes are still glistening with tears, red-rimmed. But they narrow, the soft green hardening. "But that's just it. You're not my Dom, or you won't be, after tomorrow. I'll sign that paper, and you won't be anything to me anymore. I'll be on my own."

"That's up to you. You're a beautiful woman, Fern Daniels,

and a very responsive submissive. You'll find a Dom, if you want one. Fuck, there'd be a queue."

"But you wouldn't be in that queue. You don't want me, apart from as some sort of sex toy. You bring me here, fuck with my head to make me do these things, make me actually like these things, then you mean dump me. All over again. Still, I suppose I should be grateful that you're being honest about it this time. I know what to expect."

"It was always temporary. Just the weekend. You know that."

"I do know that. A means to an end. You want to shut me up, get me to stop banging on about what happened in Las Vegas. Don't worry, I'm not going to beg or anything embarrassing like that. And I won't show you up in public again. It's just... I love you. I always have, even though you're a complete bastard. But I've just realised that I really don't like you at all."

"Fern, I—"

"You've fucked with me one last time. Enough. I want to go home."

"I know you do. Harry will take you. Tomorrow."

"I want to go now." She shoves away from me. "Where are my clothes?"

"Fern, for fuck's sake, it's after midnight."

"I don't care." She spots her clothes on the footstool and makes a beeline for them. "I want my phone back. My credit cards are in the case. I can get a train from Edinburgh."

"I'm not letting you just walk out of here in the middle of the night. Anything could happen to you."

"Like you care! If it bothers you that much, Harry or Jared could drive me to the station. I'll be all right from there."

I shake my head, adopt the stern tone that normally drops a sub to her knees. "No, it's not happening."

She whirls on me, hands on her hips and auburn hair flying. "It *is* bloody happening. Unless you decide to lock me up again, I'm leaving. I've had enough of your...your games."

She bends to tug on her jeans, then her vest top. "I want my jacket, too."

"Fern, I—"

"No! Enough. I was mad to agree to any of this. Desperate, even. I thought you might…we might…But I was wrong. You just wanted to scare me off. Well, job done." She marches to the wardrobe and drags her holdall down from on top of it. "Where are my things?"

I shrug. Her stuff seems to be scattered everywhere.

She starts flinging things back into the bag. Her hairbrush, her crumpled clothing from yesterday, her toothbrush and the denim skirt which looks so fine pulled up around her waist.

I try one final time. "Are you sure about this? Can I convince you to stay until morning? In a guest room if you prefer…"

She sends me a fulminating glare. Yup, she seems pretty certain. I give myself a mental kicking for misjudging the situation so badly but I know when it's time to retreat.

I dig in my pocket for my own phone and tap Harry's name in my speed dial.

He answers on the second ring. "Hey, boss? Everything all right?"

"Hi. I know it's late. But what are you doing right now?"

"Nothing much. Just watching football."

"Are you okay to drive?"

"You know I am, boss."

Harry is a recovering alcoholic, sober for over nine years now. It was a stupid question.

"I need you to take Miss Daniels back to Stockport."

"Right now?"

"Yes. Right now."

"Out front in ten minutes?"

"Perfect." I end the call, then drop the phone onto the bed.

"The station would be fine," she insists.

"Harry has his instructions. He'll see you safely home.

Here's your phone." I retrieve it from a drawer and drop it on top of her bulging bag. "Where did you last see your jacket?"

"In that room, downstairs. Where you spanked me."

The drawing room.

"I'll get it. Can you find your own way down to the foyer?"

"I expect so."

I march out and try not to slam the door behind me. Christ, this woman infuriates me! How did she ever manage to get under my skin like this? She makes me do crazy things.

Bringing her here in the first place was a mad idea. Letting her go like this is even more deranged.

I find the leather jacket on the floor behind the sofa in the drawing room and return to the foyer, just as Fern descends the stairs, hauling her bag down each step.

"Let me take that..."

"I can manage," she snaps.

Harry comes in from outside. "Car's ready..." He looks from Fern to me and back again. "Is everything all right?"

"Yes," I say.

"No!" Fern speaks at the same time.

"Right." Harry takes the bag from her and makes his exit. I don't blame him.

"Fern," I begin.

"What? Are you going to ask me to stay?"

"Yes. Until tomorrow..."

"Fuck you, Caleb McPherson. This time, it's me who gets to walk out."

She snatches the jacket from me, shrugs into it, and marches across my marble tiles, her head high and her spine ramrod straight. I have to hand it to her, it really is quite an exit.

. The crunch of her heels on my gravel, followed by the car door closing, is the last I hear before the car purrs away.

. . .

My bedroom feels eerily empty. I pour myself a couple of fingers of fine single malt and sink into the chair. My phone is still on the bed where I left it. I resist the temptation to call Harry and order him to return, to bring Fern back here.

We have unfinished business, me and her. Except, she doesn't agree. As far as she's concerned, we're done.

The sheet of paper propped behind the clock on the mantelpiece says it all. She signed the agreement and left it there where I'd be sure to see it the moment I walked in.

She's gone. Really, truly gone. I got what I wanted.

How come, then, my success tastes so fucking bitter?

I take the sheet of paper, open it out. Her signature is small and neat, precise. I swear under my breath as I rip the agreement to shreds and dump the pieces in the bin.

I take another sip of my whisky then begin to tidy up. I like my space to be clear, uncluttered. I allowed my standards to slip while Fern was here. It seemed less important, somehow.

I pick up the discarded shirts, pausing over the one she wore, then toss them into the laundry basket. My jeans are half under the bed. I drag them out and shake them in a fruitless attempt to get rid of the creases. I'm about to bundle them into the washing basket with the rest when something drops to the carpet from one of the pockets. Shiny and golden, I crouch to pick it up. It's Fern's chain with the palette charm attached, the one given to her by her father. I know it's an item she treasures, she'll be gutted to have left it here. I guess that's a sign of how upset she actually was, that she would walk out, leaving something so precious behind.

I rummage in my desk and find a small envelope. I scrawl her name on the front, then drop the chain inside and seal it up. I'll ask Harry to deliver it to her when next he is in the area. I prop the envelope on the fireplace where the agreement had been.

CHAPTER 14

Boss, do you have time to talk?
I frown, reread Harry's curt text. Then I hit reply.
Go on.
Sending you some pics.

I wait for a few moments, until my phone pings to signal the arrival of an email from Harry. There's no message, but I download the three photographs attached.

What the fuck...?

I'm greeted by the smiling if somewhat grubby face of a small boy. In the first picture, a close-up of his face, he's sucking on an ice lolly. If I'm not mistaken, it appears to be a truly disgusting shade of electric blue. I briefly wonder who would feed something so vile to a child before swiping to the next shot.

In the second, taken from behind, the same little boy is trotting along a street, holding someone's hand. The third picture is captured from the front. The child is wearing a royal-blue sweatshirt with a crest of some sort on the front. School uniform, probably, And, he's holding hands with...Fern Daniels.

I swear, enlarge the shot to be sure. Yes, it's her. And she's carrying what looks to be a child's school bag in her other hand. I rake my fingers through my hair.

Holy fuck.

My phone rings. It's Harry. I answer at once.

"What the fuck is all this?" I demand before he can get a word in. "Why are you sending me pictures of Fern and some random kid?"

"Random kid? I suggest you take a closer look, boss."

"Harry…" I growl.

"Better still, show the picture to Sally. Ask her who that kid reminds her of."

"What the fuck are you babbling about?" I'm totally confused. Has Harry lost the plot? "I don't have time for this."

"He's the spit of you at that age, boss."

I don't pretend to misunderstand. "No, he isn't."

"Ask Sally," Harry repeats. "She'll tell you."

I've been pacing my office while I speak to Harry, but now I sink back into my chair. "Tell me what happened."

"Okay. You remember you asked me to return Miss Daniels' chain to her?"

"Yes." That was almost a fortnight ago, but Harry has been occupied on other work. It was only now, when he had to make a trip to Manchester, that he's been able to find time to make the detour to Stockport. "I take it you managed to do that?"

"I did. I arrived here at about three. Middle of the working day. You specifically said I was to deliver the envelope to her personally, so I thought I had a better chance of catching her at work rather than at home. I went to the warehouse where her studio is."

"Right." Sounds reasonable so far.

"I got there, but she wasn't about. The place was open, though. Some of her tenants were there. Bloody odd bunch, too, if you ask me. All dreadlocks and face piercings…"

"Harry…." I almost snarl in impatience.

"I found some skinny kid with blue hair, making wax sculptures or something of the sort."

"Wax sculptures?" *Have I slipped into a parallel universe?*

"Yeah, so I asked her if Fern was about. She said she just slipped out, but she'd be back soon, and I was welcome to wait. Doing the school run, she said."

"School run?" I parrot.

"That's what Miss Blue Hair said. Anyway, I'd noticed a school in the next street when I was driving around looking for somewhere to park. I asked if that was the one, and the wax lady said it was. So, I decided to take a little stroll myself."

"Okay, and you saw Fern. With this kid...?"

"I did. I clocked them coming out of the school. Before I could get a picture, they stopped at an ice cream van by the gates and she bought him a lolly."

"A blue one," I reply. "Whoever thought that one up? Vile."

Harry doesn't comment on the abomination which is blue ice lollies. He continues his account. "Then they went off together. I got a few more shots of them walking away. They went into a shop, so I was able to get in front to take the last couple of pictures."

I let out a breath. There must be a reasonable explanation for this. It's not so strange, after all, to be picking up a small child from school.

"So, she probably agreed to do a favour for a friend. Especially if her studio is so close to the school. It doesn't mean the kid is hers. And even if it is...*he* is," I correct myself, "what does that have to do with me?"

Harry lets out an exasperated sigh but has the good sense to refrain from again telling me to ask Sally.

"I followed her back into the studio. Her reaction when she saw me was priceless. She snatched the necklace from me, told me to thank you for it, but she couldn't hide the kid fast enough. Bundled him into the studio where the wax sculpting was going on and told him to stay put. Naturally, I asked who he was."

"Naturally."

"His name is Archie, I gather, though only because I heard Miss Blue Hair call him that. Miss Daniels totally clammed up, refused to tell me anything about him. She said to thank you for returning her necklace, then pretty much threw me out."

"So, you got precisely nothing. This kid could be anyone."

One thing is for certain, he has nothing at all to do with me.

"Not quite nothing, boss.

"Oh?"

"Young Archie has been well trained. Quite the little eco-warrior. He dropped his lolly stick in the bin just outside the studio. It's in a plastic bag in my pocket now and probably teeming with DNA. Do you want it?"

"ARCHIE KEEPS ASKING ABOUT YOU. He's scared you'll be ill and miss his birthday."

I reach for my mother's hand and squeeze it. It's been a month since her surgery, and she's still weak as a kitten, though she insists she feels fine, considering.

Considering she's had a mastectomy and is just starting her second cycle of chemotherapy.

She said she'd be okay on her own, but I insisted on coming with her to the ward and sitting with her during the long hours of having the chemicals pumped into her through a drip. It took five hours last time, and I see no reason to assume this will be any quicker. Fighting cancer is grim enough, without doing it on your own.

The first dose of chemo wiped her out. She didn't get out of bed for three days and felt nauseous for a week. Her appetite disappeared, and she was utterly exhausted. She had a couple of weeks to recover, and the side-effects stopped. She felt sort of

What Happens in Vegas…

okay, for a while. We've both been dreading this next round, and the five more that are to come over the next few months.

The surgeon told us that the prognosis is good. The surgery was successful, they got all of it, so I suppose we should be thankful. And we are. But my mum looks so frail, so delicate. The slightest breeze would blow her away.

"I'll be all right again by next week," she replies, her voice cracking as she tries to speak. "The doctor said…"

I manage a smile. It's important to stay cheerful, to help her keep her spirits up and look forward to better times. Even if the worst effects of the chemo are abating by next week, I doubt she'll be up to blowing out birthday candles or helping Archie to open his presents.

Archie's fifth birthday… We'd hoped to be able to celebrate with a party, but I had to explain to him that we would have to delay that. He wasn't too disappointed, but when I also said that the puppy he's set his heart on would have to wait as well, he sobbed and pleaded with me to let him have his dog. I had to take a firmer stand on that. A puppy in the house is just too much, what with having to take care of my mum and Archie, too, as well as hold things together at the studio.

"Soon," I promised him. "As soon as Grandma is better, and we have time to look after it properly. We'd need to take it for walks, feed it, and everything."

"I'd do all of that," came the tearful reply. "Please, Mummy."

It broke my heart to say no. I had promised him the dog and I hated breaking my word. We'd even talked about what sort he wanted. He had his heart set on a St Bernard because he'd seen one in a film, but I'd convinced him to compromise on something more modest, a spaniel, maybe, or a terrier of some sort.

But all of that is on hold until my mother is fit and well again. I'm having to deal with everything single-handed, and she has to be my priority, just for now. Archie is a good boy, a lovable kid. He'll understand. Eventually.

I hope.

"Don't you need to be getting off? He'll be finishing school soon." My mum settles back in the large, plastic-covered hospital chair, her drip to the side of her. She closes her eyes.

"I asked Jade, at the studio, to pick him up. He can help her until we're done here."

"It's not right, relying on other people…"

"Sometimes, you have to. And Jade doesn't mind. Really, it's all fine and under control." Not quite accurate. I've yet to find someone to care for both of them when half term comes around in a couple of weeks. Or, more likely, I could just take time off from the studio, though I'm bombed out with work right now.

It didn't help having that great goon Harry show up out of the blue. He actually saw Archie, though not close up, so hopefully he won't have spotted the resemblance. He was full of questions, though, and I had the impression he might suspect something. Even though I told him nothing and managed to get rid of him pretty damned quick, I half expected Caleb to arrive, demanding to know why I hadn't told him he had a son.

He still might, but it's been a fortnight and no word. Maybe Harry didn't pass on the information. Or, more likely, Caleb McPherson is as interested in being a father as he was interested in being a husband.

Archie is better off without him, and I sure as hell am.

My reasons for keeping Archie to myself are simple. For the first five years I had no idea how to contact Caleb, even if I had wanted to. And, once I'd found him, met up with him again, it soon became obvious that he was not father material. The way he treated me at the shareholders' meeting in Manchester was bad enough, but that was nothing compared to the time I spent at his home in Scotland.

What Happens in Vegas...

How can a man be so...nice one minute, such good fun to be around, so sexy and...

Something curls and clenches deep in my core as I remember the hours we spent together. It was good, some of the time. Better than good. I remembered exactly why I married him. But he could turn on a sixpence and become an absolute dick. Arrogant, manipulative, ruthless, he played his games with my body and fucked with my head. It was all a game to him, a fun way to pass a weekend.

And like a fool, I let him break my heart for a second time. The bastard...

"What time is it, love?" My mum's voice sounds...weary.

I check my phone. "Quarter past three."

"A couple of hours still to go, then."

"Yeah. It'll soon pass. I thought I might make vegetable lasagne for our supper. I have a nice recipe someone gave me."

"That sounds nice. Archie likes pasta. It'll take his mind off everything, especially if I'm poorly again."

Which we both know is a knocking bet.

"He'll be okay. I've explained to him that you're not very well just now, but that you'll soon be better."

"It's such a lot for a little one to take in...."

Not just a little one.

"I need to nip over to the studio later, once Archie is in bed. I've been expecting a delivery today, all that glaze I ordered to replace the stock I shifted at Camden. Jade can take it and put it in my storeroom, but I need to go through and check everything."

"You work too hard, love."

"Running my own studio is what I want to do. You know that."

"I do. And it all sounds to be going very well, love. Do you have any more fairs lined up?"

The Camden event netted me a profit of over three thousand pounds. My mum was ecstatic, convinced I'm on the road to much greater things. I haven't had the heart to tell her the truth about how I landed that gig, or where I really was that weekend. Best to just bury the entire affair. Still, the money has come in useful, and at last I can stop fantasising about what might have been.

Caleb McPherson is history. Time to dust myself off and move on.

"I have a stall booked at the Cheshire Show, and there's a crafting convention in Harrogate I have my eye on. I need to build up my stock again. Camden cleared me out."

"Aye, well, all the more reason for you not to be at home running around after me. You have your own life to lead."

I RIP open the envelope marked: Strictly Private and Confidential. Instantly, I recognise the logo of the private DNA testing lab and scan the page.

Harry knows me well enough to be sure that I would agree to the test, if only to get him and Sally off my back. Both of them insist that the child in the photographs looks exactly as I did at around the same age. So, when the ice lolly stick arrived, wrapped in cling film, I immediately sent it off for analysis.

And now, the results are back.

I frown, read the report again, more slowly, the sheet laid flat on my desk.

Impossible!

Utterly bewildered, I rake my fingers through my hair. How is this even possible? I wasn't there in Las Vegas. I only met Fern Daniels a few weeks ago. But it's right in front of me, in black and white. Ninety-nine point nine-nine probability.

Archie Daniels, Fern's five-year-old son, shares my DNA.

He is my son.

What Happens in Vegas…

ARCHIE BOUNCES out of the school doors, his book bag in one hand and his coat in the other and a beaming smile on his face. He's only in the first year, Reception, but he already loves school. A bit of a loner, he doesn't have a special friend yet but seems to get along with everyone. His favourite lessons are Reading Time and Colours, which is what the school calls art. He loves books and can already read a few words as well as write his name. He likes to paint, my influence, I like to think, and he already has his own corner at the studio set aside for his projects.

He digs in his bag and pulls out a sheet of paper covered in rows of letters.

"We did writing, Mummy. Look."

"I examine the carefully formed but wholly illegible characters. "These are really neat," I say. "You must have taken a lot of time over them."

He shrugs. "I got bored, and Mrs Thompson told me I had to sit still and stop chattering to Mason."

"Ah." I eye the sheet again. On second thoughts, it does seem a bit tedious. "Never mind. Shall we go home and see how Grandma is today?"

"Is she still sad?"

"Perhaps, but she's a bit better and looking forward to seeing you. Maybe she'll read you a story."

"Grandma tells good stories. She does the voices."

One of my mother's hidden talents, a flair for mimicry. She's a far better storyteller than I am.

"We need to take care of her, not let her get too tired. Just a couple of stories, and you can show her your lovely writing." I crouch in front of him and help him to shove his arms into his coat, though he insists on zipping it up himself.

He slips his hand in mine. "Do we need to tell Grandma about Mrs Thompson?"

"No, we don't need to mention that."

"Or the chattering?"

"Or the chattering," I confirm. "The car's just along here…"

We cross over the road and start to walk away from the school. I parked a few minutes' walk along the road to avoid the congestion near the gates. The school is always on at the parents to be considerate, to think about pollution and road safety. I try to do my bit. Archie chatters happily about his day, and I answer when I can get a word in, which is rare.

I never hear the sound of the car engine. Nothing, not a hint until the final moment. There's a scream, someone farther up the road must have seen what was happening behind me, then the harsh grating of metal on stone. I whirl at the last moment. There's a car, coming at me, sideways. Its red paintwork gleams in the late afternoon sunshine as it bears down on us.

Too fast. No time…

I give Archie a shove, I think. I try to. Then, pain. Mind-numbing, bone-shattering agony.

Everything goes black.

CHAPTER 15

"Thank you, everyone. I think we're about done here." I glance up and down the boardroom table in my Edinburgh headquarters, checking that no one else has anything to add to today's proceedings. They don't, so I close the meeting. Simon and his team can tie up the legal loose ends, and within a month another small firm of chartered accountants will be added to the McPherson group of companies.

There will be minimal job losses, none at the lower levels. The clients will see a seamless transition to the new and more efficient arrangements. Everyone's a winner. Well, more or less. The previous senior partner will be out of a job, but his payoff will fund a decent retirement, so he should be all right. I have it on good authority that his wife has already put a down payment on a villa in the Algarve.

I gather my papers together. "I'll leave it with you, then, Simon. When you need my signature, I'll be at home. Send the documents by courier."

"Of course. It should all be fairly straightforward from here." He closes his briefcase with a resounding click and walks with me to the door. "By the way, do you still have an interest in Miss Daniels? You remember, the woman who stood up in the meeting in Manchester and—"

"Fern Daniels." I interrupt him. "Why? What has she been up to now?"

"It's not so much been up to anything. I had a report earlier, from the private investigator we had tailing her."

"Private investigator?" I glower at him. "I thought we were done with all that when she signed the agreement."

He shrugs. "You never actually said to end the tail, so he's been keeping tabs."

"End it," I snarl. Apart from the fact that whatever Fern Daniels gets up to has fuck all to do with me, what sort of an inept private investigator fails to notice that the subject has a son, who happens to also be the son of his fucking client?

"Okay." Simon makes a note on the corner of the file he is holding. "Our man went to the hospital, but I'll tell him we're not concerned with the outcome…"

I turn on my heel. "Hospital? What hospital? What the fuck is going on?"

"Miss Daniels has been hit by a car, apparently. A drunken driver, according to our source. She is not expected to survive…"

The pit of my stomach drops. My head is suddenly light, spinning. My ears are ringing, and I think I might throw up.

Not expected to survive.

"Sir? Mr McPherson? Simon sounds concerned. "Shall I get you a glass of water?

"Yes. No. Find Harry." I give my head a shake, try to clear my wits. "When did this happen?"

"A couple of hours ago."

"Where?"

"Stockport."

"Where is she now? Which hospital?"

Simon consults his phone. "Stepping Hill, in Stockport. But our man says they are considering transferring her to Manchester Royal Infirmary. It's a head injury, I gather."

"Get back to him, find out the latest information." I set off at a sprint. It's almost six o'clock, but with luck I'll catch my PA before she leaves for the day. She's putting her coat on when I burst into my office.

"Mary, I need you to do something for me. It's urgent."

She takes her coat off and sits back at her desk. "Of course, Mr McPherson."

"I need a helicopter. I have to get to Stockport, or possibly Manchester. Now."

She never turns a hair. "It's short notice, so I'll try Sloane's first."

I nod. Not the cheapest, but they have their own fleet of corporate helicopters as well as access to a wide network of other companies and pilots. I need to get to Stockport fast, and they're the ones to make it happen.

"I'm setting off for the airport now. Phone me when you have a flight confirmed. Oh, and track down Harry when you've sorted the helicopter. Tell him I need him, in Stockport. Get him to phone me."

"Leave it with me, Mr McPherson." She is already on the phone to the helicopter charter company.

Twenty minutes later, my speedometer is touching eighty-five as my Audi purrs along the dual carriageway heading towards the airport. My phone rings. I hit the hands-free.

"Sir?"

It's Mary.

"Yes. Do you have a helicopter for me?"

"Runway six, in thirty minutes. They'll wait for you to get there."

"Thank you. I'm only about twenty minutes away from the airport now, but I'll have to get through security." I bless the fact that I always carry my passport in my briefcase. Even for a private charter I'll need it for identification at the airport.

"I'll advise the crew of your estimated arrival time. I have Harry on the line. Shall I patch him through?"

"Yes, do that, please."

"Boss?"

"Harry? Where are you?"

"Glasgow."

I waste no time in small talk. "Fern was hit by a car this afternoon."

"Jesus! How bad?"

"First report sounds serious. I'm on my way there now."

"Do you need me to drive you?"

"I have a helicopter booked. I'm almost at the airport. But I'll need a car when I get there. Can you follow me down?"

"You got it. Where will you be?"

"The hospital, but I'm not sure if it'll be Stockport or Manchester. I'll text you."

"Sure, boss. I'm setting off now."

The call clicks off. With the possible exception of Simon, I've managed to surround myself with exemplary staff, and at a time like this I truly appreciate them. The practical arrangements in place for now, I concentrate on navigating the lanes of early evening traffic to get to the airport as quickly as I can.

IT'S GOING up to nine in the evening when I leap out of a taxi at the entrance to Stepping Hill hospital, the main accident and emergency facility serving the people of Stockport. I checked in with Simon who confirmed that Fern is still here, as is the private investigator. Her condition remains critical.

"I'm here to see Fern Daniels. She was admitted earlier today, road traffic accident." I present myself at the main reception desk.

The young man on duty glances at his computer screen, then back at me. "Can I ask your name, sir?"

"Caleb McPherson."

"And your relationship with Miss Daniels?"

I pause, then, "I'm her husband."

"I see." He consults his screen again. "It's just that yours is not the name listed as next of kin."

"No. We're...separated. Her next of kin will be her mother, I expect."

"Yes, that's right."

"So, where is she? I need to see my wife." I know the National Health Service do a sterling job, they are little short of angels, but I am coming seriously close to grabbing this particular young man by the throat.

"She's been moved to the Intensive Care Unit for further monitoring," he concedes at last. "Take the lift to the second floor, then follow the corridor to the right. It's sign-posted, but it's up to the discretion of the staff if they let you in."

"Thank you," I growl, already heading for the lift.

The double doors marked Intensive Care Unit are locked, as I expected. I press the bell and wait. Within moments, a nurse decked out in pull protective clothing opens it to peer out at me.

"I had a message that my wife has been in an accident," I say. "I understand she's here."

"What's your wife called, sir?"

"Fern. Fern Daniels."

She steps back and opens the door wider. "I'll should warn you, she's very poorly just at the moment."

"Can I see her?" I ask.

"Of course. I just wanted you to know. She's unconscious, and we have her wired up to a lot of equipment. It can all appear very daunting."

"I understand." I follow the nurse along the corridor and into the main Intensive Care ward.

Six beds are arranged down each side, each of them surrounded by what looks to me to be enough technology to launch a mission to Mars. All but two are occupied. The centre of the ward is dimply lit, but each occupied bed is in its own pool of bright light, and each is attended by two nurses, attired exactly the same as the one who let me in. She gestures to one of the beds on the left.

"Miss Daniels is there, sir. Her mother was here earlier, but she had to go."

I nod and murmur my thanks, then I approach the bed.

Both nurses acknowledge my arrival. One of them gestures me to an empty plastic seat.

"I'm Beth, this is Julie. We'll be taking care of Miss Daniels between us. The consultant will be back soon, so you can speak to her."

"How…how is she?" I ask, though at first sight I know the private investigator wasn't exaggerating. Fern looks like death. She is pale as a sheet, and her blood-stained hair is flattened against her head. A large bandage swathes much of her face. Some sort of frame beneath the bedclothes holds the covers up and away from her legs, which I suspect must be fractured.

The other nurse, Julie, jots something down on a clipboard which she hangs from a trolley, then she pulls a stool out from under the bed and sits next to me.

"Fern is your wife? Is that right?"

I just nod.

"Okay. She has multiple lower limb fractures, and there is some internal bleeding. She may need to go to theatre to control that, but we're monitoring it here for now. And, as you can see, there's been some head trauma. She took a very nasty blow to the left side of her skull, and she hasn't regained consciousness yet. Just now we have her heavily sedated, but she may be able to hear you if you speak to her."

"I…oh." For once, I am speechless. I have no idea what I want to say, apart from 'get well. Please, get well'. I reach for Fern's hand but don't dare to take it for fear of dislodging one of the drips or cannulas or whatever these things are that seem to be attached everywhere. "Can I touch her?"

"Of course. Just, be careful. Obviously. But really, the best thing is to talk to her."

What Happens in Vegas…

"Will she really be able to hear me? With the sedation and everything?"

"We don't know. Perhaps. Patients often say they did hear the voices of those around them. You just need to ignore us. We're part of the equipment."

I stand, lean over the bed, and lay my hand on the undamaged half of her face. "Sweetheart? It's me. Cal. I heard what happened and came straight away."

There's no response from the bed. She lies there, as still as a corpse, her breathing low and even through the tube inserted into her nostril. Above her, the machines work frantically. Lights flash, numbers flicker across the many screens, and a green line moves across from left right in rhythmic waves. I spot the blood pressure gauge, and my heart sinks. Ninety-one over sixty. That's too low. Far too low.

"Is she going to be all right?" I ask.

"She's very poorly, but she's in good hands. Mrs Mansour is one of the finest consultants for head injuries like this," Julie assures me as she checks the readings again, adjusting a dial here, a setting there.

I have never felt so utterly helpless, or so in awe. I watch the two nurses go about their tasks. It's obvious, even to my untrained eye, that Fern is hovering on the very edge of life, but they manage, somehow, to anchor her to this side, to keep her with us.

If she survives the night, surely that's a good sign…

And I'm going nowhere until I know that she has.

---

*H*URTS.
So sore.
Tired.
Heavy. Can't move.
Don't want to move, too sore…

There are voices, loud voices, shouting from a long, long way away, but I don't understand their words.

Leave me alone. I want to sleep. Need to sleep now.

More voices. Different, quieter, but still too far to hear.

And...pain. Everywhere. Is this what it feels like to be dead?

I CHECK MY WATCH. It's after ten o'clock. The morning seems a lifetime away.

By three o'clock I've run out of optimistic platitudes. Bone weary, I rest my forehead against the edge of the bed and close my eyes. I waken with a start an hour later to see a middle-aged Asian woman peering into Fern's eye, the one not covered in bandages.

She glances at me when I sit up with a jerk.

"I apologise. I did not mean to disturb you. I am Mrs Mansour, your wife's consultant."

"How is she? Is there any improvement?"

"Her condition remains much as it was when she was admitted. The sedation means she is comfortable, but she shows no signs of coming round yet."

"The nurse said she had broken legs. What will you be doing about that?"

"Yes, three fractures in all. She will need to go to the fracture clinic at some stage to have those properly set, but they are not the most pressing of our concerns."

"Then, what is?"

"The blow to the head, and the possibility of damage to the brain. She has fractured her skull, we know that, but we will need to run tests over the coming days to determine the level of brain activity."

I gape at her, horrified. "You mean, even if she survives, Fern may not properly recover?"

"Let us not get ahead of ourselves. Mr Daniels."

"McPherson."

"I beg your pardon."

"Her name is Daniels, my name is McPherson."

"I see. Well, as I was saying. It's very early days. We need those tests and time to study the results before I can offer you an accurate prognosis."

"But you must have some idea…"

"I am sorry, but we can only be patient."

"There was talk of moving her, to Manchester."

"Yes, that is an option. It will depend on the test results and the best treatment plan once we know exactly what we are dealing with. In the meantime, we shall monitor her condition here and proceed to treat her fractures as quickly as possible."

"What about the internal bleeding?"

"That is a concern. I intend to monitor the situation for another two hours, then, if it has not stopped, I shall take her to theatre."

"I see." I get to my feet. "Thank you, Doctor."

"You are very welcome. Please, do not hesitate to ask me or the nursing staff if you have any questions at all."

My head is whirling with questions, but for the most part I can't find the words to be able to ask. In any case, there are only two questions I want the answer to.

Will she live? And if she does, will she still be the Fern I knew? And loved.

And I know that I will have no answers until Mrs Mansour has her test results. She moves on to the next bed, and I resume my vigil.

At six o'clock, Julie does her fifteen-minute blood pressure check. I watch the gauge carefully. It's dropped. Ninety-six over fifty-five. Julie notes the reading, then goes to the central consul and makes a call.

"Mr McPherson, we need to take your wife to theatre. The internal bleeding isn't showing signs of stopping, so we need to investigate further." Beth sits beside me to explain what's to happen. "We'll take her up there now."

I scrub my hands over my eyes. "How long will she be gone?"

"It's impossible to say. If you want to go and get a bit of breakfast, you could do that. There's a place that does decent coffee and bacon rolls, down near the main entrance. You're welcome to wait here, either. Or you could nip over to the paediatric accident and emergency ward to see how your little boy is. They should be opening about now."

I sit bolt upright. "Little boy? You mean, Archie was with her?"

Beth nods, slowly. "I assumed you knew that. They were admitted to A and E together."

"He was hit by the car, too?"

"He was involved in the accident, but I think the car missed him."

"Oh Jesus. I never thought… I mean, it never occurred to me to ask…"

"Mr McPherson, I understand his injuries are fairly minimal. Eye witnesses said Miss Daniels pushed him out of the path of the car and took the brunt of the impact herself."

"You said he's okay. Not too badly hurt?"

"That was what we had from A and E. His grandma was here, with Fern, but she went up there, to be with him overnight. The poor woman couldn't be in two places at once, and obviously, she's not too well herself, as you probably know."

I nod. Fern told me her mother was fighting cancer. "I need to go and see him."

"Of course. In fact, why don't you go up there now, and I'll give the ward a ring when Miss Daniels returns from theatre?"

"I will. Yes. Thank you."

"You're welcome. But, Mr McPherson…do get yourself a coffee on the way."

CHAPTER 16

I detour to the main entrance to seek out the coffee and bacon roll. I realise I haven't eaten since lunchtime yesterday and my stomach is growling.

Beth was right, the classy little stall does an excellent latte and bacon in a half baguette. I ask for one of each, then rethink and double the order, throwing in a carton of blackcurrant juice and a small cheese sandwich. Thus armed, I make my way to the paediatric ward.

Again, I have to ring a bell and wait to be admitted. The nurse who lets me in is wearing a casual, child-friendly version of the uniform—sweat top and trousers in a bright-yellow fabric—and wears a multi-coloured badge in the shape of a rainbow, declaring that her name is Molly and that she is a staff nurse.

"I'm here to see Archie Daniels," I explain.

Her smile is welcoming enough. "Okay. Are you a relative?"

"I'm..." I hesitate. Even with the DNA evidence to back me up, I can't quite bring myself to say the words. Still, it's obvious that Staff Nurse Molly isn't about to let any old Tom, Dick, or Harry into her nice, safe ward. She has vulnerable children to protect. "I'm his father."

"Oh. I see." The smile vanishes, and she peers at me, obviously puzzled. "It's just that Archie's grandma told us her daughter is a lone parent, and that Archie doesn't have any other family."

"His mother and I are separated. But he does have me, and I'm here to see how he is." I hold up the bags of food. "I brought him some breakfast. His favourite…"

Staff Nurse Molly is still not convinced. "Do you have any form of identification?"

"I have my passport and driving licence. And a DNA report that will bear out that I am his father. I could get that emailed over in the next few minutes."

She offers me an apologetic smile. "Would you mind doing that, then, sir? I'm sorry if I seem picky, but you have to understand, we can't be too careful."

"Give me five minutes."

I park myself in the corridor and get Sally on the phone. She's the only person likely to be at Linn Mill at this time in the morning. I hope I'm not getting her out of bed, though I do think she's usually up and about early, organising the daytime crews.

She answers at once. "Mr McPherson? Where are ye? I had a message from your office that ye'd been called away suddenly."

That will have been Mary, thinking on her feet. I make a mental note to increase her salary.

"Yes, a family emergency I had to deal with. And I need your help."

"Is something wrong, Mr McPherson?"

"It is, yes, and I'll explain soon. For now, though, I need you to go to my office. You have a key?"

"Of course. I'm on my way." This is one of the things I value most about Sally. Once she decides something needs to be done, she doesn't waste any time.

I remain on the line while she hurries from her kitchen to the business suite. Her heels tap on the hardwood floors as

What Happens in Vegas...

she makes her way along the main corridor to my private office.

"Okay, I'm in your office..."

"Go to my desk and open the second drawer from the top, left-hand side."

I know Sally would normally rather have her hand cut off than rifle through my private papers, but she does as I ask without comment.

"There's a report from a company called Heritage DNA. Do you see it? A red letterhead?"

"Aye, I have it."

"Okay. Now, I need you to scan it, then email it to me. Do you know how to use the scanner?"

She sniffs. "I think ye'll find I'm not completely computer illiterate, Mr McPherson."

Thank goodness for that.

"I'm sorry. The scanner is—"

"In the printer, next tae your desk."

"Right. Do you know my laptop password?"

"No, Mr McPherson, I dinnae."

I reel off the sequence of letters and numbers, then give her a few minutes to complete the scan and send the document to my laptop. At no stage does she pass comment on the contents of the report, though she must have read it.

"It's done, Mr McPherson. I just emailed it tae your private address."

My phone pings to signal an incoming message.

"Thank you, Sally." I end the call, quickly cast my eye over the email, then I press the button on the door to the paediatric ward.

Nurse Molly returns, all smiles again. I hand my phone to her, the DNA report on the screen.

She takes a few moments to read it, then hands the phone back. "I apologise for any inconvenience, Mr McPherson. Would you like to follow me?"

She leads the way along a central corridor brightly decorated with scenes of pirate ships and dinosaurs. Boxes of large picture books seem to be everywhere, and several low tables are laid with craft activities and children's games. This is clearly a place designed to entertain as well as to heal.

"This is Archie's room. I'm not sure if he's awake yet." She stops at a door and opens it to peer inside. "Good morning, Mrs Daniels. You have another visitor." She stands aside to let me pass.

I draw in a breath, stiffen my shoulders, and step into the room.

A woman of perhaps fifty is seated on a hospital chair, a magazine open on her lap. She greets me with a smile, though her welcome quickly fades.

"What are you doing here?" she demands. "We don't need you."

I'm guessing she's seen the wedding photos. How else would she recognise me on sight?

Whatever Mrs Daniels might say, I sincerely doubt that I'm not needed here. I don't need to be a medic to recognise a seriously unwell woman when I see one. Mrs Daniels is deathly pale. Her green eyes seem too big for her face; her mouth is turned down as though she's actually in pain right now. Her hair is greying, though not yet showing signs of being affected by the chemotherapy she must be on. She looks so frail it's actually frightening. I'm not convinced she even possesses the strength to get to her feet, but if she did I am quite certain she would have thrown me out on my ear.

"You shouldn't have let him in," she levels at Molly. "Tell him to go. Now. I won't have him upsetting Archie."

"I'm not here to upset Archie. Or anyone else. I just need to know that he's okay."

"What do you care? You've never even seen the boy. We've managed fine on our own up to now. We had to…"

"I know that, but—"

What Happens in Vegas...

"Nurse, you need to call security."

Molly crosses the room to the single clinical bed which dominates the space. In it, a tiny figure is wrapped in a pristine white blanket. He is stirring, disturbed by the raised voices, no doubt.

"How did he sleep?" Nurse Molly addresses the question to Mrs Daniels, ignoring her earlier demand.

"Very well. Not a peep all night, once he got settled."

"Poor little mite. It's not going to be easy, and he'll need his family around him." She is clearly trying to pour oil on troubled waters.

"*He's* not family," Mrs Daniels insists, jerking a bony thumb in my direction. "First time he's ever shown any interest at all."

I can't believe she doesn't know that Fern never told me about Archie, but I let that lie for now. I have no intention of airing all of this in front of Staff Nurse Molly. Instead, I add my efforts to the peace talks.

"I brought breakfast. A bacon roll and coffee for you and me, and a sandwich for Archie."

"The hospital will give him his breakfast."

"Please, take it. It's really very good." I hand her one of my sandwich bags, but she refuses to take it. I leave it, along with her latte, on the bedside cabinet just by her side.

"Grandma...?"

All three of us turn to face the small form in the bed. Archie's eyes are open, and I note that they're a deep brown.

Like mine.

His hair is dark, too, not a hint of the auburn his mother carries off so well. And he is staring right at me.

"Who are you?" he demands to know, with all the steady, unashamed the directness of young children everywhere.

I pull up a stool and sit so as not to seem to tower over him. "I'm Cal. A friend of your mother's. And you must be Archie."

He doesn't answer, but his gaze is unwavering.

"I brought you breakfast. Juice, and a sandwich. Are you hungry?"

He nods and takes the sandwich from me.

"It's cheese," I say. "I hope you like cheese."

"He prefers ham," his grandma announces.

"I can get ham next time," I reply.

"I like cheese, too." Archie unwraps the sandwich with a bandaged hand and takes a bite out of the sliced bread.

I savour that minor victory while I scan what I can see of Archie for other obvious injuries. He was, after all, hit by a car less than twenty-four hours ago.

"How is he?" I direct the question to Staff Nurse Molly. "His hand…?"

"He's been very lucky," she replies. "A few abrasions to his hand and a bump on the head, but no concussion. He'll be ready to go home sometime today. The doctor will need to see him again, then we can discharge him."

"No!" This from Mrs Daniels. "He needs to stay here, near his mother."

Neither me nor the nurse argue, though I suspect we both agree that the Intensive Care unit is no place for a small child.

"I want to see my mummy. Can I see her yet? Did she wake up?" Mention of Fern has obviously reminded him of the accident and his mother's injuries. Archie drops his sandwich onto the blanket and directs his demands at his grandma. "You said I could go. I want to see my mummy."

"I'll have to check with the nurses looking after her." She turns to me with a glare. "You need to leave us alone now. We have a lot to sort out."

I ignore her. I'm going nowhere just yet. Instead, I turn my attention to Archie. "I was with your mummy all night. She's still asleep and the nurses are taking very good care of her."

"Can I see her? I won't wake her, I promise. I'll be quiet…" His little face crumples, and he swipes at his tears with his hands.

His grandma wastes no time in gathering him in her arms. "It's okay. It's all going to be okay, Archie. I'm here, and your mummy, too. We'll take care of you."

The nurse bends to speak to me. "I wonder, could you stop at the nurses' station before you leave? We need to discuss Archie's care when he's discharged."

I nod, though what any of that has to do with me I can't quite fathom.

The nurse leaves, and I decide to apply myself to building bridges. I start with the bacon.

"Eat your sandwich, Mrs Daniels. It really is very good."

"I don't want anything, thank you."

I lower my voice, my words for her alone. "Shall we not argue in front of Archie? All of this is hard enough on him." I unwrap my own bacon roll and take a bite. It's been a good half hour since I bought it, but even cold, the tangy flavours are delicious and the aroma even better. I take a sip of the latte and smile at my adversary. "I didn't put sugar in yours, but I have a couple of sachets in my pocket."

She makes a sound, somewhere between exasperation and frustration that I'm not taking the hint and clearing off. "Well, I suppose a coffee would be nice. Just one sugar."

We sip in silence for a while, and Archie finishes his sandwich before asking his grandma to open his juice for him. He turns to me again. "Do you think they will let me visit Mummy?"

I'm honestly not sure, but I decide there and then to do what I can to make it happen. Maybe just a peek, if we explain to him what all the tubes and equipment are for.

"I'll ask."

"There you go, making promises you can't keep," Mrs Daniels snaps. "Your sort never change."

I turn to her, a polite smile plastered across my face. "I said I would ask, and I will. That's a promise, and I *will* keep it. My smile for Archie is somewhat warmer. "You have my word."

"Will you come and see me again?" he asks, dribbling juice down his hospital-issue nightgown.

"No!" Mrs Daniels glares at me.

"I will, yes. I need to go back up to the ward where your mummy is to see how she's doing and ask about you visiting, but I will be back."

He gives me a watery smile, and something deep in my core flutters and melts just a little bit. Suddenly, nothing is more important to me than making sure this small boy is all right.

I finish my breakfast and note that Mrs Daniels makes short work of her coffee, too. I suspect she might even relent on the bacon roll, but not until I'm gone.

"Can you play Snap?" Archie hands his empty juice carton to his grandma. "I can. And Snakes and Ladders. They have a table here, and the top is all snakes and ladders. I'm the champion."

"A whole table full of snakes and ladders. I'd like to see that. Will you show me, next time?"

He nods enthusiastically. "We could play, but I'd probably beat you because I'm the champion."

"We'll see. I can be pretty nippy up those ladders myself." I stand. "Laters."

"Laters, Cal." He grins at me. There's a large gap where his two front teeth should be.

I offer a polite nod to Mrs Daniels. "Will I see you upstairs?"

"Perhaps, though I don't suppose you'll be staying long. Fern told me you're very busy."

"I'll be here as long as need be," I assure her. I get a measure of perverse satisfaction from the scowl she gives me as I leave the room.

The nurses' station is deeper into the ward. I pass the Snakes and Ladders table on my way there. Nurse Molly greets me with a smile.

"Thank you for this. I just wanted to discuss with you what you want us to do about Archie."

"Do about Archie? What do you mean?"

"As I said, he's ready to go home, but of course, he can't. There's no one there to care for him."

"I thought he and his mother lived with his grandma."

"They do, but Mrs Daniels is barely well enough to look after herself. You must have noticed."

"Yes," I agree. "The cancer?"

"The chemo, more to the point. Her treatment is quite aggressive, and she's right, she can't carry on her treatment and care for her grandson."

"Mrs Daniels said that?" The implications of her statement hit me like a wrecking ball.

"Yes. I gather she means to abandon the treatment, but in the longer term that could be disastrous."

"I see. So, what's the alternative?"

"I was going to talk to her about foster care, just for the next few weeks. Until her treatment ends, or Mum is better."

"Foster care? I don't think—"

"Mrs Daniels is adamant that Archie has to go home with her, but as things stand, that's just not possible. In a week or so, and assuming she misses the next cycle, she might be up to it, but there's no way I can let her take Archie now. She's just not well enough. It wouldn't be safe, for either of them. I have a duty of care, you see."

"So, where do I come in?"

She comes straight to the point. "You're his father. Can you look after him?"

"But, as Mrs Daniels so helpfully pointed out, I don't even know him."

"You do. Well, you do now. And you could get to know him better."

"I'm not sure that's what his mother would want. I have to respect her wishes."

She sighs. "I understand. "But I had to try. I hope you don't mind me speaking to you."

"Not at all."

"I'll get on to Social Services now, then."

I MAKE my way back to the Intensive Care unit, the nurse's final words ringing in my ears.

Social Services. Foster care.

However kindly it's meant, however temporary, unless I do something to stop it, Archie will end up in care.

I can't let that happen. And it doesn't need to happen. I have more spare rooms than I can count at Linn Mill. I could easily hire a nanny or whatever, and provide for him while his mother recovers, however long that might take. But I'd have to get past the formidable and hostile Mrs Daniels first. I'd take Archie over her dead body—quite literally, possibly.

Fern's little oasis in the Intensive Care unit is empty when I go back in there, so I sit down to wait. It's over an hour before the doors at the end of the ward clatter open and she is wheeled back in, still deeply unconscious.

"How did it go?" I ask Beth who is hurrying along beside the trolley.

"Very well. We stopped the bleed, and her blood pressure is already rising. The orthopaedic surgeons will get their hands on her this afternoon."

"Still no sign of her regaining consciousness?"

Beth busies herself reattaching the various tubes and leads, checking her monitors and gauges, before giving me her attention again. "Mr McPherson, I think you need to expect something of a long haul there."

"The consultant said something about tests."

"Yes. We should know more in the next few days. Already, we can tell there is brain activity, but we need to know how much, and what sort. But, in my experience, these sorts of injuries take their own sweet time."

"She has a son. He's only little."

"I know, but that changes nothing. Fern is very poorly, and she won't be up and about anytime soon. You can only wait. And hope. And let us do our jobs."

I CAN HEAR the voices again, softer, and closer. Still can't hear what they're saying.

Less pain, now. Sort of...hazy. Pink fuzz.
Legs hurt. Can't move them.
Scared! Try to move but...nothing.
Am I paralysed? Stuck here, in here, not able to get out?
Another voice, closer. A man. Familiar. A friend? No, a lover.
It can't be. I don't have a lover.

HARRY ARRIVES AT ABOUT ten o'clock in the morning. He texts me, and I nip out to meet him at the coffee stall. I fill him in on the situation.

"Poor little kid. And poor Grandma, too. I mean, I know she's given you an earful, boss, but you have to feel for her. She's between a rock and a hard place. What will happen if she doesn't complete the treatment?"

"I don't want to think about it." I remember Fern telling me they were going to fight the cancer, her unfailing optimism in the face of the disease. "She has to finish. It's a matter of life and death."

"I assume the lad will be coming with us? To Linn Mill?"

"He'd be miserable. His grandma might loathe me, but she adores him. She's ready to sacrifice everything for him. They're a close family, the three of them. Archie doesn't really know what's going on, but he expects to be with his grandma. He'd never understand why he was being taken away from his family. I can't do that. I'm just some stranger.

Shit, he's probably been warned to run a mile from men like me."

"I don't see that you have any alternative. Didn't you say that the hospital won't let him go home with Grandma in any case?"

I've had since first light to consider the options and the angles. I have the germ of an idea forming but I have no way of knowing if Mrs Daniels will buy it or not. There's only one way to find out.

"Harry, are you any good at Snakes and Ladders?"

I NEVER REALISED that Harry has a way with small children, but within minutes of the pair of us entering his hospital room, he and Archie are firm friends. We've exhausted our Snakes and Ladders prowess, not to mention Snap and Ludo. Now Harry is chuckling through an episode of *Peppa Pig*. Archie is sprawled on a beanbag in the children's television room.

Mrs Daniels took the opportunity, while Archie was otherwise entertained, to go up to the Intensive Care ward, though I could tell she was reluctant to leave her precious grandson with us. She's short of options, though, and I need to make sure the appreciates that. I watch out for her returning and ambush her by the door to the ward.

"Can we talk?"

"I have nothing to say to you. Neither does my daughter."

There has been no mention of the weekend Fern spent with me. I get the feeling she never shared that bit of the story with her mum.

"I have something to say. A proposal if you like. A way of solving our current dilemma."

"You don't have a dilemma, Mr McPherson. This is my problem, mine and Fern's. Archie is our responsibility, not yours."

I pull out my phone and locate the DNA report. "This says different." I hand it to her.

She studies the report with care, then meets my gaze. If anything, if that were possible, her features are even paler, even more gaunt than before.

"You'll never get custody. No court would award it. We'd fight you, and your fancy lawyers."

I shake my head. "This isn't about custody. Archie is Fern's son. His place is with her. And he will be with her, when she's well enough." I don't care to think about what might happen if she doesn't recover. I put that nightmare scenario from my mind. Best to cross one bridge at a time. "This is about who is the best person to care for Archie right now, while his mother is in hospital."

"If you think for one moment that I'm going to let you—"

I interrupt her tirade. "That person is you. Obviously."

She gapes at me. "Me? But I thought... I mean..."

"Or it would be, if you weren't ill yourself."

"I told you. I told the nurses here. I mean to stop the treatment. Archie comes first."

"He does, and he needs his grandma. Not just now, but in the future, too. You have to do all you can to get well again. For Archie, and for Fern."

"It's not that simple. The chemo, it makes me feel so ill..."

"I know. But you need to have the treatment if you're going the beat the cancer. And you also need to be there for Archie now. It's a lot to expect, but I think you could manage to do both. If I help you."

She gapes at me, incredulous. "You? How could you help me? Why would you want to?"

"You saw the DNA report. I'm not about to walk away. And I owe it to Fern. I know how desperate she is for you to beat this disease. She wouldn't want you to stop the treatment."

"I don't understand. What sort of help do you have in mind? We don't need money."

Actually, she does. Money would enable her to buy in the help she needs. A nanny. Nursing care for herself. It's my Plan B.

But I'd rather go with Plan A.

"Archie needs to come and stay with me for a while."

"No! I won't—"

"And so do you."

"Me?"

"You. Let me guess. Fern was nursing you, wasn't she? Before the accident."

"She was helping out, obviously."

"So, who's going to help now?"

"I can manage for myself."

"You don't need to. I have a house, a large house, close to Edinburgh. There's plenty of room for you and Archie, and I can hire a nurse to care for you when you need it. Think about it. No cooking, no cleaning. Just quality time that you can spend with Archie. Time for you to recuperate, to get well again. And Archie would be happy with me as long as you were there, too. He needs you, but right now, he needs me, as well."

"But how would I get to the hospital for my treatment?"

I notice she's not refusing, just concerned with practicalities.

"We could get your care transferred to a specialist in Edinburgh and you could have the chemo there."

"But Archie's school…"

"It might not be for that long. But there's a nice school in the village near where I live."

"Our house…"

"…will still be there when you're better. You can move back whenever you like."

"How would me and Archie get all the way to Scotland?

"I have a car outside. Or I could arrange a private ambulance if you need one. We'd be there in a few hours."

She frowns, falls silent for several seconds, then. "It's out of the question, What about Fern? I can't just leave her here, on her own."

"I've been thinking about that, too. We've no idea how long it will be before she's up and about again but, as soon as she's stable enough, I could arrange to have her moved to a hospital closer to us. We could visit often. Archie, too, because he will need that."

"You've really thought of everything, haven't you?"

"I hope so."

"It must be nice," she observes, her tone bitter, "to have so much money that you can afford to do just what you like."

I shrug. "It helps, certainly. And yes, there are some problems that you can throw money at and they go away. This isn't one of them. I can't buy your good opinion. Or Archie's, for that matter. And I can't pay to make Fern well again. I wish I could. I'd do it in a heartbeat. But I am in a position to make sure that you and Archie are cared for. I owe Fern that much."

CHAPTER 17

"Do you think she's going to agree?"

Harry and I are back at the coffee stall, nursing cappuccinos and a cheese-and-ham toastie each. For fast food, it's okay. We have blueberry muffins and a millionaire's shortcake to follow.

I shrug as I stir the foam into my coffee. I never could stand those moustaches you get when you try to drink it through the froth. "I couldn't tell. I'm hoping the staff on the children's ward might be able to talk some sense into her."

"I don't think she lacks sense, boss."

I meet his gaze. "No. But she's stubborn. And she's convinced Fern would want nothing to do with me." In fact, she might be right there, though Mrs Daniels appears not to have an inkling about the most recent encounter between myself and her daughter. "Problem is, we're running out of time. The ward want to discharge Archie. They need the bed, and if his grandma won't shift, he could end up in care."

"You won't let that happen, though."

"No. But it will start World War Three if I take him against her wishes. I'm still hopeful for a diplomatic solution."

Harry nods. "Uh-oh. Incoming. We might be about to hear the verdict."

He nods in a direction over my shoulder. I turn to see Mrs Daniels approaching our table.

I stand and pull over a vacant chair from the next table. "Hello. Can I get you anything?"

She sits. "A cup of tea, thank you."

She seems less hostile now. I call this progress. I go to the counter to order the tea and throw in a toastie as well. I'm ready to bet she's eaten noting since the bacon sandwich, and I'm not a hundred percent sure she ate that.

I return and take my seat. "The lad on the counter will bring it over."

She contemplates her hands for a few moments, then, "I went up to the Intensive Care ward. There's no change."

"No. Unless you count the orthopaedic work on her fractured legs." Both Fern's legs are now in plaster.

Mrs Daniels blinks back a tear. "The driver was drunk, you know. Three times over the limit, the police told me. He could have killed her, killed them both..."

I've had a similar report. I'm every bit as angry as Mrs Daniels, though I manage not to show it.

"They're all I've got. If she doesn't..." She bites back a sob. "If she doesn't get better, I don't know how I'll cope."

"We have to stay positive. The staff up there are fucking miracle workers. If anyone can pull her through, it's them."

"I know that, but—"

"You *will* cope. You'll have to. We both will. For Archie."

"But it's my little girl..." She starts to sob in earnest, and all I can do is grab a handful of serviettes and shove them towards her.

It's Harry who really rises to the occasion. He moves his chair closer and wraps a beefy arm around her thin shoulders. "Come on, love. Everyone's doing all they can. We have to just hope. And with any luck they'll throw away the key when that bastard gets to court."

Amen to that.

After a few minutes the sobbing subsides. Harry presses more serviettes into her hand, and Mrs Daniels dabs at her eyes and nose. "I just came to talk. When you weren't upstairs with Fern, I thought you might be here. I only meant to…"

"Ah, here's your tea. And something to eat."

The lad from behind the counter arrives with a tray which he sets on the table. He doesn't seem especially surprised to see customers weeping into his coffee, but I suppose he encounters a lot of grieving relatives.

"Thank you. You shouldn't have." Her response is decidedly more gracious that before. Is she perhaps relenting? Just a little?

I pour her tea, and she adds her own milk and sugar. She tries a tentative sip, then sets it down.

"I can't do with it too hot these days."

"Try the toastie. They're good," Harry urges.

She cuts hers in half and takes a bite. She nods and has another mouthful. The three of us continue to eat in silence until the plates are cleared, and Mrs Daniels pours herself a second cup of tea.

"You said you came to talk," I prompt her.

"Yes." She wipes her mouth with a serviette. "About your offer. You know, what you said, earlier."

"Yes. About you and Archie coming to stay with me for a while."

"It's just…it was kind of you to offer, but I've never been one for accepting handouts. It doesn't seem right to take advantage."

"Take advantage? Of what?"

"Of you. Fern told me you're quite well off."

"So?"

"Fern never wanted anything from you. She was always very firm about that, never asked for a penny."

"I know. But even if she never asked, that doesn't mean she wasn't entitled to anything. For Archie, at least."

Mrs Daniels hesitates. "You didn't know about Archie, did you? Fern never told you."

"No. She didn't."

"But you found out. She told me someone came to the studio and was asking about him."

"That was me," Harry says. "I took one look at the lad and I knew. You must see the resemblance yourself."

"I suppose I do. But still, you had the DNA test?" She meets my gaze. "You needed the proof."

I shrug. "That's the sort of man I am. But the results were clear enough. And I'm here, now, wanting to help." I don't bother to add that the DNA results can't be worth the paper they're written on, as I was nowhere near Las Vegas at the fateful time, but that hardly seems relevant or helpful right now.

She starts to shake her head, but I have to take one last stab at convincing her.

"Archie is my responsibility, too, now. I want what's best for him, and I honestly think the solution I'm offering is the best. It will help you, too. And I do genuinely believe it's what Fern would want. She loves you. She would want you to be okay as well as Archie."

She contemplates her cooling tea for a couple of minutes. The clock on the wall ticks slowly as I wait. Harry, too.

"It would only be temporary," she says at last. "Just until my treatment is ended, or Fern recovers. And there's one other condition."

"Go on."

"You're not to tell Archie that you're his father. That's for Fern to decide on when she's better. She should make up her own mind what to tell him, and when."

"I can agree to that." More readily than Mrs Daniels could possibly know. "I can be Uncle Cal, a friend of his mother's."

She nods. "I'll need to go home first, collect a few bits and pieces for me and Archie."

I suspect she'll need more than a few bits and pieces. "Harry will drive you, and he'll help you to pack what you need."

"There might be things for Fern, too. A nightie, that sort of thing."

"You just take your time. There's no rush. While you're doing that, I'll try to persuade the consultant to let Archie in to see his mum."

"I ought to be there. He might get upset…"

"I'll wait for you to get back."

"Thank you, Mr McPherson."

"Cal," I correct her. "Or Caleb, if you prefer."

"Caleb. And I'm Poppy."

I hold out my hand. "I'm glad to get to know you, Poppy."

MRS MANSOUR SURPRISES ME. She's perfectly happy to allow Archie into the Intensive Care ward but insists upon speaking to him first.

"You need to understand, Mr McPherson, that this is a very frightening place for most people, but small children, especially. That said, it often helps the little ones if they can actually see their relatives, to see for themselves so they can stop imagining much worse things. I can explain to him about the tubes and the equipment so none of that will be too much of a shock. So, if you wouldn't mind bringing him to my office when you arrive…?"

"That's fine. Thank you."

I spend a few more minutes at Fern's bedside, then go back down to the children's ward to tell Archie the good news.

Nurse Molly has gone off duty. Her replacement, a male charge nurse called Darren, makes a beeline for me as soon as I enter his domain.

"Ah, you must be Archie's father. Have you come to collect him?"

"Collect him?"

"Yes. The consultant has signed the discharge papers. He's ready to go."

"Ah. Right." Over Darren's shoulder I can see into the room where Archie spent the night. Except, it's now occupied by a little girl and her parents. "Where is he?"

"In the playroom. We just have a couple of forms to sign, and he's all yours. We'd recommend having him checked over by your own GP in about a week's time, but we don't foresee any issues."

I sign where required, then make my way to the playroom. I find Archie seated at the Snakes and Ladders table. He grins happily when he sees me.

"Do you want to play?"

I sit, and we have a couple of games. I'm not expecting Harry and Poppy back for a while yet.

"Do you fancy something to eat?" I offer as I slither down the longest snake on the board. "There's a nice cafe here."

"Are we allowed?"

I nod. "The hospital has said you can go home. We're just waiting for your grandma, then we'll be off."

"Can't you phone her. Tell her I'm ready to go home?"

"She knows." I pause, then, "Archie, you're going to go on a little holiday. You and your grandma. She's gone back to your house to pack your things."

"Where are we going? Grandma's poorly. She can't go on holiday."

"You're both coming to my house, to stay with me. And you and me are going to look after your grandma because you're right, she's not very well."

"What about my mummy?"

"She has to stay here a bit longer, so the doctors and nurses can take care of her. But the doctor in charge said you can go and see her. When your grandma gets back, we'll all go."

"Will we tell Mummy about going on holiday?"

"Why not? It might cheer her up."

"Can she come, too? When the doctor says she's better?"

"Of course."

"I'll tell her that. So she won't be upset."

"Good idea. So, what about that cafe, then?"

He gets up from the Snakes and Ladders table and slips his small hand into mine. "Do they have chips?"

HARRY AND POPPY find us in the cafe. Archie has made short work of a bowl of chips covered in cheese, and I'm on my second latte. I tell them the good news about visiting Fern.

"We ought to be getting on with it," Poppy says. "We have a long journey ahead."

I consider hiring the helicopter again but wonder if that might look a little ostentatious to Poppy. I doubt if she'd appreciate my playing the millionaire.

"There's no rush," I reply. "Archie can sleep in the car. You, too, if you like. I've phoned ahead, and there will be rooms ready and a meal waiting for us whenever we arrive."

Sally was horrified to learn of Fern's accident and her present condition, and not at all put out at the prospect of a small boy taking up residence at Linn Mill. Neither did she seem unduly concerned at having Poppy Daniels convalescing with us. I asked her to contact a staffing agency and engage a nurse with experience of post-surgery cancer therapies, and a part-time nanny. I don't doubt we'll have both within a couple of days.

"Can I see my mummy now?" Archie asks.

That clinches it. We put the empty plates and cups on the clearing trolley and set off for the lift.

We have a short wait outside Mrs Mansour's office. She is all apologies as she bustles towards us. "So sorry to keep you waiting. I was called away to check up on a patient. Come in, come in. And you must be Archie..."

What Happens in Vegas...

She beams at him, and Archie manages to smile back, though I can tell he's nervous.

We troop into the tiny, cluttered office. Mrs Mansour seats herself behind her desk, and Poppy takes the only other chair. She pulls Archie up onto her lap.

"So, Archie," Mrs Mansour begins. "I'm the doctor looking after your mummy. You remember she was hit by that car?"

Archie nods, slowly.

"She banged her head," the consultant continues.

Archie nods again.

"She's been unconscious since the accident. That's because her brain has gone to sleep. It's a way that people have of getting better after something like this, but while she's asleep, your mummy can't look after herself. So, we have to do that for her. Do you understand that?

"I... I think so. But, if she's asleep, why can't she come home and just go to bed?"

"It's a very deep sleep. She might need us to help her to wake up."

"When will she wake up?" Archie asks.

"No one really knows. It might be soon, or it might be several weeks, even months. If she stays asleep for a long time, she will need us to help her to eat and drink because she won't be able to just wake up and have her dinner."

"How will you do that?" Archie demands.

The consultant leans down and tugs a large shoe box from under her desk. Inside are a variety of tubes, syringes, drip bags and other bits and pieces of medical paraphernalia. She selects a length of tube, picks it up, and hands it to Archie.

"We use something just like this to feed her and give her plenty to drink. You'll see it, sticking out from under her blanket. You don't need to be worried by it, though. It's there to make sure she doesn't get hungry."

The doctor selects another piece of tubing, narrower this time. "She has a tube just like this going up her nose. That's to help her breathe. And one like this goes into her hand, just here." She taps the back of Archie's small hand. "That one has medicine in, to make sure she doesn't hurt anywhere and can sleep nice and peacefully."

Each time she mentions a tube, she places an example of it in Archie's hands so he can touch, feel, explore. I witness his anxiety settling as the unknown, the feared, becomes ordinary and functional.

"Your mummy has a big bandage on her head and face, because when she fell she scraped her face on the pavement. It will heal up, but we need to make sure no germs get in. Just like your hand, really."

The dressing on Archie's hand has been replaced by a smaller, less dramatic sticking plaster.

"There are lots of screens, too, like a tablet, or a laptop computer. Do you sometimes play with one of those?"

Again, he nods.

"They are there to tell us what's going on, just so we know that everything is all right even if your mummy can't tell us herself. They make odd noises sometimes, and there are flashing lights, but that's just the way they work and nothing to worry about. Does your tablet make noises sometimes?"

"Yes, when you burst a jelly bean."

"Ah, Candy Crush. One of my favourites, too. So, shall we go and visit your mummy, then?"

Archie wriggles off his grandma's lap and takes the doctor's hand.

"I like to play a little game," she says as we walk along the corridor and through the door onto the ward. "All those tubes you have in your hand... I wonder how many of them you can spot near your mummy. Do you think you can remember what each one does?"

Archie nods, his little face determined. And I silently applaud the doctor, who has obviously done this sort of thing lots of times and is skilled at putting frightened, worried children at ease.

We reach Fern's bed, and I pick Archie up so he can see her properly. I feel his small body flinch at the sight of her bandaged face, but he rallies quickly and is soon peering with curiosity rather than fear.

"Is that the breathing tube?" he asks. "The one in her nose?"

"Yes, it is." It's Beth who answers.

"I can't see the food one."

"It's here." Beth shows him the tube running from somewhere behind the bed and disappearing under the blankets.

Archie nods, satisfied. "That one has the medicine," he announces, pointing to the drip and cannula on the back of Fern's hand.

"That's right," Beth agrees.

"Can I touch her?" he asks. "Can I cuddle her?"

Beth smiles at him. "Yes, if you like. You can sit on the bed, on this side." She directs us away from the cannula and drip. "You can talk to her if you want. She won't answer, but she might hear you."

I help the nurse to settle Archie on the edge of the bed, staying close to make sure he can't fall. Where I was completely tongue-tied when they told me to try talking to her, Archie just starts chattering at once. Fern is treated to a blow-by-blow account of his stay in the hospital, including his mastery of Snakes and Ladders, my visit, and Harry's, and the cheese sandwich. He tells her about the cafe, and about his holiday.

"Me and Grandma are going to stay with Uncle Cal. You can come, too, when you're better. It's a long way, but we're going in his car."

I watch carefully for any change in her expression, any sign at all that she heard and understood. There's nothing. She lies there, still and silent, in her halfway place, hovering between the living and the dead.

I've never been one for praying, but I consider it in that moment, since I can come up with no other strategy that might make a difference. I desperately want her to get well, for Archie's sake, and for Poppy's. But most of all, for mine.

I can't lose her again.

ARCHIE. My Archie.

My little boy.

I can see him, across the water. A lake. An endless lake, and he is over there, on the other side. So far away...

His voice carries across the vastness. I open my mouth to answer, to call him closer, but I can't speak.

I try to wave, but my arms are too heavy.

I'm screaming, but no one hears, not even me.

CHAPTER 18

I make my way upstairs from the gym having completed ten kilometres on the bike followed by a one-mile swim. I don't manage to fit in my regime every day, but I like to start the day with a workout when I can. My hair still damp, I'm ready for one of Sally's breakfasts.

Poppy is already in the kitchen when I arrive, seated at the table nursing a cup of tea. I'm glad to have caught her.

I help myself to coffee, then sit opposite her. "Is Archie still in bed?"

"Yes. I let him stay up quite late last night. That will have to stop when he starts school next week."

I've managed to get him a place at the village primary school. We're not certain how long he'll be staying here for, but Poppy and I are in agreement that he ought to go to school. He seems happy enough at the prospect.

I'm not sure if I am. I've quite enjoyed spending time with Archie over the last few days. We've swum together, kicked a ball about, and I've introduced him to my horses. He's lively, and curious about everything. But under his natural cheeriness and enthusiasm for life, I know he misses his mother and worries about her. He hasn't mentioned her much, and that concerns me. It's a sure sign we'll need to pay another visit to the hospital soon. This week, probably, so as not to miss school.

Sally hired a nanny who comes in for the afternoons, which gives me a chance to keep up with business. Still, I've enjoyed taking time out to get to know Archie, the sort of time my own father never found for me.

He was a great role model for how *not* to be a parent. I learned a lot from him.

"What can I get you to eat, Poppy? You need a decent breakfast inside you today." Sally is beside her stove, stirring eggs for my omelette.

"I'm not very hungry. Just a bit of toast, please."

I don't need to ask why she's lost her usual healthy appetite. "Today's the day, then?"

She nods. "I can't say I'm looking forward to it."

She's due at the hospital in Edinburgh for her second cycle of chemo, a daunting prospect, especially, as I gather, she was violently ill following her first dose.

"Is Harry driving you there?"

"Yes, but I could have taken a taxi.

Harry is under strict instructions to see her right to the door of the cancer care department, and to stay with her if she wants him there. Failing that, he'll be waiting outside for her when she's done.

"It's no trouble. And when you get back we'll have Jilly on hand to take care of you."

Jilly is the agency nurse, hired to attend Poppy for three days following each round of chemo, and longer if she needs it.

"I managed without a nurse before. It's just sickness and fatigue. A nice lie down will do the trick.

"We can manage that as well. Indulge me. I promised to make sure you were looked after, and I will."

She pours herself another cup of tea, just as Sally sets a plate of buttered toast in front of her. It doesn't seem like much of a breakfast to me, but I suppose she knows best.

She glances across at me and stirs her tea. "You do know that it's Archie's birthday on Saturday."

I pause, my coffee cup halfway to my mouth. "No, I didn't."

"He'll be five," Poppy continues.

"I see. Could you organise a cake, Sally?"

She nods. "Definitely. I'll ice it, too. Does he have any favourite television characters? Sporting heroes?"

"I know he likes football," Poppy replies.

I'd already gathered as much from the Manchester United shirt he insists on wearing most days.

"What about a present?" I ask. "What do you think he'd like?"

"Fern had planned to get him a bike," Poppy tells me. "I think she actually ordered it but I'm not sure where from. He really wants a dog, and Fern was going to let him have one. That was before my illness, though, and she didn't think she could manage a new puppy in the house as well as running around after the pair of us."

"I bet he was gutted."

"Probably. I know Fern was. She hated breaking a promise. I wish I knew where she was buying that bike from."

"There can't be that many suppliers. I'll see if I can track it down and get it delivered here." It's important to me that Archie should have his mother's birthday present even if she's not in a position to see to it herself. Perhaps especially because of that. It's the least I can do for her. I make a mental note to get Mary to identify the bike shops in Stockport and start phoning round.

POPPY ARRIVES BACK JUST BEFORE five o'clock. I spot the car from my office and go down to the foyer to meet her. Jilly and I arrive as Harry helps her through the door.

"How did it go? I ask, although I can tell the answer at a

glance. Poppy appears about ready to throw up all over my marble tiles.

"The treatment went well enough, but she's wiped out," Harry answers. "Jilly, can you help me to get her upstairs?"

"No," Poppy rasps. "The drawing room. I...I like to look out of the window."

"Perhaps tomorrow," Jilly suggests.

"No," I interrupt. "If she wants to be in the drawing room, then she can. Harry, could you help me to move the chaise longue closer to the windows?" I've noticed over the week or so that she has been in residence that Poppy seems to enjoy this room the most and spends a lot of time gazing out at the view. If it's a place where she feels happy, then that's good enough reason for her to be there when she is at her lowest.

Harry follows me into the drawing room. By the time we've rearranged the furniture a little, Jilly and Poppy have joined us. Jilly assists Poppy onto the chaise longue.

"Would you like a blanket?" I ask.

"Yes, please."

"I'll get it. And I have something that should help to settle your stomach." Jilly hurries off.

Harry is still carrying Poppy's bag. He sets it down on the floor beside her. "Is there anything I can get you? A nice cup of tea, perhaps?"

She shakes her head, then lies back, her eyes closed. "I don't think I could keep anything down right now. I'll be all right soon, after a little rest. It's just the effort of getting out of the car and up those steps..."

Jilly returns, a soft blanket bundled in her arms. She spreads it over Poppy, who looks to be asleep already.

By mutual, unspoken agreement, Harry and I make ourselves scarce.

. . .

What Happens in Vegas...

MARY HAS MANAGED to come up trumps. She found the cycle shop in Stockport where Archie's bike was on order. It took a bit of negotiating, and I had to pay off the balance owing, obviously, as well as a hefty whack for next-day delivery, but the bicycle arrived at Linn Mill yesterday. Sally hid it in one of the store cupboards, and Poppy, feeling somewhat restored after three days of rest and cosseting by Jilly, Sally, myself, and much to my surprise, Harry, helped me to wrap it up after Archie had gone to bed. It now stands, resplendent in bright-crimson paper adorned with dinosaurs, waiting to be unwrapped and taken for its first adventure.

The worst of Poppy's nausea seems to have passed. She still feels a little queasy at times, but she seems to be able to live with that. She is far more upset that her hair has started to fall out. Not in big chunks, but enough to be noticeable. Sally mentioned to me that she has made an appointment with the hairdresser in the village and intends to have it all cut short. I suppose that's the wise thing to do, though it does seem a pity. I can see where Fern inherited her gorgeous auburn hair from.

By way, I suspect, of demonstrating to us all that she is on the mend, Poppy was the one to go and wake Archie and chivvy him downstairs for his birthday breakfast. Sally has set out his favourite, Cocoa Pops swimming in milk, and a glass of blackcurrant juice. He bounces into the kitchen to be greeted by a chorus of 'happy birthdays'.

A stack of smaller gifts waits for him next to his cereal bowl. A couple of large picture books from Sally, some fancy lighting-up crayons from Poppy, and one of those handheld electronic games from me. I always fancied one, now I have the perfect excuse to stalk the Nintendo website. Archie beams as he opens each one, his diligence interspersed with enthusiastic eating.

As soon as he finishes his breakfast, he wants to head off to the drawing room where there's a large flat-screen television. I decide to let him have a few minutes, then I'll take him outside to see the bicycle. Later on, I have a special treat planned for him, an outing I hope he will love.

"Oh, wow! Is that mine?" I managed to cajole him outside onto the driveway, where he now circles the gift-wrapped bike with wide-eyed reverence. Despite our combined efforts with the wrapping paper it's still perfectly obvious what's inside.

"Your mummy bought it for you, before the accident," I explain.

"It's a bike! It *is* a bike, isn't it?" he squeals.

"Looks like one, " I agree. "Have you ridden a bike before?"

He shakes his head, at the same time trying to scramble on, and somehow ignoring the wrapping paper.

"Okay. In that case, let's get it unwrapped and we'll see how you do. I have some stabilisers if we need them." Fern took the precaution of buying a set, just in case. Clearly, she likes to be prepared.

Archie lets out a scornful hoot. "Those are for wussies." His right leg is already over the cross bar again, ripping the colourful paper..

"Okay. We'll get the paper off first, though," I insist. "It'll go faster, then."

Archie is literally dancing from one foot to the other with excitement as I rip the paper off, but he manages to help with the wheels. Then, he jumps on properly and immediately lifts both feet onto the pedals.

I manage to catch hold of the back of the saddle to stop him toppling over. "You need to pedal it to stay up," I explain. "When you stop, you put your feet down."

"I know that," he informs me haughtily, and starts to pedal.

I hang on to the back of the seat until he feels a bit more stable, then I let go. Not for long. He wobbles violently, so I grab the saddle again.

"Are you sure about those stabilisers?" I ask him.

"I can do this. I need to practice."

What Happens in Vegas...

"Fair enough." I admire tenacity. "Let's go onto the grass, then."

We spend the next half hour or so mastering the bicycle. Or Archie does. I just chase him around, trying to catch him each time he's about to fall off. I succeed some of the time, but he's covered in grass stains before he decides he's had enough for now and maybe he'll play with his Nintendo instead. We troop back indoors, and I leave him in the drawing room with Poppy.

"We're going out later," I say. "You have half an hour, then you need to go and get changed."

"I'll make sure he's ready," Poppy promises. "He wouldn't want to miss his birthday treat, would you, Archie?"

"Where are we going?" he demands.

Poppy and I exchange a smile. "Wait and see," she tells him.

I CATCH up on a few bits of paperwork until it's time to leave. When I get down into the foyer, Archie is already there, sporting his usual Manchester United top, his Nintendo tucked under his arm.

"If you want to take that, you'll need a backpack. Do you have one?"

He shakes his head.

"I'll lend you one, then." I nip back up to my room to grab a small rucksack, one I use on the occasions I decide to go out on a longer ride on Roman. I return and hand it to Archie. "Tuck your Nintendo in here, and anything else you think you might need. We'll be out all afternoon."

Under his grandma's careful supervision, a couple of drinks cartons find their way in, as well as a chocolate biscuit and a packet of crisps. Thus supplied, we head outside. I can already hear the drone of the helicopter, which hovers into view as we reach the steps.

"Oooh, look." Archie points and hops up and down. "Where is it going?"

"It's coming here."

Archie watches, open-mouthed, as the helicopter gently comes to rest on my front lawn. The rotors are still spinning when I reach for his hand and start to jog towards our transport. By the time he's safely seat belted inside, Archie is near bursting with excitement.

"Is this it? My treat? We're going on a helicopter ride?"

"Well, we are," I explain. "But that's not really the treat. Or, not all of it. "Where I want to go is a long way, too far to drive there and back in one day, so I hired the helicopter."

"It's so cool," he breathes. "Wait till I tell Mummy."

Funny you should mention that...

The helicopter soars into the air. I think there must be a little kid in all of us because I get almost as big a buzz out of the trip as Archie does. I point out landmarks—Edinburgh Castle, Hadrian's Wall, Scafell Pike in Cumbria. We watch the traffic, tiny cars on the motorway, and see the towns laid out below us like model villages. Archie is excited to spot Blackpool Tower and tells me of the weekend they stayed there in a caravan, him, Fern, and Poppy. I get the impression he spent most of his time digging holes on the beach and eating Blackpool rock. I make a mental note to make sure we go back there before long.

After about an hour we reach the outskirts of Manchester and circle around to land at the heliport to the north-east of the city. There, I have a car waiting to take us to the first of our destinations.

Archie recognises the familiar roads of Stockport. "Are we going to see Mummy?"

"Yes, I thought you might like to drop in and say hello. You can thank her for the bike and tell her you've already learned to ride it."

"Yes. And I can tell her about the swimming pool in your cellar. And the ponies."

"You do that. Tell her to get well soon so she can come riding with us."

We arrive at the hospital and check in with the main desk. The receptionist informs me that Fern Daniels has been transferred to the High Dependency Unit, a step down from Intensive Care. I already knew that but thank her for directions to find the new department.

Fern has her own room in the HDU. There are still lots of wires, tubes, and equipment, but it's all rather less formidable. She's still deeply unconscious, the combined effect of the ongoing sedation, and her injuries.

I take advantage of Archie's preoccupation with telling her all about his exciting ride in a helicopter to quiz the Senior House Officer in charge of the ward. He tells me that Fern's condition is stable, no longer considered to be life-threatening, and they have every reason to believe she will regain eventually consciousness. But they have no idea when that will be or if she will suffer any lasting damage.

"I was thinking we might move her closer to Edinburgh," I explain. "Would that be safe, now that her condition has stabilised?"

"How soon do you want to do this? he enquires.

"As soon as possible. Her little boy needs to be able to see her often, and her mother, too. There's a good private hospital not too far from where I live, Halstead Grange. Do you know of it?"

He shakes his head. "I could speak to Mr Jordache. He's Miss Daniels' consultant. If he thinks it's safe to move her then I would see no problem. I'll let you know what he says. You would need a private ambulance, though. We couldn't transport her all that way on the National Health."

The least of my concerns. "I look forward to hearing from you soon, Doctor Gibb."

CLOSER NOW. *Louder. The voices ...*

I see Archie again. I've seen him many times, but he's clearer now. I can...feel him. His voice, his breath on my cheek.

His hand, in mine. I try to hold him, but he slips away.

Gone.

But the other is still here. The man. The lover. He touches me, my hair... Kisses my cheek.

Then, he is gone, too. I am alone. Silent. Cold. Still as the grave.

I weep, but no tears form. No one hears me.

FERN'S COMPLEXION is less pallid now, a more natural colour entirely, but she's still breathing through a tube and being fed intravenously. I get some measure of satisfaction from knowing that the maniac who caused all of this is looking at a ten-year prison sentence, but that won't help Fern. Maybe I can, though, by having her brought close to her family. If she really can hear us, she'll have plenty of opportunity at Halstead Grange. It's only about a twenty-minute drive from Linn Mill. Someone will be able to visit more or less every day.

"Can we go to the nice cafe?" Archie asks as we make our way back down to the main entrance.

I check my watch. It's almost two o'clock.

"Not this time, Archie. There's somewhere else we need to go, and we need to be there in less than an hour."

"Where is it? Where are we going?"

"It's still a surprise. Come on, I'll race you to the car."

I'm glad I hired a driver. If nothing else, it saves me having to find somewhere to park. And the local knowledge helps us to thread through the heavy Manchester traffic a lot quicker than I could have. Soon, the streets around us are teeming with people, football fans wearing the same red uniform as Archie.

Even when the looming facade of Old Trafford comes into view, he doesn't realise what our destination is. It's not until the

What Happens in Vegas...

driver brings us to a halt before the VIP entrance to the stadium that Archie finally lets out a squeal of pure joy.

"We're going to the match! Are we? Are we really?"

"We are indeed." I open the car door and get out, followed by a very excited little boy. McPherson Holdings retains a corporate hospitality package which means on most match days I can get myself and up to six guests into the VIP lounge at the back of the grandstand, and into the special viewing area. On this occasion I have just one very special guest. We'll have a fabulous view of the play on the pitch, Archie can cheer for his heroes, and he might even get to meet one or two of them as they do sometimes come upstairs afterwards to mingle with the rest of the rich and famous.

Today, we are sharing the VIP area with a couple of lesser royals, several politicians, a party from British Petroleum, and a celebrity chef. I also recognise a Formula One racing driver and, if I'm not mistaken, last year's Wimbledon Champion. We are in excellent company, but Archie is oblivious to all but what is happening on the pitch.

It's almost three o'clock by the time I have Archie nicely set up in a corner of the viewing area, a glass of blackcurrant in one hand and a traditional meat pie in the other. He almost wets himself with excitement when the players troop out, each of them hand in hand with a small child wearing the United colours.

United are up against Chelsea today. I'm no follower of football myself, it never really captured my imagination the way cricket did, or any sport concerning horses, but even I can tell it's a hard-fought contest. United come off best and win the encounter by two goals to one. Archie is ecstatic.

"Did you see that? Did you see Lukaku"

I nod. I expect I did see Lukaku though I can't be sure. I certainly don't know all the players by name.

Archie does. "And what about Pogba?

"He was good," I agree, hoping not to be quizzed more closely.

"And Lindelöf, and Marcus Rashford."

"Them, too. Do you want another blackcurrant?"

"Yes, please. Did you see that save? David de Gea is the best goalkeeper in the world."

"Very probably," I concur. I'd be hard-pressed to name another.

"Can we come again?" Archie wants to know. "Can we come every Saturday?"

"Not every week," I reply. "But quite often, yes. Sometimes I can bring you, other times it might need to be Harry." I happen to know Harry is an ardent Manchester City fan but choose to skate over that inconvenience.

"Will we come by helicopter?"

"Again, not every single time. But on special occasions, like a fifth birthday."

"This was the best birthday ever," he announces as we finish our drinks.

"So, ready for the helicopter flight back home?" I've arranged for the helicopter to pick us up here, which means we have to wait for the general crowds to drift off and the car park to empty. There will be several choppers landing in the parking areas, most of them taking the players and other top brass away from the ground, avoiding the throngs of fans waiting outside.

We join the more select group waiting in the main foyer, and suddenly Archie stiffens. "That's him," he hisses, squeezing my hand.

"Who?"

"David de Gea. The goalkeeper."

"Ah." The streaked brown hair and Spanish good looks do rather make the man stand out in a crowd, come to think of it.

"Can I get him to sign my rucksack?"

"*Your* rucksack?"

"Please, Uncle Cal. Please…"

What Happens in Vegas...

"Okay. Come on."

I do a quick check of my programme and find that his first name is David. With Archie in tow, I waylay the goalkeeper by the cold drinks vending machine.

"Excuse me. I don't suppose you'd do an autograph for the lad, here?"

"Eh?"

"An autograph," I repeat, offering him a pen by way of further explanation. I do a writing gesture, for good measure.

"Oh, yes. Yes, of course."

Archie offers up his rucksack like a sacrificial lamb. I wince as the footballer scrawls all over it, but one look at Archie's delighted features dispels any doubts. David de Gea, his duty done, hands me back my pen and darts for the door. We watch as he clambers aboard a small chopper and soars away.

"I got his autograph. I actually got his autograph. That's so cool."

I grin. His joy is infectious. "Come on, that one's ours."

CHAPTER 19

"Where's Archie?" I ask, entering the kitchen and finding only Sally and Poppy there.

It's the Sunday morning following our trip to Old Trafford. Archie was still buzzing with excitement when we got back, and the special birthday tea which was waiting for him did nothing to dampen his spirits. He finally had to be carried up to bed, still clutching the rucksack with de Gea's scrawl all over it.

"He's outside, on his bike, Harry's with him."

"I see. How are you feeling today, Poppy?" She certainly looks better. Hopefully the effects of the latest cycle have finally subsided.

"I'm fine," she assures me. "I told Jilly she needn't come in anymore."

"That's good. I'll get the agency to send her after your next lot. When is that?"

"A fortnight tomorrow." She grimaces. "Then another three after that."

I send a sympathetic smile her way. "It will be worth it. Eventually. Whilst Archie's outside, there was something I wanted to discuss with you."

"Oh?"

"At the hospital yesterday, I asked about having Fern moved closer to here. Her condition is stable, but she shows no signs of coming round. If this is going to be a long haul, and it's starting to appear that way, it would be better if we could all visit her more often. You've not been to see her since you came here."

"I know. It's just so far…"

"So, would you have any concerns about moving her?

"Would it be safe?"

"I have this, from the consultant." I pull my phone from my pocket and open up my email app. I find the message I received yesterday evening from Mr Jordache in which he states that, assuming the proper transportation is arranged, he has no objection to the move. He has already been in contact with Mr Trent, a colleague of his, a consultant who has beds at Halstead Grange and who would be prepared to take Miss Daniels as a private patient. It seems that all we need do is say the word.

And agree to pick up the bills, obviously.

"Won't all this be very expensive?" Poppy asks.

"I think you must know by now that I'm good for the money."

"I know, but—"

Poppy." I take her hand in mine. "There's nothing I want more than to have Fern well again. I honestly believe this will be best for her, to have her family near. Even if she doesn't want to see me, to have you and Archie visiting often will speed her recovery, I'm sure of it. And Archie needs her."

"He seems fairly happy at the moment."

"I'm not surprised. Birthday treats, a swimming pool in the basement, horses. What small boy wouldn't be in his element? All the more reason for him to see Fern often, to remember her and keep her in his life."

She eyes me quizzically. "You are a man full of surprises, Caleb McPherson. And insight."

I'm not so sure about that. What I am sure of is that my

strategy for seeing Fern back on her feet again requires that she be moved to within easy reach of my home. *Our* home, for the time being.

"So, you don't object?" I press her.

"Would it matter if I did? I can see you're determined to move her."

"I do think it's for the best, but that doesn't mean I won't listen to anyone else. I know you love her, too."

She regards me for several moments, then, "Okay. Do you need me to help?"

"If you wouldn't mind, I think it might be best if you were to ride with her in the ambulance."

"Of course. Just let me know when."

"How would the day after tomorrow be?"

She grins. "You don't waste time."

"Is that okay, then?"

"Yes. It's okay."

"There's one other thing I should mention."

"Oh?"

"I intend to set up a trust fund for Archie. Money he could have when he turns twenty-one. Or maybe eighteen."

"You don't have to do that. I know Fern never intended to ask you for anything."

"That's why, at least in part. She never will ask me to contribute, but that doesn't mean I won't. This is one way I could do it. I'm going to ask Simon Waters, my corporate lawyer, to inquire into the best financial model, but I'm thinking something in memory of my late mother. Something not connected to McPherson Holdings so it would be safe from any upheaval in the economy."

"You've clearly given this a lot of thought already."

"I have."

"Fern might have something to say on the matter."

"I will talk to her, eventually. When I can. But I want to

make a start on this now. At least establish the administrative side of it."

"You don't need my consent, though. Do you?"

"I want to know you approve."

She nods slowly. "I think I do. At least, I understand why you think this is right and I have no quarrel with it."

"Thank you." The pressing business of the day settled, I move on to my next subject. "I mean to take Archie to get his dog today. Do you fancy coming with us?"

"His dog?"

"Yes. You said that Fern was going to let him have one but had to put it off to look after you."

"I know, but—"

"Well, now that that issue is resolved and you are being looked after, I see no reason not to let him have the dog. Do you?"

"I suppose not. Although, what if Fern isn't...if she isn't... quite herself, when she wakes up?"

I take her hand again. "We don't know what the future will hold, but we have to hope for the best. And live for now. And, if Fern finds herself struggling, well, I'll be here. So will you. We can manage, don't you think?"

She nods and swipes away a tear. "I'd love to come with you."

I TOOK the precaution of phoning Dogs Trust earlier in the week, to make sure they had puppies available for adoption. Apparently they have five, as well as any number of older dogs. I bundle Archie into my car, strap him into the child's seat I had sent over from the store in Edinburgh, and set off for the city. Poppy is seated in the back with him, and I leave it to her to explain where we are going this time.

There's an excited whoop from behind me.

"A dog? I'm really going to have a dog?"

"Just a small one," Poppy tries to suggest.

"Yes, a puppy. But it will grow. Won't it, Uncle Caleb?"

Personally, I don't mind if he gets a dog the size of a donkey, but I can see that there may be issues in a terraced house in Stockport. "How big is your garden at home?" I ask.

"Not very big," he replies. "But there's the park at the end of our road. And a playing field behind. I'll take it for walks every day. Or it could stay with you when I go home. Your garden is huge."

Over a hundred acres, in fact, but that's hardly the point. His dog needs to be where he is. "Let's look for one that won't be knocking the furniture over, shall we?"

"Okay. Furniture. That means wardrobes. And beds. And tables…"

I sigh and resolve never to try to do a deal with a small child.

I pull up outside Dogs Trust. Even as we get out of the car, we can hear the barking from inside. We go into the reception area, and I give my name.

"I phoned last week. We want to adopt a puppy."

"Very well. There's this form you need to fill in." The girl shoves it across the desk, along with a ballpoint pen." And, you'd have to pay two hundred and forty pounds. That's our rehoming fee, and if you feel like it you could make a donation towards his keep, inoculations and so on."

"No problem." I take a seat and fill in the form, promising to take responsibility for the pup and to return it to Dogs Trust if for any reason find I can't manage to take care of it. I hand the forms back and find myself the proud possessor of a bunch of leaflets in return, ranging from requests for a hefty donation to Dogs Trust, to adverts for holistic dog food and pet insurance.

I'm minded to be generous, if we can find the right dog here. I stuff the leaflets in my jacket pocket. "Okay, shall we have a look around, then?"

We are accompanied into the bowels of the rescue centre by

What Happens in Vegas...

a kennel maid in a stained polo shirt and jeans. She introduces herself as Stacey.

"What sort of a dog are you after?" she asks.

"A young one," I tell her. "A puppy, preferably."

"A black one," adds Archie.

"A small one," is Poppy's contribution.

"This way," Stacey says, unlocking a metal gate and leading us through to a narrow corridor with pens on both sides. In each enclosure is a dog, sometimes two dogs.

"Do you have any other pets?" Stacey asks.

"Just horses," I reply. "But they don't live in the house."

"I see." Stacey's expression remains perfectly serious. "We always try our dogs with cats, and sometimes rabbits. But not horses. You'll have to see how that goes." She stops by one of the pens. "This is Penny, a cross Labrador bitch. She's about a year old."

The dog seems friendly enough but is already fully grown. I glance at Archie.

"I want a puppy," he says.

Stacey nods and moves on. I spare a final thought for Penny. Better luck next time.

The next pen Stacey stops at is home to three small dogs, all running around, yapping and chasing each other. Stacey tells us they are Yorkshire Terriers, all from the same litter, four months old.

"One of them would do nicely," says Poppy.

Archie and I both shake our heads.

Stacey moves on.

We reach the end of the corridor.

"There are more out the back," Stacey says. "I just need to get another set of keys."

"What about that one?" Archie asks, pointing to a dog of indeterminate colour but definitely not black. It is a puppy, though, and comes rushing to the front of the pen to greet us.

"You said you wanted a small dog," Stacey reminds us. "He's

going to grow to be huge."

"But I love him. He's the one I want." Archie is on his knees, reaching into the pen. The puppy is nibbling his fingers and rolling onto its back.

"He certainly looks friendly enough. How big would you say he'll be? Eventually."

"Going by the size of his paws now, I'd guess about the size of a German Shepherd. Maybe a bit bigger."

"He's not a German Shepherd, though, is he?"

Stacey shakes her head. "He's a cross between a Border Terrier and, I'd say perhaps a Newfoundland. It's the size that gives it away, and the long, thick coat. Newfoundlands are black, but he's got his mother's brown as well, gives him that tawny appearance."

"Is that the mother?" Poppy asks. She points to a skinny brown dog curled up in the corner of the pen.

"Yes, that's Tara. Came in half starved. We had to deliver her puppy by Caesarean. Luckily there was only one, or I doubt she'd have survived. She's been a good mum, though, but I reckon she's about ready for a break. The puppy is eight weeks old."

"What will happen to her? Won't she miss the pup?" I wonder.

"She'll be offered for rehoming. She has a lovely nature, nice and quiet, and she's only about a year old herself. Someone will take her."

I crouch beside Archie and hold out my hand to the mother dog. She regards me with suspicion, then uncurls herself and makes her way towards me. She gets close enough to let me tickle her ears.

"See. Lovely nature. A bit shy. She needs to be someone's only dog, probably. A nice, quiet home," Stacey burbles on. "So, will you be taking the pup, then?"

I look to Poppy for guidance.

She shrugs. "He'll need training."

What Happens in Vegas...

I can't argue with that. A dog this size needs to know his place.

"Please," is Archie's only contribution.

"Yes, we'll take him," I say.

"Right, well, you've been checked out and the home visit went okay, so you can take him today if you like."

I recall the brief visit a few days ago by the Dog's Trust volunteer. She took one look at Linn Mill and decided we ticked all the boxes.

"I suppose you'll sell collars and leads. And a dog bowl?"

"You can buy everything you need in our shop," Stacey assures me. She produces a key to unlock the pen and marches in to pick up the squirming fluffy bundle.

The mother dog, Tara, stands motionless while her baby is taken away. She begins to whimper as the pen door closes. We can still hear her when we reach the end of the corridor.

Archie has a good time in the pet shop, choosing the lead he wants, a nice collar, and a name tag which we get engraved with the name he insists upon—Ollie.

"Why Ollie?" I ask.

"He has tawny fur, like an owl. Ollie the owl," he explains.

"Oh. Okay. Ollie's a good name. Have we got everything?"

"You'll need some food. And some worming tablets. He's been wormed already, but you'll have to do it again." The girl behind the shop counter passes me a small pack of tablets. "Crush one and put it in his food."

"Okay." I add it to the pile on the counter.

"Have we forgotten anything?" Poppy asks.

I cast an eye over the pile of pet supplies and the squirming fluffball now wearing his new collar and tugging at his lead. "We have," I say. "We forgot Tara."

"Tara?" The girl at the till appears bemused. "I don't think we sell..."

"The mother dog. Tara. We'll take her as well."

. . .

"That was unexpected, "Poppy observes as we drive home. "Two dogs."

I shrug. "There was something about her. I couldn't leave her behind."

"Well, she's sweet, I'll grant you that. But yours isn't a quiet home, exactly. And won't she be bothered by Ollie being around the whole time?"

"She'll have plenty of chance to get away from him. He'll be with Archie, I expect, and she can stay with me. She'll be good company. Anyway, I don't think she's timid. I think she just chooses her friends carefully."

Poppy nods. "You could be right."

Archie's first day at his new school goes without a hitch. I'm relieved. I half expected to get a call by lunch time asking me to pick him up. As it is, I'm outside the school gates at three o'clock, his pup in the back of my car, waiting for him to emerge.

He does, with another boy of about the same age. The pair of them sprint over to me.

"Uncle Caleb, this is Thomas."

"Hello, Thomas."

"Thomas sits next to me," Archie goes on. "He's in Mrs Arnold's class, too. He has a pet rat."

"Oh. I see." I hope Archie isn't getting any ideas. I draw the line at rats.

"Can he come to tea?"

"To tea?"

"Yes."

"What about his mum? She'll be expecting him home."

"We can stop and tell her where I am," Thomas assures me. "She works in the cake shop."

I can't help feeling that a cake shop might be a better bet for a nice tea, but in the interests of helping Archie to settle in here

I agree to call in and introduce myself and ask if her son can come home with us for a couple of hours.

It turns out Mrs Ferguson, Thomas' mother, owns the cake shop, with her husband, Lewis. They are perfectly amenable to allowing him to come to Linn Mill, and insist on contributing some eclairs to the teatime fare.

"Bring your swimming things," Archie tells him. "We have a pool downstairs."

"A swimming pool? Oh, well, yes, I suppose you would have, up there in that nice house." Mrs Ferguson bustles off after her son. "I'd better make sure he has his armbands."

THE NEXT DAY IS MOMENTOUS, too, though for a different reason. Harry drives Poppy to Stockport, then drives back alone when she transfers to the ambulance to make the return journey with Fern.

The trip up the motorway is slow. The drivers have been told to keep it sedate, avoid bumps. I'm sure they are very diligent, but I've been waiting at Halstead Grange for almost two hours by the time the dark-painted ambulance with blacked-out windows pulls into the stately grounds of the hospital.

Mr Trent is with me in the doorway. We both hurry down to examine the small figure on the stretcher.

"Any issues on the journey?" the consultant asks.

"None, sir," comes the reply from the paramedic assigned the task of seeing Fern safely to Scotland.

"Very well. Let's get her settled, and I'll examine her properly."

The driver and the paramedic manoeuvre the trolley up the ramp and into the hospital entrance. Mr Trent walks beside them, Poppy and I bring up the rear.

"How was it?" I ask her.

"So weird," she replies. "Anyone would think she was just sleeping…"

"I know." I slip my arm around her. "I know."

Fern's accommodation at Halstead Grange is more like a five-star hotel room than a hospital ward. Her bed is relatively normal to look at, though it can be raised or lowered as required. It is queen-size, though, and the bedding is pretty flowered pastels rather than austere white. There are bright-blue curtains at the windows, matching carpets and cushions, and a fifty-inch television on the wall. She is on the ground floor so she could, if she opened her eyes and there was nothing she fancied on the television, have a nice view of the garden outside. Well, an oak tree, and a bench. But it's something. The furniture in her room is made of pale ash, and there are several comfortable chairs and a sofa for guests. No more of those hard but serviceable plastic seats.

I will forever be in debt to the National Health Service for the care they've given Fern, but having spent a night in one, I haven't a good word to say for those bloody chairs.

COLD. *It's so cold.*

I shiver.

I'm tired, leave me be. Everything is moving, swirling. I need peace. I need the pink fuzz that wraps everything up so warm, the silence.

The voices are back, loud, shouty, close. Too close. I want them to go away, to let me sleep.

Just one voice, now. Quiet, soft. A nice voice, familiar.

Mum. I see her, feel her. But she's so far away. The lake, I see the lake again, and the far shore. She's there, waving, calling to me.

I try to wave back, but she doesn't see. I call out. No one hears because there is no sound. Not here, not where I am.

OVER THE NEXT FEW WEEKS, we settle into a routine, of sorts.

Every three weeks sees Poppy laid low by another chemo cycle. Her hair had gone by the fourth cycle, and she has taken to wearing a scarf wrapped turban-style around her head. It rather suits her. Jilly tends to be with us one week out of three. I'm not sure how much difference she actually makes, but she has a very pleasant bedside manner, and Poppy seems to enjoy the cosseting. Chemo or not, Poppy spends most of her time on the chaise longue in the drawing room watching the summer go by, often with Archie, his rumbustious dog and his new best friend charging in and out of the French windows.

They all seem content enough, though a cloud of uncertainty and apprehension hangs over us all. Fern casts a long shadow from her hospital bed.

Poppy and I have become friends, or so I like to think. We talk often, especially when she is feeling well. She tells me stories of when Fern was young, and of the times before her husband died of his heart attack. In one particularly honest exchange, she tells me of her intense disappointment to learn that her only daughter had married in secret, to a man she had never even met. Gone at a stroke were her dreams of being the mother of the bride, of wearing a fancy hat, maybe making a speech. Not for the first time since I became involved with this family, I am lost for words. I settle for an apology, though I'm not quite sure why I feel compelled to offer regrets for something I had no part in.

And we go to visit Fern together, usually after dropping Archie off at school. We chat to her, and about her, both of us convinced that something must get through. The medical staff provide us with regular reports, always a variation on the same theme.

No change.

She had a comfortable night.

Miss Daniels' condition is stable.

Archie comes to the hospital a couple of times a week. I

don't push him to visit more often. I know he prefers to be with his friends, his dog. It's enough that he knows where she is, and how she is.

Ollie the pup is growing bigger every day. I've had to step up my training regime or my home would be reduced to chaos. He is a bright dog and after some initial resistance is becoming fairly well-mannered, at least when I'm around. Now I just need to instil the same standards in Archie.

The real surprise, though, is Tara. She has become my shadow. She is in the office if I'm working, and always waiting by the car if I go out. She's content to just ride around in the passenger seat all day, and when I'm at my headquarters in Edinburgh she is usually under the boardroom table. She sleeps in a basket in the corner of my room. I can't recall ever hearing her bark, though when I took her and Ollie for their check-up and final inoculations, the vet assured me she's fine. Just calm and laid-back, content with her life.

Both dogs are fine with horses. Tara enjoys the long runs, trotting along beside Roman until she's exhausted. Then she will either sit and wait for me to come back or allow me to lift her onto the saddle and continue on horseback. Ollie just runs and runs, his supply of energy seemingly boundless. The dogs enjoy each other's company, but spend a lot of time apart, an arrangement that seems to suit them.

Thomas is around most evenings and weekends. Both boys have learned to swim, so armbands are a thing of the past now, though I keep the door to the pool locked unless I'm there, or Harry, or Becky, the part-time nanny. I don't want any tragic accidents.

As luck would have it, Mr Ferguson is an ardent supporter of Heart of Midlothian Football Club and never misses a home match. He takes Thomas and Archie with him so Archie's craving for The Beautiful Game is satisfied and Harry is spared the ordeal of cheering for his archrivals. I half expect Archie to be weaned off Manchester United, but we shall see.

CHAPTER 20

September 2018

I SEE THEM EVERY DAY. My eyes are closed, or open. I don't know, can't be sure anymore. Does it matter?

I see them.

I see him.

He is close. Too close. He scares me. I left him, but still, he's here. He left me, but he's back.

I try to talk, to tell him to go. Never come back.

Others, too. My mother. My child. Very close. I hear them. I smell them. I can almost taste them.

I need them, need to see them, to touch them.

I strain, stretch for the light. There's no pain, now, but still, I can't move. I will, though. I have to.

I can see it, see them, just an arm's length away. If I reach for them, I can... I can...

"Mr McPherson? This is sister McCarthy, from Halstead Grange."

She's caught me on the way from back to Linn Mill from a meeting in Glasgow. I sit back in the rear seat of the car, driven by Jared. She has my full attention.

"Is this about Fern? Is there a problem?"

"No, sir, not a problem as such. But there has been a change."

"What's happened?" My heart sinks. Fern has been holding her own for almost five months now.

"Over the last couple of weeks or so we've been detecting raised levels of awareness. Miss Daniels is beginning to respond to stimuli. Maybe you've noticed some of this yourself."

"I thought I saw her fingers move the last time I was there, but I've seen her do that before. The nurses said it was just involuntary movement."

"On its own, yes. But we have other tests delivering similar results. Her pupils respond to light. She will move away from a pinprick. These are relatively new signs. They suggest she is making progress."

"She's coming round? Is that what you're saying?"

"Not exactly. The sedation we're giving her will ensure she doesn't regain consciousness, but Mr Trent considers it time to start reducing that medication and allow her to surface if she can."

If she can?

"Oh, I see. So, is that what you mean to do, then?"

"Only with your consent, sir. That's why I'm calling, to ask how you feel about us changing her treatment. Do we have your consent to reduce the sedation?"

"I'm not her next of kin. Her mother is."

"Yes, sir. But you are the one paying for her treatment."

"I'd prefer to consult her mother. Can you give me half an hour or so?"

What Happens in Vegas...

"Of course, Mr McPherson. That's not a problem. We'll expect to hear from you shortly, then."

"You will."

BY THE TIME I get back to the house, Archie has had his tea and Thomas has gone home. I find him with his grandma, watching television in the drawing room.

"Can I have a word?" I speak quietly into Poppy's ear so as not to alert Archie.

Poppy nods and follows me out into the foyer.

"I had a call today, from the hospital."

"Is Fern okay?" Her reaction is exactly the same as mine.

"Yes, but they want to reduce the sedation to see if she might be ready to wake up. Apparently they've been detecting signs that she may be more alert."

"Oh." Poppy clasps her hands together, tears in her eyes. "Could she... Do you think...?"

"I don't know. But I intend to go over there and see for myself. Are you coming?"

WE ARRIVE at Halstead Grange less than half an hour later. We decided to bring Archie, too.

The three of us, and a nurse, cluster round the bed. Is it my imagination, or is Fern looking just a little bit better? Is there a shade more colour in her cheeks?

"Sister McCarthy said something about tests," I say. "Light, and pinpricks."

"That's right," the nurse replies. Her name is Rachel, and we've seen a lot of her over the last few months. In fact, we must be on first-name terms with most of the staff by now, even the lady who comes in to vacuum the carpets. Rachel continues. "And her blood pressure has increased slightly. It's approaching normal now. She had a scan yesterday, one of our routine checks, and it showed distinct signs that more areas of her brain are functioning than when she arrived here." She checks the notes. "That's a seventeen percent improvement so far and gaining steadily."

"Does that mean she's better?" Archie demands. "Can she come home?"

"She's not better yet, but we think she might be improving," the nurse agrees. "We have a way to go yet, I think."

"Oh." Archie clambers onto the chair closest to Fern's shoulder. He kneels on the seat, leaning over her, his small hands cradling her jaw. "Mummy, wake up. You have to wake up and come home. You need to see Ollie, and Thomas. And, Mummy, I can swim now. And ride my bike without anyone holding on. Please, you have to come and live with us again." He stops, turns his tearful face to me. "Why won't she listen? I tell her, every time. Why won't she listen to me?"

"I—"

The platitude dies in my throat. Before my eyes, Fern lifts her hand. Just once, then it flops back to the duvet. But it was a definite movement, and much more than I've seen previously.

"Did you see that? Poppy?"

"I did."

"Me, too," the nurse adds, moving to the bed. "Let me just check her responses now." She peels Fern's eyelid back and flashes a torch at her pupil. "Okay, that's good." She scans the array of screens, more discreetly tucked away than those at the hospital in Stockport, but there all the same. "Blood pressure stable, heart rate slightly elevated…"

"Is that good?" I want to know.

"It's promising. I'm going to call Mr Trent. He'll be able to tell you more."

The consultant arrives within a few minutes, dressed as though he's just been called away from the golf course. He greets us cordially enough, then sets to examining all the notes

What Happens in Vegas...

and checking the various screens and monitors. At last, he turns his attention to his impatient audience.

"She's showing clear signs of being more alert. Nurse Manford tells me you all witnessed a distinct hand movement, made seemingly in response to her son."

"That's right. We all saw it."

"Has someone spoken to you about reducing the dosage of the sedative?"

I nod. "Yes. Sister McCarthy phoned me today."

"We haven't started to reduce the dose yet, but I believe we should. At once. Are you in agreement?"

"Yes," I say, then I turn to Poppy. "Are you?"

She nods wordlessly.

Mr Trent alters something on one of the notepads, then adjusts the drip. "It will take several hours for the reduction to take effect. You are welcome to wait, of course. We can even wheel a small bed in here, for the little lad. Or, if you prefer to go home, we'll phone the moment she starts to wake up. If she does."

"We're staying," Poppy announces. "I want to stay here."

"Me, too. And yes, a camp bed or something would be very welcome." I expect this will be a long night.

ARCHIE DRIFTS OFF TO sleep by about eleven in the evening, and we tuck him in the temporary bed which the staff have provided. I shall have to phone the school tomorrow. He'll be too wiped out, or too excited, to attend.

Poppy and I are seated on either side of Fern's bed, our eyes rarely leaving the still form lying between us. Poppy starts to nod,off and I suggest she climbs onto the bed with Fern. There's plenty of room. I might manage to doze off in the chair, which does at least have the reclining function. So much better than those in Stockport.

If anything happens, we'll know.

I'm woken by a tugging on my sleeve. I prise my eyes open. It's Archie.

"I need to wee," he says.

There's an en suite in the corner of the room. "Use that toilet," I say.

"It's dark…"

It isn't, not really. We left one lamp on, enough to find our way around. But Archie is only five, and in a strange environment. And he's probably scared stiff of what could be about to happen. We're all talking as though Fern will simply wake up, like the Disney princess in the fairy stories, and everyone will live happily ever after. But, this is real life, warts and all, and none of us really knows how it will end.

"Okay." I get to my feet and take his hand, lead him over to the small bathroom in the corner. I switch on the light for him. "Can you manage now?"

He nods and ambles inside, leaving the door open. He emerges a minute later, and I send him back to wash his hands. When he returns the second time, I beckon him to me.

"Do you want to sit on my knee?"

He nods sleepily, snuggles in, and we both fall asleep again.

I'm startled into wakefulness by a cough. I open my eyes. Poppy is still asleep, Archie, too.

But Fern is staring straight at me.

She coughs again, obviously struggling to breathe.

I hit the red button on the bed head then, Archie still in my arms, I sprint to the door.

"We need help in here." I glance up and down the corridor and would have yelled out again, but a nurse appears at a run.

"In there," I gesture through the door. "She's awake."

The night duty nurse, called Carol, hits the red button again to stop the wailing noise I've set off, then bends over Fern. Moments later, the breathing tube is out of her throat and Fern is taking her first, independent gasping breaths.

"It's up to her now," Carol mutters. "If she can't manage, I'll have to sedate her again and replace it."

"Breathe, baby. Breathe for yourself. You can do this." Poppy grasps Fern's hand and squeezes it. "Come back to us, love. We're all here, waiting for you."

"Mummy…" Archie is starting to cry. I hug him closer.

"It's okay, little man. She's going to be all right?

Is she? Christ, I hope so. And have I done the right thing, letting her little boy be here to see this?

I slump back into my chair and let Poppy do the talking for all of us.

Carol, meanwhile, is on the phone to Sister McCarthy, the most senior person on duty. "Can you come to room eleven please? Miss Daniels appears to be regaining consciousness." A pause. "Yes, I've removed it." Another pause. "No, she's making an effort, but struggling." She ends the call. "Sister is on her way, and Mr Trent has been called."

The reinforcements arrive within fifteen minutes. I can only assume the consultant lives on the premises. Carol ushers the three of us from the room.

"Let Mr Trent take care of her for now. I'm sure you all could do with a nice cup of tea. We have a guests' sitting room, just through here…"

The guest facilities run to a comfortable lounge and a tiny kitchen, where bread, butter, and a toaster are supplied as well as teabags, milk, and coffee.

"I can offer you something more substantial in a couple of hours, when the kitchen staff start work," Carol says. "Until then…"

"This is fine. Thank you." Poppy drops four slices into the toaster. Her hands are still shaking.

I settle Archie in one of the chairs near the small table and pour him a glass of milk. His eyes are red, glistening, and his lips are quivering.

Am I such a rubbish father, to expose him to all of this?

I pull myself up short. I'm not his father at all. I'm just a bloke, doing his best to put one foot in front of the other, with no idea what the end destination is or the best route to get there.

I sit next to the boy and wait for news, and my toast.

An hour passes. I wander out into the corridor a couple of times, to find the door to Fern's room firmly closed. My instinct is that if something was wrong they would tell us, so I leave them to get on with their tests and their measuring and their examinations.

"When can we see her?" Archie demands, for what must be the hundredth time.

"Soon," Poppy assures him, though she meets my gaze and shrugs.

We decide to keep him with us today, so I phone the school to let them know. The staff are aware of our situation and send their best wishes.

Sally phones, Harry, too. Everyone is on tenterhooks, just waiting, needing to know and dreading the news when it finally comes.

I GASP, desperate for air. My lungs are tight, I can't fill them, or empty them.

I start to panic, and a mask is suddenly over my face.

Someone is speaking to me, a woman's voice, soft, concerned. She tells me to calm down, and to breathe slowly.

I try, but it's hard. My body doesn't work, won't do as I want.

"Breathe in, one, two. Now out, one, two. In, one two, out one two..." The rhythmic chant penetrates the fog of despair and panic. I obey her, manage to breathe to her tune. Each new breath is easier than the last one. Manage to fill my lungs, then exhale slowly, under control.

"There. She's breathing on her own."

The mask is removed.

I open my eyes, then slam them shut again. The light is too bright, too dazzling.

There's a sound, a mewling. I realise that it is me.

"Can you tell me your name?"

This time it is a man who speaks. He is asking questions. I need to think, to concentrate. I need to remember...

"Can you tell me your name?" he asks again.

Can I? I should know. I'm sure this is something I should know. I shake my head, the effort of remembering just too great.

"Okay. Get some more rest for now. We can talk later."

Grateful, I drift back to sleep.

"GOOD NEWS." Mr Trent joins us in the sitting room. "Miss Daniels is breathing on her own, and without difficulty. The monitors indicate near normal levels of alertness, but she is very tired and has gone back to sleep."

"Sleep?" I ask. "Just sleep?"

"Yes. Just sleep. She'll wake up again in due course, but I should warn you, she's likely to be drowsy and probably a bit confused. Disoriented. The important thing is to keep her calm and allow her to catch up at her own pace. She's been away for...what has it been, almost five months?" He consults his notes. "Yes, so, we need to take things slow."

"Can we see her? Poppy asks.

"Of course, though as I said, she's sleeping now. A nurse will be with her round the clock, just until we know she's properly back with us. It might be best not to crowd her, just one at a time, for now."

"Me! I want to see her. Please, can I? Can I?" Archie is desperate to get back in there.

"He'll be very quiet," Poppy promises. "Won't you, Archie?"

He nods, fighting back tears again.

"Why don't you take Archie in, just for a quick peek? I'll wait here, and you can bring him back once he's satisfied himself that she's still there and okay."

"Are you sure?" Poppy asks. "Don't you want to be there, when she wakes up?"

"I'm pretty sure it won't be me she wants to see, at least not at first. She needs you, and Archie."

"I'll leave you for a while now, but I shall be back later to check on her. If you need anything, my staff are on hand. They can contact me." Mr Trent gathers up his papers and beams at us all. "This has been a very promising start. Very promising indeed. We have reasons to be optimistic." He gives us a general nod and bustles off about the rest of his business.

"What's optimistic?" Archie demands to know.

"He means your mummy is going to get well again, love." Poppy takes his hand. "Shall we go and see her?"

CHAPTER 21

There's still fuzz, but lighter now, a delicate mist rather than the deep, heavy, cloying fog of before. I purse my lips and blow. It disappears.

I lie still, aware of myself, of my body which doesn't feel entirely as though it belongs to me. I'm...stiff. It doesn't hurt to move, but my limbs are heavy. It takes effort, just as it takes effort to open my eyes.

So, I do neither. I lie still, just...being.

There are voices occasionally. Women. They speak softly, in whispers, as though they don't want to wake me. They don't know that I'm here, with them. Listening.

"How old is her little boy?" one of the voices asks.

"Just gone five," comes the reply.

I know that voice. I struggle to remember. It's important. She knows about my little boy. She can tell me if he's all right. Where is he?

"What? Did you hear that?" The familiar voice is very close to me now, but still I don't open my eyes.

"She tried to speak," says the other one. "I didn't catch what she said."

Where is he?

"She's asking where he is. Who does she mean?"

"Archie. I bet she means Archie."

Yes. Archie... I open my eyes.

A woman is there. I recognise her, very nearly. Her eyes are the same, the same green as mine. But her face is thinner, and she wears a scarf around her head. She never wore a scarf before. She liked to show off her hair...

"Fern? Can you see me?"

I nod, slowly.

"Do you know who I am?"

"Yes."

No.

"We've been so worried..."

I lower my eyelids again. It's easier to think in the dark.

"Let's try to sit her up and see if she wants a few sips of water." It's the other voice now, sharper, more...purposeful.

Gentle hands are behind my shoulders, easing me forward, propping me in place. There's a glass, by my lips. I have to think for a moment, but then I remember how to drink from it, and the cool water is delicious. I clutch at the wrist of the person closest to me, an anchor in a world suddenly beyond my understanding.

"I'll stay here, you go and fetch her little boy."

Archie? Is he here?

"Mummy! *Mummy...*"

Everything jolts. Hands grip my face, and the familiar, unforgettable aroma of my son fills my nostrils—a heady blend of sweat, soap, and the blackcurrant drinks he loves.

"Is she awake? Mummy?"

I raise my eyelids again, and my lips curl into a smile. "Archie...?"

"Mummy! My mummy..." He flings himself across me, his little arms around my neck. And he's sobbing.

So I cry, too.

"Archie, love, you're upsetting her. The doctor said—"

What Happens in Vegas...

I shake my head and wrap my arms around his small, shaking body. I won't ever let go of him again. Never.

"Let them be. Let them get it out." The other female voice is calm, as ever. "You and me, we'll go sit over here, by the window."

I cling to my son and allow my eyelids to drop. Again.

THE LIGHT IS NOT AS bright when I next open my eyes, or maybe I'm getting used to it. I'm still propped upright, better able to see around the room.

I'm thirsty.

"Ah, here she is again." It's the same voice I've been hearing, but now I can see that it is a nurse. She smiles at me and pours a glass of water as though she read my mind. "Just a few sips, to help soothe your throat..."

I gulp the cool liquid down. It's good, but I've soon had enough.

"Can I just check you over?"

The nurse seems to be asking my permission for something, but I don't know what to say. I nod. It seems to be sufficient.

Cool, competent fingers check my pulse. She listens to my breathing, notes my blood pressure, and checks the drip rigged up beside my bed.

I take the opportunity to glance around me, and I'm puzzled. I must be in a hospital, because there's a nurse here and she has medical equipment. But why? Am I ill?

I don't feel ill. I feel...tired. And confused.

And this room doesn't look much like a hospital. It's more like an ordinary bedroom, but nicer than mine at home. There are pictures on the walls, and pretty curtains. They're fluttering, so I assume the window must be open.

There's a soft tap on the door. The woman in the scarf enters.

"Oh. She's awake again."

"Aye, she is." The nurse packs her things onto a trolley and moves away from the bed to make room for the other woman. "You two just have a nice little chat now."

The woman sits and takes my hand. It feels natural and right, so I let her. I know I should recognise her. Her features are familiar, but different, not quite as I remember...

Mum!

It hits me with the force of a sledgehammer. I stare at her as realisation dawns. She's thinner. A lot thinner, And the scarf...

It all floods back. I cry out, stunned that I could have forgotten, even for a moment.

"Are you...? How are you? The cancer?"

She pats my hand. "Much better now, love. It's been rough, but I'm through the worst."

"The treatment? The...the chemo...?"

"All done. I had the last cycle nearly two months ago. Just waiting for my hair to grow back now." She pats the scarf.

I blink, not comprehending. *Two months ago? How is that even possible?*

"I don't understand..."

"I know that. You've been... You had an accident. Do you remember that?"

I shake my head.

"You were hit by a car, picking Archie up from school. A hit-and-run."

"Hit-and-run," I repeat, stupidly, trying to take all of this in.

"Yes. Drunk, the driver was. They caught him, mind."

"Oh, But how...?"

"You had a nasty bang on your head. Out cold, you were. Broken legs, too, and some internal bleeding. It was touch and go for a while."

"Broken legs?" I lift each in turn under the light duvet. "My legs aren't broken."

"Not now, but they were. The fractures have healed up, but you were in plaster for weeks."

Weeks? I feel sick.

The nurse returns to my bedside. "It's a lot to take in, all at once. Don't you fret, lass."

"Oh dear, I'm sorry. I shouldn't have blurted everything out like that." My mum looks almost as stricken as I feel.

"How...how long have I been here?"

"Here at Halstead Grange? About four months," the nurse replies. "You were a few weeks in the hospital in Stockport as well. It's been almost five months since your accident."

"But I don't remember anything. Nothing at all."

The nurse offers me a reassuring smile. "That's not uncommon in cases like yours. Tell me, love, what's the last thing you can recall?"

I think. Hard. It's difficult to pin down any specific memories, to select what might be relevant.

"Can you remember anything about the last time you picked Archie up from school?" my mother prompts.

I probe around, sifting memories, seeking something, anything to make sense. "I went to the school, I think. I must have done. I always go to pick up Archie at three o'clock. It was the same most days, but this time we were in a hurry. There was somewhere we were supposed to go after school. I can't remember where. Or why that was. We walked along the road towards the car. Then, nothing."

"Probably just as well," my mum observes. "There were witnesses, though, and they said you shoved Archie out of the way, so you must have seen it coming."

"He was with me?"

"Aye, he was. But he wasn't seriously hurt. Spent a night in hospital for observation, that's all."

"He could have been killed. We could both have been killed." Stunned, I lie back and stare at the ceiling, my thoughts whirling as the shock of what has happened starts to hit home.

"But you weren't killed," my mum insists. "Archie's fine, and you're going to be."

Five months. I've been in a coma for five fucking months.

"Now, we just need to concentrate on getting you well."

Five months gone. Lost. Just...not there. The world carried on without me, for five whole months.

"We need to get you back on your feet, and home. With us."

Holy shit, I need to go back to sleep. I wish I'd never woken up.

THE NEXT TIME I open my eyes the artificial lights are on in my room, and it is dark outside. The nurse is seated beside my bed, but no one else is here.

She smiles at me and sets aside the magazine she had been reading. "Good evening, Miss Daniels. How do you feel?"

"Fern," I mumble. "My name is Fern."

"Would you like a drink, Fern? More water, or perhaps a cup of tea?"

My mouth waters. "Tea would be nice. Did my mum leave?"

"She had to nip home to collect some things. A change of clothes, some cartons of juice for the little lad. She won't be long."

"I see. Will I...will I be able to see Archie again?"

"Of course. He's in the guest lounge, with his uncle. I'll tell them you're awake."

"His uncle? Archie doesn't have...he has no uncle. We have no other family, it's just me and my mum and him."

The nurse frowns. "Oh, well, maybe I got it wrong, then. Archie calls him uncle, so I assumed... I'll tell Mr McPherson that you're asking to see Archie."

Mr McPherson. I know that name...

"Is he...who is Mr McPherson? Why is he here?"

"I'm not sure I can answer those questions, Fern. You'll have to ask him. All I can tell you is that Mr McPherson has visited almost every day, usually bringing Mrs Daniels or Archie with him, but not always. And he's paying for your treatment here."

"Paying for my treatment? Why would he do that?"

"I'm afraid I have no idea. Shall I ask him to come in?"

I shake my head. I need to think, to work out who this man is and what I need to say to him.

"Can I just see Archie, for now?"

The nurse nods. "I'll go fetch him. And your tea."

She returns after a few minutes carrying a tray. There's a small teapot and a jug of milk on the tray. Behind her, Archie trots along carrying a cup and saucer.

It's just the two of them.

"Archie, pop the cup on the bedside cabinet, please."

He rushes to do as the nurse asked him, then clambers onto the chair she vacated a few minutes ago. From there, he launches himself onto the bed.

"Is he allowed...?" I ask.

The nurse grins at him. "We've never managed to stop him yet." She pours my tea and sets the cup close, where I can reach it. "You two have a nice chat. I'll go sit over there. Just yell out if you need anything. My name's Carol, by the way."

"Thank you, Carol."

At first, it's enough to just stare at Archie, to take him in, every detail. He's grown, and he feels heavier, sturdier somehow. I try to count the months in my head...

"You had a birthday." And I missed it.

He nods. "I got a dog. And we went to see Manchester United. I got de Gea's autograph."

"A...a dog?"

He nods. "Ollie. He's quite big, and sort of black and brown. Uncle Cal got Tara. That's Ollie's mum. He felt sorry for her and took her home as well."

"You got a dog? For your birthday?" I remember talking about this, about letting him have a puppy. But we couldn't, not yet. Because…because…" There was a reason, but I can't call it to mind now.

"Uncle Cal said it would be all right, because he's looking after Grandma so you don't have to. And the nurse."

"Nurse? You mean, the nurse here?"

He shakes his head. "No, the nurse at home. She came to look after Grandma when she was poorly. But she's not poorly anymore so the nurse stopped coming."

"I see." I try to piece something together from all of this. The main gist seems to be that my son now has a dog, apparently, and Mum isn't poorly anymore. And Uncle Cal figures prominently in all of this.

"Tell me about Uncle Cal."

Cal? Cal? I should know who that is… It's there, on the very edge of my memory, peeping around the corner.

"He came to the hospital, that first day. I didn't know who he was, but he said he was your friend. He had his friend with him, Uncle Harry. We played Snakes and Ladders. Uncle Cal and Grandma were arguing, then they stopped. I wanted to come and see you, but they wouldn't let me because you were too poorly. I was scared, but Uncle Cal got them to let me in. We came to see you with all the tubes and wires and everything."

"Oh. That must have been frightening. I'm sorry you had to see that."

He shakes his head. "The lady doctor told me all about it before, so I knew. And Uncle Cal held on to me." He adopts an exasperated expression I recall vividly. "And, Mummy, remember, I was almost five, not a baby."

"I know that, but even so…"

"Then we left the hospital, but we didn't go home. We came here."

"Here?" I'm bewildered. We're still at the hospital, surely…?

Archie prattles on. "To Uncle Cal's house. In Scotland. It's a holiday, but it's gone on a long time. Until you're better, he said. I'm glad you're better, but I don't want to go home just yet."

I can think of nothing to say, so I simply hug him.

PATIENCE.

Give her time.

I repeat these wise words to myself, but nothing helps. Every instinct screams at me to march in there and tell her how things are going to be. That she needs me, and I'm going to be there for her. For Archie, and for Poppy, come to that.

It's been over twenty-four hours since Fern first opened her eyes and looked right at me. Until now, she's drifted in and out of sleep. I know she has trouble remembering, but she did recognise Archie, and Poppy. She asked to see them.

She hasn't asked for me, but that won't stop me for much longer. She can't hide away from me, not this time.

There's a movement outside in the corridor. I glance up as Poppy enters, carrying two bags. She sets them down, then goes to the kitchenette to fix the pair of us a coffee.

"I assume Archie is in with her," she calls over her shoulder.

"Yes. Carol came for him about an hour ago."

"Have you been in yet?"

"No."

She comes back into the lounge with two mugs. "You parted on bad terms, you and Fern. She won't expect you to be here. She may not ask for you, so you'll have to be a bit pushy."

I can do pushy, but I don't want to upset her, or do anything to cause a relapse. But Poppy is right, the longer this goes on, the more difficult it becomes. By now, Fern must be starting to piece things together, and she'll need explanations.

I hope.

If she's ready to listen.

"Do you mind looking after Archie for a while?"

"Of course not. I brought some books, and his Nintendo thing."

She leaves her coffee here, but I take mine with me. I may be glad of the sustenance.

The door to Fern's room is closed, and there is no sound of voices from inside.

"Should we knock?" Poppy asks me.

I nod and tap on the panel. It's answered a moment later by Carol.

"They're both asleep," she says, gesturing to the bed where Archie is curled up into his mother's side.

"It seems a shame to wake them," Poppy whispers.

"Yes. Shall we just pull up a couple of chairs and wait?"

"I'll go get my coffee."

Carol goes off to take her break since we are both here with Fern and can sound the alarm if anything goes wrong. Poppy settles in with a book, and I have some work to get on with, so I fire up my laptop. The next couple of hours pass in relative silence, broken only by the sound of keys tapping, gentle breathing, and the turning of pages.

"Mum?"

We both turn, hearing Fern's voice. Poppy is closer, so Fern's gaze falls on her first. I am seated by the window, and Fern doesn't realise I'm there until I stand and move towards her.

"You! What are you doing here?"

Not especially encouraging, but I decide to take it as a good sign that she actually recognises me.

"I'm here because I've been worried about you."

"Why?" she demands.

"Because you've been very ill."

"No. Why would *you* care about *me*?"

Archie stirs He sits up, rubbing his eyes. I'm not prepared to have this conversation in front of him. Poppy either, for that matter.

"Poppy, could you and Archie give us a few minutes, please?"

"Of course. Come on, you." She holds out her hand to Archie. "We can play with your game thing in the lounge."

"But I want to stay with Mummy and Uncle Cal."

"We won't be long," I tell him, beckoning him to come to me. He does, and I scoop him from the bed. He links his arms around my neck.

"I told Mummy about Ollie. I think she's cross. You won't let her take him away, will you?"

"It'll all be all right, squirt," I tell him. "You go with Grandma so that me and your mummy can have a talk."

"You'll tell her I've been good, won't you?"

"Of course." I set him on his feet. "You're not to worry about anything, do you hear. And definitely not about Ollie."

He gives me a sad little smile, so I hug him, hard. He's come through a lot these last few months with barely a word of complaint.

"Your mummy and me will make it all okay."

He seems to accept that and trots of with Poppy. I wait until the door shuts behind them, then I perch on the edge of the bed.

"Are you really cross? About the dog, I mean?"

She regards me for several seconds, then slowly shakes her head. "I would have bought him one. I was going to."

"I know. Poppy told me."

She narrows her eyes at me. "You've been talking to my mum?"

"Yes. A lot, as it happens."

"I suppose you managed to charm her, and Archie. Just like you always do."

"We've been getting on okay, if that's what you mean."

"But Archie thinks you're his uncle. Not his father."

"That's right. He does."

"Still lying to people then? Still denying what you are? What you did?"

"Not exactly. It was Poppy's idea. She felt it should be up to you to tell Archie who his father is, not me. I respected that. It makes no difference. I still love him as though he were my own."

She shakes her head, but I notice she doesn't contradict me, try to point out that, at least as far as she's aware, he *is* my own. "No. It would never work. I decided, years ago, that he was better off without you in his life. That hasn't changed. I still—"

"Everything has changed, Fern." I keep my tone low, but not soft. She needs to hear this, needs to take it in, because I'm going nowhere. "Archie and I have got to know one another. He has two parents now."

She shakes her head and glares at me. "What do you know about being a parent, lording it in your mansion in Scotland?"

"I confess I've been on a steep learning curve, but we're getting by. Poppy helps."

"My mother loathes you nearly as much as I do. She knows what you did."

I suppress a grin. "Not quite all of what I did. She doesn't know about the days you spent at my house. She doesn't know that I spanked you, and fucked you, and put plugs in your arse. You didn't share those little snippets with her."

She flushes and glares at me. "That was a mistake. I should never... You...you kidnapped me."

"You chose to stay. And you chose to leave."

"Exactly. It's over between us. That was what you wanted, a clean break. I signed your agreement..."

"I tore it up."

She gapes at me. "Why? Why the fuck would you do that?"

"I changed my mind."

"You...? You changed you mind? When? Why?"

"Right after you left. As for why, that's simple. I love you."

She shakes her head again. "No, you don't. You don't even like me."

I shrug. "You drive me crazy, make me want to tear my hair out, but that doesn't mean I don't like you. Or love you."

"You think I'm a liar, trying to trap you."

I lean forward to bring my face close to hers, capture her gaze and hold it. "I know you're not out to trap me. The fact that you kept quiet about Archie proves that. And as for being a liar, well, that's more complicated. But understand this, if you can make any sense of it, because I can't. I wasn't in Las Vegas. I never married you there, then walked out. I told you when you were in my office at Linn Mill, I would never have done that. If I'd married you, it would have been for keeps and I'd have considered myself a lucky man. That's not how it worked out. But I know you well enough by now to believe that *something* happened in Vegas, and that you believe every word of what you're saying. What's more, you have compelling evidence to back up your version, enough to convince any court of law. Even the DNA evidence is on your side. You can convince anyone, except me, but only because I *know* I wasn't there. I've still to unravel how that could all be true, but that's where I am with this whole bloody clusterfuck right now."

She glares at me, her mouth working. She's trying to come up with a response. I'm dying to hear it.

"Grandma, did Uncle Cal say a naughty word?"

We both turn. Archie, Poppy, and Carol are framed in the doorway, varying degrees of astonishment plastered across their faces.

CHAPTER 22

Carol breaks the silence.

"We heard raised voices. Miss Daniels is to be kept calm. Mr Trent was most specific."

Cal rakes his fingers through his hair. "I'm sorry. I'll go."

It was me doing the shouting, not him. But I want him to leave. I need more time to think, to re-evaluate. To try to make sense of what he just said to me.

"Uncle Cal...?" Archie is close to tears again.

I want nothing more than to go to him, but my legs feel like lead.

"It's okay, squirt. I'm sorry about the naughty words." Caleb drops to his haunches in front of Archie, who moves into his arms for a hug.

It's clear to me that they've been doing a lot of hugging. I'm not at all sure how I feel about that.

"Archie, I—"

"Can I keep Ollie? Please?"

I nod. "Of course."

"Ollie will be wanting a walk by now. Tara, too. Why don't you two go and see to them while I keep Fern company?" My mum pats Caleb's arm by way of reassurance, then bends to kiss the top of Archie's head. "Go on, off you go."

What Happens in Vegas...

Caleb seems to be in agreement. "Good idea. I'll send Harry with the car later, to pick you up." He stands, lifting Archie with him. "Come on, you, and I'll explain to you how it is that grown-ups get to say naughty words occasionally and you have to forgive them." He turns in the doorway. "I'll see you soon, Fern."

Carol insists upon running through her checks once more as soon as Caleb and Archie have left and repeats her admonishments regarding my getting 'agitated'.

"I know it's difficult, and everything must seem so strange, but you really do have to stay calm, my dear." She replaces her stethoscope in its plastic case. "Tension will hinder your recovery, prevent you from remembering..."

I don't know what to say, I certainly can't promise to remain calm around Caleb McPherson.

"It's all very complicated," my mum settles herself in the chair close to me, "but I'm sure it will all work out."

I can't believe what I'm hearing. On what planet could this possibly 'work out'?

"I don't want him here." On this, at least, I am certain. "I don't want him around Archie. He...he's taken advantage because I'm injured."

My mum shakes her head. "No, it's not like that. But I can see why you would think it. I did, myself, at first."

"It's obvious. How can you not see it? He wants to take Archie from me. I'm not having that. I'll fight him if I have to."

Carol opens her mouth, doubtless ready to issue another homily on the virtues of keeping calm, but my mum forestalls her. "Let me explain some things to you, sweetheart. You need to understand how it was back then, right after the accident."

I scowl, but if my mum wants to say something, I've learned it's generally best to let her get it out. I nod, though with little conviction that anything she can say will soften my attitude towards Caleb McPherson.

She waits until Carol has completed her checks.

"Is everything all right, dear?" my mother asks the nurse.

"It seems to be, but—"

"Excellent. In that case, you can maybe take a break while I have a chat with my daughter."

"I think it's best if I—"

"We can call you if we need you. I expect you'll be close by?"

"Hrumph." Carol is clearly reluctant to leave me again, but my mum offers one of her sweetest 'don't mess with me' smiles. I've never really managed to emulate them myself, but I've seen those innocent little smiles bring grown men to their knees. My father was always a sucker for it. Carol has no chance.

"Very well. I shall be back in an hour. Call me if you need anything."

"We shall, dear. We surely shall." The smile never wavers until the door closes behind the nurse. Then, she turns to me. "I truly believe I would not be here talking to you today, if it weren't for Caleb McPherson."

I eye her warily. "Where would you be, then?"

"Back in hospital, the cancer in full flow. Or more probably dead. And I don't want to even think about what might have happened to Archie if Cal hadn't stepped in when he did."

I gape at her. "What are you talking about?"

"Think about it, love. Five months ago, I'd just had surgery and was still feeling like death warmed up after the first round of chemo. I was in a right state but managing to get through because I had you to rely on. Then two policewomen came to the door. They told me you'd been mown down by some drunk, you and Archie. I was still in shock when they drove me to the hospital, but they told me I needed to come straight away. You weren't…you weren't expected to survive the night."

There are tears in her eyes, but she manages to continue.

"You were in such a bad way. Your face, all bandaged, and your legs broken. There was talk of spinal injuries at first. And you were unconscious and showing no signs of coming round.

Those first few hours were awful. Terrifying. I sat there, willing you to fight, not to give up. Not to leave us. The X-rays came back. Your spine was all right, but the head trauma was life-threatening. They sent you off to the Intensive Care Unit where you were deeply sedated. So, I sat with you up there while they pushed tubes in everywhere and hooked you up to machines to keep you alive. I know that they knew what they were doing, but still... I have never been so scared in my life. Never felt so helpless..."

"Mum, I never realised..."

She waves her hand, clearly not yet finished.

"A nurse from the children's ward came up to ask if I could find a few minutes to come visit Archie. He was staying with them overnight, just for observation, but had become very distressed. He saw everything, you know. He sat with you, in the road, until the ambulance arrived."

"Oh God..."

"I didn't want to leave you, but I had to go to him. I thought, if I could get him off to sleep I could come back up and sit with you. Anyway, I was so exhausted myself that I fell asleep in the chair next to him. I woke up the next morning, when Cal came into the room. He brought breakfast for the pair of us, a bacon roll and coffee for me, juice and a sandwich for Archie."

"But what was he doing there? How did he know...?"

"He had word of the hit-and-run the previous evening, not long after it happened, I gather. I don't know how, he never said. But he got the same information I had, that you were badly injured and might not survive. He flew down from Scotland by helicopter because it was the quickest way to get to Stockport from Edinburgh. It was Cal who was at your side all through that first night."

I can only stare at her, bewildered. "I don't understand. Why would he do that?"

My mum shrugs. "It seems to me that he loves you. At least, I think that now. I wasn't so sure then. I didn't trust him, because of all that you'd told me, and I thought he might want to lay claim to Archie. I wasn't having that. I told him as much. And I told him what he could do with his bacon roll, too, though I confess I did eat it after he left."

"But he ended up taking Archie to Scotland anyway?"

"The hospital needed to discharge him. He wasn't really hurt in the accident, just shaken up. He'd be better off at home. The trouble was my illness. The staff in the children's unit could see that I was ill, and they were reluctant to let me have care of him, especially as I was only at the start of my treatment and things were going to get a lot worse before they got better. Even before Cal showed up there was talk of a foster home."

"A foster home? They would have put him in care?"

She nods. "Just temporarily, they said. But I wasn't having that. So, I decided to cancel the rest of my treatment so that I could look after him."

"Oh, no. Mum, you didn't..." I grope for her hand. "I need you to be well. Please, tell me you had the treatment."

"Cal's response to that suggestion was much the same as yours. He said that you and Archie needed me, would need me in the future, so I had to get well. But he also agreed that the right and proper person to take care of Archie was me. Cal might be his biological father—oh, yes, he had the DNA results to prove it—but he was still a stranger to Archie. He convinced me that I could take care of my grandson and complete my treatment, if I would let him help me."

"Help you?" I am totally mystified now. "What do you mean, help you?"

"He helped me by taking both of us, me and Archie, back to Scotland with him. He has a lovely big house there..."

Don't I know it?

"There's a lady who does the cooking, and any number of cleaners and such like who do all the housework. All I had to do was concentrate on Archie and myself. And on getting better. Cal arranged for my treatment to be done in Edinburgh

What Happens in Vegas...

and hired a nurse to look after me on the bad days. He also hired a part-time nanny, but me and Cal have managed mostly between us. He does the school run. I keep an eye on Archie after school. On my bad days, the nanny steps in, or Sally, the housekeeper. Not that I have so many bad days anymore. We let the nanny go a couple of weeks ago, and the nurse."

I can only stare. This is a picture of Caleb McPherson I just cannot get my head around. A man who would open his pristine, stately home to a sick woman he barely knows and a small boy. Allow his graceful, elegant hallways to be smeared with sticky fingers, his ordered existence disrupted by the vagaries of an illness as unpredictable as he apparently is.

And...the school run?

"Archie goes to school? In Scotland?"

"It has been five months, love. We both thought it best. It's a nice school, in the village."

"I suppose I should be glad he didn't pack him off to boarding school."

"I don't think that ever occurred to him. If it did, he never mentioned it."

"But Scotland is so far away..." I am suddenly struck by a sense of not being in control. Of bitter, cloying loneliness. My son, my family, are miles away, and I'm stuck here, in a hospital bed, useless, my life passing by while they just get on with things without me. I know how wealthy Cal is, the sort of life he can offer Archie. And I've seen for myself that Archie trusts him, has learned to turn to him when he's unhappy or scared.

That should be me!

I would have fought tooth and nail to keep Caleb McPherson out of Archie's life, but how can I compete now? He's become some sort of hybrid of Superman and Mother Teresa.

I lean back against my pillows and let all of what she has said sink in. I try to reconcile the Caleb I know with the one described to me by my mother, the man who stepped in and prevented further tragedy from engulfing my family. I should be grateful, but my overwhelming reaction is one of resentment.

He's taken over my life. He just sauntered in and threw money at my problems, made them go away. The people who matter to me are his now. As if that bloody agreement wasn't enough...

Something occurs to me, something else doesn't make sense. When Caleb left, there was some talk of walking the dogs. But the last time I looked Stockport was a four-hour drive from Edinburgh.

"Where did they say they were going? Home, was it? To walk their dogs?"

"Yes, dear."

"How long will it take them to get home?"

"Not long. Twenty minutes or so."

The penny finally drops. "I'm in Scotland, too?"

"Yes. None of us wanted to leave you behind, but we had to get things sorted out here. My treatment, settling Archie down after all the trauma he'd seen. It was too far to visit often, though I know Caleb did drop in a few times while you were still at Stepping Hill, and he took Archie to see you on his birthday, although he had the helicopter again for that. But it was just too far. Not practical. Cal was worried that Archie might start to forget about you, especially as he settled in so quickly here. So, as soon as your condition was stable enough for you to be moved, he had you transferred to this hospital. It really is a lovely place, and they've taken absolutely excellent care of you."

"A private hospital. And that's why he's paying the fees."

"They're very good here. I know we wouldn't normally go private, but..." She shrugs by way of an apology. "It meant me and Archie could visit whenever we want, and I'm sure, from what the staff here tell us, that having people come and talk to you has helped you to come round, so it was worth it." She

What Happens in Vegas...

pauses, then, "Caleb's family use this place a lot, I gather. He was actually born here."

I struggle to take in this latest bombshell. Not only has he taken control of my family, but of me, too. I quell the softer voice within which points out that he could have left me behind. He could have taken my son so easily, and there would have been nothing I could do, lying unconscious in hospital. My mother, too, would have tried to put up a fight, but deep down I know she would have failed. He would have hired better lawyers. And, he had the DNA evidence. Christ only knows how and when he got that, but it would have swung matters his way.

But he didn't do any of that. He managed to keep all of us together. I just need to get well enough to leave hospital and...

"Mum, have they said how much longer I'll need to be here?"

She shakes her head. "The consultant, Mr Trent, was here when you first started to come round, but I don't think he's been since. I've not seen him."

"I want to talk to him. Can you call for Carol and we'll find out when his next visit will be?"

"Of course, dear." She presses the bell to summon the nurse back.

IN PRIVATE MEDICINE, it seems my wish is their command. Less than an hour after I said I'd like to speak to him, the auspicious Mr Trent arrives. He is all smiles, wearing a three-piece suit, which will have cost all of a thousand pounds, and an even more valuable Rolex watch. Tending to the wealthy clearly pays well.

"How nice to meet you properly at last, Miss Daniels. Tell me, how are you feeling just now?"

He somehow manages to keep his attention on me whilst at the same time skimming over the notes and records kept by the staff. He checks my pulse himself, peers into my eyes with his little flashlight, and listens to my breathing.

"No fluid on the lungs. That's good. Have you experienced any headaches? Any tingling in your limbs?"

"No," I reply.

"Have you been out of bed yet? Used the toilet?"

"Um, no. All the tubes…"

"Quite. I shall ask the nursing staff to remove the catheter and we shall see how you go on. And the feeding tube. I see you've managed some liquids."

"Just water. And a cup of tea."

"Excellent. We need to be sure your digestive system is working properly. And, of course, you will require physiotherapy for your legs."

"My legs? But I thought they were fixed."

"Fixed, yes. But you had a double fracture of the left tibia and fibula, and a compound fracture of the right femur. The X-rays suggest all is well now, the bones have knitted nicely, and the legs are stable, but in any patient recovering from such injuries there would be a prolonged period of physiotherapy to enable full mobility to be regained. I can arrange for this to be started at once, but you should expect several weeks of work before you are able to walk independently."

"But that's no good. I need to go home. I have a little boy, and—"

"I'm sorry, Miss Daniels, but there is no way of making your recovery any speedier. Now that you have regained consciousness, we can make a start on the rest, so you have made a massive leap forward. But you will require the physio, and your body will mend at its own pace. We also need to assess the extent of any residual head trauma and if this is likely to impact on your cognitive abilities. So far, according to the reports from the nursing staff, there is no sign of such impairment, but we should run some tests to be quite certain. Sometimes there are other effects following a blow to the head and prolonged coma

—memory loss, disorientation, mood and personality changes. Again, there are no obvious early signs, but we must be sure."

I resign myself to what I cannot change. "How long will I need to be here for?"

"I can arrange for the tests over the next few days. But the physio will be a long-term prospect. That said, there's no reason why you should not complete the treatment as an out-patient, though I should warn you, at first you will find you need to use a wheelchair, then you will graduate to crutches before finally being independently mobile. But you *will* get there."

I cheer up at the mention of out-patients, but my spirits drop when he tells me I'll be in a wheelchair.

Does this nightmare never end?

CHAPTER 23

Carol meets me at the main entrance to Halstead Grange, barring my way.

"I'm sorry, Mr McPherson, but I distinctly heard Miss Daniels tell her mother that she didn't want you to visit her. She doesn't want to see you, sir."

I pause, manage to keep a lid on my irritation. "I appreciate that yesterday didn't go as well as I hoped, but—"

"I can't allow you to come in. I'm sorry."

"Are those Mr Trent's instructions?" I demand to know.

"No, not exactly. But we have a general policy that patients should select which visitors they wish to see, so—"

"If Mr Trent thinks I am going to continue paying his not inconsiderable fees, he needs to get down here right now and explain to me why I cannot come in and see my wife."

"Mr Trent isn't available. He—"

"Right. Now," I repeat. "I'll wait in my car."

The dark-burgundy Rolls-Royce glides through the main gates eleven minutes after I issued my ultimatum, proof if it were needed that money talks. I exit my car and approach the doctor.

"Ah, Mr McPherson, thank you so much for waiting." His usual polite demeanour not dented in the slightest, he offers

What Happens in Vegas...

me his hand, so I take it and we shake. "I gather there has been some sort of misunderstanding."

"Your staff appear to be of the opinion that I am banned from the premises. Is that the misunderstanding you mean?"

"Indeed." He eyes me with quiet calm. "Are you able to shed any light on why the nursing staff might arrive at that view, sir?"

"Fern and I had words yesterday. Not surprising, in the circumstances. But I know I can make matters right if I talk to her."

"What circumstances would those be, if you don't mind my asking?"

I do mind his asking, but I suppose he is owed some sort of explanation if I want him to overrule his staff and the hospital policy. "Fern and I are...separated. Her feelings towards me are somewhat conflicted, I imagine. But I do care for her. You must have seen as much in the time you've been treating her. I would never hurt her or upset her on purpose."

"The staff here have reason to be concerned. I have stressed the importance of allowing Miss Daniels to return to us at her own pace, to avoid any form of agitation. I cannot allow you to provoke or upset your wife. This would undo all the work we have done, all that she has achieved over the last couple of days. I must put my patient first, despite your remarks regarding the continued payment of our fees. I do hope you understand."

"Of course, but you need to understand that—"

"I visited Miss Daniels yesterday evening. We discussed her future treatment. I gather she is anxious to leave hospital, which is to be understood. But we will require further tests before that can happen. We must be quite certain what, if any, long-term effects she will have to contend with. And she will need intensive physiotherapy in order to regain full mobility in her legs. At no time during our discussion did she express the view that she did not wish to see you."

"Oh. I see. Well, then..."

"Perhaps if we both go in to see her now, sir, and she will say for herself what she wishes to do. If she is adamant that she does not wish you to be there, I will have no choice but to ask you to leave. My patient comes first."

Nothing will be gained right now by issuing further threats, and I can't help but respect his concern for Fern's welfare and her wishes. I'll cross any future bridges when I come to them.

"Thank you. I do understand that. So, shall we go in?"

I follow Mr Trent up the steps and into the main entrance. Carol glowers at me from the nurses' station but makes no further attempt to intervene. We troop along the corridor and pause outside Fern's door. Mr Trent knocks softly.

"Come in."

At the summons from within, he opens the door and steps inside. I go in with him.

Mr Trent starts cheerily enough. "Ah, good morning, Miss Daniels. I found Mr McPherson in the entrance. So, how are you feeling this morning?"

"I'm...fine. I think."

"Good, good." He perches on the edge of the bed and gestures for me to be seated in the chair. "How did you sleep?"

"Like a log."

"I see the catheter and feeding tube have been removed." He smiles at her. "You're entirely independent again, Miss Daniels."

"I don't feel independent. I still can't get out of bed."

"It will come. Have you eaten anything?"

She shakes her head. "I'm not hungry."

"It will take a while for your normal appetite to return, but if there is anything you especially fancy to eat, just say so and we shall endeavour to provide it."

"Could we bring food from Linn Mill?" I ask. "Fern particularly likes my housekeeper's cooking."

Her eyes swivel in my direction for the first time, but she says nothing.

"I don't see why not. Whatever Miss Daniels fancies. And as for getting out of bed, the sooner you do manage that, the better. You will need to use the toilet, and although we can make do with bed pans for a while, I prefer you to be mobile if we can manage it. I shall ask the nursing staff to assist you to the toilet if that's all right with you. And if you'd like to get out of bed and sit in the chair during the day, I see no problem with that either."

Fern is looking much happier suddenly. "Thank you, Doctor."

"I mentioned a wheelchair when I called yesterday."

"I don't think I—"

"I know, I know. But it would only be a temporary measure. And it would make you mobile again. You could even go outside, sit in the gardens, perhaps."

"How temporary?"

"Well, that depends on you. On how hard you're prepared to work, and how determined you are to get back on your feet. I suspect weeks, though, rather than months. Shall I order one for you?"

"I suppose so." She looks as though she would rather eat a rat sandwich. "When can I start the physio?"

"At once. The sooner, the better. We have an excellent physiotherapy department here. If you're ready to begin I shall request an assessment by the head physiotherapist, and we can go from there."

She nods. "Yes, please. I just... I want to get better so I can get out of here. No offense, everyone has been wonderful, but... well, you know..."

He pats her hand. "I do know. I need to run some additional tests and scans to make sure there's no permanent damage from the blow to your head. Are you happy to crack on with that, too?"

She nods. "Anything, yes. I just want... I *need* to get back to normal."

"I'll sort out a slot with the radiography team, then. We can probably get that out of the way today."

"So quick? Still, I suppose this is the advantage of going private."

"Quite." Mr Trent gets to his feet. "Nothing but the best for my favourite patient. I shall leave you with Mr McPherson now but I'll be back later with the results of the scans and the recommendations of our physio team. Then, we can start to plan your great escape."

I've been listening carefully and formulating an escape plan of my own. Best to wait until the test results are back and the physio has done his assessment before making any suggestions, though.

Even so, I am already planning a temporary wheelchair ramp at Linn Mill, and some remodelling of the ground-floor rooms.

"I'M SORRY. About yesterday. I upset you, and I shouldn't have." I blurt my apology as soon as the door closes behind the consultant. I don't want to have this discussion with the nurses hovering, so I guess we haven't much time.

"It was me doing most of the shouting," she concedes.

"Still, I said more than I meant to. I just... I just want us to get along. As friends if nothing more. For Archie's sake."

"You've obviously won him over," she replies. "And my mother. I think she'd marry you herself if that were possible."

"They've both been good company at Linn Mill. I've enjoyed having them there."

She nods. "And, according to my mum, they've enjoyed it, too. You've been...very kind. And generous."

"Generosity doesn't come into it. I had to help. I had a responsibility. I did what I thought you would have wanted."

What Happens in Vegas...

"I never wanted Archie to live with you," she replies.

"Ah, well, yes, but—"

"But, you were right yesterday, when you said everything had changed. My accident changed everything."

"So, you're okay with it? With Archie being with me?"

She shrugs. "I wouldn't go so far as to say that, but I can see how it happened. And I do appreciate the help you gave when my mother was faced with an impossible choice." She meets my gaze. "She was here, yesterday. We talked for a long time, or she did. She told me about her decision to abandon her treatment, and how you talked her out of it. I... I don't know how to thank you for that."

"You don't have to. I just—"

"No. You did a good thing, and I *am* grateful. Please, let me be grateful where it's due."

I know when to quit while I'm ahead. "Okay. So, can we start again then? As friends?"

I offer her my hand.

"There's just one thing I need to know."

"What's that?"

"Tell me Archie has no idea about your playroom. My mother, too, for that matter."

I'm not in the least ashamed or embarrassed about my sexual choices and preferences, but I do agree that there is a time and a place. And some things are just plain private. I put my hand on my heart. "I swear they don't. It's strictly out of bounds."

"Okay, then. Friends." She offers her hand, and I take it.

THE REST of the day passes quickly. I'm transferred onto a trolley and wheeled through the hospital to the radiography department, where they shove me into one tube after another. A full-body CT scan is followed by various angled views of my head and an MRI scan. The whole procedure takes quite a while, and I'm feeling shattered by the time I find myself back in my comfortable room.

Caleb is there, waiting for me, and so is my mother. I've no sooner settled back in bed than there's a knock at the door. I call out for this latest visitor to come in, and a woman of around thirty-five enters.

Miss Truelove introduces herself as the consultant clinical psychologist at Halstead Grange, called in by Mr Trent to assess any long-term effects on my mental abilities, behaviour, or emotional state.

"I feel fine," I tell her. "Just the same as before."

As far as I can remember...

"Yes, of course. But the staff have said you seem somewhat...anxious. This can be a sign of other issues, so it's best to be certain."

"I'm anxious to get well again, if that's what they mean."

"I daresay. Miss Daniels, you don't have to undergo any tests if you prefer not to, but Mr Trent did recommend it. I could conduct the tests here, and it would only take a couple of hours or so. Then, if any issues do emerge, we can address those in your recovery plan. If there's nothing, well, we can forget all about it."

"Will it get me out of here any quicker if I do the tests?"

"I don't know," she replies. "That would depend on the results."

At least she's honest.

"Fern, love, I do think you should take the tests. Better safe than sorry," my mother offers her opinion.

"But there's nothing wrong with me. Well, nothing that a bout of physio won't put right. I don't need all this psychology stuff."

"Please, love. To put my mind at rest." My mother can be very persuasive when she decides to turn it on.

I know when I'm beaten. "A couple of hours, you said?"

"Yes," Miss Truelove confirms. "And you can have someone with you throughout. It's best if it's someone who knows you very well and would notice if there's anything different about you."

"I could do it." Of course, my mum volunteers like a shot.

Miss Truelove beams. "Excellent. Shall we say tomorrow, then? About eleven o'clock?"

I'M EXHAUSTED by the time the physiotherapist arrives, all bouncy and energetic, and resplendent in his white clinical tunic and pants.

His name is Terence—Terry to his friends, which apparently now includes me.

Despite my protests, he rolls up his sleeves and insists upon tugging each of my legs at impossible angles, ordering me to bend them as far as I can—which is barely at all—and raising them off the mattress one at a time, then both together. I have to rotate my ankles and wriggle my toes, then we play a game where he touches the sole of my foot with a pencil and I have to say if I can feel it. He has me sitting up, then lying back down, and lifting various weights in each hand, all the time asking me to rate the degree of exertion required on a scale of one to ten. Most of my scores are above five, which I gather is not good. He nods frequently and makes a lot of non-verbal sounds as he notes his findings down on a clipboard. Eventually he fixes me with a steady gaze.

"We have a lot of work to do."

"Oh." I'd already arrived at that conclusion. Even I'm not impressed by scores of above five.

"The original fractures have healed nicely, but there has been some considerable weakening of your leg muscles, through prolonged disuse, and your body in general."

That doesn't surprise me either. Five months in bed is not

exactly a recipe for marathon training. I flop back against the pillows to await his verdict.

"I would want to suggest we concentrate on building the large motor movement and strength in your lower limbs to get you walking again but combine this with a general fitness regime. A high-protein diet will help, too."

"Will I have to go to a gym?"

He smiles. "I think we're some way off that, still. But we do have a wide range of suitable apparatus in the physio department here which we can get started with. And we have a therapy pool as well, which I think you will find especially beneficial in the early stages. The water supports your weight, so your muscles don't have to. You can get a great cardiovascular workout without causing undue stress anywhere else."

"Sounds wonderful," I reply with little enthusiasm. I can see myself being trapped here for several weeks, if not months, until my fitness levels can be dragged up to the required standard.

"Shall I book you in for daily sessions with me and the team?" he asks brightly. "The sooner we start…"

"Yes, I suppose so. I can—"

Caleb stretches his long legs out and crosses them in front of him. "Once Fern's routine is established and she knows what she's doing, is there any reason why you couldn't supervise her progress as an outpatient?"

"An outpatient?" Terry turns to regard Caleb. "Oh no, that wouldn't do, not really. You see, she will need intensive therapy, at least initially, daily sessions. It just wouldn't be practical to be coming backwards and forwards."

"Could you send a physiotherapist to her. At home?"

"Well, we do do home visits, of course, but it's the use of the equipment really. It's not portable, in the main…"

"I already have a home gym with some fitness equipment. I could add other items, according to your advice. And I have a pool. Is there anything special about a therapy pool?"

"Well, the temperature, probably. We tend to like them quite warm."

"I'll turn up the heat, then."

"Hmm. Well..."

"I'll tell you what. Why don't you come and do a home visit to assess the existing facilities, advise me on what additional items will be required, and we'll take it from there. Fern could be discharged to Linn Mill, and her treatment could continue. As an outpatient."

I listen to all of this in astonishment. Is Caleb McPherson completely delusional? In what universe did he dream I might want to return to his bloody house?

"Look here," I begin. "Hold on a moment..."

"Oh, what a grand idea. It will be so nice to have Fern back with us," my mother gushes. "We can take proper care of her at home. No offence, mind, you've all been wonderful here, but she'll do a lot better with her family around her."

"I've no intention of—"

"Well, it could work, I suppose," Terry concedes. "I'd want to consult Mr Trent, obviously."

"Obviously," Caleb agrees. "Am I right in thinking we have a meeting with him the day after tomorrow, once the clinical psychologist has done her tests?"

"I can let him have my report by then," Terry says. "Would it be convenient to call at the premises tomorrow morning to do the initial assessment and follow that up with recommendations?"

"Of course. I'll make sure my housekeeper is ready for you."

"Whoa. Now hold it," I manage to shout above the rest of the chatter. "I'm not moving into your house."

They all turn to regard me with varying degrees of puzzlement, apart from Caleb himself. His expression is inscrutable.

"But why, dear?" my mother wonders. "It seems to be the perfect solution. I can help look after you. And Archie. He'd be so excited..."

I experience a sharp pang but squash it. "No. It's out of the question."

Terry shrugs. "Very well. My report will be finished tomorrow in any case."

"Would nine-thirty suit? For the home visit?" Caleb asks him.

The physiotherapist glances from Caleb to me and back again. "Yes, sir. Nine-thirty is fine."

Shit! I open my mouth to deliver the sharp retort required, but Caleb forestalls me.

"Perhaps if I could have a word with Fern. Alone. It's been a long day, and she's tired…"

"I'm not tired. I just…" My protest might have carried more weight had I not yawned right at that moment.

"Of course. I need to be getting back to the department. Can you text me the details for tomorrow?" Terry hands Caleb his card.

"And I'll be getting off, too. I daresay Archie will be back my now and wanting his tea." My mother kisses me on the cheek. "You get some rest, love."

Caleb treats the nurse to one of his winning smiles. "Carol? Will you excuse us for as few minutes?"

The nurse is showing no sign of taking the hint. "I need to be here. In case of…"

"Of…?" Caleb regards her with one raised eyebrow.

"In case of emergencies," she clarifies. "Miss Daniels is still under close observation."

"I can observe her and call you at once if anything happens."

"I'm not sure Mr Trent would approve of that. It's most irregular."

"Why don't you check with him? From the nurses' station?" my mother suggests. She already has her coat on, ready to leave. "I'll come with you."

She somehow manages to usher Carol out of the door, on

the heels of the physiotherapist. Caleb and I are left alone, and I round on him at once.

"If you think I'm going back there..."

"I understand. Sort of. But just have a think about this first."

"There's nothing to think about. I won't—"

"Even if it means you could get out of here almost immediately? Within days, certainly."

"It wouldn't be that quick. I'd need nurses, and..."

"I can hire nurses. I did before, for your mother. And Mr Trent can do his house calls just as easily at Linn Mill. Easier, probably, as he only lives a mile and a half away."

How on earth does he know that?

"Last time I was there, you treated me like...like..."

"Last time I made a lot of mistakes. I don't intend to do the same thing again. Last time, I brought you to my home by force. This time, you would be my guest. And my friend. In any case, things would have to be different. Poppy is at Linn Mill now, Archie, too. And..." he flashes me that sexy smile, "it wasn't all bad. Was it?"

"If you think you can take advantage of me...of this..." I gesture to the bed and my useless legs, "just to get me to sleep with you again..."

"The sleeping arrangements will be perfectly respectable. You could have the room adjoining Archie's. He'd love that."

I shake my head. "It feels all wrong. You and I...we're strangers. You said so yourself."

"We have a lot on common, though, and I don't only mean the fun to be had in my playroom. We have other shared interests, you might say, and Archie is the chief among them. He wants his mummy back, and I want him to have that."

"Your playroom isn't always fun."

"I had the distinct impression you liked it, but still... If I recall, it was what happened in my bedroom that you found harder to tolerate."

"You treated me very badly," I say, stiffening my spine. "I still... I don't like to think about it."

"I pushed you too far."

"Yes. You did."

"I apologise for that." He reaches for my hand. "You must know, especially after what happened between us before, I would never touch you without your consent. You would be safe at Linn Mill."

"I'm safe here," I point out.

"But not happy. You're worried about Archie, about him becoming too attached to me while you're stuck in hospital."

"I never said that."

"No, but it is what you think. You want your little boy back. Don't you?"

"Of course. He belongs with me."

"I know that. And he needs you to be fit and well. That's what I'm offering."

"Even if..." I hesitate, but some things just have to be said. We have to understand each other properly. "If I do come to Linn Mill, you know I won't stay. I'll leave, eventually. I'll go back to Stockport and I'll take him with me."

"We'll cross that bridge when we come to it."

I shake my head. "You need to understand. I signed that agreement. There's nothing between us. I never intended you to even know about Archie. We *will* leave."

"To leave, you have to be there in the first place. I'll take that as a 'yes' then."

CHAPTER 24

Fern is to be transferred from Halstead Grange to Linn Mill by ambulance. Mr Trent insisted upon it. Once again, Polly will make the journey with her.

The various scans and clinical psychological tests showed up nothing of note, so the consultant was happy enough to agree to Fern's early discharge, provided she came to Linn Mill and continued her rehabilitation from here. Needless to say, his fees for treating her as an outpatient are only marginally less than it cost to keep her in hospital, but I'm not complaining.

Archie and I are waiting by the door. Ollie, as usual, makes laps of my entrance foyer, skidding on the marble flags. I am beginning to wonder if he will ever completely master control of all four of his legs. Tara, in contrast, sits quietly beside me, her shoulder resting against my calf. I reach down to tickle her ears, just as the sound of an approaching vehicle reaches us.

"Is that them?" Archie chirps up. "Are they here?"

I open the door and manage to grab Ollie before he charges out. We have made progress with his education, but he gets excited easily. His rear end bumps to the floor at my command to sit, but I take the precaution of hanging on to his collar as the dark-maroon taxicab purrs up my drive.

Not an ambulance this time then, after all. Mr Trent has

opted for a normal taxi adapted to take a wheelchair. The vehicle glides to a halt, and Poppy emerges first. The driver is not far behind. He walks around to the rear doors, opens them, then operates the hydraulic system which slowly lowers a platform which makes up part of the rear portion. Fern's wheelchair is on the platform, secured in place. She is seated in the chair, gripping the arms like grim death.

"Mummy! Mummy's here." Archie bolts down the stairs and runs across the gravel to reach the taxi, then flings his small arms around his mother's legs. "You were ages," he complains. "We've been waiting all day."

Fern pats his head then leans forward to kiss him. She murmurs something which makes him grin, but I can't catch it.

I decide to take the risk with Ollie and let him go. He charges over to the pair, licks Fern's hand, then lurches off into the rose bushes in pursuit of an imaginary rabbit.

"That's Ollie," Archie announces proudly. "My dog."

"He's very...bouncy," Fern observes.

"We're working on that," I assure her as I approach. "Welcome to Linn Mill."

She meets my gaze but says nothing, just scans the facade of the house and the ornamental terrace. If she spots the newly completed ramp giving access to the main entrance, she chooses not to comment.

The driver retrieves a large holdall from the boot of the cab. "Do you want this inside?"

"Yes, please. How much do we owe you?"

"Twenty-five, mate."

"I hand over two twenty-pound notes then grasp the handles of the wheelchair. I push it up the wooden ramp, Tara still trotting along at my side and Poppy and Archie bringing up the rear.

"You'll love the house, sweetheart," Polly calls to her. "The decorations are gorgeous. And there are antiques everywhere..."

What Happens in Vegas...

"You've been brave, letting Archie loose among your precious collectables. And that dog..." They are her first words directed at me.

"Archie's been fine, and the dog is a work in progress. Do you want to go straight up to your room, or would you like a tour first?"

I'm sure we both remember vividly the last time I gave Fern a tour of my home, but of course we don't refer to it.

Poppy has another suggestion "Shall we have a nice pot of tea in the drawing room? I asked Sally to set it out for us."

"Fern?" I pause just inside the door.

"Tea would be nice," she replies, so I angle the chair towards the drawing room.

"Over there, by the window. I had Harry move the sofa along a bit so there would be room for Fern's wheelchair next to my chaise longue. It's such a lovely place to sit, dear. I thought you might like it."

"You have a chaise longue?" Fern smiles at her mother. "Since when?"

"Well, since I came to stay here, I suppose. I've always loved this room the best, and on those days when I felt really ill I preferred to be in here rather than upstairs. There's a view of everyone coming and going, and the gardens beyond. It made me feel a part of everything. Caleb kindly dragged the chaise longue over to the French windows, but there's plenty of room for you, too. I thought you might like it better than being confined upstairs."

Trust Poppy to think of that. I've been preoccupied in making sure the ramp was constructed in time and the lift was wheelchair accessible. Apart from the kitchen, perhaps, these days the drawing room is the heart of the house, so naturally, Fern would want to be here. I manoeuvre the wheelchair into the gap between the chaise longue and the sofa and apply the brakes.

The tea and some cakes have been set out on a tray. I place

them on a low table next to Poppy, then drop onto the sofa while she pours tea for each of us.

"It's nice to be finally out of hospital," Fern murmurs. "Thank you, Caleb."

"You're welcome. I want you to feel at home here. If there's anything you need…"

"Ask Sally," Fern finishes for me.

"Oh, you've met Sally, then?" Poppy asks. "I didn't realise."

"Yes, I… I mean, Caleb has mentioned her. She's a very good cook, I gather…"

"Yes, she is. And very pleasant company, too. We're good friends now, me and Sally. I know you'll like her."

Fern was adamant that only she and I should know of her previous visit here, so I asked Sally not to make reference to it. Trust Fern to let the cat out of the bag herself!

"These will be Sally's cakes. You should try one." My attempt at a diversion works.

Poppy selects a small cupcake decorated with icing sugar seashells and takes a bite.

"Delicious." She shoves the plate closer to Fern. "Try one of the chocolate ones."

Fern has the cupcake halfway to her mouth when her eyes narrow. "Who is that?" she asks.

I glance out of the window at the small figure trotting up my drive. "That's Thomas Ferguson. He's Archie's best friend at school."

Archie has spotted him, too. He lets out a whoop and darts off, shouting his friend's name. We watch from the French windows as the boys meet on the drive, collecting Ollie from the rose bushes on the way. Thomas has brought a football with him, so they start up a dribbling game on the lawn.

"Best friend from school? He seems so…settled here."

"It's been five months, love," Poppy reminds her. "Life goes on."

"I suppose it does. But I'm back now and that changes everything. It has to."

Poppy and I exchange a look. Neither of us asks her to elaborate.

THE FIRST SESSION in the pool is conducted under the watchful gaze of Terry the physio. He shows Fern how to do some general muscle building and cardio-vascular workouts in the water but seems satisfied that she'll be able to continue on her own, as long as she doesn't come to the pool unaccompanied.

"I can come with her," I promise. "I'm here most days with Archie anyway."

"Archie needs to be careful in the water," Fern remarks. "He can't swim yet, and I won't be much use."

"He can swim," I correct her. "He can do three lengths of this pool, and one in the big one they go to from school. He... we've spent a lot of time down here."

She regards me oddly. "Oh," is her only comment.

We move on to the gym. As well as the treadmill and bicycle I already had, I've had a weights system installed, on Terry's advice, and a set of steps with handrails on both sides. For now, Terry insists that Fern remains in her wheelchair, concentrating on building strength and stamina.

He wraps weighted cuffs around her ankles and has her raising her legs, five repetitions on each side.

"Do that each day. After three days we can start increasing the reps," he says. "Once you've got some decent muscle tone, we'll get you back on your feet."

"Thank you," she replies. "I can't wait."

"I'll be over twice a week to assess your progress and provide you with new exercises. But it's vital that you do your workout every day without fail. Any problems, give me a ring."

"We will," I assure him. "And don't worry, we'll make sure she keeps up the good work."

. . .

FERN NEEDS no encouragement from me or anyone else. On the contrary, she works like a demon, completing her set exercises and then doing it all over again. She and Archie do lengths of the pool. She hoists her feet up and down with the weights attached and adds far more reps than Terry suggested.

"Don't overdo it," her mother advises, but Fern isn't listening. She's determined to get out of that wheelchair, then, I assume, to get out of Linn Mill. For good.

"IS THAT YOUR SLIMY LAWYER ARRIVING?" Fern and I are sharing a late breakfast in the drawing room. I'm just back from dropping Archie at school, and Fern has already completed her first workout of the day.

I glance outside to see Simon Waters emerge from his red Porsche. Fern has never warmed to him. "Yes. I wonder what he wants." As far as I can recall we don't have a meeting scheduled. "Excuse me."

I meet him at the door. "Simon. Good morning. What brings you here?"

"There's some paperwork we need to get sorted out. For the trust fund you wanted me to set up."

"Trust fund?" The problem with wheelchairs is they make little or no sound on carpets or marble floors. I hadn't realised Fern was right behind me. "What trust fund would that be?"

Might as well meet the issue head-on. "For Archie. He'll be able to access it when he's eighteen."

"What? You want to buy him his first car? Is that it?"

I suspect the value of the fund will be sufficient to cover rather more than the cost of a clapped-out Volvo but decide to leave that aside for now.

"Yes. If that's what he decides to use it for."

"We don't need your money."

"No, but that doesn't mean it won't be useful." I firm my tone. "I'm setting up the fund. It'll be for Archie to decide if he uses it, and what for."

"I never expected—"

"I know you didn't. But it's happening anyway. Did you say there were some documents to be signed, Simon?"

"Not signed," he replies. "Provided. As the trust is in your late mother's name, I need to include her death certificate in the documentation submitted to the fund management company. I wondered if you might have it to hand."

I furrow my brow. "I can't recall having ever seen it, but it must be among my father's private papers that I had shipped back from Manhattan after he died. Everything was stored in a filing cabinet in my office."

"Okay. Well, if you could look it out and drop it off with me, I can complete this application and get it all set up for you.'"

"I'll do that. Is there anything else?"

"Just a bunch of stuff that does require your signature…" He produces a sheath of papers from his briefcase. "Do you want to borrow my pen?"

THE NEXT COUPLE of weeks pass in a flurry of activity. Fern's hard work pays off. She graduates from seated exercises to being allowed to haul herself onto the treadmill where she limps along at a snail's pace for the first session or two, then she seems to find her confidence and her strength. She is soon walking briskly, then running, not to mention skipping up and down the steps two at a time.

Within a month of leaving Halstead Grange, the wheelchair is history and the crutches have been discarded. It's clear to all of us that she could, just about, return home to Stockport. This is a fact not lost on Fern who raises the matter at lunchtime one day.

"My studio needs me," she explains when Poppy asks her what the rush is. "I have a business to manage."

"It's doing okay, Caleb got someone to keep an eye on things…"

"He did what?" She rounds on me. "Have you been meddling with my business?"

"I appointed an agent, that's all. Someone to make sure the tenants paid their rent and the bills were kept up, too."

"There was no need. My tenants are all honest, and Jade would have kept an eye on things."

"That's pretty much what the agent reported," I reply. "Do you want to go there yourself to check on everything? Harry could drive you."

"Yes. Yes, I think I would. I could check on the house as well, see what needs doing to get it ready for us to move back in."

"Move back in?" Poppy appears less than thrilled at the prospect. "Are you quite sure about that, love? I mean, are you well enough?"

"I'm perfectly fine now. And what about you? Surely you want to get back to your hairdressing?"

Poppy shakes her head. "Not especially."

Fern sighs. "Look, I know you like it here. So does Archie, but it was only ever temporary. We can't impose on Caleb forever."

I shrug. "There's no rush. Why don't you stay until after Christmas?"

"But that's another six weeks."

"Archie's already planning his round of parties with his friends," Poppy puts in. "He'd be heartbroken to be wrenched away so suddenly."

"He has friends at home, in Stockport."

"He's been away from them for months."

"Let's discuss this later," I suggest, seeking to take some of the heat out of the conversation. "I was thinking of going out on

Roman this afternoon and I expect Bella would appreciate an outing, too. Would you like to come?"

Fern seems apprehensive. "I'm not sure that's a good idea. What if I fall off and I'm back at square one?"

"Ah, not quite so confident in your recovery after all, then?"

"It's not that. I mean…"

"We'll take it slow. Come with me. The exercise will do us both good."

WE TAKE both dogs with us. Neither of them is in the least bit fazed by the horses, and they behave well around them. Even for all his exuberance, Ollie seems to instinctively know to be calm in the stables. Tara, naturally, never puts a paw wrong.

"I knew you loved horses, but I hadn't realised you had a thing for dogs, too," Fern says as we set off across the springy grass in the direction of the grazing meadows.

"Not dogs in general. It seemed important to me that Archie should have his dog. It had been promised to him, and he seemed so lost and forlorn when he first arrived. Ollie changed all of that overnight."

"I'm not sure how we'll manage him at home."

"You will," I assure her. "He's young and excitable, but he's bright enough and eager to please. He can learn to behave himself. And if not, he can stay here, but I know Archie will fret for him. He'd have to visit often."

"You have all of this worked out, don't you?"

I wish I had.

Fern goes on. "Playing daddy. Letting him have anything he wants…"

"Apart from a helicopter trip, I wouldn't say he's been enjoying a lavish lifestyle. He goes to the local school, plays with local children, has a dog, and a bike. He goes to watch football with his friend's dad. It's not so different from how he would spend his time if he lived with just you and Poppy."

"Are you mad?" She glares at me. "What about all of this? The house, the land, the horses...?"

"He doesn't seem that interested in horses."

"You must be disappointed," she says, the bitterness evident in her tone.

"Not especially. I just want him to be himself. To be happy, well-adjusted. To grow up with family who love him."

"Just the way you didn't?"

I stop, rake my hands through my hair. Fern lacks nothing in the way of insight and has hit the nail squarely on the head. "My father was crap at the job. I've tried to do better. It helps that I have money, but all I ever really wanted was for my father to spend time with me. He never did. I've tried not to make that mistake."

"You've done well," she concedes, at last. "Archie adores you."

"The feeling is mutual." I take her hand, relieved that she doesn't drag it away immediately. "I'll be honest with you. I want him to stay. I want you to stay, and Poppy."

"We can't," she whispers.

"Why not? We get on okay, the four of us."

"I have a life. A business..."

"Practicalities. We could manage that somehow. We have been managing it."

"You and me...we don't just 'get on okay'."

"You think not?"

"That weekend...the things we did. The things you did to me..."

"We should talk about that, talk through what was good and what wasn't. I need you to tell me where it went wrong, for you. We can work out how we want it to be between us."

"It can't be anything. I'm not...like that. Not like you."

Now I can't stop myself chuckling. "Sweetheart, I get it that forced orgasms are not your thing, and that's fine. We'll put that on your hard limits list. But the rest...the spanking, the flogging, the sensation play, the playing out your fantasies—that was absolutely your thing. Wasn't it?"

She shakes her head. "It's impossible."

"Not impossible," I press her, sensing her ambivalence. "Come back into the playroom with me. Explore some more."

"I can't."

"Can't?"

"Don't want to. It...it scares me."

"Do I scare you?"

"Of course not. Not anymore."

"Do you trust me?"

"Yes. No. Sometimes."

"When do you not trust me?"

She meets my gaze. "When...when I think you might take Archie from me. If you apply for custody, I would—"

"That will never happen."

"You say that now, but who knows? In the future..."

"He belongs with you. Ideally, he belongs with both of us, and I mean to remain in touch with him, but I will never fight you for custody. I'd be prepared to sign an agreement to that effect if that's what you need."

"A legal agreement."

"Yes."

"Like the other one? The one I signed?"

"Not like that one. For a start, there would be copies, so neither of us could tear it up." I take her face between my palms. "I do mean what I say, Fern. I'm not looking to take your son from you. I will never do that."

She meets my gaze, peering at me, searching...for the truth.

It's there. I hope she can find it.

"Okay. I believe you."

"You do?"

"Yes. I trust you."

"I'll talk to Simon about that agreement."

"Okay, if you want."

I kiss her forehead, and we resume our walk towards the meadows.

Just as we crest the hill and the horses come into view, she slips her hand into mine. "Maybe we can talk about that other stuff. The playroom and...everything. But Archie and my mother had better not find out. Not ever."

CHAPTER 25

Fresh out of the shower following a gruelling workout, I tighten the belt on my towelling robe and ease myself back on my mother's chaise longue. I consider getting up to close the curtains. It's mid-November and after four o'clock. Already it's dark outside. I suppose I really should go up to my room and get dressed, but I decide to take a few minutes here in the peaceful drawing room, my mother's sanctuary.

I can easily tell why my mother loves this room so much, especially this spot by the French windows, with the view of the gardens and endless quantities of her favourite tea to hand. I can hardly blame her for not being eager to return to her job, up to her armpits in perming solution and colour rinses. It's not even as though she owns her own salon. She rented a chair in a place down the road, and the salon owner has most likely let it to someone else by now.

As for my own business, I took Caleb up on his offer of lending me Harry and a car, and I dropped in on my studio. Jade has really come into her own and is running the place as well as I would have. I confess I have mixed feelings about this, but as she has found me two new tenants and finished fitting out the gallery space, I can't really complain. She's even managed to attract a few exhibition bookings. I gave her carte blanche to continue the good work, agreed to increase her salary by ten percent, left her my contact details, and headed back to Scotland.

I don't only have myself to consider, though the prospect of an extended stay here is becoming more attractive by the day. My mother loves living here at Linn Mill. Archie is thriving. I close my eyes and allow my body to relax.

If it ain't broke, why mend it?

Except, I can't imagine that a relationship with Caleb could ever work out. I tried that; it was a disaster. A sexy romp is one thing, I'm as keen on good sex as the next woman, and a bit of kink thrown in sweetens the deal, but a relationship is more than that. It has to be more than that.

Car headlights split the inky darkness outside. I recognise the engine tone even before Caleb's Alfa Romeo pulls up on the driveway. He had meetings today at his business headquarters in Edinburgh and is back earlier than I expected. He exits the car, glances up at the drawing room windows, and takes the steps outside two at a time. The outside door opens and closes, then his footsteps sound on the marble tiles of the foyer.

The drawing room door opens. I sense his presence before I see him.

Caleb strolls into the drawing room, handsome as sin in his slate-grey business suit and pearl-pink tie. I'm accustomed to seeing him more casually dressed these days, but I have to admit, he fills out a suit to perfection. He sheds the jacket and drops it over the arm of the sofa, then leans on the frame of the French windows, his arms folded as he regards me.

"Where is everyone?" he asks.

I swallow hard while a bolt of pure lust punches through my core. "My mum picked Archie up from school. She's taking him and Thomas to Alphabet Zoo."

"Pardon me?"

"It a soft-play gym. It opened a month ago, in one of those

refurbished mills at Kirklington. Archie loves that sort of thing. He's been pestering his grandma to take him."

"I see."

"What about you? What brings you back so early?"

"I need to look out some documents in my office."

"The death certificate?" I guess.

He nods. "Simon has been pestering me."

"Is there anything I can do to help?"

He raises one eyebrow. "Have you come around to the idea of the trust fund, then?"

"Not exactly. But I want to make myself useful."

"There's no need."

"I'm not used to just sitting around all day. I want to…contribute."

"Fair enough, although if this is your idea of sitting around all day, I have no objections." He rakes his dark gaze over my loosely fastened robe, taking in my damp hair and bare legs. "Still, there was something I was wondering if you might be able to help me with. How are you on cataloguing and valuing artworks and antiques?"

"Cataloguing?" I sit up straight. "I could manage that. As for valuing, that tends to be a specialist area."

"Yes, I daresay. The thing is, I need to produce a detailed inventory of the contents of this house, for my insurers. If you want to lead the project, I'd appreciate it. You would need to catalogue all the items—works of art, antiques, collectables, anything that might be of value—then put each in front of the right valuers and get them to assess the items. Do you think that's something you might like to do?"

"It's a big job." *Big enough to give me a reason to stay here for several more months, at least.*

"I know. It would take a while to complete, but even if you just made a start that would help."

No pressure, then. Except, "I always like to finish what I start."

His lip quirks. "So I've seen. You'll do it, then?"

I pause, then nod. "I will. I'd enjoy it."

He tips his chin in the direction of the teapot on a side tray. "Any tea left in that?"

"No. Shall I go and ask Sally for more?"

"Later, perhaps." Then, in a sudden change of subject, "How did Poppy and Archie get to Kirklington?

"Harry drove them. I hope that's okay."

He smiles. "It's fine. I told Poppy to just ask if she needs transport anywhere. There's no bus service out here, and she doesn't drive herself."

"That reminds me, I don't suppose you've any idea what happened to my car, do you?"

"Your car?"

"I parked it near the school in Stockport and I was walking towards it when I was run over. I expect it got towed away eventually."

"Ah, right. I confess I never gave it a thought. I should have. Leave it with me. In the meantime, there are four vehicles in the garage. Take your pick, I'll sort out insurance."

More of his careless generosity. I should be used to it by now, but it never gets old.

"Thank you."

"I think I passed Terry's car in the lane on my way home."

"Yes, you just missed him. He left about five minutes before you arrived. Today was probably his last visit here."

He lifts an eyebrow. "Oh?"

"He wants to sign me off. He doesn't think I need him anymore."

"That's good news. Worth celebrating." He glances over his shoulder into the darkness outside. "Do you mind if I close the curtains?"

I shake my head. "I was about to."

He uses the pulley system to draw them closed, then sinks onto the sofa close to me. "Terry is right. You do look well, Fern."

"I feel well."

He smiles. "Thank you for staying."

"I should be thanking you."

"Don't. I enjoy having you here. All of you."

I sit up to face him. "I wish we'd been like this before. Friends."

With benefits?

As if he reads my mind, he leans forward to cup my jaw in his hand. "If you don't want me to kiss you, you need to say so. Now."

I remain silent.

His lips brush mine, slow, lazy. Exploring. His palm is still on my chin, angling my face up. I raise my hands to place them on either side of his head, framing his beautiful features like a prayer. I take in his masculine perfection, comb my fingers through his hair, and I remember how it used to be between us for those few heady weeks. Before...

"Christ, Fern, you take my breath away..." His voice is low, closer to a growl. "I thought I might never..."

"Don't. Don't say it. That's over now. I'm well again, fully recovered. It's official, Terry said so."

His lips close over mine once more. I open for him, greedy suddenly for this. For all of this, all he has to offer and everything I've missed. Everything I so nearly lost.

He moves from the sofa to kneel beside the chaise longue. "What are you wearing under this?" he murmurs, his fingertips nudging the collar of my robe.

"Nothing. I just had a quick shower, after my session with Terry."

"Ah, there is a God..." He parts the two halves to reveal the swell of my breasts. "So pretty..."

His mouth closes over my nipple, while he uses his fingers to toy with the other. He increases the pressure. Both buds tighten and swell, and I arch into him.

"Caleb..." I groan.

"Mmm?"

"I need…"

"What?"

"This. It's been so long…"

He unties the belt of my robe to bare me completely. I lie still, let him look his fill. The longing in his eyes makes me powerful.

"You lost weight." He trails the backs of his fingers over my stomach.

"Must have been the liquid diet. I've been making up for it with Sally's cooking."

"We still have work to do." He cups my breast in his palm, rubs his thumb across my nipple until I gasp. His lip quirks and he draws his palms lower, across my ribs, my abdomen, then past my navel to rest on my smooth mound. I part my legs instinctively.

"So eager," he breathes.

"Yes. Why are you taking so long?"

"And impatient. Were you always so demanding?"

"Cal…"

He lowers his head to kiss me again, simultaneously driving two fingers deep into my pussy.

"Yes, yes, yes!" My inner walls quiver and convulse. I'm instantly on the brink. "Caleb, I need to come…"

"I know." He twists his fingers within me, adds a third, and slows his driving motion.

"No, don't stop. Please."

"Not stopping, just slowing down. We're in no hurry."

I am. I've never been in a bigger rush. I grind my hips against his hand, seeking more of the friction I crave. He concedes only enough to lay the pad of his thumb on my clit, so my frantic efforts do succeed in creating something of a sensation there. It isn't enough, though. Nowhere close.

"Cal, please…"

"Please what?"

What Happens in Vegas…

"Please make me come. Now. Then, fuck me."

"Mmm, that's definitely the best offer I've had all day."

He drives all three fingers deep again, angling to find that sweet spot inside, at the same time rubbing my clit with his thumb. I shatter almost instantly, my senses whirling. White light explodes, then shrinks to a kaleidoscope of vibrant colours as the tremors subside.

Long moments later I lie, spent, my eyes half closed.

Caleb, on the other hand, is still fully dressed apart from the tie he must have shed at some point, and his shirt sleeves are now rolled back. He looks the picture of male elegance.

"How do you manage to do that?"

"Do what?" He unfastens the buckle of his snakeskin belt.

"Totally unravel me and stay pristine and tidy yourself."

"Sweetheart, I'm a mess inside. I need to fuck you, now, or my balls will explode."

"Ah, then I win, because I feel fabulous. Inside." I send him a slow smile. "Care to check for yourself?"

"Holy fuck, Fern. That blow to your head has made you start talking dirty. It's a good thing Doctor Truelove didn't spot this unfortunate tendency. She might have kept you in hospital, and you're a lot more fun here, at Linn Mill." He unbuttons his trousers and lowers the zip, then pulls his wallet from his back pocket. He extracts a condom and offers it to me. "Will you do the honours?"

I take it, snap open the wrapper, and kneel. I have exactly nil experience in this particular art but seem to manage without mishap. Desperation will do that, I suspect. It affords me ample opportunity to admire his cock, take in the wide girth, the velvety softness of the skin, the smooth crown, already leaking clear droplets. Caleb always did have a gorgeous dick. On impulse, I lap the droplets away, savouring the salty tang.

"Fern," he growls.

I take the hint and finish rolling the latex down the length of his shaft.

"On the sofa. And spread your legs." His tone has taken on that air of command I recognise. And respond to. I shift quickly, dropping the robe as I go.

"What if Sally was to come in?" I ask, somewhat belatedly.

"I expect she'd leave again pretty fast." He moves between my spread thighs, his fist wrapped around the base of his cock. He positions it at my entrance. "No last-minute reservations?"

"None," I whisper.

"Thank God for that." He tilts his hips and drives the full length deep inside me.

It hurts, briefly, the sudden stretch and burn causing me to cry out. He pauses, balls-deep, allows me a few moments to adjust, then he starts to move.

Short, sharp thrusts at first, followed by longer, slower strokes. Any initial pain evaporates to be replaced by the first curls of orgasmic pleasure. I lift my bare legs and wrap them around his waist, sink my fingers in the silky softness of his shirt.

Something clenches low in my belly. Warmth, a gentle, wet heat, building, spreading, rippling outwards.

"Cal," I moan. "I..."

I love you. I always did.

"Fern," he replies, "Christ, Fern..."

I deliberately squeeze hard around him, my hips rolling in a sensuous dance, aligned to his thrusts.

He slips his arm under my knee to lift my leg higher and withdraws almost entirely. He waits a moment, then slams his cock back inside me, deeper, harder.

"Come for me," he rasps. "Do it now. Come on my cock."

My inner submissive leaps to obey. The familiar ripples curl and tighten low down in my core. My body clenches, stretched to the maximum, wrapped around him like a velvet vice.

He alters his angle, only slightly, but enough to rub my inner sweet spot with every powerful stroke.

I scream, grab his shoulders, and hang on as Caleb tumbles the pair of us over the precipice. His cock lurches inside me. He lets out a guttural curse, thrusts once more, then again, then goes still.

Long moments pass. We lie motionless, bodies joined, panting. Caleb is the first to move.

He pulls out of me and disposes of the condom, then rights his clothing and restores order. He gets to his feet and retrieves my discarded robe from the floor.

"Do you want to take this upstairs?"

I peer up at him, his powerful frame silhouetted in the light cast by a single standard lamp. "I'm not sure if I can…again. Not yet."

"Me neither. But soon. We have a lot of lost time to make up. I need a shower, though. Join me?"

I smile, and nod. "Yes. I'd like that."

AN HOUR LATER, both of us freshly showered, I kneel on the floor in Caleb's office surrounded by piles of paper. I'm wearing nothing but the shirt he discarded for the shower. In just jeans and a T-shirt, he lounges in a chair close by, leafing through yet more documents.

We found his father's death certificate, Caleb's birth certificate, and his parents' wedding certificate easily enough in a file marked 'family papers'. Those are set aside carefully as we continue to sift through the documents left by the late Mr McPherson.

Most of the documents relate to business deals, the buying and selling of property both in Scotland and in the US. Businesses, too. The senior Mr McPherson was every bit as acquisitive as his son, and from what I can tell, he made some judicious investments. Seven- and eight-figure numbers seem to leap off every page.

"He was quite the tycoon," I murmur.

"That he was. He could sniff the air and smell money." Caleb sets one file aside and picks up another to check. "Problem was, that was just about his only talent."

We continue in near silence until every file has been sifted through and still we haven't found the death certificate.

"That's odd." Caleb rakes his fingers through his hair. "I'd have expected it to be in here, with the rest." He picks up his parents' marriage certificate. "Look at this. It's dated June, nineteen eighty-nine. Just over a year before I was born, and she died. It was a short marriage."

I take the paper from him. "Meryl Baxter. That was her name? And he was called Alister."

"Yes, although barely anyone ever used his first name. My father appreciated formality."

"She was only nineteen when they got married, and he was thirty-seven. That's quite an age gap."

"I suppose so, though it sometimes works."

"But not for them?"

He shrugs. "It's hard to be sure. He never spoke about her, and there are no photographs, nothing to remember her by. If they'd been happy, well, you might have expected…something, some small memento."

I tend to agree, but we'll never know. "Can you do this trust fund thing without the death certificate?"

He shakes his head. "Not according to Simon. But it should be possible to get a replacement since the original seems to have gone astray."

"Oh? Right."

"I can order one online, I think." He moves across to his desk and fires up his laptop. "Ah, right, here's the site for Scottish death certificates. I just need to fill in a few details…"

I remain kneeling on the floor while he deals with the form-filling. It only takes a few minutes, then Caleb leans back in his chair, frowning.

"Is there a problem?"

"You could say that. The system can't find any record of the death certificate."

"That's weird. Like, it was never registered?"

He shrugs. "It must have been. I'll try another site."

I wait as he keys in the details again. His brow furrows when he arrives at the same dead end. I come to stand behind him and peer at the screen. This time he is on the ScotlandsPeople official government site and can still locate no record of his mother's death.

"Aren't death certificates usually issued by doctors?" I ask. "Hospitals?"

"Maybe. Yes, I expect so as they have to be signed by a doctor confirming the cause of death."

"And, you're saying that she died at Halstead Grange?" I point to the box asking for the place of the event.

"She did."

"That's a coincidence, don't you think? The same hospital where I was cared for."

"Not really. Halstead Grange is far and away the best private clinic in the region. It was a no-brainer for me to get you in there. My parents were wealthy, they wouldn't have considered using any other facility either."

"It doesn't have a maternity unit now, does it?"

"I don't know."

"But they did back then. Will they keep records, do you think? Maybe they could issue another certificate, or at least shed light on why your mother's death wasn't registered."

"I wouldn't mind betting it was my father's responsibility, and he just didn't bother. Like I say, he seemed to simply wipe her from his memory."

"But, if we can access the hospital records which will confirm that she died there, and from what cause, maybe the death can be registered, even now, after all this time."

He looks up from the screen and meets my eyes. "It's worth a shot. I don't have any better ideas."

CHAPTER 26

"It seems odd, being here and not a patient." Fern squints through the windscreen of my Alfa Romeo at the front entrance to Halstead Grange.

"Yes, I can imagine. Do you prefer to wait here?"

"Not a chance. I want to solve this mystery as much as you do."

"Hardly a mystery, sweetheart. Probably a simple cock-up where each side assumed the other was doing it."

I'm making light of this deliberately. In truth, the more I think about it, the more bemused I am. A death certificate would have been required by an undertaker in order to organise the funeral. I have no details of my mother's funeral, but she must have had one. No one is left lying around for the best part of thirty years!

I open my car door. "Coming, then?"

"Too right." Fern exits the car and comes around to take my hand.

Together, we walk up the main steps to the entrance.

The nurses' station is right in front of us. We head towards the 'Patients and Enquiries' sign where a familiar face greets us with a smile.

"Good afternoon, Rachel." I return her warm welcome.

"Mr McPherson. Fern." She nods to each of us in turn. "Were we expecting you?"

"No," I reply. "We're not here about Fern at all. It's another matter."

"I see." It's clear from her expression that she doesn't. "How can we help you, then?"

"Do you still have a maternity unit here?" I ask.

She shakes her head. "Not since… I think it would have been about two thousand and one or two. The consultant who ran the unit had to give up the practice, and there was no one else available to take it on."

She's being a little economical with the truth. I've done my own research, naturally, before coming here. The consultant in question, one Aldrich Digby Saunders, despite being a renowned obstetrician with a multi-million-pound private practice, also had a taste for high-stakes gambling. For some years he managed to fund his expensive habit through the exorbitant prices he charged, but eventually matters got away from him. He was under pressure to repay his debts, which ran into tens of millions, and in the end was easy prey for an organised crime gang wanting to develop a trade in human body parts. In payment for what he owed, Saunders performed several illegal kidney transplants, operations where the unfortunate and unwilling organ donors had been attacked and their organs extracted. Then they were dumped outside NHS hospitals to take their chances while wealthy clients benefited from the stolen kidneys. Saunders was sentenced to fifteen years for his part in the scam, and his unit closed down under a cloud of scandal.

Of course, I don't regale poor Rachel with all of this. I'm only interested in accessing Saunders' records.

"I'm looking for information about a patient who was treated here, in nineteen ninety. She gave birth. To me, in fact."

"Oh."

"Sadly, tragically, she died in childbirth."

"I'm so sorry..."

"Thank you. But the reason we're here is that we want to know more about the circumstances of her death. How she died, exactly. So, I was wondering who I need to speak to in order to access the medical records."

"The medical records?"

"Yes. Please..."

"I'm not sure. It's a matter of confidentiality, you see."

"I'm her son. Her next of kin."

"Well, yes, but even so... I think you'll need to speak to the hospital administrator."

"Excellent. Can we make an appointment with him?"

"Her. I'll see if she's free." Rachel uses the internal telephone system to consult the admin department, eventually putting down the phone with a smile. "She can see you in ten minutes."

We're directed upstairs, to a plush office suite, where we spend the next twenty minutes balancing on overstuffed armchairs and helping ourselves to freshly filtered coffee from a glass jug. I'm on my third cup when a young woman appears and asks us to accompany her. We do so and are shown into the cluttered office occupied by the hospital administrator.

She, too, greets us cordially enough and offers yet more refreshments, which we decline.

"Miss Forbes," I begin, reeling off the name from her badge. "Thank you for seeing us at short notice. We won't take up much of your time. We just need to access some medical records. It concerns my mother, Mrs Meryl McPherson. She came here to give birth but sadly died."

"My deepest condolences, Mr McPherson. Please, be assured that I will help you as far as I am able, but I'm not in a position to release confidential records, even to members of the deceased's family."

"In that case, perhaps you could home in on one key question."

What Happens in Vegas...

"Of course. What question would that be?"

"My mother was under the care of Aldrich Digby Saunders when she died. That's not in dispute, is it?"

"One moment, if you please..." Miss Forbes turns her attention to the desktop computer before her and types a few lines. Her lips purse. She glances up at me, then at Fern, then returns to tap a few more keys. At last, she lifts her gaze to us. "I can confirm that Mrs McPherson was an inpatient here from May nineteenth to May twenty-seventh, nineteen ninety. Her consultant obstetrician was Mr Aldrich Digby Saunders, as you know."

Beside me, Fern has produced a small notebook. "So, the date of Meryl's death was May twenty-seventh," she says.

Miss Forbes doesn't answer.

"Do the records show her giving birth? To me. On May twenty-second?" I ask.

Miss Forbes consults her screen again, then nods. "They do. The baby was delivered by Caesarean section."

"And, presumably, there were complications. That would explain why Meryl stayed in hospital for another five days," Fern suggests.

Again, Miss Forbes declines to comment.

"Well?" I demand. "Is that it? She died of complications five days later?"

"I'm sorry, Mr McPherson, but I can't help you any further." She gets to her feet and offers me her hand by way of terminating the meeting.

"One more question." I ignore the outstretched hand. "Can you explain to me why my mother's death was never registered? Was that not a statutory obligation of this hospital, since she died here, and Mr Saunders must have signed her death certificate and confirmed the cause of death?" I'm by no means sure that it was their responsibility, but a little bluff sometimes comes in useful.

Miss Forbes sits down again. "Yes, I can explain that."

I wait.

"No death was registered because Mrs McPherson did not die here. She was discharged from Halstead Grange on May twenty-seventh, nineteen ninety.

FERN and I make our way outside with barely a word exchanged between us. I can't speak for her, but I'm numb. Never, not once, did I contemplate an outcome like this.

My mother died giving birth to me. I have known this all my life, borne the guilt of it, in fact. My father was most explicit on the matter, he never wavered from that fact. No one else ever cast any doubt. So, how can it be that the hospital records say something quite different?

I'm still reeling when we reach the car and Fern turns to meet my gaze. "What do you suppose happened to her? After she left hospital?"

"She's dead," I reply. "She must be."

"Perhaps, but not at the time or in the way you always thought."

"Do you believe all of that?" I gesture with my thumb over my shoulder, back in the direction of Miss Forbes' office.

"Why would she lie?"

"To protect the hospital from a lawsuit. What if my mother died because of someone's negligence?"

"Do you honestly think they'd do that? I mean, it's one thing to somehow disguise the cause of a death so as not to get the blame, but to conceal that death entirely and get away with it for thirty years? That's quite another."

At some level, I know Fern is talking sense, but I'm still not buying it. There has to be some other explanation. There must be.

"And they didn't conceal a death, did they?" she goes on. "Just the opposite. They falsely reported a death, to your father, and concealed evidence of recovery."

"Holy fuck..." My eloquent contribution.

"Would you like me to drive?" Fern offers.

It's a measure of my utter confusion that I hand her the keys.

BACK AT LINN MILL, we return to my office and I get out the file with the family papers in. I spread the wedding certificate out on my desk, the last tangible link I have to my mother. Her signature is scrawled on it, next to my father's neater hand. I always imagined her to be more exuberant than him, livelier, with an unquenchable zest for life. In contrast, I know that he was dour, predictable, serious to a fault. They say opposites attract, but even so, if I'm right they must have been an unlikely pair.

"Do you recognise either of these names?" Fern points to the witnesses' signatures.

"I know him." One of the witnesses, a Mr Leonard Ferrands, was an old business associate of my father's. "They did a lot of business together. Len Ferrands used to come to dinner when we lived in Aberdeen. He owned a string of hotels and casinos."

"Owned? He's dead now, then?"

"I don't think so. He retired and his son took over."

"What about the other one? Vivian Valence?"

I shake my head. "No idea. I don't even know if it was a man or a woman."

"Okay. What about the people who worked for your father before they worked for you? Sally? Harry?"

"What about them?"

"Would any of them remember Meryl?"

I shake my head. "Neither of them was around back then. Why do you ask?"

"I'm thinking, if we want to track her down, we could

maybe start with people who knew her, who might have some idea where she would go."

"Track her down?" I shake my head. "Even if she is still alive, and I'm by no means convinced, she certainly doesn't want to be found. If what Miss Forbes said was true, she handed me over to my father and walked away. From him and from me. Maybe it's best to let it stay that way."

HE'S HURTING. I can see that. The pain in his eyes grieves me, too.

I can understand, to an extent. It's the pain of being deceived, lied to by one or both of his parents, for his entire life. The pain of rejection, of learning that during all those years he spent alone, yearning for his father's affection, there was a mother out there, somewhere.

Someone else he could have turned to, someone who should have loved him.

My own family may not be perfect, though I can't really come up with any major flaws. My parents loved each other, and they loved me. I grew up secure in that knowledge. We weren't wealthy, but we got by. We cared about each other, that much is absolutely certain in my mind. We made sacrifices sometimes, put each other first. Because families do that.

It amazes me that, given the role models he had, Caleb managed to become such a well-adjusted and, frankly, nice man. Setting aside the Dom traits, he's kind, generous, sensitive to the needs of others. I don't quite know where he learned those skills, but he did, and I'm thankful for it. Thankful for my mother's sake, and for Archie's.

I have no experience of the sort of dysfunctional arrangements that passed for family life in Caleb's childhood, but I can imagine it, and I can appreciate the emptiness, the sterile loneliness. I can share the hurt.

Quite literally.

I reach for his hand. "Let's go to the playroom."

He shoots me a glance, one eyebrow arched. "Are you sure?"

"Yes. We both need this."

"I know why I might have a twitchy palm, but why do you need a spanking?"

"To celebrate being alive. I want something...sharp. Edgy. Something I can feel."

He grins. "Fair enough. I get that. A crop should do it. Or maybe a cane."

A tremor ripples through me. Yes. *Yes!*

"Where's your mother?"

"In the drawing room."

"Okay." He tears a corner off a sticky note on his desk and scrawls a six-digit number on it. "Here's the combination to unlock the playroom door. You go on ahead and wait for me. I'll just text Harry and ask if he'll pick up Archie from school."

"Trust you to think of the practicalities." I close my fist around the scrap of paper.

"Dom's responsibility. Now, go."

I use the lift which takes me straight to the basement floor, then hurry along the tiled corridor to the locked door at the end. I punch in the digits on the note then try the handle. It opens readily, and I step inside, pulling it closed behind me.

I walk to the middle of the room, stop, and turn through three hundred and sixty degrees. The playroom is much as I remember it. The spanking bench is still here, the cross in the corner, the large wooden chair in the centre, and the rather austere bed over to my right with the stocks built into the footboard and the cage underneath. I'm still not keen on the cage, but the stocks might be interesting.

The rack of implements still fills one wall. I move in that direction to get a closer look. Caleb has ordered his collection neatly. Leather items are together, and so are the wooden paddles. Several crops of varying lengths occupy hooks next to each other, and he has a selection of canes, too. I choose one, a particularly slender bamboo-style example, and swing it through the air.

"You wouldn't like that one."

I whirl. I never heard him enter.

Caleb smiles at me. "That one may appear light, but it's too thin, too stingy. You'd be screaming your safe word by the second stroke. A slightly thicker, shorter one would be better for your first experience of a caning."

"Okay. What about...this one?" I pick up another and hold it out to him.

"Better. Yes, we can work with that. Now, what about the warm-up act?"

"A crop?"

"Fair enough. Take your pick."

I settle on a leather one with a suede handle and a fairly long tongue at the end.

"Nice choice. So, I haven't forgotten what happened last time we tried this, but you did say you wanted 'edgy'. Will you accept two strokes with this on each nipple, then present your arse for punishing?"

That tremor from earlier seizes me again. My pussy is already leaking. I nod, my mouth suddenly too dry to speak.

"Ah, Fern, we are going to have some fun together, you and me." He frames my face between his hands and kisses me, lightly, almost chaste. "Undress," he whispers.

I'm still wearing the casual top and jeans from our visit to the hospital. I pull the top over my head and set it neatly aside. Next, I toe off my training shoes and socks, then my jeans. I place them on the tidy pile of clothing. Finally, I remove my underwear and add bra and knickers to the pile. I place all of my garments on the spanking bench and await further instructions.

"On the bed. Kneeling. Close to the foot."

I clamber onto the mattress and kneel.

"I think a blindfold would enhance this experience. Any objections?"

"No, Sir." More tremors…

A selection of coloured scarves is bundled on a shelf beside the bed. He selects a dark blue one and folds it diagonally, then again to form a thick band of fabric which he ties around my head. "Is that okay? Not too tight?"

"It's perfect," I reply,

"Good. Put your hands behind your head and thread your fingers together nice and tight. You'll need to stay perfectly still for all four strokes. If you want me to stop, use your safe word, or your slow down word."

"My slow down word?"

"Yellow. Yellow means 'Whoa, slow down, need to talk'. Red means 'stop'."

"I know that."

"And green means 'All's good. Happy to continue'."

"Okay. I've got it."

"I must say, Fern, you do seem much more enthusiastic than you did on your previous visit here."

He's right, and I can't entirely account for it, apart from thinking that a near-death experience will tend to put matters into perspective, perhaps clarify others. "I may come to regret this, but right now, I do feel good. I want this, sir."

He bends to kiss my mouth. "Me, too. Ready?"

I nod.

"Say it."

"I'm ready, Sir."

The floor creaks slightly, which is how I know he is moving about the room. I listen, try to follow him, but I sense rather than hear when he is beside me again. He cups my left breast in his hand, presses his fingers into the flesh, then pinches my stiffened bud.

"Mmm, nice and hard. Beautifully swollen and ready."

He switches his attention to my right breast, teasing and pinching until that nipple, too, is rigid and throbbing. He releases me, and I gnaw on my lower lip, tense, apprehensive, but at the same time eager for this. I roll my shoulders back and push out my chest in invitation.

"Be absolutely still, now," he warns me, an instant before fire explodes in my left nipple.

"Christ," I hiss. "Christ, that hurt."

"Settle down. We're not done yet."

I drag in several breaths, panting as I work to process the pain, only to lose all the air in my longs when he swipes my left nipple with the tongue of the crop.

"Jesus! Ow, ow, ow." Despite the sudden flare of agony, I don't move.

"Good girl. Now just once more on each, then you can turn around."

Somehow, I manage not to squirm away or shout my safe word when he repeats the torture on each nipple. At least I have the measure of this and can temper the pain with growing arousal. My breasts are throbbing, aching for his touch by the time he tells me to get on all fours.

He leaves the blindfold on then helps me to shuffle a bit further towards the foot of the bed. "Lift your bottom up nice and high and keep still. This will sting, but not too much. I'm preparing you for the cane."

"How many strokes, Sir?"

"I don't know. As many as it takes to properly set you up for your first caning."

"I see. Thank you."

The first few strokes are light, teasing, almost. I'm tempted to writhe and wriggle a bit but I remember his instructions and try to remain quite still.

The intensity ramps up. Each stroke offers its own delicious bite, adds to the heat in my buttocks and thighs. He leaves no spot untreated, dropping quick little strokes everywhere, covering every inch of my tender flesh.

"Oh! Ow!" I squeal when the sensation builds to the point of real, enduring pain.

"Almost there." He lays his palm on my sizzling buttocks and presses hard. "Ah, yes, I think you'll do."

"Oh God," I moan. *Why did I get into this?*

"Five strokes will be the maximum. If you want to stop at any time, say 'red'."

"I...I'm okay."

"I know, but this will be intense. If you need me to stop, I expect to hear that safe word."

"I will," I promise.

I flinch when he lays the cane across my buttocks, not hitting me with it, just slowly, gently stroking.

"Just concentrate on the sensation. Let it seep into you." He draws the cane back and forth across my throbbing skin. It's almost hypnotic, calming me, soothing me, grounding me. Then, he lifts it and brings it down hard across both buttocks.

I scream. This is like nothing I ever imagined. The agony seems to be suspended for a moment and the breath rushes from my body, then it hits me like a tsunami, setting my bottom on fire as the rush of pure white heat engulfs me.

"Ohh," I moan. "Oh God, oh God..."

"Ride it out, Fern. Breathe through it."

It's easy for him to say, but I do try to concentrate on drawing in each breath, then exhaling calmly. It works, after a fashion. The pain doesn't so much subside as seep into my flesh to become part of me.

Caleb draws the flat of his hand through my folds. "Jesus, you're so wet. So hot. Again?"

"I..." Words are lost on me. I simply nod. "Again."

He repeats the caress, the seductive dance where he rubs the cane back and forth, then, just when I drift into a relaxed stupor, he delivers the second stroke.

Once more there is that moment of...nothing, then agony

flares again. I gasp for air. My throat closes around a silent scream. I breathe in through my nose, then exhale through my mouth, reaching for the sense of control he gave me before.

I grab it, ride it, hold on as the pain morphs into perverse pleasure and sinks into my flesh.

"One more, then we're done here."

Caleb's voice is soft but determined. I want to argue, to demand the five he promised me, but I know better.

"Thank you," I sob.

The final stroke is cruel, excruciating, and utterly exquisite. I have never understood how pain can be cleansing, but I do now. There is a purity in it, a soul-deep honesty that leaves me feeling both refreshed and exhausted. I collapse forward onto the mattress, weeping from an excess of elation because no other outlet will suffice.

Caleb lies down behind me. He removes the blindfold, then turns me and holds me against his chest. He doesn't speak, doesn't try to shush me, just lets me cry out the pent-up emotion released by the caning.

Long moments pass. I lose any sense of time. My thoughts begin to align themselves again and just one overriding urge consumes me.

"Cal," I whisper.

"Yes?"

"Fuck me. Please. Fuck me hard and fast. I... I want it to hurt."

CHAPTER 27

I answer my phone on the third ring. An unfamiliar number is displayed on the tiny screen.

"Caleb McPherson," I say automatically.

There's a silence at the other end, then a tentative, "Hello?"

"Hello. This is Caleb McPherson."

"I... I need tae talk tae ye." It's a female voice, not young, I'd say, with a strong Scottish brogue.

"Can you tell me your name, please?"

"Me name doesnae matter. An' if ye try tae trace this call ye'll get nowhere. It's a pay as ye go, an' I'll dump it."

What the...?

"Now look," I reply, seriously irritated by now, "I don't have time for this."

"Then ye'd do well tae make time, lad."

"If you have something to say to me, spit it out. What is this concerning? Maybe one of my staff could help you."

"No! No, it has to be ye. I'm no' talkin' tae anyone else."

"Get on with it, then. I'm listening."

"This is...about Meryl. And the hospital."

The dismissive response dies on my lips. I pause, take a breath. "Meryl? You mean Meryl McPherson? My mother?"

"Aye. That I do."

"What do you know of her?"

"Enough. An' my information's worth a pretty penny, I'd say. Five grand, at least."

"Five thousand pounds?"

"That's right. In cash. Ye pay me, an' I'll tell ye what really happened at Halstead Grange."

I pause again, try to process this, to digest what this stranger is saying to me. My business instincts kick in.

"Information first. If it's good enough, and if I believe you, then I'll consider what to pay you."

"That's nae the deal. Ye'll leave the money in a rubbish bin outside Waverley Station. Tomorrow. Five o'clock, when it's nice an' busy, like. Once I've checked it, I'll be back in touch tae tell ye the tale."

"Now, hang on. You can't expect me to—"

The line goes dead.

I waste no time in bringing up my speed dial to call Harry.

"Hi, boss."

"I need you to find the owner of this phone." I reel off the number which was recorded in my incoming calls. "It's a pay as you go."

"Leave it with me."

He ends the call. I sit back in my chair. Nothing to do for the moment except wait.

Harry calls me back a couple of hours later. "Hi, boss, about that phone..."

"Yeah?"

"It's registered to a Martha McKenzie. Age fifty-seven, a retired nurse."

A nurse? Interesting.

"Do you have an address?"

"Yes." He rattles off the name of a tower block in Glasgow. "Do we need to go and pay her a visit?"

"I think we do. Are you in the area?"

"I could be in Glasgow in an hour."

What Happens in Vegas...

I glance at my watch. "I'll see you there. Three o'clock."

I grab my jacket and head for the lift to the foyer. Just my luck to meet Fern coming out of the drawing room.

"Hey, where are you off to?"

"Business," I reply, barely breaking stride.

"What sort of business?" She matches my step. "You look upset."

"I'm fine. I shouldn't be too long."

"Caleb, stop. You're scaring me. What's happened?" She grabs my sleeve.

Short of shaking her hand off, I have no choice but to stop.

"Something urgent came up. I need to go to Glasgow."

"I'll come, too," she replies, her smile bright.

"You can't." For all I know, this woman who thinks nothing of trying to blackmail a perfect stranger could be dangerous. I can't expose Fern to possible harm.

"Of course I can." Already, she has skirted the car and is getting into the passenger seat. "I can wait in the car while you have your meeting. Or maybe wander around the shops."

"It...it could take a while. You'd be bored."

"But you just said you wouldn't be too long." She meets my gaze and is not backing down. "Tell me what's really going on, Cal. You're not dressed for a business meeting..." She gestures to my casual Levi's and black T-shirt. "And you left your briefcase behind."

"Fern, I—"

"Just tell me. I'm not letting up until you do."

I groan, but there's clearly not going to be any way short of physical force that I can eject her from my car. Neither can I sit here arguing while Harry waits for me in Glasgow, and Martha McKenzie gets up to Christ knows what.

"Okay, but you'll have to promise to stay out of it and let me and Harry handle everything."

"Harry? He's involved, then?"

"Yes. I'm meeting him in Glasgow."

"Right. Go on."

I start the car and set off along the drive. "Okay. I had a phone call, about two hours ago…"

Fern listens in silence while I relate the details of my conversation with Martha McKenzie. When I finish, she twists in the seat so she is facing me. "You think there might be something in this, don't you?"

I shoot a glance her way. "She knows my mother's name, and the name of the hospital. And she's a retired nurse."

"A retired nurse ready to resort to blackmail. It hardly speaks of caring and honesty."

"There is that."

"Will you pay her?"

"Possibly. If I think she's telling the truth and the information really is helpful."

"And if you don't. Or it isn't?"

"Then I'll probably leave the matter with Harry to settle. Unless you'd prefer I report her to the police."

"Let's meet her, then we'll decide."

HARRY IS PARKED in the street outside the tower block. I pull up behind him. He looks surprised to see Fern but greets her politely enough.

"Fern insisted on coming along, but she's going to wait in the car."

"I see. The flat is on the thirteenth floor, boss. Number forty-nine."

"Any way of knowing if she's in?"

He shrugs. "Knocking on the door is the usual method."

"Smartarse." I set off for the main entrance. "I hope the bloody lift works."

It does. Harry manages to key in the correct code to gain us entry to the building. I have no notion how he does this stuff and no intention of asking. The lift is tiny to the point of claus-

What Happens in Vegas...

trophobic, and we're both relieved to step out onto a landing that smells suspiciously of disinfectant mixed with cat pee. The bare concrete walls are covered in graffiti detailing the romantic entanglements of local youths, as well as several gang-related tags. I shudder. This is not a salubrious neighbourhood.

"Let's get on with this." I spot the number forty-nine on the door closest to us. I march up and knock.

Several seconds pass. There is silence from within. I knock again, harder.

"I could break in, boss."

I consider Harry's offer but shake my head. "What would be the point? We need to speak to her."

He shrugs, and I knock one last time before finally admitting defeat.

"Bugger." I start to bark out orders. "I want someone watching this place. I want photos. I want someone tailing her when she goes to Edinburgh to collect her money tomorrow."

"I'll sort that, boss."

By mutual agreement, we don't use the lift to go down. We're on the third flight from the bottom when we meet Fern on her way up. I suppose I should be surprised, but I'm not.

"She's not in," I say, before she can ask.

"Oh. Right. Maybe that's for the best..." She takes my hand, and we head on back to the ground floor.

The woman carrying two bags of shopping along the path outside is nondescript. Middle-aged, hair grey, wearing a waterproof coat which has seen distinctly better days, she struggles to operate the keypad with both hands full. Harry opens it from inside, and steps aside to let her pass.

"Thank ye, lad." She shuffles past us, heading for the lift.

Maybe it's her voice. Maybe it's the way she calls Harry 'lad'. I watch her as she presses the button to select the thirteenth floor.

Four flats to each storey. We already worked that out. A one-in-four chance, then...

"Hey, Martha, do you need a hand with those bags?"

Fern steps forward, all smiles. The woman turns, peers at Fern as though she should recognise her. "It's right kind o' ye tae offer, lass, but I'm almost there now." The lift door opens, and she takes a step forward.

Harry is faster.

"No, we can't let you carry all this on your own." He is already in the lift with her, deftly relieving her of one of her bags. "The thirteenth, was it?"

"Aye," she confirms, "but ye dinnae have tae..."

Fern and I rush the lift, too. All four of us huddle in the cramped space. Any further objections raised by Martha are shelved until the lift pings to a halt, back on the thirteenth floor.

"You'll be in number forty-nine, is that right?" Harry dumps the shopping bag on her doorstep.

"How d'ye ken that?" she demands, glaring at each of us in turn.

"You knew my mother, I believe." I hold out my hand. "I'm Caleb McPherson. We spoke earlier, on the phone."

Martha McKenzie pales and staggers backwards. At first, I think she might be about to faint, but she manages to remain upright.

"How...? How did you...?"

"That doesn't matter. You *are* Martha McKenzie?"

"N-no. I dinnae ken what—" Her eyes dart from me to Harry, then to Fern.

"Let's go inside. We need to talk."

"Ye cannae just—"

"The keys, please?" Fern holds out her hand. "Unless you'd prefer me to go through your handbag."

The woman mutters something which I can't quite catch, but I have no doubt it was both obscene and deeply offensive.

She does, however, reach into her pocket and produce the door keys.

"Thank you." Fern unlocks the flat, and Harry leads the way carrying both shopping bags. WE all trail behind him.

Harry deposits the bags in the kitchen, then follows the rest of us into the small but mercifully clean living room. There are two chairs, one of them cluttered with magazines and several Mills and Boon novels. The other chair is the only one that appears to be used for its intended purpose. I assume Martha McKenzie lives alone.

She sinks into the one usable chair and folds her arms. "Ye'll have tae leave. My son is due back any time, an' he'll—"

I remove the obstacles from the other chair and sit. "Tell me, Martha, what's your connection to Halstead Grange?"

"Halstead what?"

"Let's not play games. You phoned me this afternoon and offered me information regarding the death of my mother, in exchange for five thousand pounds in cash. Is that not the case?"

"No, it isnae. Why would I—?"

I pull out my phone, bring up the list of recent callers, and hit 'return call' next to the number which called me. Moments later, the strains of *Daydream Believer* fill the room.

I cringe. I was never fond of ringtones. But my point is made.

"Martha, unless you prefer to discuss this matter with the police, I suggest you start cooperating now. I'm not a patient man at the best of times, and so far you've done nothing but piss me off. So, I'll ask once more. What's your connection to Halstead Grange?"

She glares at me, her mouth working as though trying to formulate some new lie, anything to throw me off the scent.

"Martha? Now," I warn her.

Moments pass, then, "Oh fuck, all right. I used tae work there."

"You were a nurse, I believe," Harry says.

"How d'ye ken that?"

I honestly don't know how Harry found out. I turn to him for an answer.

"Social media," is his succinct explanation. "It never ceases to amaze me how much information people put online."

I return to the matter in hand. "So, you worked at Halstead Grange. As a nurse. Go on."

"I'll still be wantin' me money."

"Really? Tell me what I want to know, and we'll discuss money later, if you have anything useful to offer."

"Oh, it'll be useful all right." She pauses, seems to be considering where to start, then, "I were a midwife back then, trainin' like. An' yer ma were a patient."

I narrow my eyes. "When was this, exactly?"

"Nineteen ninety. I remember the exact year because it were when our David got wed."

"David?"

"Me brother. 'E's dead now, mind." She shakes her head. "Cancer it were. Anyway, yer ma'd been comin' tae the hospital for months, for the scans an' such like. We ran an antenatal clinic as well as a delivery ward."

"Okay. And Mr Saunders was her consultant?"

"That 'e was, aye. An' 'e were a good doctor, i' spite of everythin'."

I suspect she's referring to his ill-fated career as a transplant surgeon. "I'm sure. So, Meryl, my mother, came to you for antenatal care?"

"Aye, she did. An' that was 'ow we kenned. An' she did, too, mind. It were only yer da who didnae ken. He must not ha' known…"

"Known what? What did you all know that he didn't?"

"We kenned aboot the twins."

There is silence. Total, deathly silence. If I found yesterday's revelations in Miss Forbes' office stunning, that was nothing compared to this. Fern is the first to gather her wits.

"Meryl McPherson was having twins?"

"Aye. She were. An' when it were 'er time she came tae Halstead Grange tae give birth. I attended tae her, along wi' another midwife, more senior than me."

"Go on," Fern presses her. "What happened?"

"She were in labour, an' struggling. It went on for a day, then another. Mr Saunders decided tae do a Caesarean. An' not before time if ye ask me. So, that's what 'appened. A little boy it were. Ye, I suppose." She meets my gaze. "But she wouldnae even hold 'im. Just shoved 'im away an' told Mr Saunders tae do what 'ad been agreed."

"And what was that, Martha? What had been agreed?" Fern's voice is soft, but her tone is strong. She is as determined as I am to get at the truth.

"Mr Saunders told Mrs Cox, that were the other midwife, tae take the wee laddie an' get in touch wi' 'is father. Alister McPherson. She were tae tell 'im that 'is wife 'ad died and that we were all very sorry, but could 'e make arrangements tae collect 'is son."

"Alister McPherson was told that his wife was dead?" Fern's expression betrays nothing.

"Aye. 'E was. That was what she wanted."

"Meryl?" Fern locks eyes with Martha McKenzie. "Are you absolutely sure about that? Meryl wanted her husband to be told that she was dead. Even though she wasn't?"

"Oh, aye, nae doubt o' that. It were all 'er idea. She paid Mr Saunders tae do it 'er way an' tae keep 'er secret."

"What happened to the other baby? There were twins, you said."

"Aye. That's right. As soon as the first wee one were out o' the room, Mr Saunders delivered the second lad. Mrs McPherson held that one, an' she fed 'im. She'd given one bairn tae her husband, an' she kept the second one for herself."

"Mrs Forbes never mentioned twins," I say, mainly for Fern's benefit.

"Who is Mrs Forbes?" Martha asks.

"The hospital administrator," I reply. "We went to see her."

"There were nae records kept. Meryl insisted. Nae paperwork that could ever let 'er 'usband find out what she did. Mr Saunders was paid tae cover it all up, make sure it stayed a secret. The only ones as kenned were me an' Mrs Cox, Mr Saunders, an' the anaesthetist. Me an' Mrs Cox each got fifty pounds in exchange for our silence. I expect the anaesthetist got more, an' Mr Saunders kept the rest. Mrs McPherson an' her baby stayed a few days, then left."

"Where did they go?" I ask.

Martha McKenzie shrugs. "I've nae idea. What I do ken, though, is that she changed 'er name. At least, 'er last name. It were like she meant tae just disappear."

"What do you mean?" I demand. "What name did she go by after?"

"It were Meryl something. Began wi' a V. I saw it on the cheque she 'anded tae Mr Saunders. That were the last I saw of 'er. She didnae come back for any follow-up appointments. At the very least there's usually a six-week check-up, more probably after a Caesarean. But she ne'er came back."

The woman falls silent. Fern, Harry, and I exchange stunned looks.

"So, me money?" Martha tips her chin up at me. "Ye said ye'd pay, if the information were good enough."

I ignore her demand for money. "What made you contact me today? Why wait all these years?"

"What does it matter?"

"I'm puzzled. Why not sell the information to my father? I'm sure he'd have paid you well for it."

"His wife 'ad 'er reasons fer wantin' tae disappear, I dinnae doubt. I wouldnae ha' told 'im. But 'e's dead now, so..."

"He's been dead for five years. I repeat, why now?"

"I didnae need the cash before."

"What do you mean?"

She gestures around her. "Look at this place. Thirty years I worked as a midwife. I helped birth thousands o' bairns an' this is all I can look forward tae fer my retirement. Me sister lives in a lovely wee place, just outside Stirling. What wi' the little bit I have saved up, five grand would be enough fer me tae rent a wee cottage near 'er and live out me days in a bit o' comfort. I think I earned it."

I daresay she has a point but resorting to extortion seems excessive.

"I didnae plan it. I just…well, when young Rachel phoned me tae say as ye were askin' aboot yer ma, well, the notion just suddenly came tae me."

"Young Rachel? You mean the nurse at Halstead Grange?" Fern turns to me. "You remember, we talked to her when we first arrived."

I nod. "Do you keep in touch with the staff at Halstead Grange, Martha?"

"One or two. Me an' Rachel's ma worked together. She knew I used tae work on maternity so she thought I might remember Meryl McPherson. She rang me yesterday evening."

"And you hatched your little scheme overnight," Fern murmurs. "You didn't waste any time."

Martha shrugs again. "I'm no' gettin' any younger. So, are ye goin' tae pay me?"

I consider that for a few moments. There's no earthly reason why I should, and every good reason to report her to the police. But still…

"I'll pay you, but it won't be in cash left in a litter bin. Let me have the details of the cottage you want in Stirling, and I'll pay the first year's rent."

"But…" Martha's expression is one of utter astonishment. "That'll be more than the five grand I asked for."

"You kept my mother's secret. As I say, my father would

have paid far more." I produce a business card from my wallet. "Contact my office when you've chosen your cottage. I'll see to the rest."

"IT WAS HIM, wasn't it? Your twin brother?"

We're halfway back to Linn Mill, and this is the first time Fern has spoken.

"In Las Vegas?" I shoot her a quick glance. "Yes, I think it must have been. It fits all the facts."

"I'm sorry," she whispers.

"What do you have to apologise for? It sounds as though he set out to deliberately impersonate me and made a good job of it. How were you to know?"

"I don't mean that. I mean, about Archie. You…you believed he was your son."

I shake my head. "*You* believed that, but I knew all along that he wasn't. He couldn't be. Whatever the DNA said, it didn't alter the fact that I was never in Vegas. I couldn't be his father and I never claimed to be. Well, I might have let the hospital think that, back in Stockport, but only because it seemed simpler that way."

"But you took him in anyway. After the hit-and-run."

"Of course. The DNA evidence was proof of…a connection. I didn't understand what that connection might be, but Archie was clearly my flesh and blood somehow, and I wasn't about to abandon him."

"This is all so bizarre. Who would ever have imagined…?"

"True. It is bizarre. But it also makes sense. In fact, it's the only thing that does make sense, and I should have worked it out. Someone else, with DNA identical to mine. It's the only explanation that stacks up and accounts for all the evidence."

"What are we going to do about it?"

"Do? I honestly don't know."

CHAPTER 28

"So, there you have it. The facts as we now understand them."

Caleb leans back in his chair and sweeps his gaze over the rest of us assembled around his boardroom table back at Linn Mill. Archie is tucked up asleep in bed, but everyone else is here. I sit to Caleb's right, and next to me is my mother. Then Harry and Sally. Simon Waters, the solicitor, sits opposite me, making copious notes.

Caleb has outlined our recent discoveries. He invites any questions.

"So, it was your brother who got married to our Fern, in Las Vegas?" Poppy says. "Not you?"

"Not me," he confirms.

"Then, we're here, under your roof, under false pretences," she continues.

"Why is that?" Caleb asks gently. "I always knew I wasn't Fern's husband, but I invited you here anyway."

"But we—"

"Setting all of that aside," Harry interrupts, "the question now, surely, is what do we do next."

Simon looks up from his notes. "Presumably, you intend to track this individual down. At the very least we need to ensure that there is no repeat of this...this deception. The next time he decides to play at being you, the consequences could be far more serious."

"Thank you very much," I mutter.

Caleb lays his hand over mine and squeezes. "That's a fair point, but to the best of our knowledge he hasn't tried anything else. It's been nearly six years. I see no cause to assume my... brother is a danger to me."

"But—" Simon starts to protest, but Caleb quells him with a glance.

"Firstly, we have absolutely nothing to go on. My mother disappeared leaving no trace, no trail. We don't even know her name. Unless, and until they surface again, what prospect do we have of locating either her or my brother?"

His question is met by silence. Caleb continues.

"And second, apart from the point made by Simon, what would be the purpose of tracking them down? My mother could have made herself known to me at any time in the last few years, certainly since my father died. She chose not to. She knows about me, knows who I am, because it's obvious that she told her other son. Why else would he have used my name? There appears to be no desire for a family reunion on their side, so why would I seek them out?"

I return the squeeze of his hand and meet his gaze, For the first time, perhaps, I see the hurt there, and the latent bitterness. I see the lonely, abandoned and ignored little boy, and I know without any shadow of doubt that he doesn't mean it. He wants his family. He wants that reunion. He wants answers to so many questions.

"You can't mean to just let it lie? To leave it like this?" My mother shakes her head. "I don't believe that."

"As I say, what would be the point?" Caleb replies. "At least now we know the truth about what happened in Vegas. Fern and I can move on, and—"

"My Fern can't move on. She's stuck, married to a man she

can't contact and will like as not never see again. What if she were to meet someone else?"

"Mum, I—"

"I can sign the divorce papers, if that's what Fern wants. The courts would certainly accept that. She needn't be shackled to this...this situation for good."

Simon clears his throat. Caleb turns to regard him. "You have a point to make?"

Simon nods. "I do. And it is simply that this latest revelation obviates the need for a divorce, since the marriage is and has always been, invalid."

"Invalid?" Caleb narrows his eyes. "Explain."

"One of the parties, your brother, committed a fraud when obtaining the necessary documentation. He then participated in the marriage ceremony under an assumed name. I would be happy to confirm following consultation with US colleagues, but I am quite certain that such a union is not valid and would not be recognised as such on either side of the Atlantic."

"You mean, I'm not married. And I never was?" *After everything, I suppose I should be pleased. I'm not. This knowledge leaves me suddenly desolate.*

The lawyer inclines his head. "That is the case, Miss Daniels."

My mother gives an unladylike snort. "I don't know whether to congratulate you or not."

I shake my head. "I can't believe it. I was so sure. How could I have not known? Not realised you weren't the same...?"

"I think it's fair to assume my brother is my identical twin," Caleb offers. "And by the time you and I met, it had been five years..."

"Even so..." I meet Caleb's gaze. "We have to find him. I need to see him again and ask him why he did it. What did he have against me that made him want to ruin my life?"

"I wouldn't say your life is ruined, exactly," my mother observes. "For a start, we wouldn't have Archie but for...this."

"Well, I suppose that's something," I concede. "But it's hardly closure, is it?"

"Closure?" Caleb turns to me. "Is that what you want, Fern? Closure?"

Yes. And so do you if you would but admit it.

"Yes," I reply. "Yes, I want closure. I want to…to find that man and ask him why he did it."

"Okay, I do understand that. And if he pops his head up again, we can—"

I shake my head. "There must be a way. There must be something to lead us to them. No one can just disappear…"

Simon appears to agree with Caleb. "It's been what, over thirty years since she disappeared and not a word. For all we know, Meryl McPherson might be truly dead by now."

Caleb shakes his head. "I don't think so. Or, at least…Fern, didn't you tell me once that you met me…sorry, my brother, when he came into the gallery where you worked? He wanted to buy something?"

I nod. "Yes. He bought a birthday present. He said it was for his mother."

"Exactly. So, why would he lie about that if he didn't know you, and at that stage you had no connection to me? And, if we assume he wasn't lying, it's fair to also assume that Meryl was alive and well and having a birthday about six years ago."

"Cal!" I grasp his sleeve. "He bought a figurine, of a ballerina. And you found the ballet slippers. You said you always had the idea she was into ballet, somehow. Your tattoo…"

He nods, slowly. "And Meryl is a fairly unusual name…"

"It's still a massive pool to search in," Simon points out. "If we could just narrow it down a bit more."

"The last name she adopted began with a V," Harry adds the next bit of the jigsaw. "Remember, Martha McKenzie told us that."

Simon is scribbling his notes again. "You said you have your parents' marriage certificate?"

Caleb nods. "In the filing cabinet."

"May I have it, please?"

"What for?" Caleb is already on his feet and heading for the cabinet.

"There are agencies that specialise in tracking down missing or disappeared persons. I suggest we brief one of them. I know of one that comes highly recommended. We would need to give them what we have so far, along with any primary source documents..."

"Primary source?" I ask.

"Something directly linked to the missing person," he clarifies. "In this case, something with Meryl's signature on it, as well as information about her immediate family."

Cal returns to the table with the folded document. He hands it to Simon. "Keep me updated. Any progress, however slight, I want to know."

"Of course. And if there's anything else you think of, or come across, you'll let me know. The slightest detail could be crucial..."

TWO WEEKS LATER...

"MERYL VALENCE," I breathe, scanning the pages of the investigative agency's report. I look up at Caleb. "This is astonishing. I mean, how did they...?"

"Remember the wedding certificate? Vivian Valence, one of the witnesses? We had a hunch about her, and it seems we were onto something. The agency interviewed Len Ferrands. He was easy enough to track down, he's still on my corporate Christmas card list. He told them he'd never met Vivian before the ceremony, but he did chat to her that day, and as far as he could recall she was a relative of the bride. An aunt, he thought. He was right. The agency managed to establish that Meryl's mother's maiden name was Valence. Meryl was close to her Aunt Vivian so it was natural that she would be a witness at the wedding, and apparently they did remain in touch until Vivian's death about ten years ago. Meryl is named in Vivian's will, I gather. She inherited ten thousand pounds and an antique clock."

"A clock?"

He nods. "At that time, she was living in Ashburton."

"Ashburton," I repeat. "Where...?"

"A few miles south of Christchurch. New Zealand."

"I see. She couldn't have got much farther away." I scan the report slowly, picking out salient details. The agency describes their detailed social media trawl and other online research which has turned up a life story, of sorts.

Meryl Baxter, daughter of Isabella Valence and Edward Baxter, had been a promising ballerina, and aged sixteen won a place with the Scottish Ballet Company in Glasgow. Four years later, aged twenty, she was managing to break out of the chorus line and had even performed a couple of solos by the time she met and married Alister McPherson in nineteen eighty-nine. For no obvious reason, though, her promising career seemed to stagnate from there and was abruptly cut short by a nasty fall down the stairs at her home about two months after her marriage. She shattered her kneecap, an injury which meant she would never dance professionally again.

There follows a gap of about five years during which the agency could find no trace of her apart from the records we already turned up relating to her brief stay at Halstead Grange. The agency concentrated on the New Zealand connection they had discovered from Vivian Valence's will and eventually found Meryl running a small school of ballet in Wellington. From there they were able to trace her moving around the country, ending up in Christchurch where she apparently holds the position of Head of Dance in a school for performing arts.

"So, she's still working," I observe.

"Looks like it."

"What about her other son? What did the agency find out about him?"

"Nothing much until he finished high school in two thousand and eight and went on to university. His name's David Valence. He graduated four years later with a degree in English Literature and a teaching diploma and moved to the US. The agency finally located him teaching English Literature in a high school in Mesquite, Nevada."

"Nevada? Is that—?"

"About eighty miles from Las Vegas. An hour and a half by car."

"Did he work there when…?"

Caleb nods. "David Valence was appointed to his job in two thousand and twelve. And here's the clincher. The following year the school was closed for the summer recess from the beginning of June until early September."

"So, he was on holiday from work. That's why he was in Las Vegas, probably, and why he had the time on his hands to spend with me."

"David had the opportunity, certainly. And the means. The missing bit is motive. Why would he do it? What did he stand to gain? Why impersonate me? And how did he get away with it? I mean, what about his accent if he grew up in New Zealand? And mannerisms?"

"He did have an odd accent. I noticed soon after you and I met, that you didn't really sound like you had before. But I assumed you had been imitating an American accent in Las Vegas, and probably not very well. I'm not sure I'd recognise a New Zealand one, especially if he did try to disguise it. Maybe he put on his best English accent for my benefit. As for mannerisms, I had nothing to compare to. How would I have known?" I pause, considering all the questions we need answers to. "We need to ask him." I grab Caleb's hand. "Or I do. Did the agency find his address?"

"Yes, it's here. But—"

"I'm going there. To Nevada. As soon as I can get a flight. Can I leave Archie with you?"

He shakes his head. "Not a chance. You're not the only one with unfinished business to settle. I'm coming, too."

"Wow! I never knew what it was like to fly first class. I must do it more often."

Fern beams up at me as we make our way through the new arrivals lounge at McCarran International Airport, dragging our wheeled suitcases behind us.

I wrap an arm around her shoulders. "Stick with me, kid."

I'm not really joking.

She yawns, a reminder that, however luxurious the accommodation, overnight flights are still a bitch.

We exit the airport into the balmy Nevada sunshine. Although this is December, the coolest time of the year, it's still a desert out here and the sun shines all year round. A row of taxis snakes around the front of the terminal, and we join the queue. A few minutes later we're in the back of a yellow cab.

"Where to, folks?" the driver asks.

I didn't bother to book ahead. I reckon it should be easy enough to find accommodation. "We need a motel, in the Mesquite area. Can you recommend anywhere?"

He grins. "Sure can, sir. You'll be wantin' the Blue Falls out on Highway Eighty. It's a fair way, though..."

"Will this cover it?" I hand him a five hundred dollar bill.

"Sure will." The driver pockets the cash and starts to pull out onto the main driveway heading for the exit into the city.

"How long will it take to get there?" Fern asks, yawning again.

Our driver threads the cab through the teaming traffic with

effortless ease borne or years of practice. "You'll be there in time for lunch, lady."

"I'm not interested in food. I just want a soft bed and a shower. In that order."

I tuck her up against me, and she's asleep before the car reaches the Las Vegas Strip. I settle back to enjoy the scenery and plan how to handle my first meeting with a brother I never even knew existed until two weeks ago.

THE BLUE FALLS is reasonably upmarket, if that's a phrase which could be properly applied to a drive-in motel. We rent a small suite consisting of a bedroom, sitting room, bathroom, and kitchenette, available for hire by the day. The rooms are clean, modern, and everything works. There's also a diner selling Tex Mex food on the site, a laundrette, and a beauty salon.

I peer at my phone. "According to the maps app, David's apartment is about half an hour's walk from here."

Fern has just woken from a couple of hours sleep. I pass my phone to her so that she can see where we are. "Do you want to go and look him up today or leave it until tomorrow?"

"Today," she replies. "Definitely today."

"Fair enough. Let's get something to eat, then we'll take a stroll round there. Unless you want to phone for a cab?"

She shakes her head. "I fancy a chilli dog followed by a nice walk."

The diner serves up a fine late lunch of nachos loaded with cheese and salsa, and a foot-long hot dog doused in chilli sauce, that we share. Fern swallows the last of hers and puts her napkin aside.

"Time to go."

I leave a couple of twenty-dollar bills on the table, nod to the waitress, and we exit into the pleasant afternoon sun. Fern lifts her face and smiles.

"I'd forgotten how warm it is here. Even in the winter."

"And I'd forgotten about the monster portion sizes they serve on this side of the Atlantic." I rub my stomach. "I don't think I'll eat for a week."

"Well, the walk should keep us on the right side of obesity. Which way is it?"

I consult my phone again. "Out onto the main highway, then turn left."

"Well, it looks..." Fern hesitates, clearly unsure how to describe the nondescript three-storey block facing us.

"Unpretentious?" I offer.

"Modest," she clarifies. "Modest and unfussy."

"Right. Well, according to the internet, schools here finished for the Christmas holiday two days ago, so we know he's not working today. Shall we see if he's at home?"

She nods, resolute. "Let's do this."

The glass doors are controlled by a secure entry system. Alongside the keypad is a row of doorbells. The third one in the row bears the name 'Valence'. I press it and step back.

Moments later there's a faint buzz, then a voice. "Hey, what happened?"

"I beg your pardon?" I reply. Fern and I exchange puzzled glances.

"Did you miss your flight? And lose your key? What're you doing back here?" the disembodied female voice demands.

"She thinks you're David," Fern whispers. "There must be a camera or something..."

For want of a better strategy, I opt to come clean. "My name's Caleb. I'm David's brother..."

"Holy shit," the voice concludes. "Well, I suppose you'd better come on up."

There's a short but loud buzz, and I push on the door which opens readily.

"His apartment is on the first floor." I take Fern's hand, and we climb the short flight of stairs.

A girl of about seventeen sporting more facial piercings than I can count greets us on the landing.

"Fuck, you certainly look like him..." She peers at me with undisguised curiosity. "You two twins or something? Davey never said nothing about a brother."

"I...we're not close," I explain. "Are you a friend of his?"

She shakes her head. "Not really. I live upstairs. I'm just here to feed the cat." Right on cue, a large grey feline appears through the open door behind her. The girl bends to scoop it up in her arms.

"Ah. I see. He's away, then?"

The girl nods. "They went to spend Christmas with his mother."

"They?" I frown at her.

"Davey and Harper."

"And Harper is...?"

"Davey's wife. Gee, you meant it when you said you two weren't close. Anyway, they're not due back until New Year's Day. I could leave a message. Or, I have Davey's number if you want to call him..." She pauses. "I guess he'll be real sorry to have missed you."

I'm not so sure of that, but I keep my opinion to myself.

"You mentioned a flight. They went to New Zealand, then?"

The girl nods. "To his mother's place. Well, your mother, too, I suppose, since you're brothers an' all."

"Er, yes. Quite. I—"

"There's no need for a message, but we'll take that number, please," Fern interrupts, smiling brightly at the girl. "Lovely cat. What's she called?"

"Felix. It's a him." The girl shoves the cat back through the door from which he emerged and produces her mobile phone. She rattles off a number, which Fern keys into her own phone.

"Well, thank you." Fern offers her hand. "We're sorry to have disturbed you. Have a nice Christmas."

"You, too. And if you do call Davey, tell him Felix knocked Harper's lamp over. And the vacuum cleaner's broken."

BACK OUT IN THE SUNSHINE, Fern slumps to sit on the wall. I sit next to her.

"Did you hear that? He remarried."

"Sounds like it."

"But he can't. He's already married. To me."

"Not according to Simon."

"Well, yes, but—" Fern's jaw flexes. "We need to see him. Talk to him."

"I agree. This needs sorting, and the sooner the better. He'll be back at New Year. We could wait."

"But that would mean being away from home over Christmas. I'd hoped to be back, for Archie."

"Me, too. So, it seems to me we have three choices."

"Okay?" She regards me, her expression puzzled.

"One, we go home and come back after the new year. By then, it's a knocking bet that the human pincushion up there will have told him his identical twin came calling. I suspect my brother Davey will be keen to avoid me if he can."

"And we'll have lost the element of surprise."

"True, although he won't be able to avoid us for long. If need be we'll camp out at the school where he works."

"Okay. What's our second choice?"

"We stay here and make sure we're on his doorstep to say 'hi' when he gets back."

"But—"

"I know. Christmas with Archie. So that's a non-starter. Agreed?"

"Agreed. Number three?"

"We check out flights to New Zealand."

CHAPTER 29

We're lucky. Caleb manages to snag us the last two business-class tickets on a flight from Las Vegas to Queenstown on New Zealand's South Island. It's not ideal as we'll have a six-hour drive ahead of us to get to Christchurch, but it's preferable to waiting another day for a direct flight.

"I'll book us a hire car. And a hotel in Christchurch," he says, tapping away on his phone. "And a return flight to the UK the day before Christmas Eve."

"That only gives us one day in New Zealand. Will it be enough?"

He meets my gaze. "I'd say it'll be ample."

APART FROM MY gap year in America, I've never been that much of a traveller, so I'm not prepared for the weird sensation of jet lag that assails me when we arrive in New Zealand at what Caleb insists is just after nine in the morning. I'm completely disorientated and could sleep for a week, whereas he seems as bright-eyed and bushy-tailed as usual.

Caleb steers me towards the car hire kiosk where a smart little Suzuki awaits us. He bundles our cases into the boot and me into the passenger seat.

"Sleep," he instructs me.

"But don't you need me to navigate?"

He grins. "I'd rather take my chance with the satnav. I'll wake you when I spot somewhere decent for us to eat."

"I'm starving."

"I'll bear that in mind." He starts the engine, and that's as much as I remember until he wakes me in front of a cheerful roadside pizzeria. I make short work of a *quattro stagioni* washed down with ice-cold cola before settling down in the car for the second leg of the journey.

"How much farther is it?"

"A couple of hours," he tells me, "assuming the traffic stays light. We should be there by three o'clock, local time."

"Which is what, really?" I yawn.

"Never mind. Just get some sleep."

"Fern? We're here."

What? Where?

"Wake up, love. We've arrived." He gives me a gentle shake. "You'll have time for a shower, and we can grab a bite to eat, too, if you like."

Shower? I'm tempted, but more sleep sounds better.

"Come on. We need to check in, freshen up, then go and find this pretend husband of yours."

I open my eyes. "Check in?"

"Yes. We're at the hotel." He drops a kiss on my mouth. "Come on, Sleeping Beauty."

"Christ, I feel so strange…"

"It'll wear off in a day or so…"

"By which time I'll be on another plane."

"I'm guessing we'll never make a globetrotter out of you." He gets out of the car and opens the boot. Soon our cases are perched on the steps to the small but stylish hotel he's found for us. I stumble out and try to clear my head, while Caleb chats easily to the uniformed doorman.

He wraps his arm around my shoulders and guides me into the foyer. The ambiance is one of understated elegance, though I barely have time to take in my surroundings as Caleb deals with the paperwork and hands over our passports in exchange for the room key.

"First floor," he murmurs. "The cases have already been taken up." He leads me up the thickly carpeted stairs and along an upper hallway, stopping before room number one zero four. "This is us."

The queen-size bed looks tempting, but Caleb urges me in the direction of the en suite. "You'll feel better after a shower. They serve food from the bar downstairs. I thought I might order us a sandwich."

I nod and drag myself off to do as I'm told.

In fact, he's right. A good, hot shower succeeds in clearing my head better than hours of sleep have done. I'm thinking far more clearly by the time I amble back into the bedroom swathed in fluffy white hotel towels to find Caleb tucking in to a plate of cheese and ham sandwiches.

"Ah, there you are. I ordered hot beef for you. Is that okay?"

My stomach growls. "Wonderful."

"And a pot of tea." He pours me a cup. "Help yourself to milk and sugar."

I savour my first sip and manage a smile. "Don't you need a shower, too?"

"In a minute." He helps himself to another sandwich. "Go on, dig in."

"So, are we ready for the confrontation?" His jaw flexing, Caleb picks up his jacket and passes me mine.

We are both suitably refreshed and ready to leave. I shrug into my coat.

"Do you think that's what it will be? A confrontation?"

"I'm assuming the worst."

"Your mother might be delighted to see you."

"Yeah, right." He snorts in disbelief. "She could have arranged that happy event at any time in the last thirty years. And I doubt if David ever expected to have to face you again."

"Tough." I harden my attitude. "I've chased him, quite literally, right to the ends of the earth so I intend to have my say."

"Exactly," he agrees. "Ready?"

I shrug into my jacket. "Let's do this."

"It's number two one seven," I say, twenty minutes later, checking the details provided by the investigation agency.

Caleb slows the Suzuki to barely more than a crawl, and we both scan the numbers on the doors and gates as we cruise down the suburban side street. This is a pleasant enough area, quiet, well-kept gardens in front of smart, single-storey dwellings, and little in the way of traffic.

"There. That's number one nine three," I say. "It can't be much farther."

Caleb nods and continues on a few more metres, pulling up in front of a neat bungalow set back from the road in its own grounds. We both peer at the house from the safety of the car.

"There's a light on in the window." Caleb kills the engine. "Looks like they're in. Let's get this done."

We both exit the car, and I join him on the pavement. Despite being after seven in the evening, it's still light because of the reversal of seasons here. It's mid-summer in New Zealand, which does nothing to help my jet lag. I link my arm in Caleb's, and he reaches for the gate latch.

"So, y'all decided to take a walk after all."

We both spin around at the unfamiliar voice, heavily laden with a Southern American drawl. A woman of perhaps thirty smiles at us over a bag of shopping.

"Here, you take this, sugar." She dumps the bag in Caleb's

What Happens in Vegas…

arms. "I'll get the gate. Nice jacket, by the way. Y'all must have sneaked it in while I had my back turned.

She opens the gate and marches along the neatly swept path leading to the front door. Caleb and I exchange a glance and follow her. We are becoming accustomed to Caleb being mistaken for his brother.

Our companion produces a key and unlocks the door. She steps inside, leaving the door swinging open, so we follow her into the hallway.

"Guess who I found outsi—" She pales as she takes in the two people already seated in the sitting room. Her eyes widen, and she spins around to face us again. "Who…? What the…?"

Caleb steps forward to dump the bag of shopping on a side table, then offers his hand to the woman. "My name is Caleb McPherson. This is Fern Daniels." He lifts his gaze to lock with eyes across the room, eyes identical to his own. "And this, I assume, is my twin brother. David."

The man in question rises from an armchair. "What the fuck are you doing here? How did you find us?" He does not appear exactly thrilled at the reunion, nor even unduly surprised. I wonder if his cat-sitter phoned him already.

"We'll come to all of that soon enough. For now, I'll be the one asking the questions."

I'm impressed by his calmness when Caleb turns to the only other occupant of the room, an older woman with the same dark eyes as both her sons. Her features are narrow, delicate, even. Her hair shows signs of greying at the temples but is still mostly the same glossy black as Caleb's. It is perfectly obvious which parent both sons take after. She, too, gets to her feet. Her build is slender, still that of a dancer.

"Caleb?" She extends her hand, palm up as though expecting the mirage to evaporate before her eyes. "Is this real? Are you…? I don't understand."

Caleb closes the distance between them and takes her

hand. "Sit down." His tone is gentler now. "We only want to talk."

She slumps back into her seat, still clinging to Caleb's hand.

"You've no right to just come bursting in here." This from David. "You need to go. Now."

Caleb opens his mouth to reply, but I get in first. "Don't you have anything to say to me, David? Surely, you must remember me?"

He narrows his eyes, and I'm sure I detect some hint of recognition there. He chooses instead to shake his head.

"I don't know you. Get out."

"Well, that's odd, as I haven't changed my name. I'm still the same Fern Daniels you met and married in Las Vegas five years ago. Except that you weren't using your own name at the time, were you?"

"What the fuck are you talking about? I'm married to Harper here." He gestures in the direction of the woman we met at the gate. "We've been married for over two years. We're having a baby."

Caleb chuckles, not a particularly pleasant sound. "Is that right? Well, brother David, I think it's fair to say that at least one of your marriages is invalid."

Harper groans and lays a protective hand over her abdomen. Of all the people affected by this debacle, she's the one I feel most sorry for right now.

Harper glares at her husband. "Davey, what's this all about? What have you done?"

"Nothing, I swear. It was…a mistake. Not important." Physically, the man might be identical to Caleb, but there the similarity ends. The individual now slumped in a chair in his mother's crowded living room is an empty, weak shadow of the man I have come to know. Where Caleb exudes self-confidence and assurance, David appears…defeated, a victim of his own self-doubt and anxiety.

My anger at him evaporates. He simply is not worth it.

Caleb has apparently arrived at the same conclusion. He shifts his attention to his mother.

"I have questions. Do you feel up to answering?"

She just stares at him, shaking her head.

"I realise it's a shock, me just showing up like this. If you want me to leave, I will, and I promise not to bother you again. We just need to settle the unfinished business between Fern and David here, and then we can—"

"No!" She grabs his hand. "Don't go."

"Okay?" He offers her a lop-sided grin.

"I don't want you to go. I need to... I need to tell you I'm sorry. I need you to know that I never stopped thinking about you. Every single day. I... I always loved you..."

There is silence.

Caleb looks to me, briefly, his brow furrowing, then he turns to regard his mother. "Start at the beginning. Tell me about my father, and why you married him."

She takes her time, which I suppose she is entitled to do. When she speaks, she is looking away from us, somewhere into the middle distance.

"I was young, only nineteen. Ballet was my life, always had been. I started dancing when I was five..." She flattens her lips. "I was good. Really good, and not just because I worked hard, though I did. All my teachers said I had talent, and when I managed to get a place in the Scottish Ballet Company, my future career was assured. I would progress to become a principal ballerina, travel the world and perform in all the greatest theatres. It was all coming true, everything I dreamed of. All that I worked for. Then, I met him."

"My father?" Caleb prompts.

"Alister McPherson." She almost spits the words out. "He came to a performance, saw me dancing a solo in *Sylvia*. He sent flowers, asked if he could come backstage to meet me. That wasn't unusual, a lot of men do that. It doesn't always mean much. But, from then, he hardly missed a performance.

He sent gifts all the time, showering me with accolades. He was so charming, and so very, very determined. And persuasive. He said I was beautiful, and I was, I suppose, in my own way. He called me his treasure, the most precious thing he could imagine, an exquisite work of art. I was just...swept away."

I stifle the caustic remark that springs to mind. Suffice it to say, David did inherit some qualities from his father.

Meryl continues. "We were married within three months of our first meeting, a lavish, society affair, although the guests were mostly his friends and associates. Apart from my parents, there was only Aunt Vivian there."

"Yes," Caleb agrees, "she witnessed the marriage."

Meryl nods. "He changed, instantly. The ink was barely dry on the marriage certificate before he insisted I start putting his needs first. His career, his business interests. I was a society bride, and he demanded that I act the part. And I did try, for a while. I accompanied him to functions, did my best to entertain his associates even though it interfered with my rehearsal and training schedules. But Alister didn't care about any of that. He considered me his property, bought and paid for. He wanted his money's worth. Within weeks I was no longer being selected for solo parts. I couldn't let that continue so... I confronted him. I tried to explain, tried to make him see how important my career was to me."

"And he wouldn't listen?" Caleb says.

She shakes her head. "He laughed at me and said my days of prancing about for other men to ogle were over. He ordered me to withdraw from the Scottish Ballet Company and devote myself to what really mattered—him."

She drags in a shuddering breath. "We argued. It was a vicious, ugly row. He called me...names I will never forget. And in that moment, I knew I hated him. Marrying him had been a dreadful mistake. I told him I was leaving. I even went to my room and packed my bags, but he wasn't having that. He

What Happens in Vegas…

stopped me on the staircase and ordered me to go back. I was his, he said, and he never let go of what was his."

"So, what happened next?"

"There was a struggle. On the stairs at our home in Aberdeen. After, he told everyone I slipped, but I didn't. He grabbed me, by the arms, and told me to choose. Him or my ballet. The choice was obvious, I'd already made it. He…he grinned at me, kissed me on the mouth, then flung me down the stairs."

"He did it on purpose?" Caleb leans in. "Are you sure?"

"Oh, yes. Absolutely sure. I lay at the bottom, my knee shattered, and he actually laughed at me before he called the ambulance. I was in hospital for a month while they did what they could to repair the damage, but it was no good. He'd ended my career, just as he said he would. And just to round everything off perfectly, I learned that I was pregnant."

"But you did leave him. You'd left by the time your baby, sorry, babies, were born."

Meryl nods. "Alister went back to his apartment in New York while I was still in hospital, so when I was discharged, I went back to my parents' home. I never actually saw him in person again, but I did my best to play the dutiful wife, tried not to let him know what I was planning. I went to functions on his behalf, smiled when necessary, did what was needed to keep him happy. I wasn't sure, not at first, how I would escape, but I was determined to get away. When I was told I was having twins, the plan sort of formed. I could contrive to give him something, enough to satisfy his greed, his possessiveness, and at the same time fake my own death. With the help of the hospital, and the few people close to me, I could make it convincing. My parents and Aunt Vivian even organised my funeral, a cremation, naturally. Alister attended, briefly, but he had other places to be, so…" She shrugs and falls silent for a few moments.

"By the time they were burning an empty coffin in

Aberdeen, I had left the UK with David and changed my name. I used my mother's maiden name, settled in Australia for a couple of years, then I moved here, to New Zealand. I was reasonably sure that Alister had no business interests here, no reason to ever come here. I couldn't dance anymore, but I could still teach, so that's what I did. I started a small ballet school and made a decent living. Every few years, I moved on, just in case."

"You thought he might track you down?"

"Well, you did."

"Only because of the unfinished business between Fern and David. But for what had happened in Las Vegas, I would have been none the wiser. I thought you were dead. I never questioned it. No one did. No one would have looked for you."

She nods. "But I never felt safe. I never dared return to the UK, or the US, because I knew he might be there. He might have found me. Even after he died…"

"You knew he was dead?"

"Yes. I saw it in the newspaper."

"But still, you stayed in hiding?"

She nods.

"Why?"

"It had been so long, nearly thirty years. I… I abandoned you, and I wasn't sure how you might feel about a mother coming back from the dead. And there was David. He…he hasn't always been well. He gets anxious, worked up, sometimes. And he was very bitter about his father, growing up, and about you. I was never sure how he might feel about actually meeting you. Somehow, it just seemed better, safer, to let things lie."

"You make it sound as though I had no reason to be bitter. While he grew up in the lap of luxury and we had to worry about every penny, always running scared, never really settling anywhere." David scowls at his mother and Caleb from across the room. "And all because he was the one lucky enough to be pulled out first."

"There's more to life than being wealthy," Meryl replies, her tone sharp.

I suspect she has heard these complaints before.

"And we were comfortable. You lacked for nothing."

"Except maybe the private education or flashy cars. The corporate jet, the yachts..." David reaches for a bottle of something and pours himself a generous measure. He doesn't offer anyone else a drink.

Caleb shakes his head. "Private education isn't all it's cracked up to be. And I don't have a yacht."

"Fuck you," is David's less-than-eloquent response. "You had it all, on a plate."

"Is that why you decided to impersonate me?" Caleb asks, his voice low and soft. "Out of jealousy and a sense of entitlement?"

David shrugs.

"You did what? You impersonated your brother?" Meryl looks from one son to the other. "But...why? When did you do that? Even knowing how I felt, how frightened I was of being found, you would tempt fate like that?"

"I waited until after the old man was dead, and then only did it a couple of times. I could have done much more if I'd wanted."

"What else?" Caleb demands. "Apart from forging my name at a wedding chapel in Las Vegas when you married Fern, what else did you do?"

"I just took out a couple of loans. Not much. A car, and the deposit on my apartment. You never even noticed."

"And that makes it all right?"

"Why not? You inherited everything. I've had to work for all I've got. I was entitled to something, surely."

"I can't believe you would do this." Meryl appears

genuinely stricken. "I never brought you up to be a thief, or a cheat. How much did you steal?"

"A few thousand bucks. Small change, to him. A drop in the ocean."

"I shall pay it back. Every penny."

Caleb shakes his head. "That's not necessary, Meryl. I'll write it off. I just want to be certain it won't be happening again."

"It won't. Tell him, David." She glares at her younger son. "David?"

He shrugs. This seems to be his stock response when under pressure.

"Are you...are you going to the police? About any of it?" The question comes from Harper, who has been silent throughout most of this. She turns to her husband. "What about me? What about our baby if you end up in jail?"

More shrugging. "He said he's going to drop it. You heard."

"The stealing, yes. But what about Las Vegas? The fake wedding? Oh, my God, are we...are we even married?" She slumps into a chair, tears streaming across her cheeks.

For the first time, David does appear genuinely concerned. "Of course we are, baby. It's like you say, that first time was fake. It doesn't count. Only you and me matter."

I shake my head in disbelief. *What a charmer.*

"We already took legal advice back in the UK," I say, passing a handful of tissues to Harper. She and I have a common enemy, so to speak. "You'd do well to check for yourself in the US, but as I understand it, because he forged his identity, the marriage between myself and David was never valid. For that reason, I think there's a good chance that your marriage is legal, but as I say, you should check."

"Thank goodness," she breathes.

I find it incredible that she would want to remain married to this slimeball, but I suppose love is blind. And deaf.

What Happens in Vegas...

Harper mops at her face with the tissues. "Why did you do it?" she sobs. "Why get married?"

Ah. The six million dollar question. We all wait, silently.

"I didn't plan it if that's what you mean. It just...happened."

"Five years ago?" Harper snuffs. "You and I were together then."

"Yes, but don't you remember, we had a fight? You stormed out, went back to Atlanta. You were gone for weeks, the whole summer, in fact."

"Yeah, I remember that. But I called you. You knew I was coming back. I only stayed out of town so long because my mama was ill."

"Well, in any case, I was bored on my own for the holidays. I went to Vegas, just meant to stay a few days, cruise the casinos, play a few slots, but I met this kid when I was out shopping. She seemed sweet, and we got along. And, she had an apartment. Just a tiny place, but she let me stay there so I didn't have to fork out for a hotel. So, I extended my trip. We had a good time..." He meets my eyes. "You have to admit that."

"Oh, we did. You were on your best behaviour. Looking at you now, though, I can't even start to remember what it was I saw in you."

My scorn earns me another of his customary shrugs. "Me, too. But you were a good lay, I'll grant you that."

Caleb snarls, but I lay my hand on his shoulder. "No, my love. He isn't worth it." I return my attention to the important matter in hand. "Go on. Why did you pretend to be Caleb? I assume you meant to dump me all along."

"Sure I did. I had students older than you were. The last thing I wanted was you trailing after me, tracking me down in Mesquite. And I didn't mind if it caused problems for him. So, two birds with one stone. I already had a copy of my brother's birth certificate, I got it so I could take out the loans. The rest of the paperwork was simple..."

CHAPTER 30

Fern has hardly spoken a word since we left Meryl's house. But now, back in our hotel room, I need to know what's going on in her head.

"Talk to me." I drop to my haunches in front of her as she perches on the edge of our bed and take both her hands in mine. "Tell me what you're thinking."

"I'm thinking...your mother is lovely. I like her."

I nod. "Me, too. More than I expected I would."

"What she did was extreme, but I can sort of understand. She really, really hated him."

"I know. I do get that. It's just that..."

"She abandoned you."

"Yes."

"She wants to see you again. To stay in touch. Will you do that?"

"I'm not sure."

"You should. You really should."

"It's too late. Over thirty years. Me and Meryl..."

"Your mother," she reminds me.

"I suspect it will be a long time, if ever, before I can think of her as 'mother'."

"Okay, I get that. I expect she does, too. But if you stay in touch, get to know one another, well, who knows?"

"Who indeed? But what about you? And...him?"

"David? What a total prat. I feel such a fool for ever being taken in by him. He's...vile. So self-obsessed. He makes my flesh crawl." She looks up at me. "I'm sorry, he's your brother, I know that, but..."

"Hey, you'll get no argument from me. I'd quite happily deck him. If I ever see him again it will be too soon."

"Do you suppose Harper will stay with him? After all of this?"

"I honestly don't know. She seems to be in love with him..."

"I hope she doesn't. She's better off without him. I liked her as well."

"I did, too. And, with that in mind, we have some decisions to make."

"You mean, do we report what he did? The fake wedding?"

"Exactly."

"What do you think?"

I rake my fingers through my hair. "I confess, I'm tempted. I'd like to wipe that sly grin off his face."

"Well, a brush with the law would probably do that."

"True, and he'd probably end up with an eye-watering fine, but it would hurt Harper. And Meryl. And the publicity wouldn't do either of us any good. My main worry, though, is Archie."

"Archie? What do you mean?"

I draw in a breath, then go for it. "He's my son. In every way that matters, he's mine, and I want it to stay that way. I don't want to confuse the issue by going public about your previous relationship with my git of a brother."

"You want to adopt Archie?"

"As I say, he's mine already. But yes, I'd be happy to make it official. Nice and low-key, obviously. I could get Simon to deal with the paperwork. As for you and me, I see no problem between us that can't be sorted by a quick trip to the register office, though if you want a bigger, flashier wedding, I'd go along with that."

"You want to get married? To me?"

"You know I do. I said so all along."

"But, what about…all our baggage?"

"Ah, that. Well, we already know that your previous marriage is invalid, so there's nothing to stop us. And, the way I see it, what happens in Vegas, stays in Vegas."

She is quiet for a few moments, absorbing what I've said. "You mean, we just forget about it? Pretend it never happened?"

"In a manner of speaking, yes. Apart from Meryl, Harper, and David, who I'm certain won't say a word, the only others who know what happened are Poppy, Simon, and Harry. They can be trusted to keep it to themselves. So, I think we should leave it at that. Yes, David gets away with it, but there are others involved in this who I care about a lot more than I do him."

"What about Archie? What will we tell him?"

I pause, less certain about this question. I fully intend to be a father to him. I already think of him as my little boy and that will never change, but it feels wrong to lie to Archie about who his biological parents really are.

"I think we should tell him the truth, eventually," I say. "Obviously not yet, but when he's old enough to understand. Do you agree?"

Fern nods. "We'll know, I think, when it's time…"

"So, now that we have that settled…?"

"What happens in Vegas stays in Vegas?" she repeats. "Do you really think we could get away with that?"

"I see no reason why not."

There are another few moments of silence, then, "Okay. Ask me again."

"Ask you what?"

"Ask me to marry you."

I furrow my brow. "Will you say 'yes'?"

She punches my arm. "Just bloody ask me."

EPILOGUE

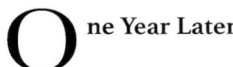ne Year Later

"Rosie wanted to see her daddy."

I look up from the screen. Fern is at the door to my office, a tiny bundle cradled in her arms. Our daughter is one month old today.

"Hey, give her to me." I hold out my arms, then smile as the now familiar gush of unconditional adoration engulfs me. I love Archie, too, but there's something about a tiny baby, and a daughter, at that. The miniscule fingers and toes, the fresh, clean, milky smell of her. How my own father resisted this I will never know but I was a goner from the first moment I set eyes on her. "How's the most beautiful little girl in the world, then?"

Rosie peers up at me, with what I like to think of as a smile on her perfect face, though in my less besotted moments I suspect that could be wind.

I kiss my daughter on the forehead, then glance over at Fern. "What are you doing up here, anyway? I thought you had pots to cook, or whatever you do with them."

We converted the old laundry at the rear of Linn Mill into a studio and ceramics workshop for Fern. She still has her premises in Stockport and her business there is doing quite nicely, offering an incubator space for young creatives under Jade's management. Fern drives down there every couple of weeks or so, but she prefers to do most of her own artistic work here as it means she can spend more time with the children. And, I suspect, Sally's cooking may have influenced her decision to install a kiln in my outhouse.

Whatever the reasons, it's an arrangement that suits all of us very well.

"I finished early because today is a big day. Rosie's been bathed and fed, all ready to meet her grandma. When will Meryl get here, do you know?" Fern perches on the edge of my desk and drops a kiss on my mouth.

"Harry texted from Glasgow Airport just as they were leaving." I glance at my watch. "Another fifteen minutes or so."

"I'm looking forward to seeing your mother again. Skype and FaceTime are okay, but it's not the same, is it?"

"I suppose not." I lean back in my chair, wishing I could share my wife's enthusiasm.

She and Meryl have spoken a lot in the year since our surprise visit and do seem to have become friends. I've made an effort, but it's hard. I find it difficult to shake off the memory of a childhood spent alone and ignored. For all his bitching, I'm still not convinced that David didn't get the better part of the bargain. He had his mother's love and attention. He knew he was wanted, that he mattered to someone apart from the servants.

I know that we can't undo the past, and we have to go forward, look to the future. I mean to try, if for no better reason that Fern will never let up if I don't make a decent effort with Meryl. Mind, even she was astonished when I transferred two million pounds into David Valence's bank account, and the same amount into Meryl's.

What Happens in Vegas…

"I've become a lot wealthier in the years since he died, but that's two thirds of what I inherited from my father," I explained to her when she demanded to know what the fuck I was thinking of. "Split evenly, now, between the three of us"

"But you don't need to do this. No one expects—"

"Meryl is refusing to touch any of it, and I suspect her share will eventually end up with Archie. But money is all that matters to David. If this makes him feel less badly done by it's worth it. I hope he can make something of his windfall, though I wouldn't be surprised if he blows it all within five years. Still, it's his choice. If he takes good investment advice, his share will be enough to ensure he'll never need to get up close and personal with the students of Mesquite again. I think he and I are even now."

"What do you mean? You didn't owe him anything."

"Ah, but I did. I owe him you. If he hadn't got up to his pranks in Las Vegas, you and I would never have met."

"I never thought of it like that.

David hasn't been in touch since he came into his money, not with me and, I gather, not with his mother, either. He and Harper did go their separate ways, and she went back to Atlanta. I suspect he's in Las Vegas and having a great time, but I can't be certain. I don't intend to waste much mental energy worrying about him. And I certainly don't want him at my wedding.

Fern agreed with me on that but absolutely insisted that we invite Meryl.

"It's time to build bridges. Archie needs his grandparents. And so will this one, when she's born." She patted her curved abdomen, glared at me, and the argument was lost.

We agreed to delay the ceremony until after our baby was born, and I was relieved that Fern was content to keep it simple. Just immediate family and friends will be joining us at the register office in Edinburgh followed by a lavish meal back here. The big day is less than three days away now. Sally has been cooking for weeks.

Fern heads for the office door. "Come on, shall we go down to the foyer to meet Grandma?"

Poppy is already in the foyer when we descend the stairs, Tara at my heels. Archie is hopping up and down at her side, his big, daft dog joining in the fun. The pair of them look just about ready to burst with excitement.

"We saw the car from Grandma's window," Archie yells. "They're here."

Fern grabs the door handle and throws the door open, just as the car pulls up. She rushes out to greet our guest, Poppy and Archie at her heels.

Meryl appears suitably awed when she emerges from the passenger seat, then pauses to take in the grandeur of Linn Mill. Meanwhile, Harry is dragging her two huge suitcases from the boot of the car.

"Hello, it's so good to see you. How was the journey? We've been so excited..." Fern flings her arms around Meryl, who returns the hug. "This is my mother, Poppy Daniels...and of course, Archie. Our son."

Meryl is aware of the true circumstances surrounding Archie's birth and has taken a philosophical approach. He's her grandson, whichever of her sons is his natural father.

Poppy and Archie join the welcoming party, while Harry drags the first of the cases up the stairs to the door. I'd offer to help, but I'm still holding Rosie. I nod at him as he passes me.

"Front bedroom, east wing," I inform him.

Fern leads our guest inside, Archie and Poppy adding to the excited chatter.

"Do you want to go straight up to your room," Fern asks, "or would you like a cup of tea first?"

"Tea would be nice. Thank you."

"Excellent. I have a tray already set out in here." Poppy links arms with Meryl and ushers her into the drawing room she has

What Happens in Vegas...

claimed as her own. "You sit there, dear, on the sofa. It has the best view..."

The rest of us make ourselves comfortable while Poppy fusses about ensuring everyone has tea to their exact taste. Milk and sugar are passed around. The slices of lemon, as usual, remain undisturbed on their plate.

"So, how long are you able to stay, Meryl?" Poppy smiles brightly. "I'm sure there must be lots of people you'd like to see again."

Meryl shifts uneasily. "Not really," she mumbles.

I'm grateful for small mercies. I hadn't exactly relished the prospect of introducing Meryl to old associates of my father and trying to explain the somewhat awkward matter of her having been dead for thirty years. There would be many who would feel moved to observe that she looks remarkably well, considering.

"Even so," Poppy continues, "it's such a long journey. You won't be rushing off straight after the wedding, surely."

"Meryl has work," I remind her. "Responsibilities back in New Zealand."

Poppy is undaunted. "Then we shall have to go there next. Let's not be strangers..."

"Well, actually..." Meryl meets my gaze. She seems distinctly nervous. "I...retired."

"Retired?" I keep my tone neutral. "As in, you gave up your job?"

"Yes. They offered me a good deal to retire early, so..."

"Well, she did right, didn't she, Cal?" Fern hands round the plate of chocolate Hobnobs. "You can't turn down a good deal. What plans do you have now, then, Meryl?"

"I was thinking about starting another dance school. I always enjoyed teaching, and—"

"Back in Christchurch?" I ask. "I suppose that would make sense, as you have a house there."

"But there's no hurry, surely," Fern insists. "Now that you're here, I was hoping that you could stay with us beyond the new year. That'll be all right, won't it, Cal?"

It's an ambush, but I saw it coming. When Fern is determined to have her way there's not much point digging my heels in. I nod, grateful that this house is big enough for everyone here to have their own space.

"There's something else I should just add, since you did mention my house," Meryl continues.

"Oh? What's that?" I ask.

"I put it on the market before I left New Zealand." She hurries on before I can come up with a reply. "It's too big for me on my own, and I felt it was time to move on..."

"Where do you mean to live, then?" It seems a reasonable question to me, but four pairs of eyes regard me as though I just kicked Ollie.

"She can live here, obviously. Just until she decides what's what." Fern clearly considers the matter closed, and Archie has taken to dancing around the room whooping about Grandma coming to the football with him and his friend. "In fact," Fern continues, clearly warming to her theme, "we have the perfect place for a dance school."

"We do?" I am at a loss.

"Yes. The ballroom. We could shift those Gainsboroughs and install a mirror. A dance studio needs a mirror, doesn't it? And a bar..."

"A dance school? In my ballroom?" I am assailed by a vision of dozens of little girls in tutus parading about in my foyer, chattering like sparrows and practising their pirouettes. There will be traffic jams on my drive when all the mamas and papas drop off their little princesses.

"*Our* ballroom. And yes, that's if Meryl wants to stay in Scotland, obviously..."

We all look to my mother for some sort of signal of intent. She says nothing but shifts awkwardly in her seat.

"Meryl," I say, as calmly as I can manage. "You did buy a return ticket, didn't you?"

"Well, I wasn't sure just when..."

"You bought a one-way ticket." It's not a question.

"Yes." She meets my gaze. "I'm not going back to New Zealand."

Rosie chooses that moment to screw up her little face and heave. The ensuing smell brings wrinkles to the most doting of noses.

Fern stands. "Oh dear. Give her to me."

I shake my head, silently blessing my daughter for her impeccable timing. "No, I'll deal with it. You stay here and...whatever."

"There are clean nappies in the kitchen," she says. "Shall I just—?"

"No, I can find them." I drop a kiss on her forehead as I pass. "We may be a while. Once Rosie is fit to be among decent folk again, she and I have work to do."

"Work?"

"Yes. We need to do some internet shopping. I reckon we'll be needing an extra chaise longue in here to start with. And I'll need to get someone out to measure up for a mirror. Where were you thinking of re-hanging the Gainsboroughs, my darling?"..."

The End

FROM THE AUTHOR

Thank you for reading *What Happens In Vegas*. If you enjoyed the story, I would really appreciate it if you would leave a review. Reviews are invaluable to indie authors in helping us to market our books and they provide useful feedback to help us work even harder to bring you more of the stories you love.

ALSO BY ASHE BARKER

The Black Combe Doms
- Dark Melodies
- Sure Mastery
- Hard Limits
- Laid Bare
- Black Combe Doms box set

The Doms of Skye
- Highland Odyssey
- Above and Beyond
- The Doms of Skye box set

Contemporary
- A Dom is for Life
- Innocent
- Broken
- Tell Me
- Her Two Doms (also in audiobook)
- Capri Heat
- Making The Rules
- Faith
- Spirit
- Hardened
- First Impressions
- The Three Rs
- Chameleon
- La Brat

Historical
Surrender to the Viking
Right of Conquest
Deeds Not Words
The Laird and the Sassenach
Sassenach Bride
Seducing His Sassenach
Mightier Than The Sword
Her Celtic Masters
Conquered by the Viking
Her Rogue Viking
Her Dark Viking
Her Celtic Captor
The Widow is Mine (The Conquered Brides collection)
A Scandalous Arrangement
The Highwayman's Lady
Her Noble Lords

Sci-fi
Her Alien Commander
Theirs: Found and Claimed

Paranormal and Time Travel
Resurrection
Shared by the Highlanders
Held In Custody
Under Viking Dominion

LGBT
Gideon
Bodywork
Hard Riders

Short Stories and Novellas
Viking Surrender (The Prologue) (also in audiobook)

Brandr (Viking Surrender, Book 1) (also in audiobook)
A Tale of Two Pirates
Brigands, Thieves and Lawless Ladies
Rough Diamonds
Re-Awakening
Carrot and Coriander
In the Eyes of the Law
The Prize
A Very Private Performance
Yes or No?
Rose's Are Red

Manufactured by Amazon.ca
Bolton, ON